STARTING OVER

THE
Carrero
SOLUTION

The Carrero
Series

L.T.Marshall

The Carrero Series

Jake & Emma
The Carrero Effect ~ The Promotion
The Carrero Influence ~ Redefining Rules
The Carrero Solution ~ Starting Over

Arrick & Sophie
The Carrero Heart ~ Beginning
The Carrero Heart ~ The Journey
The Carrero Heart ~ Happy Ever Afters

Alexi & Camilla
The Carrero Contract ~ Selling Your Soul
The Carrero Contract ~ Amending Agreements
The Carrero Contract ~ Finding Freedom

Bonus Books
Jake's View
Arrick's View

Other books by L.T. Marshall

Just Rose

The Elite Team, who pushed me to keep going.
And to Irn Bru – the fuel to my fodder!

Chapter 1

I'm lying in a heap on the bed, numb from endless sobbing and wracking pain. I don't know how long I've been lying, listening to my blood rush through my head as my heart self-implodes inside my body. I'm nothing but a shell. A quiet, empty shell of exhaustion and heartache rumpled beyond recognition.

I lashed out, hit at him, and shoved him away with every ounce of strength I possessed, yet still, he tried to cling to me.

My Jake, my body and soul. Now the destroyer of everything that I was.

I told him not to touch me, never to touch me again. To leave and to go away. I screamed and cried and fell to pieces on the floor at his feet. His words tumbled around me like noise that I couldn't understand, so consumed by my grief.

It's only when I whimpered and begged that he leave me alone that he finally listened, moving away so I could find my way to my feet, running into the solitude of this room ... our room. His room. Shutting him out and locking him away. I can't bear for him to be near me, touch me, or look at me anymore.

What we are is lost; his betrayal sealed our fate, and my world has been ripped apart with such devastation. I don't think I'll ever be the same again. All I can think about is his mouth against hers, over and over, and it rips through my heart. Kissing the mouth of the one woman in the world I hate beyond compare. He does not know the depth and damage cheating with her has done. He has no idea how deeply his betrayal has wounded me.

He kissed someone else. Not just anyone else but her. The object of all my hatred and pain for the last few months.

The woman who possessed his heart once upon a time. The only other woman who has been loved by him and now carries his child.

Marissa Hartley.

How can I ever get beyond this or believe his feelings for her are as clear-cut as I thought?

Her name is like a dagger in my chest, a wound so unbearable, burning, and searing, ensuring I never recover from the fatal blow.

Why, Jake? ... Why? Because you were so sure of my readiness to betray you? Fueled by insecurity because of my refusal to start a home with you or answer your proposal?

Fueled by my stupidity in making you believe I would betray you so readily over a fight.

Were we so fragile that something this stupid has ripped us in two?

There's a light chap on the door. My breath halts and my pulse stops. His closeness still affects me. Even at a distance, my body feels him in the air and trembles.

"Emma?" Jake's voice, hoarse and raw, causes sharp pain in my chest. I slide onto my side to blot him out, covering my ears, curling into a ball with a fresh wave of the unbearable aching inside me, silent tears pouring down my face. I just want this pain to stop devouring me.

"Emma, please? ... Let me in." He pleads, his voice as far away from my Jake as it could possibly be, different from how he normally sounds, crushing my soul. I'm so far away from myself that I fear I'll never find my way back. I close my eyes tight, screwing them hard, willing him to leave. My voice wouldn't come even if I wanted it to. It's so raw and painful, making it too hard to swallow, aftereffects of the wailing of a desperate woman.

There's a gentle thud against the door. It creaks with the

pressure of human weight, a noise of something heavy and soft sliding down the other side slowly.

"I'm not going anywhere, *Neonata*. I'm staying right here until you let me see you. I need to see you, Emma ... I'm going insane out here." The sadness in his tone makes me ache. He sounds as broken as I feel. His normally low husky tone is strained and hoarse, emotion breaking with every agonizing word.

He left me until I became quiet, but I couldn't lock him out forever. This is his apartment ... his home. Not mine anymore. I need to get up, take everything I own, and leave him; he's left me no choice but to go. There's nothing here for us anymore.

Fresh waves of devastation hit me, causing me to break the silence with a sob. I can't begin to think about leaving him, not yet, not while my body wants to lie here and die. The pain is so all-encompassing I can barely breathe.

"Please ... Please, *Bambina*. It's killing me staying out here listening to you cry. Let me in. Let me hold you." His voice breaks, the pain too much. I imagine him slumping against the door, his knees up and arms around his shoulders, maybe cradling his head, as broken and crumpled as me. I try to shake his image from my mind, tears consuming me; the thought hurts me more than I can imagine. I can't bear for him to be as broken as me, aching in agony outside his own door.

I'm drowning in confusion. I can't endure the pain of letting him close. The thought of his touch brings the flash of a vision into my head of him and her - him touching her, focusing on her eyes, kissing her. It slices through me like a hot poker and tortures me to my core.

What has he done to us?

"I ... I ... I can't." My voice is weak and fragile, a ghost of the normal tone I usually possess. I breathe through tears, unsure if I'm loud enough for him to hear me.

"Emma, I won't touch you. I swear. I'll keep my distance. I just need to see you ... look at you." He begs. He shifts toward the door to strain for my response, which shatters me all the more.

I don't like him this way. He's my strong, domineering Carrero, always so sure and infuriatingly confident, in control of everything.

I can't bear this sad, quiet version of him begging me, sitting slumped outside, and seeking permission to enter a room in his apartment.

This is not Jake. I want my Jake back. I want the Jake from a week ago, the one who never betrayed me and left me this way. The Jake who would move mountains to protect me, not this man sitting out there who is so far removed from the one I thought I knew.

"I can't. I can't get up." it's true. I don't have the strength to walk to the door. My body's broken. I cry quietly, tears falling freely beyond my control. I can barely lift my head, so drained of life I am beyond the point of moving. Fatigue is wracking every limb with emotional exhaustion. I don't know what time it is, but it feels like I've been here for days.

"Just tell me I can open the door, and I will," his voice is strained. He's waiting and hoping I won't hold him out while still seeking my permission.

I can't keep him out as much as I desperately want to. He's the one causing me paralyzing agony but is also the only person in the world with a hope of helping me. That's my torture. My healer is also my tormentor. When all I can feel is devastation, my heart aches, calling out for the one person who always grounds me and makes me feel secure.

"It's your house," I crumble, not deciding for him. I flinch moments later, clenching my body in surprise, as he kicks the door open with effortless force. The wood splintering and metal sheering violently; light flooded from the other room, showing his strong masculine figure silhouetted in the frame.

I curl into myself tighter, as I did when I was a child, covering my face with my arms and instinctively defending my body. The pain of him being near me is more excruciating than anything I've ever endured. I hear him moving closer. The bed dips as he slides on, keeping his distance. He sighs heavily. I can feel every ounce of strong energy radiating from him, despairing and remorseful, surging with as much heartache as I am.

"I love you, baby ... I can fix this. I want to fix this. I want you so badly that this ... What I've done ... It's killing me. It's ripping me apart that I've hurt and lost you." His voice aches and trembles, and the urge to turn and wrap myself into his safe arms overwhelms me, but I know I won't find the relief I desperately desire. His touch will only cause more devastation to my heart.

Marissa, with her nasty snarl and wicked eyes, is running through my head, smirking at me, cackling at me. I can almost sense her satisfaction coursing through me. She's won. She's taken him from me in the worst way.

"I don't know if I can come back from this ... I need time to breathe, time to think," I whisper, afraid that saying it louder will be more crushing to my soul.

"I don't want you to leave." He croaks as he tries to see my face in the gloom of the dim light, leaning closer so I can feel his body heat hovering over mine. He's caging me in without touching me, and I hold my breath.

"I can't stay." I curl up tighter, hiding what I am from the man I love most in the world, the one person who changed everything in my life for the better. Yet destroyed it all in the same gentle stroke.

"I'll do anything, whatever you ask, Emma ... Just please, don't leave me," his voice is softer, almost breathless. He sniffs, and I know he has tears on his cheek. It kills me inside, despite what he's done, I don't want him to be hurting. I've never seen Jake cry over anything before this, and I don't want to see it now. I can't bare it.

"I need to go. I need time away from you ... It hurts too much having you near me. I don't know if I can forgive you while everything is so raw and fresh. I need space and time to think." My words are empty, as though from another person. I wish I had conviction in my request, but I sound pathetic and small like I'm asking for his permission to go.

He takes a sharp breath, trying to fight the internal battle threatening to consume him, trying to keep it all in, but I can hear it in every noise he makes. His regret is the only thing keeping me sane right now. The only thing keeping my anger at bay. His obvious pain at what he's done to us is the only balm in this horrible train wreck that was once our relationship.

He stays silent. The bed moves as he clenches the sheets, his hands trawling in desperation at whatever his inner dialog is saying to him. Jake in turmoil is devastating to my soul.

"I'll have Jefferson take you back to Queens whenever you want to go." He breathes the words as though I just stabbed him through the heart with a dagger.

If I have, I've also turned it on myself, and now I'm bleeding to death.

"I think it's best if I go as soon as I can get myself together." I don't think that's possible right now. My body is detached and useless, barely wanting to move, let alone get up. My heart is aching so heavily that it throbs through my chest and stomach. I feel sick with all of it. My head is light and swimming with the effort of trying to breathe. My nose is blocked from crying, and my throat is raw and raspy.

"I can't ... I can't, Emma!" His voice suddenly turns powerful, tugging me to him in a flash, and I yelp in surprise. He buries his face into my hair, crushing me in his embrace and letting out the pain he's been holding back.

I never in my life thought I would see Jake cry, and it's the most awful thing I've ever witnessed. It has the same effect as watching everyone I love cut down and murdered while I lie useless and watch. My heart is broken in two.

I sob into his body in reaction, trying desperately to push away the thoughts running through my mind tormenting me. I stiffen against him, afraid to let him hold or let me go. Afraid to give in to the thoughts spiraling out of control in my mind. Thoughts of him and her. Afraid to try to envelope myself in him for fear of what will consume me.

"Please, let me go." I cry silently, begging him to stop making this worse for me. He has no idea of the agony that touching me is causing or how much internal pain it inflicts.

He seems to compose himself, sensing that I'm unresponsive in his arms, and loosens his grip, letting me go. He stands and quickly turns his back to me as he takes several heavy breaths. His posture is that of deflation and hopelessness.

"I'll let you leave, Emma, but I can promise you this. I'll never let you go ... Even if I need to chase you for the rest of my life, I won't stop trying to get you back." He walks off slowly. I sense it's before he does something he will regret, like pushing me further away. He pauses by the door taking a final look at my disheveled form lying carelessly on the bed. His discarded, broken woman.

Our eyes meet, and it causes the sharpest wrenching kick to my gut, so much sadness and pain mirrored there.

Why did you have to kill me so?

"If I have to spend the next sixty years begging at your feet, Emma, then I will. You're the only one for me. *The* one! ... I love you with every piece of my soul, baby. I know I fucked this up, but I won't ever stop trying to get you back in my life and your heart. Because I need you." With one final aching look, he leaves the room, walking further into the apartment, heading toward one of his many unused guest rooms to give me space. I wish his words could comfort me, but they don't; they only bring heart-ripping anger cutting through my grief.

If I really meant that much to him, then he would've never touched her at all.

* * *

I get up when my body can finally hold my weight, and I dress quickly. I can't bear to wander the apartment. I don't want to see Jake at all. I grab what clothes I can, and then, with a final walk out the door, I press the intercom button, which summons Mathews into the internal apartment. He appears, dressed in his *Men in Black* attire, informing me that Jefferson will only be a few minutes. He seems to know what I want, and I guess Jake has brought him up to speed like he always does.

Jake is nowhere to be seen, but I can sense him somewhere in the apartment. I can feel his presence. I'm trying not to give way to thoughts of him, or else I won't cope. I need to stay strong to be able to leave.

Mathews agrees to have Nora pack and send the rest of my

belongings later today. I've decided that I need to walk away, taking all that I am. I need to get organized, get back to Sarah and home, and take time to think all this through. It's a plan and all that is holding me together. The old PA Emma taking over, clinging to organized thoughts and planning to help me get through the worst moment of my life. It's all so very polite and calm. My requests come from a seemingly sane person arranging a little trip while, in sheer agony, I try not to show the tormented soul that I am. It's what I need right now since any emotion would make me crumble at my own feet.

Mathews stands politely and silently as I give instructions on certain items I don't want or couldn't bear to have with me. His black hair is sprinkled with gray, his crinkled eyes highlighting the soft blue kindness in them. He's maybe in his late forties. I've always liked him as a quiet protector, always present sort of way.

I can see why Jake trusts him to run his security both in and out of his home. He has the air and quiet gentleness of a military man underlined with a hint of danger. I've no doubt he's the kind of man who would take a bullet for Jake. I like that he has Mathews to take care of him now that I won't be here to do it anymore.

My body is held together only by sheer will as Mathews takes my case and leads me to the elevator at the outer doors of the penthouse apartment. I manage to find the old part of me deep inside that shields how I feel. PA Emma lifts her chin and sets her face in a blank mask. I take one last look around. My heart aches like a dead weight in my body, not for this apartment, since it was never really mine anyway, but for what walking out of it symbolizes. I've lost everything just like I thought I would.

Not because I let Jake seduce me into a one-night stand but because I fell in love with him. I let go of so many defenses which kept me safe. Yet the outcome was the same: I lost him, my job, and our relationship. Here I am again, walking out of his life for the second time, only this time, I don't see a way of ever coming back.

Chapter 2

It's only been a day since I left him, but it feels like an eternity. The apartment is eerily quiet while Sarah and her boyfriend, Marcus, visit his family for the next six days. I have all technology switched off, so Jake can't contact me, and I'm slowly dying inside. It doesn't feel like I belong back here, in this apartment. Queens isn't where I should be anymore either.

The anger sweeps through me, followed closely by grief, then mourning. I can't seem to be still. Every part of me cycles through emotions over and over. I feel like I'm caught in a nightmare I can't wake up from, and everything around me is surreal. My palms are cold, and my body trembles, but I feel hot and sick. I've tried to do something other than lie on the bed and sob, but I've lost all my capabilities.

The years I was hurt and abused at the hands of men used to somehow give me the strength to fight back. No matter what they did, my anger fueled me to be better. But Jake has left me barren and empty. There's nothing in me but an agonizing pit of despair and hopelessness as I lie crumpled and useless on a bed.

Food doesn't tempt me, I can't swallow water, and the thought of getting up is abhorrent to me. I've thrown up so many times since I got here. Maybe a reaction to the emotional trauma.

Thoughts of Jake and Marissa run over and over through my

head. My imagination is taking hold, running wild, seeing them kissing passionately, hands running up and down her body pushing things further. I can't shake it; every new visualization becomes more detailed and more excruciating than the last. I'm literally torturing myself into insanity.

I've no idea how far things went or how they even started, but my mind is slowly tormenting me. I know if I stay here like this, I'll slowly go insane or die from starvation. I need to get up and shower, get up and eat. Just get up and not lie, falling into oblivion. I need to start rationalizing my thoughts to help process what has happened.

You need to pick up the pieces and file them into the back of your head. You are better than this!

I finally drag myself up, sitting and watching the rain fall down the window from my padded, silver-gray headboard. The dark gray sky brings a dull light to everything around me in my stark modern room. It seems to echo how I feel inside. I've no idea what time it is; it ceased to exist the moment he told me what he did.

I pull myself to standing, ashamed that I'm still in his T-shirt and running pants, acknowledging the mess of me. I don't want his smell around me or the memory of him so close. I must pull myself together and look like I'm coping with life. Maybe by doing this, I'll find my old resolve.

I force myself into the small shower of my apartment. The confines of the cheerful pink bathroom Sarah insisted on decorating brings me a little comfort, a minor spark of happiness amid a sea of darkness. A touch of Sarah with her bright, happy face pushes Marissa aside for a moment, giving my head respite.

* * *

I'm a little saner from the harsh jets of hot water drilling into my skull, distracting me from my reality, and I stand that way until my legs go numb, like a mindless drone on autopilot.

I dress in fresh clothes and brush out my hair before moving to unpack my things into the empty wardrobe.

The doorbell ringing snaps my focus around, and I hesitate, stomach lurching in panic. Sarah won't be back for a few days, and I'm not expecting anyone I can think of. Experiencing a moment of fear as my gut tells me it might be him, that maybe he doesn't want to give me space to think, but I can't see him so soon. My insides go weak, turning to liquid mush, my legs become rubber, and my hands start sweating. I'm close to fainting when sense steps in.

Wait!

My brain snaps into focus, telling me it'll be Mathews with my belongings! I asked him to bring them to me sooner rather than later, wanting the pain of the task out of the way quickly. I feel ridiculous and try to regain some stability in my legs.

Get a grip, Emma. Breathe ... Count ... Breathe.

I stumble to the door through the open-plan lounge opening it hesitantly without checking the spy hole, willing myself to find the courage and poise to hide the internal disaster that I am.

I'm right, and Mathews stands with another man dressed in matching black, holding cases, a serious expression on his face. I know he's taking me in, trying to ascertain how I am without asking. It's what he does. He appraises people instantly, analyzing me at a glance.

"Miss. Anderson, shall I have everything brought in?" His deep gravelly voice is comforting. I smile emptily, moving out of the way, gesturing they should, finding PA Emma, pushing her out in front to take control of my lifeless body for a while.

It doesn't take long to bring the cases and boxes in; my head and heart hurt a little more each time. I didn't realize how much I accumulated moving in with Jake; ever generous, always flourishing me with clothes via Donna or little surprise things among my jewelry or shoes, even down to books I read. Always finding a new one beside my bed when I was nearing the end of the one I had.

He never ceased to anticipate my needs knowing exactly what I'd like. He never made a big thing of it, though. No large dancing gesture, presenting me with gifts he knew I'd feel embarrassed about accepting ... so he'd slot them in with my things to find while alone. I never refused anything that way, always warmed by the thoughtful touches he left for me.

God, I miss him so much. He always knew what I needed.

When the men are done, Mathews turns to me at the door, ushering his man out, and gives me a paternal, warm, sympathetic smile.

"Miss. Anderson, Mr. Carrero asked me to give you this." His steady gaze takes in the flicker of emotions across my face as he holds out the long slender cream envelope with my name on the front and Jake's achingly bold and beautiful handwritten script. My heart pangs and contracts at the sight of it. I instantly bite my lip to quell the tears. The heavy swallowing to calm my emotions doesn't go unnoticed. He gives me a sympathetic look, sliding the envelope into my palm with a brief pat on my shoulder and a nod.

"He loves you, ma'am. Men are idiots when it comes to love and relationships. We all make mistakes. Just don't dismiss all you have without really thinking things through. You are his universe, Miss. Anderson."

An interesting observation from a man who sees so much and yet is only a mere brief presence in our lives.

He smiles at me gently, and I nod too, ignoring that tug in my throat that aches so badly. Tears pool in the back of my eyes, my throat throbbing.

"Please tell Jake I need time alone. I'm grateful for my things, Mr. Mathews, and thank you, really." I smile emptily.

He understands I'm dismissing him before I fall apart because even hearing Jake's name brings an unbearable agony that cuts through my core. He nods and says a small farewell before leaving, pulling the door closed behind him.

I stand stiff and numb, staring at the door handle for a few moments, lost in an empty daydream before my head snaps into focus, and I stare down at the letter in my hand. I'm grasping it so tightly I've put a wrinkle across its smooth surface.

I walk to the couch and sit down, holding the letter in front of me as though it's some foreign object I don't recognize and don't know what to do with. I sit for the longest time and stare, my heart beating through my chest, my breathing labored.

His neat, beautiful writing scrapes at what's left of my strength, knowing whatever is inside has the power to fuel another onslaught of tears, sobs, and crushing pain that I'm just not ready for. I get up, walk to my room, and slide it in front of the mirror on my vanity instead. I need time - time to get myself together before I read it.

Jake kissed someone else, Marissa, of all people! Will I ever be ready to face that?

To some, the act is excusable, maybe even understandable, considering everything that went on leading up to it. I can't change how irreversibly it has hurt me. It's about trust, betrayal, and security. He did something as painful as full-on sex. He touched her and gave her something that should only belong to me from the second he gave me his heart, regardless of his pain. He gave his touch to someone he knew would crush me. The woman he will be tied to for an eternity because of her unborn child. I know drunk Jake can be irrational and impulsive, fueled by rage, but a part of me shakes its head sadly.

If he loved me, he wouldn't have been able to throw me aside so carelessly and cruelly, turning to that woman and doing something so vindictive.

Maybe this is what I deserve in life. Perhaps this is my retribution because of the insecure, afraid, emotional, weird mess that I am who pushed him away for so long, even though I've no doubt that Jake loves me. I've seen it so many times in the ways he's changed his life for me. I do not doubt that he regrets what he's done. I would be blind not to see it written all over him, but it's not any of that which holds me here.

It's knowing I may never be able to trust him again, letting my insecurities expand beyond control, knowing I'll always be second-guessing him anytime he leaves me alone. Always doubting if he has unresolved feelings for Marissa. He showed me that all men, even the ones who love you, can still crush you so easily. It's a black mark in our almost perfect union, a hideous, ugly scar, forever there between us.

I know I have blame in this too. Maybe that's why I can't hate him, and maybe it's why even as I'm dying inside, all I want is him.

The source of my pain is my only cure, and as much as I hate what he's done, as much anger and hurt there is inside me, I can't stop pining for him. It makes me more messed up in the head and unable to get my thoughts straight.

* * *

I spend the next several days locked in my solitude, leaving only to buy groceries and then returning home. I've mindlessly sat through so many hours of daytime TV and horrible romantic movies that make me want to throw books at the screen. Sarah should be back soon, and I don't want her to see what I've become; some slobbish, tear-stained mess of a girl living in a sea of junk food, chocolate wrappers, and screwed-up tissues.

Classy look, Emma; really holding yourself together, aren't you?

After a much-needed pep talk and a long agonizing look in the mirror, I am finally so sick of my depressive mood and disgusting behavior. I force myself to get up and stop moping around like a broken-hearted zombie, doing anything to stop mulling it over in my brain.

I busy myself with cleaning the apartment, wiping away hours of lying around sobbing into tissues, and eating carbs. I can't bear to look at the endless sea of clothes on my floor, all tied viciously to memories of him. I need to get myself together and show Sarah I can be who I used to be. I can pretend to be in control for her sake by looking as I should and having our home as neatly kept as we usually do. I won't inflict this person I've become on her when she returns. I'm ashamed of who she is.

I have texts from him and emails, all unopened. The bunches of flowers and expensive gifts sent to my door were all turned away. Jake's trying so hard to reach through my wall of silence and contact me, but as I told him on every returned gift card:

Leave me be. Give me time.

Every time the bell goes, the pain of being betrayed rears its ugly head, with each bunch of gorgeous flowers more extravagant than the last, chocolates, jewelry, and even a stuffed bear holding a broken heart. Each one causing a flood of tears and a ravaged soul. It's been hell trying to tell the couriers to take them back, that I don't want any of them. Inflicting my sobbing, manic, blubbering, messed-up self on any delivery guy brave enough to give me any of Jake's gestures. Flapping my hands to move them out of my sight. It's all too much to bear, and now I've muted the intercom, so drivers assume no one is home.

I can't fault him for trying to reach me. Not a day has passed that he hasn't tried, but I'm not ready to face this or him just yet. My head is a mess; my body is a mess; my emotions are a mess. I feel like I've been cut loose and left adrift. I can't focus on a single thing. I've never experienced this kind of torment. I thought being sent away by Jake to his dad's company was the worst pain I would ever endure in my life, but this tops that. This is excruciating.

At night, I barely sleep and reach for him when I do. I dream of him, and each dream gives way to my old night terrors, waking me up in a panic and causing me to dive toward my headboard. I pull my covers to my chest, trying to fight off the shadows coming at me as I drag myself out of my mind, desperate to wake up fully.

Those nights are the worst, drenched in sweat and fear, gasping in terror as I slap at the shadows around me. I wake up, often hoping that it's all been a dream and that I'm in his apartment again. Held captive by his limbs, and he's right there beside me to make me feel safe, but every time, my body gives way to sobbing when I realize where I am.

I've cried so much that I'm unsure how my body still has any fluid left, but it seems I have a never-ending supply reserved just for him. Exhaustion is the only thing that helps numb the pain; my head is foggy with fatigue constantly.

* * *

"Emma?" Sarah's worried voice hits me as I scrub the cooker for the fiftieth time, her arms flying around me as she sees me. I didn't even hear her come in. I finally caved a few hours ago, in a phone call while she got ready to travel home, and told her why I was here, unable to talk through tears, but she finally understood.

"Oh, my God! I was frantic the whole flight, desperate to get back to you." She croons, holding me tight, and I relax into her embrace. Holding myself together, telling myself not to fall apart. To not be the girl who crumbles when her friend asks how she is.

"I'm okay, Sarah ... Better than I was the last couple of days." a numbness has started to envelop me most of the time, making me able to cope with menial tasks and mindless routines in an almost zombie-like state.

I turn in her arms and spot Marcus scurrying away with cases to her room, a typical man avoiding female tears, a real charmer. Jake would have brushed them away for me and asked me to tell him all about it. He would've wiped the floor with the likes of Marcus and his evasive behavior to female tears.

I push down the thought and bite my lip.

I can't keep torturing myself this way. Stop thinking about him.

"Is this it? Are you really walking away from what you had?" She gazes at me with an intense frown. "He made a mistake, Emma ... He's human." Her revelation surprises me; it makes me stop what I'm doing and gape at her.

"On our call, you were all for me kicking him the balls, if I remember." I point out in surprise. Complete disbelief etched on my face. In truth, I'm more than a little hurt.

"Yeah, but then I had time to simmer and think about everything, Ems ... Jake loves you. I don't think this is something he'd ever repeat." She looks incredibly sincere at this very moment.

Why am I shocked? She's just another version of my mother, letting a man hurt you and then crawling back to him again. She's given Marcus so many chances in the past, and here he is again.

"I don't know what I'm going to do. I'm beyond confused." I admit, glancing down between us at the way she's holding both of my hands tightly, a sudden urge to haul her into my arms and cry. I don't miss the old me who never allowed this kind of touch between us. It's comforting and so necessary to me right now.

"Emma, think about it. He could've done more than a kiss ... He could've taken her back to her hotel and done the deed. As soon as he kissed her, he knew he'd fucked-up, right?" Her hopeful blue gaze bores into my face, and I try to ignore it.

I can't deny that the Jake of old would have thought nothing of screwing some girl from a bar or even screwing Marissa if he was drunk enough. He'd done that already, the baby proof of that. I quash down the vile thoughts of his body entwined with hers, revulsion pushing up my throat at the traumatic visions going through my mind.

"So, you think I should just forget it ... Brush it off as nothing?!" I snap, yanking my hands away. Of all people, I expected Sarah to be on my side.

But not this!

"No, of course, I don't. He's hurt you, Emma. But I think you can move past this and be with him again when you're ready." She sounds so young and pleading. I don't want this version of Sarah. I want her jokes on what she would do to maim him in her unrelenting loyalty to me, dragging his name through the dirt, calling him all the cusswords she can think of. Instead, she's championing him, making me feel anger that has lain dormant the past few days.

"It's not just the kiss ... It's who he kissed!" I stamp, pulling myself away, heading to the couch, and slumping down. Trying hard to simmer the wave or irritation growing in my belly. "It was her ... Marissa. The one person I hate more than anyone and the one person that can truly kill everything between us." the tears sting my eyes at the mention of that bitch's name, and I bite them back defiantly. Not while her name is on my lips, I wouldn't dare.

That bitch will never get my tears.

"It probably wasn't a choice, Emma, just a coincidence. Someone or anyone that happened to throw themselves at him because that's how much he was hurting; how irrational he was being ... There was no attraction in it." She raises her hands almost in exasperation and meets my furious scowl.

How are you so sure, Sarah, because I don't even know!?

"If he loved me, then he wouldn't have so cruelly kissed *her*." I spit, her stance unmoving, arms folded across her chest as though dealing with a petulant child. Her voice is steady and stern, with a look in her eye that belongs to a schoolmistress.

"If he didn't love you, then he wouldn't have done anything at all, Emma. He stupidly did it because he was in an incredible amount of heartache. You hurt each other. He only found out later that you were bluffing about the other guy, but you still rejected him." She walks forward, sliding beside me, regarding me, pleading, and takes my hands gently, but I turn my face away, defying her defense of him.

"He should've known I would never do anything like that, and I didn't reject him. I just said it was too soon." a tear rolls down my cheek; my head is in chaos again. I never seem to be able to get any of this straight in my head, at exactly whose fault this is, if I should've done anything differently, or how we could've prevented all this.

"Men can be idiots, especially drunk and emotional men. He was already hurting because he felt like you rejected him. With an ego like his, I'm sure that was a devastating thing, Ems and the other guy comment sent him over the edge. Maybe he just figured you had finally realized he wasn't what you wanted anymore." She's trying to sound soft, but I feel so angry and enraged.

"Well, he's an idiot because he was everything I wanted and needed. I would've followed him to the ends of the fucking Earth." I sob, unleashing a heart-breaking cry so raw even Sarah is silenced by shock. She watches me with large blue eyes, and her lip trembles.

"Emma?" she finally whispers, leaving me to calm to a gentle sniffling, my anger deflating before she continues, "If he's everything to you, then why would you reject a home with him?" She watches me closely, regarding me with a confused and gentle expression.

"Because I'm scared," I admit finally. "I'm scared I'm not enough to keep him with me for a lifetime. I'm scared of letting someone else take the lead and losing all I am. I'm scared of this new life he's offering me that could be taken away at any minute." It's then that I realize I've never believed in myself, never thought I could keep someone like him for more than a few blissful months, let alone marriage and life. That I could be more than my career and give him something equivalent to all he was trying to give me.

Even now, I feel like I never really deserved any of it.

I have so much to thank my mother and her lovers for; self-doubt is so huge I'm too scared to let myself be happy. Jake is right. I'm incapable of ever fully letting go or letting him in all the way.

"Emma, I believe he's the one for you, mistakes aside. I truly believe you'll never find another love or happiness like you did with him. He seems to know what you need, almost instinctively, and he gives it to you. He understands you. You have no idea how rare that is." She tightens her grasp on my hand and gazes at me fondly. Those tropical blue eyes twinkle with love. "You changed someone like him, Emma. He changed you. You have no idea how huge that is. I don't think he'll ever look elsewhere again if you give him another chance. No, in fact, I know he won't."

"I can't just push aside what he did." I sigh.

"But you can learn to forgive him, and you can only do that by talking to him and seeing what happens next." She strokes back my hair from my face wiping away some of the wetness on my cheek. "You can't wallow in here and hide away forever."

"It hurts me when I think of him or even see his name on a text or an email. I can't bear to open any that he's sent, not even the letter Mathews brought the first day." I shrug at her hauling my hair across my face and twisting it harshly. Lately, every anxiety-driven habit and fidget I'd learned to control has returned tenfold, reminding me of him and his warm hands pulling my fingers from my hair. I yank my hands away, clenching my fists to curb the urge.

"You're doing what you always do. You're pushing it away, denying its effect on you. It's hurting you trying to catch it all in that little black box in your head, but it won't work with this. You look awful." Sarah smiles at me, but I can see the concern in her eyes. "I'm not telling you to run back to him with open arms, just go see him ... Or let him come see you. Talking is the only way forward." How she inclines her head with a knowing look gives me a tingle of suspicion. Something in that *'know it all'* expression makes me stop and take note.

"He's talked to you, hasn't he?" I finally click that she knows more than I managed to say through hysterical tears, and she changed her whole attitude in the last few hours since my call. I'm not dumb. Only Jake could've given her the insight that I don't have. The way she's been fighting to give him a chance when only hours ago she wanted to rip that pretty head from his wide, strong shoulders.

More like his asshole head and arrogant shoulders. Man up, Emma!

"Yes, he did. I wasn't sure if I should tell you. I wanted to give him a piece of my mind, if I'm being honest. He gave me his number a while back when I couldn't get through to you at work and had to call your main office." She looks away sheepishly as though she's done something wrong.

"What did he say? How did he sound?" I can't help myself. It's like dangling alcohol in front of a drunk. Any little insight into Jake right now is what I need and crave, even if it's something I'm not sure my frayed emotions can handle right now. I know how contradictory my reaction is to what I've been thinking, but it's a spontaneous impulse I have no control over.

"He sounded so ... broken. The first thing he said was, "How is she?" ... That kind of threw me." She shrugs nonchalantly. "I was all set to yell at him, but then I sort of didn't. He sounded like a man living through hell, Emma ... Not very *Jake Carrero* at all."

I swallow hard, returning my focus to my hand as the tremble in my lips betrays my urge to cry. I don't want to hear how hurt or different he is. I want to know my domineering cocky asshole is still in there. I need him to be the Jake I love.

"Tell me ..." I stumble over the words like lead in my mouth. "... Tell me what he told you."

"Maybe it's best coming from him, sweetheart? He told me because he needed someone to offload to, someone who would be on your side. Someone he knows loves you as much as he does. I think he wanted me to see it from his side, and somehow, if I could understand it, he would have a chance at getting you to understand too." The honesty in her eyes makes me break.

"No ... I couldn't bear to hear him say any of it. I don't think I could handle it. Please, Sarah." I turn to her with watery, pleading eyes and a grim expression. My pain is so visible that she lets out a small cry of sympathy, making my heart thump harder in my chest.

She thinks for a long while before resigning herself to saying more, my begging gaze boring into her, weakening her resolve. Defeat in her eyes as she slowly gives in to my silent will.

"He barely kissed her, Ems ... seconds at most, and then felt an almighty kick in his gut. He said he knew instantly he was throwing away everything that mattered to him. That he was being an idiot, so he turned around and walked away. Left her standing in the club. He went home with Daniel until he was ready to face you."

She looks at me, waiting for some response, and she carries on when I don't give one.

"He said he switched on his phone when he couldn't stand it any longer and had two messages and a voicemail from you. It was like having his heart ripped out all over again. He knew as soon as he saw them that he'd lost you. He knew you would go the second he told you what he'd done." She sighs and raises her eyebrows in an *'I'm sorry'* gesture.

"I just don't get how he could do that to me." I sob as pain scars through my chest despite her telling me something I already know. I bite down the burning knot of agony in my throat, fighting down the words trying to come out of my mouth.

"He's a man, Emma ... He's human and not perfect. God, you've told me how many times before how imperfect your Boss was? He's still the same guy, except now you love him. We all have insecurities, and we all jump to conclusions and make stupid mistakes, even him." She hands me the box of tissues from the side. No one knows more than me that we're capable of irrationality when insecurity raises its head.

I am the queen of insecurity and jealousy.

"What if I can never forgive him? Never stop feeling this broken?" Fresh tears roll down my cheeks, hopelessness devouring me.

"I promise you that you can move on from this, and if he's the guy for you, he'll earn your forgiveness a thousand times over. I have faith that he will, Emma." She tips my chin with her fingers, so

I look at her. "He really loves you in a way that makes me kind of jealous." She smiles, casting her eyes to her shut bedroom door. "Not all men are so easy to love or show it so openly. But Jake and you, I think you're the exception to the rule. You two are the fairy-tale couple despite his impulse to fuck it up all the time. He dotes on you in a way most men aren't capable of, and he doesn't care who sees it either."

"It doesn't feel like it right now." I sigh, wiping my nose with my sleeve, ungraceful and completely angst-pushed. The old Emma would be rolling in her metaphorical grave right now.

"Don't walk away from him ... I'm not saying that for him. I'm saying it for you. I don't think I'll ever see you get over him if you do." She sets a serious look on her gentle face. "You owe it to yourself to try to forgive him. If you can't, then at least you know you tried." Sarah's warmth calms me, bringing some sense of numbness back to the ache in my chest.

"You really want the apartment to yourself, don't you?" I smile through my watery tears, and Sarah giggles.

"Totally! It is my love nest, after all." We both laugh softly, releasing a tiny bit of tension. "You know you can stay here forever. I would love nothing more, but I want you to be happy, and I think it'll only happen when you're back with him."

Typical. Find happiness in the arms of the one person who can destroy you.

"What should I do?" I finally sniff, still confused at the riot of emotions and thoughts coursing through my head.

"Read the letter, the messages, and emails. Then maybe reply to one of them and take it from there." She presses a palm to my cheek in a surprisingly maternal way. "Do what you feel is best for you. But don't just sit festering, doing nothing." Sarah gets up and walks to her door, leaving me to digest our conversation.

"I need to go unpack and see Marcus. Tell him it's safe to come out. He has a phobia of women's tears and a public show of real emotions. Just yell if you need me, okay?" She smiles at me widely, realizing she still has her coat on from coming home. She didn't even stop to take it off before coming and being here for me.

I love you, Sarah.

"I'll be in my room ... Reading." I sigh, resigning myself to following her advice for once, unable to stop the trembling in my body, but my mind is made up. Even if every part of me is screaming in fear.

Sarah halts and throws me a wink and a smile.

"I was hoping you'd say that."

Chapter 3

With shaking fingers, I stare at the folded paper in my hand. The envelope discarded, now lying on the bed with his neat scroll on the front. I take an eternity to run my fingers across the neat lettering, pain shooting through me from every angle. I inhale deeply, steadying my nerves, unfolding the thick cream paper, and biting my lip. I drag courage from somewhere, telling myself I should dive in and do it.

Emma,

I'm sorry, Bambina, so extremely sorry. I don't even know what writing to you will achieve, but I had to do something. I saw them packing up every piece of you, and I had to stop myself from tearing it out of their hands and holding onto it all. I can't bear it. I feel like everything they remove is a slash across my heart.

I know I don't deserve you, I don't deserve your forgiveness, but I'll do anything to have it, anything to get you back. I made a stupid mistake, wasn't thinking clearly, and wanted to lash out at everyone.

I'll never hurt you again, I swear. Just give me a chance to fight for you. I'll never give you a reason to doubt me again. I hurt the one person I love and need more than anything in the world.

I won't ever make that mistake again. Being here without you is torture, so unbearable I can't breathe. I can't get you out of my head or how you looked at me when I told you what I'd done. It was like a knife being thrust deep into my chest and turned; I know what I've done. You don't need to punish me, baby, nothing is as bad as this, and no punishment could come close to the pain I'm in without you. I've never felt regret like this before and never intend to earn it again.

Please. Talk to me. I just want to see you, look at you, and have you near.

I'm slowly going insane without you, baby. I need you. I love you, and I can't, won't lose you. I'll fix this.

Just give me a chance.

Jake x

Tears roll down my cheeks, dripping onto the paper, and I watch in agony as some of the ink from his signed name bleeds across the surface. I watch in dismay as his name becomes a blur of stained grey and throw the letter on the bed as though it's burned me.

It hurts more than I thought it would, reading something he wrote for me, connecting to him in some small way. It hurts because I miss him so damn much, and I'm dying of pain. Everything he wrote makes me ache, and I want to see him more. I'm so confused and in turmoil about what to do. His words have cut me to the core with longing and anger, so much love from one man. Yet he's capable of cutting out my heart in one selfish, childish act. I want him right here with me, but my mind wants to punish him by staying away.

I pull my phone out of the bedside drawer and switch it back on. After his third text, I turned it off days ago, unable to cope anymore, hoping to find relief in the silence. I needed a break to be alone and process things. It bursts back into life, and I try to steady the inner wave of tears and fear waiting to drown me. I need to do this if I desire to move forward. I need to see what he wants to say and decide where I go from there. Sarah is right. I can't dwell on hoping I'll wake up fine tomorrow and forget all about it. The only way to sort this out is to face it head-on and start taking steps to either fix us or forget him.

When my phone is fully caught up, I flick to my texts from him, opening the oldest one unread in the row on display.

I love you, and I miss you xx I'm sorry, baby. J

I bite my lip and quell the new onslaught of tears, moving to the next text quickly, like ripping off a Band-Aid fast, trying to avoid the overemotional response to each one.

I wish you would just say something, anything. Even if it's to yell at me and tell me you hate me. Silence is torture. Xxx J

My hands tremble as I trace the words on my screen. My heart is aching for him like a pathetic idiot. My fingers hover over the kisses longingly for a moment before I shake myself out of it. I notice under the third message is one more; a new one received when my phone was off, updating now.

Tell me what to do. What you need from me? Talk to me. Please. Xxx J

With another punch in the gut and another tear to my collection, I sigh, biting back the tremble on my bottom lip, and push the next one open.

I can't do this; I will end up banging down your door just to see you. Please, Emma. Reply or something. I got every bunch of flowers, every piece of jewelry, and every gift sent back to me. Emails ignored; texts ignored. You're not giving me any choice but to show up and fight for you, baby. I love you too damn much to let this go, and I'm going crazy with this silence. We had so much, too much, to let it end this way. Xxx J

My breath catches in my throat at the last one, a mix of heartbreak and something else, a tingle of something I can't even pinpoint. I should be angry with the way he's texted me, but strangely, I'm not. He should be groveling at my feet for my forgiveness.

This is the Jake I need to see. The one who ignores all and comes pounding after me regardless. The Jake who came after me to Chicago despite me saying no. The Jake who always pursues me because he can't help being the dominant one.

Do I want Jake to show up and break down my door to see me? Prove to me he will fight for me?

Maybe I do. Perhaps it's partly what I need from him - that instinctual way he cuts through everything to come for me regardless of protest.

I shake the thought aside and quickly open my email app, logging into my personal account. Before I can linger on my confusing thoughts, there are two.

Jake Carrero has sent you an iTunes song.

Jake Carrero has sent you Beyoncé-Halo.

Attached message - I never had a way to resist letting you in. You're my angel baby. The light in my world, the reason I want to be better, you're in everything I look at. You're always around me even when you're not here. You're the voice in my head that tells me to be a better man. I waited a lifetime to find you and will not lose you now. I need to know what you're feeling and thinking. I won't just lose you without a fight. Talk to me, Emma, Please. Xx J.

The use of our old mode of communication hits me like a punch to the heart, painful yet not. Memories of how sweet he can be, attentive, funny, and loving. It confuses me more, and despite myself, I press play on the song as I agonize over his sweet words.

Listening to it almost breaks me. More tears and more internal assault as I imagine Jake saying every single word to me. I can't stop the ache of longing or the insane depths to which I miss him. Each lyric clawing at me reminds me of all the good in him and how he shows me love and always expresses his devotion without hesitation. It hurts so much.

When the song ends, it lingers in my head for a while before I have the strength to read his last email. Thoughts of his touch, his kiss, his heart like bittersweet torture.

I tried your cell and got your answering machine a dozen times. I hate that you don't want to talk to me. Just tell me what to do, baby ... Please. I'm literally on my knees begging here. Xxxx J

I have no clue in which order the emails and texts were sent. My head is too frazzled to care. The point is I've done it. I've read them, despite the emotional turmoil, the tears, and the ache to see him, and yet, I'm still breathing.

The salty warm tears are pouring down my face, and I slump

back onto my bed, staring at the ceiling, my head a whirling mass of crazy emotions and thoughts.

I don't know what to say to him or what I need from him. I've never been here before, dealt with this kind of heartache, or been in a situation where I've freely given my trust away only to have it wrenched apart like a worthless rag. The thought of never seeing him again destroys me, but the thought of him brings a full vision of his mouth on hers that tortures me. I'm so stuck between two excruciating realities I can't breathe.

I hold the phone above my face and read his texts again, wanting his nearness through the only contact I've allowed. My heart constricts and twists inside of me. I devour the messages over and over, memorizing them until they are etched into my heart, absorbing the words, letting the slice of agony they cause dim. Trying to find calm in my chaos yet still being connected to him in some small way.

What do I say? I know he'll come here at some point if I say nothing. Jake won't sit back forever and wait. Do I even want him to come?

I don't know if that's what I want; my mind and body are at odds with one another, fighting a grand battle to the death. Self-preservation, PA Emma, telling me to keep him out, the new weaker me begging to let him come.

I sit up, take a deep breath, and wipe my face, steeling myself to do this, to do something. I don't want him to sit suffering in my silence indefinitely, despite the pain he's caused me. I can't do that to him. I can't keep inflicting silence when he's trying to reach out to me in any way possible. My hands tremble as I impulsively type a response.

I needed head space to think. I'm confused and heartbroken. You hurt me. I don't know what I need from you, so how can I tell you what to do? X Emma.

I look at the text before sending it, inhale heavily, emotions swirling up again, my hands shaking violently. If I don't know how to deal with my head, what chance does he have? This day may kill me after all.

My phone beeps seconds later. My heart skips a beat, and my fingers shake when I swipe my phone.

Let me pick you up so we can talk face-to-face. X J

I inhale sharply as panic sets in, knowing it's too soon. I don't know if I can handle seeing him right now. My heart bleeds that he's so quick to connect like he's been waiting. It feels like he's right here beside me. But he's not. He's somewhere alone, mirroring what I'm doing, touching me instantly when I need him like he always has done.

What happens if I can never handle seeing him again? What happens if this destroys everything, so I can never move on? Maybe it's better to see what happens rather than hide and die a slow, painful death of heartbreak.

I grab my hair at the temples of my head, tugging in frustration. My emotions and brain are tormenting me relentlessly. I can't pick one path to follow, which drives me insane.

I take my phone from my lap and stare at it, taking a deep and calming breath before deciding what to do and say.

Not yet. I need time to digest all the messages and your letter. I only just read them. Give me time. That's all I ask. My response to your song, Jake, Beyoncé's "Broken-Hearted Girl." X

I sigh with a deflated breath as it sends onto him. My heart is aching, but I can't see him yet. The song expresses the craziness of what's going on inside of me. This war raging inside me, relentlessly consuming my thoughts, needs to be dealt with first. I'm scared about his response, holding my phone with bated breath. I wonder if he'll listen to the song, pondering it, and then my phone beeps.

You're killing me, Emma. I'll do what you ask. Xxx, I love you so much.

I don't feel any better with his response, an inner wave of disappointment that he's not trying to change my mind. Anger boils up inside me, coming from nowhere, and with it, the impulse to smash my phone off a wall.

What the hell is wrong with me? What is with my undying need to make Jake come after me and devour me?

It was the same when we fought after Arrick's birthday. My anger wanted him to take me with a vicious passion, as though he had no control, and now here I am, angry because he isn't ignoring my wishes and pushing his way here to see me. It's like I need the extreme from him. Maybe the lack of real love in my life growing up has caused this deep-aching desire to have someone show their love in dominant ways. I can't begin to analyze that right now. All I know is I want him to take away my decision not to see him and let his own needs take over. That's the Jake who swept me into his world. The guy who never took NO for an answer and pursued me regardless.

God. Maybe I do need therapy after all.

There's a gentle knock on my door, and Sarah wraps her head around warily. Her eyes flicker over me very analytically; she's clearly assessing my mental state.

"Emma ... honey? Are you up for a visitor? There's someone here to see you." She looks sheepish, and my heart plummets in cold fear.

Oh, my God, he didn't?! He couldn't?! Forget all that pushing his way in stuff ... NO! I really don't want to see him.

She sees my face pale visibly and immediately cuts in.

"No, no, not him ... God, no ... That girl you told me about. Leila?" She smiles in an almost terrifying effort at bravery, and I sag with breathless relief.

Oh lord ... Leila.

I get up and start adjusting my casual, rumpled clothes self-consciously. I must look a fright. My hair is wild. My face is tear-stained and puffy. God knows how crushed and dirty my loungewear is. Sarah takes my fussing as a cue to let Leila come in.

Within seconds the whirlwind that is Leila bounds in, dressed from head to toe in a gray tracksuit with fur trim and sparkly silver trainers. She's like my modern-day Fairy Godmother. A crazy combination of a sporty woman and a cute child. She practically knocks me over with the force of her hug and over-energetic hand gestures.

"Jake is an actual fucking idiot." She releases enough to gaze up at me with angry eyes, carrying on her dramatic emphasizing sign language. "I told him as much before I threw the contents of his kitchen at him a couple of hours ago, complete fucking idiot ... I swear. Him and that shithead best mate of his both need a major fucking brain overhaul."

"Leila, you did what?!" I gasp in shock, unsure if this is what I want Jake to be enduring right now. With her mad temper, I can visualize her fiery little self causing chaos in his immaculate kitchen. Images of her mounting a full-on arsenal of pans and cutlery fly through my head as Jake ducks and weaves to avoid the collision.

"Yeah, I did! It's not like he can't afford some new gadgets and a clean-up crew. I'm just sorry I have such a shit aim. He was stupid enough to tell me why you were no longer at the apartment; fuckwit!" She grins at me, and I can't help but smile back, beautiful, crazy little Leila. I wish that smile meant she was joking, but I know it's unlikely. I would never like to be on the wrong side of that small blonde cyclone in full fury. I can only speculate that, despite his ferocity, Jake was probably slightly scared.

"Please tell me you didn't mark that face, though? As much as I hate him right now, it would be devastating to know you ruined it." I catch her wrist as she fusses with my mess of hair and shake my head out of her palms. I know this mess is beyond repair and her efforts are completely futile.

"Stop right now with that pouty look of despair, and no, I didn't ... Lucky for him, he's got fast reflexes. Pity his brain doesn't have the same skills. We'll get you dressed up and go somewhere cozy for cocktails, music, and a girl chat. It's an order, not a request." She lets me go and starts yanking through the cases of clothes on my floor that I still haven't had the heart to unpack, pulling dresses loose and holding them up to investigate.

"I don't think I'm up for this." I balk at her, my voice on the pleading side. My stomach is doing somersaults at the mere thought of venturing into the public domain.

"It's about time I made good with your side chick through there. I can't have my girl mooning around with another woman without getting a look in. Bet you're glad I like threesomes." She winks at me with that devilish air that can only be described as Leila. She's not going to take no for an answer. I sigh heavily and brace my hands on my hips, trying to look more authoritative.

"Leila. I look like crap and am just not in the mood...."

"Shh, not a word. Your job is to do as you're told and let Auntie Leila take care of everything." With one stubborn Leila look, I know I've no hope in hell of arguing my way out of this.

Chapter 4

I sigh for the hundredth time as I sit across from Leila and Sarah in a small booth at a trendy little cocktail bar. I feel like crap. I don't want to be here, but the force that is Leila not only whipped me into a dress and heels, and a face of make-up, but also cajoled Sarah out with us too. Sarah is in complete awe of this sassy, little whirlwind, and I can tell Sarah loves her, like everyone else who ever meets her.

"Sex on the beach?" Leila blinks at me innocently. I blink back, gulping, instantly incredibly awkward.

"What?" My head immediately zooms to the week Jake took me to the Caribbean, and I flush with both the memory and the heartache.

Why the hell would Leila be asking me this right now?

"It's a drink, Emma." Sarah cuts in, cupping her hand over mine. She's still being the gentle and sweet maternal one, still anticipating my moods, mothering me. Meanwhile, Leila is being a rather bossy and domineering little pest.

"Get that look off your face. By the time we leave, I will have you smiling and pissed. Broken hearts are cured with lots of delicious alcohol, and you know ... the quickest way to get over a man is to get under a new one." She winks naughtily, grinning, as my stomach hits my ankles and a cloak of dread passes through me.

This was so not a good idea. Leila is completely nuts.

Leila shoves Sarah's hand back from the top of mine with a rather sassy eyebrow raise.

"Stop coddling her. She's made of much tougher stuff, and this new, all-teary Emma is not a good look. I swear if you don't suck it up a little for one night, I may have to get my whip out." Leila's words hit me, almost like a slap, and I try to ignore the whip thing, wondering how serious she is.

She's goddamn right! I am not someone who sits and cries their way through life's upsets. I'm stronger than this.

I also think that, secretly, Leila is a sadist.

I lift my chin and paste a defiant smile on my face. Meeting Leila's approving wink instantly, her nod of pride at the show of my old self.

"Yes, sex on the beach all round!" I chirp up, trying to sound brighter, my heart desperately pushing down the resistance and tears. Sarah regards me a little warily before shrugging and leaning back into her chair resignedly.

"Why not? Been ages since I had to get through a shift with a hangover." She shrugs.

* * *

"Oh, my God! Leila, get down!" I'm laughing so hard my sides hurt as Leila dances along the bar top, shimmying and singing full pelt into the wireless mic of the karaoke machine. She's in full rock star mode, strutting her stuff like a coyote ugly wannabe. Sarah is so drunk she's sprawled over the bar, laughing at my poor attempts to control the wild petite blonde.

"Leave her alone, honey. She looks mighty fine up there." Some sleazy fat man grabs my wrist, tugging my arm from Leila's leg, and I recoil in disgust at his touch. His eyes travel under the dress she borrowed from me to wear, and my repulsion grows into something more empowering, seething anger. I elbow him hard in the ribs and stand back with a fierce glare when he comes around at me.

"What the hell is wrong with you? Crazy bitch!" He moves in

angrily, but my inner anger and psycho switch clicks on, pulling my height up to its full length in readiness, too drunk to care about what I'm doing or any subsequent consequences.

Bring it on, asshole!

"That's enough. Do you need me to escort you out, Tom?" The bartender cuts in, sliding the empty glass away from the man with a warning glare. The man snaps his attention to the burly tender, with his bulging muscles and no-nonsense expression, and sneers my way.

"Fucking bitch ... No. I'm going anyway." The chubby older man turns on his heel and stalks off, leaving me feeling a little smug. I'm trying to ignore the deep welt of pain growing inside of me, managing to convince myself that it has nothing to do with the anger inside of my broken heart. Anger is a good emotion for me right now. It's pushing away the melancholy from the last few hours. I've been thinking about Jake almost every second, despite the alcohol-fueled party mood that Leila has inflicted on me, and I'm trying my hardest not to let it show for fear of Leila's wrath.

"Try not to get yourself into a fight, honey. Some of the regulars can be prissy as shit." The tender winks at me and moves off to tend to the crowded bar. I glare after him, drink bringing out this alarming inner rage inside me rather than my merry carefree drunken Emma.

What would Jake think of drunk Emma like this? Wouldn't like her very much, would he? This is more like Drunk Teen Emma.

Leila is still singing her heart out, but the song switches to something slower, and now she's swaying around up there. I've given up trying to reach her now that she's moved further along the bar, which spans the room and turns in a U shape along the other side. I have no idea how she's still upright, considering we've been here for hours and drunk enough alcohol to render the three of us unconscious.

My legs ache from our dancing attempts, and I have the head of a drunk girl wandering around the crowded room aimlessly. I have a fuzzy, almost dream-like haze with my consciousness, and I just want to lie down. I am suffering the effects of my drink, and the room is spinning and swaying around me. I hold onto the bar for support and stand slumped, watching the room, a little detached from reality.

She starts belting out a love song rather tunefully, a little flat in places, but she's giving it her all and enjoying herself, so I sit down to listen. It takes only a moment to realize it's a song Jake has sent me in the past.

Pink, 'Give me a Reason.'

It hits me like a punch in the stomach, winding me and bringing the huge weight of agony back to the forefront of my mind. Emotion heavy in my chest, I let out a long heavy breath to hold back the new onslaught of tears prickling behind my eyes.

I miss him so damned much. I wish he were here right now. Why did he have to infect every part of me with his presence?

I realize, suddenly, I don't like being drunk anymore. I only ever drank with Jake because I knew he would take care of me and my little bubble of bravado, well and truly pops. I hate being in a bar, without my protector, surrounded by strange men who stare and sleaze over the women around them. I'm vulnerable and emotional. The last thing I should've done was come here and get drunk. I feel so powerless and small.

Now I've started this monsoon of depressed feelings. I can't seem to switch it off. I watch Leila for a moment and see, almost with new eyes, how the men around the bar are looking up her dress, checking out her ass, practically drooling with every little movement she makes. Male eyes check out every girl that walks by, all with the same leering stare and licking of lips. Like animals searching out prey, and it sickens me.

I feel nauseous, so aware now of how awful this is. We've left ourselves vulnerable in a lion's pit, too drunk to function and take care of ourselves, and at this moment, I've never wanted Jake beside me more than right now to take care of me. Sarah's passed out, hordes of drunk men surround Leila, and I'm so out of my depth that an edge of panic starts coming on, the old Teen Emma freaking in my mind.

I haul out my cell in my drunken haze, noticing the wetness on my chin and wiping it with surprise, unaware tears have even been falling. The phone sways in my vision, my focus shot, and I try to make the screen less blurry by holding it at various distances.

"You all right, beautiful?" A male voice comes considerably close to my ear. I recoil as his warm breath hits my neck, revulsion creeping over my skin like a moving tide of cringe.

"Fuck off and get away," I snarl, all claws hissing and recoiling against the bar. I'm in full defensive Emma mode and feel hemmed in by over-sexed sleaze bags who wish to touch me. I'm prickling with angry energy.

"Fuck you, lesbo!" he snaps and moves along to try his luck with the next one. That knot of anxiety stays well and truly tightened within me, my body tense.

Charming. Dickhead.

I stab at the phone manically, unsure if I'm managing to call anyone at all, suddenly desperate for him to be here. I can hear ringing, so I put it to my ear and hold my breath.

"Emma?" Jake's voice is like a complete blast of light beaming from heaven, running through me, hitting me right in my center. His low sexy, soothing tone and the way he says my name, yet with a hint of worry. Trembling rivulets of warmth run through my body at just hearing his voice.

Oh God, I miss you.

I managed to get Jake on the first try. I've never felt such relief at hearing his voice, my heart constricting in pain and longing. Now I've finally broken the silence. It feels like it's been months since that gentle tone was inside my head.

"Who else would it be...." I slur crazily. I try for light and humor, then get angry at myself for being this weak and calling him. Even now, I cannot stop the stupid onslaught of tears pouring down my face. I'm aware my mind is still in a deep pit of confusion, but my itchy hands and aching heart must've overridden my brain with the need to see him.

I hate you. I love you. God, I miss you.

"Baby, are you drunk?" I can decipher the concern in his beautiful voice, which only makes me want to cry even more.

He's still calling me baby, his baby. I want my Jake.

"I'm too drunk ... I don't like it much. You're not here to take care of me." I burst into half gasp, half sob trying desperately to right myself on my shoes, stumbling and recoiling rapidly when my arm scuffs a warm arm.

"Don't touch me," I snap, in anger, at the blurry mess of a figure to my right. Recoiling at the male touch, wishing that Jake was there beside me.

"Calm yourself, sweetheart. You fell into me. Watch where you're fucking going." The male voice snaps back angrily as they turn away from me.

Screw you, asshole.

"Who the fuck was that asshole, baby? Where are you? I'm coming to get you." Jake isn't so gentle anymore; he sounds like bossy Carrero with a serious touch of aggression. Internal me picks up with satisfying warmth. The same me who wants the Jake I know and love to raise his head. He must've heard the asshole down the cell, who is now snarling at me with evil gleaming eyes and a twisted mouth over his shoulder. I turn my back to him and stumble against a bar stool.

"I don't know." I sigh heavily, tears replaced with exhaustion. The desire to listen to his voice and hear him talk. I sigh, and the drunken wave of daydream tugs at me for a moment. My drunken mind instantly distracted by Leila hitting an impressive high note.

"Leila is singing. Can you hear her?" I lift the phone above my head and hold it at an odd angle so he can get full clarity of that wonderful sexy soulstress. She's in the full throws of Christina Aguilera's 'Voice Within.' Right now, it's all I can think about to distract me from his voice being so painfully close, too alluring, even though I wanted to drown in it a second ago, causing me more pain and joy.

Damn you, Carrero.

I sway in time to her singing a few lines, then bring the phone back down when I can stand the sound of him again.

"Emma? ... Emma?! ... Fuck's sake! Emma?!" Jake's mid-ranting and sounds overly worked up into aggressive mode.

Oops. He obviously didn't like Leila's singing.

"Don't swear at me! You, of all people, should not be swearing at me right now," I snap and immediately burst into tears. Drunk and emotional are not a good combo. Having him verbally close is just making me worse.

Does he have no clue how much he's hurt me or messed my head up?

He inhales slowly, steadily, to calm his temper. His tone lowers, but there's that sound he makes when he's talking through gritted teeth; his - *angry yet trying to control myself* tone. I get a little ripple of longing again.

"Baby, listen to me, don't cry. I'm sorry, okay? I'm really worried about you and losing my mind a little, tell me where you are, and I'll be right there. I'll come to take you home. I'll take care of you."

Home? Home sounds good. The apartment in Manhattan overlooking the sea of lights and tall buildings, wrapped in bed with Jake, wrapped up in Jake; that's home for me.

"I don't know where we are. Somewhere, Leila brought us. Sarah's here too, but I think she's dead." I watch as she slides ungracefully off the bar where her body previously was, and she ends up in a chaotic heap on the floor, behind her bar stool between two men, seemingly ignoring her.

I don't seem overly concerned for someone who thinks Sarah might've died. I trip toward her a little, stooping to see if she's breathing, almost losing my balance and nearly falling on top of her.

"Never mind. She's just snoring," I slur down the phone with a dramatic sigh of relief. I slump down on my knees beside her to peel what looks like a beer mat off her cheek.

Yay, my friend isn't dead after all. But that is disgusting.

I hold the beer mat out in front of me and squint, looking at the blurry, sticky vile thing, before tossing it casually over my shoulder and rubbing my hands on Sarah's dress.

"For the love of God, are any of you capable of something coherent? Emma, put Leila on," Jake commands, the tone of his voice riling me a little.

You're supposed to be groveling for my forgiveness, not barking commands, Dick. Asshole. You gorgeous, sexy asshole ... But I still hate you.

"Jerk." I sniff down the phone, and I swear Jake growls ... like, actually growl.

I find myself sighing and attempting to walk toward Leila, rolling my eyes, my defiant chin stuck in the air. I'm instantly confused when suddenly I'm facing down on a leather booth seat after the wall I was using to keep me upright opened into nothing. It was a splat and vertical drop without my attempting to save myself.

"Ouch," I murmur as my face peels painfully from the seat. I realize my phone is squished to my face, and I can hear Jake rather loudly on my cheek. Opening my eyes, the lit screen blinds me near my eyeballs.

"Did you just fall? What the hell ...?! Emma, hello?! Okay, look, hang up but don't leave that bar. I'll find you my way." It sounds more like a threat, and when I reply, I realize he's disconnected my call.

Asshole! I didn't ask you to come for me. I don't want you to come for me! You don't know where I am anyway, so good luck with that.

I crawl onto the booth where I'm already lying and curl up on the seat, trying to get a hold on these damn infernal tears. I should call him back and tell him to go to hell, but I don't want to. Part of me wants him to find me and take care of me. Wanting him to ignore my pleas to stay away and do what Jake does – Come charging in all dominant mode trying to bend my will to his. If he does that, maybe my confusion can take a long walk off a short pier for a while and give my mind a well-needed break.

I don't like it here anymore, and I think Sarah may really be dead. She's not moved at all, but I'd rather rest first because she's too far away to get to. I wiggle my feet out of my shoes and drop them on the floor, feeling an odd sense of heartache at this simple act. Jake always took my shoes off for me when I was drunk. He always took care of me regardless of his mood or sobriety. I hate that he plagues everything I do.

I sigh, trying to wipe away the mess pouring down my face,

resting my head against the wall and closing my eyes to block out the wave of people mulling around the bar and floor. For a small place, it's crowded and noisy, with a thick foggy atmosphere. Maybe if I drown it all out for a few minutes, I could get my head straight and get us back home. Take Sarah home somewhere safe to sleep in a position a little more natural and get Leila off that damn infernal bar, so men stop trying to grope her.

* * *

"Emma, Bambina, wake up." Jake's voice comes at me through the darkness, and suddenly I'm aware of music, people, and a lot of noise. Warm fingers trace my jaw, and I push my face into them, rubbing like a greedy cat at the touch. I choke on the atmosphere and come to in complete confusion. I find my neck stiff from the angle I've been curled up at the booth's corner.

"I'm going to lift you, okay?" warm, strong, familiar arms slide under my legs and behind my back, and I'm hoisted up against the smell of my Jake, the feel of him, his warmth, and his strength like some fantasy dream. I close my eyes, nuzzling into him, wanting this dream to last forever. I want the safe and comforting feel of him surrounding me to last, keeping the horrible ache of not being with him at bay.

I come to my senses a little, aware of movement, and open my eyes suddenly, looking right at Jake's face. Not a dream or a hallucination, but really him, and the pain of what that means right now is sheer agony. I choke back the gulf of emotions at seeing him again.

Bittersweet sums this up completely.

My chest feels like it might concave, and my heart has stopped beating. He looks beautiful if a little tired and sexy and ruffled, yet completely here and familiar and safe.

We're still in the bar, and he's carrying me out of the booth across the floor, my head is swimming, and I realize he did it; he found out where we were and came for me. Impulsively I reach out to that beautiful face and poke him in the cheek, checking that he's real and not some sweet figment of my imagination. I always did like poking that man of perfection in the face, but he frowns at me with an amused expression.

How the hell did he do that? I shouldn't be surprised with Mathews on his security; he probably tracked my cell.

Asshole! ... My asshole ... Jerk! ... My sweet jerk.

"Your face is still too pretty!" I sigh in defeat, looking for something to criticize and finding nothing.

"Glad to hear it." He smiles at me softly and lifts me with a little jerk to get me in his arms better.

"Wait, my shoes! ... Sarah ... Leila," I mumble as coherently as I can, regaining my senses, surprised at the slurring mess I hear in my own ears.

Still drunk then? How long was I out?

"Daniel has taken Sarah to the car already. He'll come back for Leila in a sec, and I have your shoes here." He lifts his fingers under my legs, and I see my shoes swinging below them.

Of course, Jake would never forget a detail like that.

"Why are you here?" I gaze up at him with wide eyes, trying to focus on the double Jake I can see in front of me. I know why he's here, but I need the words. I need Jake to be the balm that heals my wounds, and he needs to find a way to do it because trying to do it alone isn't working.

"You know why, Emma. Do you think I could sit in the apartment knowing you were out in the city somewhere and vulnerable? You may not like me very much right now, *Bella,* but I love you. I wouldn't just leave you here. I couldn't." He pulls me closer and lifts my temple to press against his mouth, closing his eyes and inhaling me. It brings me an odd sense of comfort. "You don't need to like it, but I'm taking the three of you back to the apartment. Not one of you is capable of taking care of the others." His eyes return to mine, those beautiful hazy green eyes with so much going on inside them. So much translating from him to me with just a locking of them. My heart thuds heavily, held in his arms like I have been so many times before, but this feels new.

I don't get a chance to protest because I cringe at Leila's voice piercing the atmosphere.

"I don't fucking think so!" Such a sweet thundering tone of malicious intent scouring the air; the precious little flower she is. I squirm in Jake's arms to see which direction her yell came from and catch sight of her immediately. She's still on top of the bar with mic in hand, hands on hips, glaring like a psychopath at one Daniel Hunter.

Daniel is standing in front of her on the floor, looking up, one hand attached to the hem of her short dress with a vice-like grip. He has zero intention of letting go and meets her fiery snarl with one of his own. Equally matched in the ability to throw harsh icy scowls and in the ability to handle one another.

"I'm not fucking leaving you here alone, so get down now, or I'll fucking make you. I'm not playing, Leila!" he yells back at her. Jake stiffens as a man approaches Daniel and tries to pull him back with a hand on his shoulder. It seems that someone is trying to act chivalrously by thinking of protecting my feisty little friend.

"Can you stand?" Jake turns to me, and I catch the look in his eyes that spells trouble for any guy giving his best friend grief. Jake is getting ready to kick ass, but it scares me.

"Please, Jake, don't," I whisper, sudden fear for his safety consuming me, nerves swarming up like a tornado to overwhelm me. I don't want him to fight. I don't want that version of him right now. I need him to keep doing what he's doing, sweeping me out of here regardless of my opposition.

There's an instant look of regret in his eye. He wants to help Daniel, but he's torn with me in his arms, looking at him like I'm about to cry. He genuinely doesn't know what to do. He tightens his grip on me and lifts me closer as though his decision is already made.

"Fuck," he mutters under his breath, sighing, gazing at me a little too intensely.

Luckily, he doesn't need to do anything as Leila yelps and then squeaks, spinning my head back to see Daniel walking our way with her thrust over his shoulder. Her arms and legs are flailing as she screams obscenities at his back, hauling at his shirt to fight him.

Daniel looks grim and strides purposefully past us. His face is a picture of sheer anger, yet the boy has muscles. He has Leila in a grip, which means she can't get out. He's not even reacting to her weight nor disturbed by the lashing violent outbursts on his back.

"I fucking hate you!" Leila is yelling at the top of her lungs in his strong embrace, hauling his shirt up his back, twisting it around her fists.

Jake follows at a distance keeping a tight hold of me in his arms. His expression giving nothing away. My heart is pounding so fast at his proximity, yet part of me can't tear my eyes away from the couple walking ahead. My heart is torn about where my attention should be; Jake's perfect profile and touchable face or the hellcat being kidnapped by the guy who wants her.

"Leila, I'm not against dumping your ass on the sidewalk and making you walk home if you keep that up." She's still pulling his shirt up his back, clawing at him, and using his trouser waistband as leverage to pull her weight down to smack him. He hits her ass hard in retaliation, the sound echoing across the night air, and smirks back at Jake when Leila instantly quiets and becomes motionless.

What the hell? Bastard!

I squirm in anger to be released, but Jake only tightens his hold and gives me a look that tells me to leave it alone.

"You know, as soon as you let her go, she will give you a black eye for that, right?" Jake throws back, with an edge to his tone, and follows Daniel to the waiting car. It's the black four-by-four, usually driven by Jefferson, but he's nowhere to be seen.

"Looking forward to her trying." Daniel prods Leila in the ass, looking mightily pissed. "Still with me, kitten? You're awfully quiet up there now." He shifts her weight on his shoulder for a better grip, almost as though he's trying to shake a response from her.

"Screw you," Leila mumbles from her hanging head, hair falling over so I can't make out her features. Her hands are up near her face, and suddenly I realize she's crying.

"Leila?" I reach out toward her with my free hand. My insides are hurting for her.

"Daniel ... Man ... You've fucking got that girl sobbing," Jake snaps. Daniel spins his head toward us, then looks up at the little ass on his shoulder and gives her a jiggle.

"Leila? Leila?" When she doesn't answer, he slides her down to the ground smoothly and protectively and pulls her to face him, lifting her chin in an almost tender way and meeting her wrath in the blink of an eye. She flies into all-rage hell-cat mode through tears and sobs, slapping at his arms and chest wildly, claws unleashed in full fury mode.

"I hate you! I fucking hate YOU! ... You don't give a shit who you hurt or who you use! You ever smack me like that again, and I'll tear your fucking head off!" Her tears are flowing, anger searing as she fights hard, but Daniel effortlessly restrains her, batting away her attempts to claw him and shaking her into submission with a hard jerk.

"Stop it ... Stop it, or I'm fucking done. I mean it, Leila. I won't put up with your psycho shit like Jake did earlier." He grabs her flailing hands, trying to restrain her once again, as she goes for another onslaught. I watch, holding my breath, while Jake tries to maneuver us around them, yet there are too many people trying to get past us with eyes on stalks to watch this little domestic unfold on the sidewalk.

"Done? Done?! We never fucking started. You're an asshole. You think *sex and see ya* with every girl stupid enough to come near you. You used me for sex, then dropped me like trash." She's writhing free of his hands and attempting slaps once again.

"It's never just sex with you! I fucking care about you, Leila, okay?! I just don't know what the fuck to do about it," Daniel snaps and shocks almost everyone standing here.

I don't think I've seen him more shocked at himself.

It seems to do the trick, though, Jake slides me down to my feet beside the car, and I can't help but watch with glued eyes at the pair of them standing on the sidewalk, looking at each other silently. She's stopped her assault and seems to be standing, blinking at him with her wrists in his palms; there's a moment of pause then Leila breaks the tension.

"I'm getting a cab. Go away. I don't need you to take me home, and I don't want your fucking help. I can handle my booze!" She yanks her wrists free and turns on her heels to attempt to storm away, but Daniel only grabs her by the arm and hauls her back far too easily.

"You're coming to Jake's whether you like it or not. Try fighting me on this, sweetheart, and I will literally gag you and throw you in the trunk. Don't try me, honey. We both know I'm enough of an asshole to do it." Every time she turns from him, he hauls her back, meeting another bout of her slapping and rage.

Leila, did Daniel just tell you he cares, and you're still acting crazy?

Leila seems to visibly change from sheer fury to something else, her face crumbling.

"Why would you say that to me? Why tell me you care about me? When it doesn't mean shit, Daniel! You know, no matter what, you're still going to leave me alone and fucking broken anytime I get close." Her rage has turned to angry crying, make-up pouring down her cheeks at an alarming rate, yet despite it, she still looks breathtakingly beautiful, and I soar with sheer venom at the man causing her so much heartache.

Jake is trying to get me into the car beside Sarah, but I resist, watching and waiting, wanting to see what happens next, ready to jump in and defend my friend, willing to gouge the shit out of the man upsetting her despite being Jake's worse significant other. I don't want to leave her alone to deal with him this way.

"I'm not doing this here." Daniel lets her go and turns on his heel, ready to walk off, but he catches Jake's death glare, a look that says, *don't do it, man.*

"I'll get a cab. Take her back with you and look after her. I need to think when she's not screaming in my face. She needs to sober up before we can talk."

"Danny?" Jake moves past me toward him but meets defensive palms and a look of utter emotional turmoil on Hunter's face.

"If I stay, I will make this whole fucking thing worse. She's too drunk and upset right now. I don't even know what the hell is going on in my head to begin to try to make her understand." He shrugs and shakes his head as he walks off toward the road, and Leila is left gaping after him with tears pouring down her face.

"You're a fucking coward, Daniel Hunter. You don't deserve me!" She calls after him, and he doesn't respond; he keeps walking off into the busy street without a backward glance.

Jake pushes me into the car, lifting my legs in gently, sliding my shoes into the space on the floor, not giving me any more room to fight him on this.

"Slide over while I get her." He glances over his shoulder toward Leila's sobbing figure, and I obediently move up.

Seconds later, with his arm around her shoulder, he gently guides her beside me, and I envelop her against me, letting her cry. Her petite frame is shaking with the effort of holding in so much heartache.

"I hate him so much ... I don't want to love him anymore, Emma. It hurts too goddamn much. He makes it so painful." She buries her face against me and lets it all pour out in a muffled sob.

I guess I know how that feels right about now.

I glance up, catching Jake's eyes in the rear-view mirror as he slides his seatbelt on. He looks away quickly, jaw tightening and ears moving; his body stiffens. A moment of pain runs across his face, that moment of taking Leila's words as mine.

Chapter 5

I must've gone back to sleep at some point in the car ride through the city because I wake up completely disorientated in a familiar bed, Sarah's loud snoring and body next to me. I sit up warily as spinning nausea and headache of the world's worst hangover hit me, and I push down the urge to throw up.

The room is dark and quiet, but that doesn't mean much. Jake has blackout shades on all his windows, blocking the sun whenever he wants to sleep. I scramble around under the sheets, catching the smell of him from the cushions under my head, and it instantly overwhelms me with a mix of longing, pain, and upset.

I still don't know how to feel. Great.

I slide out and carefully tread my way to the bedroom door, not wanting to wake Sarah or anyone else, especially when I've no idea what time it is. I open the door slightly and hear muffled voices from the kitchen, followed by a sudden rush of brilliant light which makes my eyes smart, and I hurry to cover them from the blinding pain.

It takes a moment to get used to the adjustment, and I check I'm still wearing clothes; last night's dress and underwear are still intact, which surprises me. I would've expected Jake to at least undress me. It's not like he hasn't seen me in varying degrees of nakedness. I guess I'm seeing how much of a gentleman he can be. The fact he chose not to sleep in the bed beside me hints at him respecting my need for space. Part of me feels disappointed, and I wonder how it would've felt waking up in his bed in his arms. The thud in my stomach hits when I realize that may never happen again. We may never sleep in a bed together again, and I try to push down the thought as a twisting wave of tears runs up inside me.

I head out in search of a drink and some pain relief in hopes of distracting myself from those agonizing thoughts.

I pause when I see Leila and Jake sitting at the breakfast counter across from one another, talking in hushed tones. They have their heads bent over coffee mugs and a plate of butter croissants, seemingly oblivious to me as I wander out quietly. Just seeing him takes my breath away, and my palms start to clam up.

"Give him time, Leila ... You know Daniel's head is royally fucked-up. He has some serious issues when it comes to love." Jake leans out and covers her hand with his in a small affectionate gesture, which makes me want him back so badly. I miss having him act that way with me. I miss his attention and soft touches, his never-ending understanding, and how he grounds me.

No! Don't even go there. He hurt you. You're not your mother, running back to men who don't care about what they do to you.

My mind slaps me hard. Somewhere old PA Emma, voice full of stern disgust, finds her way back inside my head.

I clear my throat quietly, spanning the area from his door to the kitchen, and they both look up. Leila smiles, and Jake slowly rises, not hurrying to take his hand from hers. He walks around the kitchen, making me a mug of coffee without lingering too long or looking at me. It hits me like pain under my rib cage and confounds me.

"Morning, you. How you feeling?" Leila looks freshly showered and wearing a T-shirt and shorts belonging to Jake. Her clean face, free from make-up, looks unbelievably young and cute; her blond, choppy hair is tucked behind her ears making her look ten years younger. No hint of last night's tear-stained emotional wreck, and I can only admire her for it. I've no clue how awful I must look right now, and she's making me so self-conscious. I try to run my fingers through my hair, knowing my make-up under my eyes must be smeared.

I catch Jake's eyes flicker to mine and wonder if he thinks I look like an absolute mess; maybe that's why he's trying not to look at me.

Great.

"Like I'm dying," I mumble, trying to get onto the stool beside her, my head aching and mouth dry like sandpaper. I've never felt a hangover this bad. I drop my face to avoid him. I obviously look like trash. I wish he could see me looking better or showered, at least.

Jake wanders over and slides the coffee in front of me with a glass of water. He reaches out for a pack of aspirin and places them beside me too, his eyes never leaving the task, not once looking at me.

I am stabbed with that tug of pain again. I want his beautiful green eyes to look at me the way he always does. This is just painful. I want to feel like the center of his universe again, commanding his attention and attentiveness. I want him to tell me that I look nice, even though I know I don't because that's what he does, what he's supposed to do. I miss it.

"Thanks," I utter softly, trying not to focus on him for too long. He pulls the plate of croissants over toward me.

"They're fresh; I picked them up about a half hour ago on the way back from my run." His deep voice is like molten sexiness, and I can't help but glance up at him. Our eyes meet, but he's the first to look away, and it emotionally slaps me hard across my heart.

Why won't he look at me? Because I was a drunken mess last night and now probably look a hundred times worse. Hardly the picture of beauty he probably imagined in our separation.

My head starts going crazy with suspicions, self-doubt, and panic, my stomach lurching once more, and my nerves get the better of me.

Has he been with someone else in my absence? Because he could, we're not together, and it's who he used to be. Has he decided he doesn't love me after all? Oh, my God ... has he decided we're not worth the fight?

I swallow a little too heavily, my hand trembling around the glass with shaking fingers. Wetness builds in my eyes as I try to focus on the water inside the cup.

"I love you. Even hung over with last night's make-up on, you're stunning," Jake whispers quietly, as his hand slides over mine on the glass, his face close enough for my cheek to warm from his breath; his touch is the healing balm I ache for. I flicker up sharply, surprised at how he guesses my inner thoughts, always knowing how to calm me. "Stop doubting it, Emma." Our eyes lock, and he lets me go quickly, leaving my hand cold and pining for his warmth. Then, as though nothing happened, he returns to drinking his coffee. I can feel Leila's eyes on me.

"I'm going to leave you two to talk while I get dressed. You guys need some time alone." Her hand comes to my shoulder. "Give him a chance, Emma, babes. Men are programmed to be shitheads. They can't help it." She kisses me on the cheek softly, throwing Jake a supportive wink before sliding down, and padding off toward the guest rooms at the far end of the apartment.

"If you're not ready to talk yet, I can understand. I'll take you and Sarah home when you're ready." He stays focused on swirling the coffee in his mug with a steady voice and relaxed posture. He seems to be quietly mulling over his thoughts, not letting me get any vibes into his feelings.

I swallow hard and inhale very slowly.

Decide, Emma. This is the moment to either move forward or stay here in this pain. It's time to either bite it and talk or go back to hiding in self-pity.

"Maybe when you take Sarah home, I can get a shower and freshen up here?" I can't bring myself to look at him, my insides turning to jelly. "I'll need to get her up soon anyway because she's working today." I sound feeble and unsure of myself, part of me wondering if he'll even want me to stay or if he'll just send me home.

"I'd love nothing more than to have you stay if you're sure?" the tiny hint of hope in his voice is obvious, and it hurts more than I can bear. Not in a bad way but in an 'I'm so royally broken-hearted over you, yet you still give me tingles' kind of way. We glance at one other and quickly look away, awkward and emotional, unable to stand the gaze of one another's eyes for more than seconds.

Okay, now I get why he won't look at me for long. This shit hurts.

"You don't need to get me up. I'm up." Sarah's hoarse and grumpy voice echoes our way from the bedroom door; we turn in surprise to see the disheveled mess slumped there. Her face is a makeup smear, and her hair is sticking up at odd angles. "What the hell did we drink last night?" She groans, looking around, searching for something.

"Your bags are all on the couch with your shoes." Jake points out, and I spot the little mini mountain of bags, shoes, and coats piled carefully on the sofa. Another thoughtful Jake move; any other man would have dumped them on the floor by the door.

"Thanks. I'm sure Marcus is going crazy over my whereabouts right now." She practically crawls to the couch and starts rummaging in her bag.

"I called him from your cell when we got here last night and told him I'd bring you home this morning. He was cool with that." Jake cuts in, and I find myself glancing at him with no surprise at all. This is who he is - smart, intuitive, and mature in so many ways, always thinking of every detail and doing what needs to be done. I sigh a little.

"God. Did you tell him what an absolute drunken mess I was?" She groans, trying to scroll through her phone one-handed while pulling her shoes on in a rather awkward and dangerous pose.

"I left out the part about peeling you off a bar floor and having you throw up all over the back of my car," Jake smirks at her, and I catch the grimace running across her face as she tries to remember. The look of disgust at her behavior.

"Jesus. I'm so sorry. I never drink as much as that. Leila is an awful influence on me, but damn, that girl is hilarious." She giggles and goes back to her phone.

"It's fine. The car's already been taken to get detailed. Jefferson was the only one to endure the smell, almost enough to get drunk on the fumes." Jake is smiling.

God, that smile.

Good humor from him, despite looking shattered since he hasn't slept.

"Ha. You need to let me pay for it, seriously. I can't let you pay to clean up my mess." Sarah turns our way and walks toward us, pure sincerity on that stubborn face, but Jake only shakes his head. I'm surprised at the lack of hostility toward him, especially since this very awkward scene is because of him.

"Don't worry about it. If it wasn't you, then it was going to be Emma. Kudos to her though she waited until we hit the curb." I snap up and gawp at him with a shocked flush to my face.

I threw up in front of Jake. Oh, my God.

"I'm sorry." I fumble the words out, embarrassed, my eyes hit my fingers in my lap, and I twist at the hem of my very short dress.

Great way to show the man who hurt you that you're so in control and worth every inch of the fight to get you back. Especially when you drunk dial him, need his rescue, and then throw up at his feet.

Classy, Emma ... just classy.

"Don't be. I'm glad I was the one there to take care of you. It was a drunk Emma I've never met before." His eyes linger this time, and I can feel them boring into me a little too closely, his scrutiny making me feel more awkward. I wish the ground would open below my feet and swallow me whole.

Sarah wanders over toward us and turns green at the sight of food. Jake waves a mug at her to offer coffee, his eyes finally giving me respite, but she shakes her head.

"No, really, no. If I take a sip, I'll hurl. I need to get home and get sorted out before I start the lunch rush at work. I can call a cab, so you don't have to ..." Her eyes flicker between Jake and me and the obvious tension between us.

"No, it's fine. I want to give Emma some space to get herself together, and my driver is out for now anyway. I'll take you; I'll go get my shoes." Jake pushes off the counter, glancing at me quickly, and saunters off toward his guest rooms. I can't help but watch his strong and fit body swagger, like a man with too much sex appeal, crossing the room and that ass, sighing as I watch it go.

When did he start keeping clothes down there?

"You're not coming home anytime soon, I take it?" Sarah looks me up and down warily, a slight hint of hope on her face and a smirk at where I've been staring.

What is with all these looks?

"No. I think I need to stay for a bit and see what I feel." I turn away from her, my mind getting itself out of the gutter with the memory of Jake's ass. I down two aspirin with the water and hold the pack to her, but she shakes them away.

"Don't close down on him. Give him a chance. No one's perfect, babe." She runs a hand over my hair and tweaks my cheek. "The guy obviously adores you. I mean, who else comes tearing across Manhattan to find his ex because he's worried she's in danger?"

"I'm not his ex!" I snap a little too quickly, the outburst surprising me. I've not even begun to contemplate what we are, but I am not that, not if he loves me.

"Well then, seems there's a small part of you that acknowledges it's not over." She smirks at me knowingly, then moves away as we hear Jake coming back. "Tell Leila I said thanks for a memorable night." Sarah smiles as she moves to go.

"Ready?" he asks her, bending to kiss me on the cheek impulsively as he passes. He freezes as his mouth connects with my skin. It reacts with goosebumps and flashes of flutterings deep in my stomach, my body still electrified by his touch even when things are this way between us. It hurts me knowing my body would easily fall back into his arms.

Pathetic.

"Sorry." He straightens up and looks away from me. "Habit." He mutters it so softly, almost sounding painful. He walks off, placing a hand on the small of Sarah's back, guiding her toward the door with an unreadable backward glance toward me. I've no idea how to feel about any of this, and I'm starting to wonder if it's even a good idea. I'm unsure if I have the strength to face Jake alone and fight his pull over me. I watch him from lowered lashes, and a complete pit of confused despair churns me up.

Sarah slides on her coat, picks up her oversized bag, throws me a wave, and blows a kiss with a wink as I watch them leave; a strange sense of nerves creeps up inside me as Leila comes strolling down the hall dressed in last night's clothes.

"I have my driver coming for me, so I'm going to head down, babes. Sarah still here? Has Jake gone?" She scans around in surprise.

"Jake's taking Sarah home," I say, picking at a croissant on the plate, having no desire to eat. My stomach is making a good effort to impersonate a washing machine.

"Yet you're still here?" She grins, placing her hands on her hips, and I sigh in response.

"I don't know what I'm feeling or thinking anymore. I'm giving him a chance to talk, and I guess I'll take it from there." I can't meet her eyes as she hovers beside me. Part of me feels like I'm being weak for being here after only a week of separation. I know Leila and Sarah are urging me to work this out, but I still feel pathetic.

"Make him suffer, Ems, but don't let him go. He's one of the good ones, despite all this shit, trust me. So, maybe a little messy in the brain department, but I can promise you he's worth it." She hugs me around the shoulders tightly before skipping to the couch for her shoes and belongings.

"What about you and Hunter?" I watch as her body goes rigid halfway to putting her shoe on.

"That boy has been breaking my heart since I was fifteen. I doubt he'll ever sort out the mess in his mind long enough to let me in. I need to learn to get over him," she shrugs, shoes now on, and turns to me with a resigned expression, meeting my gaze confidently. "Daniel is always going to be the first boy I fell in love with. He was my first kiss. He was my first sex, too; not even Jake knows about that time, so please don't tell him. I'm sure he would kill Daniel for it, but he's so far down that route of woman-hating and mistrust and emotionally fucked-up that I doubt we'll ever be anything more." She shrugs and continues getting ready, sliding her coat on. I blanche at her open-mouthed in shock.

"Your first time having sex?"

I just can't ... Just can't.

"Yeah, my sixteenth birthday. I saw another side to him and stupidly fell for it. I was already gooey-eyed over him because he'd kissed me senseless a couple of weeks before my party. He was eighteen and just as handsome as he is now, all muscle and big grins of self-confidence." She sighs dreamily, almost lost in memories of a boy she once knew. Then, snapping out of it, she picks up her bag and walks toward me with a tear in her eye.

"What was it like? What happened?" I can't seem to get my head around any of this at all.

"Daniel's brain happened. It was nice. None of the horror stories about the first times that you usually hear about. He was gentle and slow and made sure I was ready before he did it. It didn't hurt, and I even had an orgasm. So, I guess he was my first of those too. He kissed me the whole time and told me I was beautiful, and I felt it. He was obviously already a seasoned player by then."

I know I'm gawping, but I can't help it. I've seen the way Daniel is with women, and none of those images match up to the vision of Leila's first time.

Daniel must be in love with her after all.

"So, what then? Did he not call you after that?" I'm trying to understand how the hell he could've got that by Jake unnoticed. Jake is like a sniffer dog with his crazy sixth sense and bloodhound instincts when protecting the women he loves.

"He told me I was too young, that it was dumb, and Jake would kill him. I was so in love with him that I didn't want to argue, and it hurt like hell, but I wanted to play it cool and act mature. I think I died a little every day after that, and then the weeks passed, and he never spoke about it again. We'd fallen back into our old 'friendship,' and he went back to acting like nothing had happened. I was so confused!"

I guess that would be why no one knew!

"Oh, Leila. What an asshole." I frown at her; irritation rises from deep inside me, angry that Daniel could dismiss something this important to Leila without a care. She shrugs nonchalantly, rummaging through the contents of her bag until she locates a lip balm and applies some with her fingertips.

"It's nothing compared to what he did to me in Paris a few years back ... That time I really did think this was it, a whole night of crazy passion and drunken fun, and I was so freaking happy. I realized how crazy about him I still was. We were locked in a room for eight hours solid and had sex multiple times, making me orgasm like crazy. The best night of my life. Come morning, he gets up before I'm awake and sneaks off, doesn't speak to me for months, wouldn't return my calls, nothing. I only started being okay with him last year when Jake convinced me to try to be civil for his sake."

"Jesus." I cringe, trying to figure out how I would've felt if it had been Jake.

It doesn't bear thinking about.

"Yeah, that time hit me hard. I went on a drink-fueled binge for a few months, partying wild and man-hungry, trying to get him out of my system. My brother, Tom, and Jake came and dragged my ass back home and put me on lockdown for a few weeks until I stopped and got sober." She hauls on her coat and throws her bag over her shoulder airily, hiding her innermost feelings from sight.

"Leila, I'm so sorry." Tears catch in my throat, and I get up and walk toward her, throwing her in my arms and giving her the best Jake-style hug I can muster.

"Should've learned, huh? Giving him a chance to do it again was stupid, especially as I know what he's like. I know him." Her eyes hold a thin veil of moisture, and her lip trembles a little as she fights hard with her internal emotions, small tears in the wall of strength she always tries to exude.

"I don't know what to say, but I know it's not as simple as not liking you. He seems to feel something genuinely, maybe even love." I appraise her expression, seeing that wall of impassiveness slide back up.

"Jake's told me pretty much the same, but it doesn't change anything. I can't live my life waiting for him to sort his shit out. I'm done. Last night I finally realized it as I stood considering those devastating blue eyes of his. I'll die alone and unhappy if I don't move on." She shrugs it off and despite being sad for her, I also see her point. She deserves a man who pursues her and loves her completely.

The way Jake does with me?

Don't think about him!

"Leila, why are men so frickin frustrating?" I ask, sitting back down, staring at the hands I drop loosely on my lap.

"Don't lose him, Emma. Jake's an ass who goes into self-destruct mode when he can't handle his emotions, and that's exactly what he did. Marissa did more damage than he likes to admit, and those years of hitting back with women, booze, and drugs are still in there deep down. He's never had to face the consequences of his behavior before. Still, something inside his crazy head obviously snapped because kissing her for the briefest moment was as far as it got before he was running off and agonizing over what he'd done." She stands over me and lays a gentle hand on my shoulder.

I lock eyes with her in wide-eyed silence, the pain a little too acute to form a response.

"I'm not excusing what he did. God knows I was livid beyond belief when he told me. I'm just saying it won't be repeated. He learned a valuable lesson that night. Life without you is unbearable, and he won't ever chance risking it again if he ever wins you back." She pats me on the shoulder and tucks a stray hair behind my ear. My heart is thudding heavily as I absorb every word. Emotion catches in my throat and makes me feel a million times worse than a hangover should.

"You sound like someone who's been talking to Jake." I sniff back a tear, threatening to pour out the rising ache inside me, making my hands tremble.

"Had to return the favor. After all, he did let me cry on him when you drunk weirdos were too passed out to care."

I catch her smiling at me with fondness, and she ruffles my hair childishly.

"Go. Get cleaned up and fresh for the most important heart-to-heart of your life. I need to go." She bends and kisses me on the side of my mouth with a devilish smile. "I love you, girl, and I love that sassy Sarah. We three are so hooking up again!"

With that, she saunters off as though she hasn't a care in the world and heads out the door.

I can't help but admire her. Broken-hearted and as emotionally hurt as me, yet she has her chin held high and a smile on her face as though everything is right in her world.

I could learn a lot from Leila.

Chapter 6

I stand in the shower for an unbelievably long time. The hot water pouring down me refreshingly helps to push the nausea down. I'm aching at everything so familiar about being here, so many memories and thoughts of Jake beside me. I feel like I've woken inside a dream, some strange alternate reality I never left, and this feels like where I should be. It's disconcerting and doesn't help my emotionally confused state of mind at all.

Fully cleansed of my shameful drunken night and drying myself, I can hear noise in the apartment. The sound of music drifting through the walls, and I know Jake must be back. I pause for a moment listening to the faint drifting of one of his favorite songs and the sound of a juicer going in the kitchen, emotion swirling in apprehension in my stomach. I'm nervous about being with him, being alone, and facing him.

I pull on an oversized white bathrobe and wander cautiously out to the large open-plan lounge, looking around for him, holding my breath. I'm like a jittery teen going on a first date.

He has his back to me, dressed in a fresh T-shirt and jeans, and seems to be making a smoothie or some healthy drink. The blender is going strong, so he doesn't hear me approach. I can't help but watch how his strong, wide shoulders move and flex under his body-hugging T-shirt or how his arms and biceps tense and grow with every bend and stretch. His masculine mannerisms, strong with effortless ease and grace, are the signs of a man confident in himself without the malice of cocky arrogance.

I must admit, he's the perfect specimen of manly form. Just the thought of it makes me depressed. Every nerve in my body is torn between lust and betrayal, I want him, yet I don't. I long for his touch, yet I know it will only bring me pain. I miss those arms and hands on me, but I know having them back would break me.

The machine stops, and I watch from the other side of the counter as he pours half into a tall glass before turning my way with a flicker of surprise.

"Hey, didn't hear you coming through." He smiles in his shy and charmingly beautiful way; it has the same effect on me that it always has. I clamp my knees together as a wave of hot warmth rushes through my veins.

Seems he hasn't lost that ability over me anyway.

"Here, your favorite smoothie. I figured you may need it, seeing as you haven't eaten anything yet." He nods toward the plate of croissants on the counter, now covered in plastic wrap. I take the tall glass, carefully avoiding his hand so we don't touch, and smile shyly. I pull my robe tighter across my chest and slide onto the bar stool trying with every ounce of self-control to stop trembling and acting as awkward as hell.

"Thanks. Not sure I can drink it right now, but I'll try." I take a sip of the forest fruits, mango, and banana smoothie, touched that he would do it for me; but I gasp and swallow hard when the bile rises from my stomach. I put my drink down grimly and hold my throat until the nausea calms down.

"Maybe just water?" He nods at me with a slight frown before getting me a glass of iced water from the machine on the refrigerator.

There's a weird quiet atmosphere as he watches me sip. Tension and awkwardness, as though neither of us knows what to say first. I turn away from him and around the room to find something to rest my eyes on that isn't six feet two, sexy as hell, with an ability to break me into a million pieces. I can feel his body heat across the kitchen bar and the tingle of electricity in the air. Drawn back to him like a moth to a flame. I glance up and down at his fresh clothes and know for a fact he never came into his room for them. I motion with my glass at his attire shyly.

"Why are you keeping clothes in the guest rooms?" I ask gently, confused by this unusual fact. He frowns at me for a moment before answering.

"Because I can't bear to be in there." He nods toward his bedroom. "Without you ... I had Nora move some of my things so I wouldn't need to go there at all." He looks down at his hands awkwardly. I flinch like he's just sucker-punched me in the stomach. It's such a painful response. We look away from each other instantly.

"I see." I choke back the tears threatening to break loose and clear my throat to try to shift them away again.

"I brought you something to wear when I took Sarah home. The bag is by the bedroom door." He nods toward the pink hold-all that belongs to Sarah, changing the subject quickly, and I smile gratefully; only Jake would've had that kind of foresight.

"Figured you would keep me in that dress if you had a choice," I smirk at him and catch the tension in his face, ease a little. Trying to lighten the heavy mood I created with my question.

"I would have, but I think it needs dry cleaning first. You smelled like a brewery last night." His devilish smile melts the pain in my heart slightly, and I slide off the chair. Jake's trying for the light, easy humor we used to have. It's a little warming and helps with easing my nerves.

"I think I'll go get dressed. I don't feel too comfortable like this." I point out an instant pain in my heart at the hint of disappointment across his face. Jake used to love me in nothing more than bathrobes, easy to peel apart and access me underneath. This is a sign of how things are between us, and without trying to wound him, I have.

"I'll be here." He throws on a brave smile that doesn't reach his eyes. I nod and move off, grabbing the bag as I pass, trying to remove the spike wedging itself in my heart.

* * *

He chose one of my casual 'lounging at home' outfits, whether it was deliberate or Sarah had chosen it, but I'm comfortable. I feel much better dressed in leggings and a silky camisole under a long, oversized cashmere jumper. I pull on the long thick socks, leaving them wrinkled at my ankles. They're my much-needed hugs from clothes I would've chosen myself.

The nausea, headache, and overwhelming hangover are still lingering, but that constant hunger I seem to have is starting to battle with it, urging me to eat after all. I'm unsure how well it'll go down, but I'm ravenous despite what awaits me out in the kitchen.

I pad out into the lounge and see Jake hovering in the kitchen, messing with the expensive coffee maker and filling up the small compartments. I never see much of his domesticated side when Nora is around, but he shows his competence on the rare occasions she has a day off.

He turns with a timid smile, sensing my presence, and puts down the packets he's holding. We both know it's time we talked and stopped evading this. I walk past him, retrieve the smoothie from the fridge, and take a proper drink, and he smiles at my efforts.

"Do you want to sit here or in our room?" His gentleness makes me waver; he's still calling it 'our' room, and I can't trust myself not to fall under his spell almost instantly if we were near that bed.

"The couch." I nod in the direction of the white leather and chrome behind him, and with trembling legs, I make my way to the padded seat and sit down, hating the tension that has suddenly thickened in the space between us.

I push around some of the fluffy cushions I picked out a few weeks ago, nervous anticipation and stomach butterflies returning, and nestle myself near the side table so I can put my glass down. I haven't upchucked it yet, surprisingly, it seems to be soothing my stomach. The aspirin is helping my head a little.

He waits, then sits near me, still giving me space. His whole body is turned to me, focusing solely on my face. This close, I can almost feel his touch. His smell is intoxicating, and his nearness is a little too suffocating. I tip my head down, letting my damp hair cover me, suddenly aware of how tired and pale I must look.

I don't want him to see me this way. I should've worn make-up or paid more attention to my appearance earlier!

"You look beautiful, *Neonata*," he says, almost as though he can read my mind. I swallow hard as the lump of emotion threatens to rise through my throat at the fact that he always knows.

Is there another human being alive so effortlessly in tune with me? Who always says just what I need to hear?

"I look tired and awful," I reply quietly. "I haven't been sleeping a whole lot lately." I bring my hands to the hem of the cozy long jumper dress, fiddling with the soft wool, and chew my lip. Now I'm here beside him and ready to get this out. I don't know what to say or how to say it; I don't even know what I want.

"Makes two of us." His voice is lighter, and without looking up, I can tell he's staring at me with his beautifully gorgeous green eyes.

God, I miss him so much.

Even his smell and closeness are aiding wounds that have opened over the last few days. The eternal despair and loneliness that consumed me are fading with his mere presence and him being his normal gentle self. I can almost forget the past few days of unbearable loneliness.

"You hurt me." It's the only thing I can think of to say to get this in the direction it needs to go. I'm so used to Jake leading conversations that involve feelings but not this time. I need him to understand what I'm feeling and thinking and not let it bubble inside me.

"I know ... I hate myself right now, Emma. You have to believe me. If I could go back and stop it, I would, in a heartbeat." He shifts closer, his leg on the couch, so he's fully turned to me. I can't bring myself to turn to him, tears welling inside me now that we're doing this. "I can't function without you ... I miss you like crazy, *Bambina,* and I'm losing my mind not being able to touch you." His nearness causes waves of tingles and cold to run over me, my body as confused as my mind, turning into a chaos of mixed signals. Lust, fear, longing, defiance, love, hate, heartbreak. I've no idea what to feel about him.

"I don't know if I can ever forgive what you did." A silent tear rolls down my cheek. "I trusted you." I lift my hand, tangling my fingers into my hair, turning the strand, and twisting it absent-mindedly, trying to focus on something else rather than the erupting chaos inside me. Jake leans out over me automatically, taking my hand in his, and slides the last gap between us, holding my hand to his chest and over his heart. His touch is searing yet comforting but pushes the vision of his hand on her into my head, and I pull it away as though it's been scolded. He says nothing and doesn't react but sighs gently, accepting that I can't have him holding my hand.

"I'll spend the rest of my life trying to earn it back ... I'll do anything, Emma. I'll go anywhere. If you want me to cut all ties with her, then I will." His voice only holds strong conviction.

"What about the baby?" I croak, my heart thudding like a war drum. I can't look at him when he's sitting so close, but I can feel his eyes burning into me, devouring me.

"If you asked me to walk away from that too, I would. I know how bad it will be for us to have that connection with her. All I want is you back in my arms, Emma." He leans closer, almost touching my hair with his nose. I hold my breath, fighting with myself to move away, but my body stays still, betraying my mind. My body wants this even if my brain screams to get away from him. I feel so powerless.

"I wouldn't want you to do that. I don't want you to abandon it, despite me not wanting the baby to be there." My hands are shaking so badly I push them between my knees and press my legs together to hold them still.

"I know you wouldn't, but I need you to know I would do anything for you."

"I need you to tell me why." The tears spring out without warning, my voice crumbling, and I tense away as his hands rise to hold me. He stills and puts them back down.

"There is no why, baby. Only a stupid drunken mess who

convinced himself that you didn't want a life with me. I wasn't just drunk, Emma. I went off the rails and took shit I hadn't touched since my teens. I got completely shit-faced and got into a fight with two men during that one night." The regret in his voice causes me to look at his hands. It's the first time I notice the faint bruises and healing cuts across his knuckles. That inner weight gets heavier, and my heart bleeds a little more, a surge of disappointment at knowing he'd taken drugs. The Jake I loved didn't do those things anymore, and I don't like that he's admitted it.

"I didn't say no to a life with you. I didn't say no to marriage. I said it was all happening so fast, and I was scared." I leave my focus on his hands. They're sitting on his knees. It's a better, safer view than his green eyes deeply boring into me.

"I know." He sounds ashamed, deflated, and devoid of hope; the tone of his voice yanks through my chest, tugging painfully at my emotions.

"I need to know what you were thinking, how far it went. It's all that goes through my head all the time. You and her and I can't bear it." I don't hide my tears, and my voice is trembling as much as my hands. He lifts his hands automatically, fisting them, and puts them back down. His urge to console me and touch me is torturing him as much as his closeness is torturing me.

"I wasn't thinking, Emma. There was just rage and mess and a lot of pent-up anger. The more wasted out of my head I got, the less logical everything became. It could've been any girl. It just happened to be her. She appeared almost out of nowhere and was trying to get me to talk to her. I don't remember much of what happened, only her kissing me, and I didn't stop her for a minute. Jesus, this is so hard to say to you." His voice breaks, his body tense beside me, yet I stay focused on my lap.

"I need to know. I need to hear all of it," I whisper, tears coursing down my face. My heart has finally met so much pain it's temporarily gone numb, a deep hollow of disbelief taking over me and giving me a moment of respite before it wears off.

"I guess she thought there was a chance for her. I knew I was making a mistake, even as messed up as I was, so I pushed her away after seconds, baby, I swear. Nothing else happened. I didn't even touch her. I didn't stick around either ... I stormed outside and ended up beating the shit out of a security guard in pure anger because I was so fucking mad at myself. I knew I'd fucked-up, even in that state, baby. You must believe me, Emma. I've never felt so much disgust at myself." He shifts, getting as close as he can to feel my heat, still unsatisfied with his inability to touch me. Part of me longs to feel his arms around me, but I ignore that inner defiance.

"Did you do it to hurt me? That's what you said that night. To lash out." I look away from him toward the kitchen and focus on the bedroom door I left open, trying not to think of the first time he carried me in there. So long ago, yet still there to visually torture me.

"I worded it badly, Emma. I never did it in such a calculated way. I was acting up and lashing out at everyone because I was a mess. Wasted off my face on God knows what. Hitting people and kissing her ... It was all part of my *fuck you all* haze. It wasn't like that. I wouldn't intentionally do something to cause you pain or score points. I'm crazy about you. You're everything to me." He sighs heavily, voice broken, and this time without hesitation, he catches my hand, pulling it into both of his firmly and holding it tight. I don't resist this time, watching his fingers slowly move around my clenched fist and gently stroking me, enjoying how his skin always feels on mine, allowing myself this little comfort. I'm trying to take in everything he's saying, and my head is getting so fuzzy with fatigue.

"I know I always seem like the cocky, arrogant asshole who's so sure of everything. I'm that way because I've had a lifetime of being on show in the limelight. It's a part I play so well that sometimes I forget to tell you about the other side ... There is another side, Emma, the jealous, grumpy, shitty side. He's insecure and so sure that he's only holding onto you by the skin of his teeth. He's lurking inside me, telling me that I'll never be good enough to keep you, that my past will push you away. It's why I push for more, push to get you to move in, push for the house, and the dream, push for marriage."

He's gazing at me intently, squeezing my hand into his, I think he's waiting for me to say something, but I can't. I don't know what to say or how to say it. I've never been here before either. I look away, unsure of what he will profess next, but the passion in his stare pulls me back. I glance at him pleadingly, not knowing how to respond. He realizes I need something else, something more, something that brings this all back together, and he takes a deep breath, ready to continue his onslaught, knowing it's anything but unrequited, speaking to my inner soul.

"You're the one for me, Emma. The woman I want my happily ever after with, the big house full of kids. I figured rushing you into that stuff would make me feel more secure. Stuff I never imagined myself ever hoping for, but I see it all with you. It's that guy who got unleashed with force that night, and I couldn't rein him back in. The insecure guy who figured he'd been right all along and could never keep you.... That destructive me hasn't reared his head for a very long time, and he never will again ..." He leans in toward me, his voice closer to my ear, his breath tickling my face. "At Daniel's that night, while wanting to beat the shit out of myself, I realized something ...so blindingly obvious ...... I always had you, every part of you, and I was too stupid to see it or believe it until I fucked it up." His hoarse voice breaks a little, his tone deep and full of despair.

I sniff back the overwhelming wave of pain he's caused me and lift my chin to look at him, gulping back the onslaught of tears a little forcefully, his words slicing through my heart.

"I still love you, Jake, but I'm so confused right now and so hurt. I was always yours. I don't know how else I could've made you believe it. What else could I have said or done?" I've no idea what else to say after that. So many things are running through my head. Trying to process that Jake could be as insecure as me in our relationship has completely thrown me. I never imagined someone like him would doubt anything, let alone how I felt about him.

"You didn't need to, baby. I should've realized it before acting like the world's biggest asshole. I love you more than anything in the world. You have to believe that." He catches my other wrist and pulls both hands up so I'm drawn toward him, his forehead touching mine, giving me no option but to obey.

His alluring green eyes meet mine, but they are dark and foreboding with the intensity of his emotions. Emotions matching mine.

I missed those eyes so much, like doorways to my soul.

"You're mine, you'll always be mine, and I'll rip the world apart to keep you, *Bambina*." He leans in, and I know he's going to kiss me, moving in slowly, his eyes focused on my mouth with a hint of longing so intense it stings through my chest. My heartbeat rises in tempo, and my blood runs cold as fear overtakes me. My breathing hitches as he gently grazes his lips across mine, soft, warm, and tender. Familiar lips that I could almost fall into, hoping to erase the pain they caused.

Marissa floods into my head, smirking at me, pulling Jake's mouth to hers while her eyes bore into the recesses of my mind, forcing me to push him away sharply.

"I can't ... Not yet." I gasp, yanking back, trying to reel in the crazy burst of emotions that overwhelm me, suffocate me, and make my body tingle crazily. He lets me loose with a sigh and a look on his beautiful face of utter deflation.

"I understand. I told you, whatever you need, no matter how long it takes. I will do whatever it takes to have you back with me." The sincerity in his voice helps calm me.

"I can't think straight ... I'm so tired and overemotional." I sag against the couch, letting out a slow breath and wiping more tears from my already sensitive face. The hangover hits me hard again, and fatigue pushes at my eyelids cruelly. All this emotional roller coaster has done is make me crave sleep. I long for some peace in this nightmare for just a little while.

He leans out, pulling me into his arms, strong, safe, and secure. He slides back along the couch and nestles me alongside him as he lies down, his arms and legs around me, spooning me. I don't fight or struggle. I'm too tired to protest or resist. A part of me wants this. After everything he's told me, a part of me needs to feel him around me. The pain of being close and not having him touch me has been agony.

"Go to sleep, N*eonata*. I'm not going anywhere; I could use the sleep too. I was up all night checking on drunk women." He buries his face in the back of my hair and breathes me in, surrounding me with the security I've been aching for. My mind tells me to push him away, but my heart is aching with his touch. I close my eyes, trying to bring calm to my reeling mind, and ignore the way my body is relaxing into him, molding itself to his hold like a traitorous whore.

You're weak, just like her! Your mother would be so proud!

I push the voice in my head away, too tired for battle or any of this. I know I shouldn't let him touch me, but I can't compete against this. I'm tired, broken, and hungover, and right now, lying here in his arms is a battle I'm too exhausted to fight against.

"Maybe for a little while," I say. "Then I should go." I'm already relaxing into him, tiredness fuzzing out my brain, like being enveloped into a soft, fluffy, warm room after a terrifyingly cold night. It's so easy to relax in his arms. They've always been my safety net and my whole world. The fatigue is moving in with his hold over me as though I've been waiting to return to this.

Lying here like this, I finally feel able to still my mind, focusing on just the feel and smell of him. The gentleness of his breathing and the way his fingers stroke my arm. It's all so familiar and so necessary to my mental state. I don't fight sleep as it moves in, enveloped in his arms, in the warmth and security my body has longed for.

* * *

I wake with a jump, dreaming I was falling, my heart racing as I bump back to reality. Jake's arms tighten around me and hold me still.

"It's okay," he mumbles, sleepily, not fully coherent, bringing my cheek to his mouth and kissing me lightly. His warm breath giving me tingles and soothing my racing heart. "I'm here." His voice is gravelly, he's half-asleep, and I'm still held in his arms on the soft leather couch, only now there's a warm fur throw over us, and the room is so dark it's almost impossible to see. The only lights on show are coming from New York's sparkling glow through the long, wide window behind us, and I guess we must've slept for hours as it's the middle of the night. His comfort pains me how he can be asleep and still try to reassure me.

"I'm okay. It wasn't one of those dreams. I dreamed I was falling, and it gave me a fright." I try not to move, knowing I won't stay here if I turn to him. I'll leave. I don't want to face reality and do this right now or give up being in his embrace just yet.

"Do you want to get up?" He squeezes me a little, clearing his throat to sound more awake, a huge lump hitting me in the stomach. The surge of emotion at his closeness and all his Jake mannerisms. He sounds unsure, wondering if I will ask to go home. I can feel it in the tense way he's holding onto me, and my heart bleeds a little.

"Don't ever do that to me again," I cry, suddenly letting all the emotion break loose at his tenderness. He freezes, his body going stiff, a slight ripple of his muscles against me.

"Do what?" His voice is hoarse as I unleash this burst of crazy Emma who has pounced out in the dark. There's a mild hint of confusion in his voice as he tries to understand what he's done to me while lying here next to me.

"Don't ever hurt me again ... Don't ever do that to me again! Don't kiss another person, shut me out, or make me feel like I don't matter! Don't make me feel like you don't love me any more or don't give a shit about how you make me feel." The sobs overtake me, and I can't say anymore. He crushes me to him, wrapping those arms tightly around me, pulling me into his body, so we're almost one.

"Emma ..." The pain in his voice matches mine, grabbing me so close that he's squeezing me. "You think I would ever be that stupid again? This last week has destroyed me. Do you know how often I drove to Queens and sat a block away from your apartment, stopping myself from coming for you?.... About three times a day, every day.... I had to stop myself because I knew you didn't want to see me, and it killed me.... I was right there, baby, when flowers were rejected and gifts thrown back. Because I hoped one of them might make you call me, and I wanted to be there as soon as you did. I swear I'll never, ever hurt you, never betray you again.... I'm sorry, sorrier than I can ever find the words to tell you.... No one hates what I did more than me.... Please, Emma, give me one chance, and I promise you I'll never give you another reason to leave me for the rest of our lives.... I love you. You're *all* that matters to me. Nothing else is worth anything if you're not a part of it. How you feel is everything. You're inside of me; you're a part of me. My heart doesn't beat without you, baby. I need you," he says it all, barely taking a breath, clinging to me fiercely.

I turn in his arms and throw myself around him, taking comfort from the person I need most in the world. I still ache, and I'm still grieving for what he's done, but I need to be here with him to heal. The wracking pain from being away from him is more unbearable than facing the pain of what he's done to us. It's crazy and messed up; maybe it makes me weak, but it's the only way I can function.

"I don't want to leave," I whimper, with my head buried in his neck.

"No one is making you go, Emma. They're going to have to fight me to the death to try to get you out of my arms. I won't let you go." The hoarseness in his voice betrays his emotion, close to breaking down, yet with a hint of stubborn Carrero.

"I want to come home." I sniff quietly, my heart wrenching through my chest painfully.

"I want you home. I need you home." He presses his mouth to my forehead and inhales me heavily.

I sound like a broken child, wrapped in my security blanket, longing for him to take all my decisions away and take care of me. I can be angry and sort out the mess of what we have left tomorrow. Then, when I'm more able to, we can face this together, whatever 'this' is or will be.

"I still don't know if I can ..." I hesitate, screwing my eyes shut against his chest, breathing in his scent.

"I told you, I'll do whatever you need, baby. As much space as you need ... As much time as you need. Come home. I'll sleep somewhere else in here if that's what you need. I'm begging you." His voice is rough and low, his arms holding me tight, and I know he'll never let anyone take me.

My Jake. My security. My tormentor.

"Can we go to bed?" I whisper. I'm still so exhausted, I want to stop thinking, just for one moment, and forget any of this, forget everything but what he feels like. I'm not ready to be free of his arms around me, giving me much-needed serenity. I sniff back the last of my tears and lift my chin to him.

"Together? Same bed?" He's wary and gentle. He doesn't want to presume anything, so I nod and bring my eyes to his in the dim light.

"Don't do anything more than hold me ... I can't ... I can't do anything more than that. I don't even know if we can even do this."

Even though I know I need this.

I close my eyes and rest against him, trying to calm all the inner protests and voices telling me how pathetic and weak I am.

"We'll take it one hour at a time. Adjust to what you need. Just being with you is enough, N*eonata.* It's always enough." He slides up and scoops me into his arms like a child, letting the throw slide from us to the floor almost gracefully.

He carries me, as though I'm fragile and ready to break, to the bedroom and lies me down gently on the bed before moving back to give me space. Then he turns his back, so I can have privacy to change.

Without hesitation, I pull off my clothes until only my underwear and the silk camisole remains, then I slide under the sheets. Being back in this room and this bed with him makes my heart lift a little, that empty hopelessness moving away just enough to let me breathe. When he hears me sliding into the sheets, he pulls off his clothes too, keeping only his boxers on, and slips in beside me. He waits hesitantly to see if I want his touch until I tug his hand toward me, and he relaxes, takes me back into his arms, holds me tight, and then begins to stroke my hair softly.

"I love you so much." His soft low huskiness makes me close my eyes, and I trace my hands along his powerful arms around me. My body is yearning for more than his embrace but is quietened by my emotions building inside. I can't bear to do more than this until

I can push her out of my head, if I ever can. What he did with her, the confusion about what I wanted, and all the emotions swirling inside me, waiting for release.

There's a storm brewing inside of me, and she's not ready to give up the fight just yet, but she needs this for herself. She needs a break from the pain, and he's the only one capable of giving it to her. A lull in the storm to get my head straight with some much-needed rest and solitude from my own brain.

I snuggle down under the duvet and wrap my legs through his without thinking about what I'm doing like we have done a million times before. His deep, steady breathing calms me completely. The thoughts, aches, and pains, drift into numbness. I'm shocked at just how quickly I start dosing off again. Days of emotional insomnia are finally catching up with me.

Weak, pathetic girl. Mommy's little mirror image.

Shhhh, I'm nothing like her.

Chapter 7

I yawn, stretching out like a satisfied cat in the silky comfortable bed, my mind taking moments to come to terms with where I am. Fully rested for the first time in days, and for a second, I forgot everything.

Jake is close by, his arms around my waist, his legs across mine, but he's sound asleep. I take a minute to evaluate how I feel about waking up this way. I slowly pull myself free from his embrace and sit in the bed, pulling my knees to my chest and sighing.

Confusion still present? Check.

Emotions all over the place? Check.

Still not further forward in how I feel about him. Check.

Just friggin dandy!

It's late in the day, past eleven am. I don't remember the last time I slept this much, so I sit and watch him sleep a little longer. The longing to reach out and touch him overwhelms me, so I slide out of bed and go to the shower, locking the door for the first time ever. I'm not ready for anything to happen between us and need some time alone to stand under the massaging jets of water and think of nothing. I don't regret being here or sharing a bed with him, my heart needs it, and I meant it when I said I wanted to come home. This is where I belong, and Sarah is right; I can only begin to forgive him by being here, surrounded by him, and taking everything a day at a time. I don't know when things will feel better for me, but I love him, and I can't bear for it to be the end. I need him.

Does this mean a part of me has decided to give him a chance?

I stop for a moment to blink through this thought. I guess a part of me knew from drunk dialing him that I wasn't ready to end things. I wasn't prepared to live a Jake-less life, but it doesn't mean I can't walk away. I need to see how this goes, see if I can move on, and get back to what we had.

If I can't, then I'll go.

When I wander through to the bedroom draped in a warm fluffy robe, the bed is empty, and the covers are strewn messily, but the smell of coffee and food is wafting through the walls. I pull my robe tighter, rub my hair with the towel, and then leave it to air dry; it's at its waviest when damp.

The internal war inside me seems to be giving me a break for now; it's like she's holding her breath, just waiting to see how things develop. For once, I'm glad of the lack of constant emotional torture and this new relative peace sweeping through me. I guess a decent night's sleep with no night terrors has helped immensely.

I wander through to find Jake sitting at the breakfast bar drinking coffee in T-shirt and sweatpants. He looks better, is less tired and ruffled, and has damp hair. He smells divine. He's trimmed his stubble and sorted his hair. He seems like normal Jake, not yesterday's slightly tired and rumpled version. Something I wasn't aware I was aching to see until now.

He smiles at me when I approach, wide and happy, uncovering a plate of croissants, bacon, and pancakes for me, my breakfast of choice from one of my favorite local deli. I slide onto a stool beside him and watch as he pours an orange juice before sliding it in front of me with a peck on the cheek. I pause at the affectionate touch, waiting for the pain or the image of her, but nothing comes. Just the warmth of his skin on mine. He seems to sense my hesitation but returns to his coffee without a word. I've no clue about how we're meant to do this, touching or not, cuddling or not. I've no idea if I want it or not.

Despite having zero appetites the last few days, I'm ravenous and dig in in silence. I didn't eat at all yesterday. We'd slept the day and night away. Catching up on rest from days of emotional angst and insomnia, food has been the last thing on my mind.

I'm aware of Jake's eyes on me a few times, but I concentrate on eating without looking his way. My head is calmer today, and I'm more positive, but there's still a can of worms waiting to be opened; not sure I even want to try to prize it open yet.

"What do you want to do today? Stay here and talk? Or go somewhere else and talk?" Jake's voice cuts into the quietness of my brain. He drops his fork and lifts his coffee mug, eyes on my profile, watching me eat.

"Maybe we could go for a drive?" I say shyly. "I don't think there's much left to say, to talk about. I mean ... We can only see how it goes." I swallow hard. I've no idea why this makes me nervous; talking has never been my strong point, but indecision is not something I've ever dealt with. It's knocking me off kilter, so I focus, a little more intently, on eating my food.

"I told you, Emma, whatever you want. Whether it's to talk or not if it's to take you places and distract you, or even to sit in silence. Whatever you need, I need you to tell me." His fingers brush my free hand, and I watch, mesmerized, as he trails the tips over my knuckles on the countertop. So softly, it's barely a tickle, but it feels natural and right, my body betraying me once again.

Pathetic, Emma.

"Right now, I don't want to think anymore, Jake. I want to relax and not feel anything for a little while. Pretend that everything is normal." I sigh heavily, pushing away PA Emma's voice in my head.

"Don't hide inside your head, *Bambina*. I know your impulse is to block it out and push it away with all the other things that hurt you ... But please, not this. We have to deal with this properly, *Neonata*, so it never comes back to hurt us again." He turns in his seat, pulling my stool between his open knees so I'm nestled close to him. Letting him wrap himself around me all night has permitted him to proceed with his touchy old Carrero self. I know I should be setting limits, making him keep his distance, but I don't. My body is yearning for his soothing touch, a relaxing balm for me today. I went days without it, and it was agony. Now my body is making up for its loss.

"I know." I can't help glancing at him, his knuckles coming to graze my cheek gently, the fluttering inside of me at his touch even now. I pull my face away and bite my lip as his hand drops between us. Even after what he's done, I'm responding and feel angry at myself.

"Where do you want to drive to?" His voice is softer with being so close, and his gaze is intent on my mouth. I can tell how much he wants to kiss me, which only raises my fear.

That kiss invites her into my head, all the pain of what he did, and I'm not ready to deal with that right now. I turn away so I'm not tempted and push my empty plate aside. I look out across the open-plan room and sigh, knowing that he's reading every signal I'm giving off with apprehension, probably overanalyzing every one. Being so near him has my head in chaos about what I want from him, blurring the lines of how much touching I can bear to allow.

"I don't know ... just anywhere, somewhere pretty. Somewhere that's not here." I shrug. I don't know why I want him to drive me anywhere. Maybe the motion of the car and Jake being the one in control somehow make it feel better. It means I can take time out from life while he focuses on the road, and maybe we can listen to music and not talk.

I don't want to talk. I'm scared that if I start talking about everything, about her and the baby, if she still means anything to him and our life, then it will all come crashing painfully in on me like a fragile tower of cards. Today I want quiet and calm and to be with him. The past few days have taken a toll; this little respite is like a breath of warm air in the frost. I want a time out, and nowhere in the rules of whatever this is does it say that I can't have that.

"Okay ... Your wish is my command, beautiful. Do you need me to take you to Queens for clothes first?" His fake jovial tone makes me falter, and I hate that it's not genuine, that we're hurting each other this way. I inhale heavily, trying to get at least one breath that isn't laced with pain.

"Later. I'll keep on the clothes you brought me yesterday, seeing as all I've done is sleep." I can't explain the weird way I feel, but I want to get out and go somewhere where no one knows us, where I don't need to explain anything to anyone. Sarah would ask questions, but I need reflection and silence and maybe him.

Okay, definitely him.

I'm still tired, and I'm a little lightheaded despite eating. All the recent emotional turmoil and lack of food and sleep have taken their toll on me, and now playing catch up.

"Can we go now?" the apartment is closing in on me, and restlessness is kicking in. If I keep sitting here, near him, like this, I'll want to kiss him, which would lead to touching. Then I'd want him all over me, inside me, and I'm not ready to take that step just yet. I don't know if I ever will be. It's too confusing with him being close enough to inhale.

"Sure, go get ready. Which car do you want to take?" He slides his mug beside his empty plate, and I sigh, pushing myself up from the bar stool.

"The Bat-mobile." I smile shyly at him, knowing a ride in his pride and joy will make him happy, and right now, I want to hear it genuinely in his voice and not just play pretend.

"Lucky for you, I keep it downstairs." He grins merrily at the mention of his toy and slides out of his chair, stooping down to kiss me behind the ear thoughtlessly before picking up his phone and walking toward the bedroom. I falter at his touch but take a deep, steadying breath.

Make a choice; either he's allowed to touch you and throw affection your way, or he's not. You're only confusing him and yourself by not deciding whether he can or not.

I swallow the ball of emotion rising in my throat and head toward the bedroom to get dressed.

I just don't know, okay!

* * *

Less than half an hour later, we're heading out of the city onto calmer scenery. Jake suggested driving to Long Island, over an hour away, and maybe stopping somewhere to walk and take in the beautiful surroundings. He's packed a couple of warm jackets and a hat for me and looked up some quiet spots for lunch when we get there. He's being romantic and thoughtful, Jake, trying to show me how much I mean to him.

The car is stiflingly hot. Even though the weather is mild, his air con is blowing gently, and a slow heat creeps up my spine. I wonder if maybe the way I've been feeling is a sign I'm getting sick.

Yes, that's really what I need right now on top of everything else.

I'm exhausted. Even though I slept a lot last night, this fatigue can't be from the emotional insomnia I've suffered for the past week. Right now, here with Jake, listening to quiet country music as we pass through the city, I feel anything but emotional, yet my body is completely out of whack. I'm tired and sensitive. Nausea from my hangover lingering, despite sleeping almost an entire day and night, I crack the window a little for air.

"You okay, *Bambina*?" Jake's voice cuts through my inner dialog, and I glance at him quietly. "You look a little pale suddenly." He lifts his fingers to my cheek and frowns. "You feel warm too." He looks around, veering the car into a side street, and pulls over before he leans further to feel my face properly. The touch of his hands on my skin sends out another brain-filled bout of arguing voices with which I've zero energy to contend.

Fine, he can touch me ... End of!

"I think I'm getting sick. I've been feeling off-color lately." I admit, resting my forehead against his palm instinctively. The inner voices seem to have shut up now that I've given consent for him to touch me.

"I don't think a trip to Long Island is the answer, Emma. I'm taking you home, and you're going to bed." He has the serious, *don't argue,* commanding tone in his voice that, for once, I've no desire to go up against. Since getting into the car, my bile has risen slowly, and I have an overwhelming urge to gag.

"I'm not that sick, Jake. It's just remnants of my hangover and this past week." I try for a smile, but without warning, nausea rises out of me, and I jack the car door open just in time to get my head out before I throw up.

"Jesus. Emma!" Jake lets go of me and, within seconds, appears outside the car, pulling me away from the contents of my stomach to a nearby step and sitting me down. I rest my head between my knees before turning away in panic as I throw up again into nearby bushes, retching in pain as I lose the only things I've eaten over the past two days. This time Jake holds back my hair and balances my shoulder, keeping me steady.

"Can you sit up?" He pulls me back against him and doesn't let go until I nod. "I have water in the car." He jumps up, dashing to the car's open doors and back again in a flash. He takes up his position behind me, bringing the bottle to my hands, and I lean against him, sipping the burning taste of vomit away from my mouth. My head is swimming as nausea subsides, and I suddenly feel weak and tired.

"I've never seen you ill ... You're worrying me, *Miele.* I think we need to get you home and looked at." He sounds concerned, with a hint of panic in his voice. He holds me to him with his palm on my forehead, giving me more reasons to take a chance on him and get this between us to work. He's taking care of me, just like he always does.

I love you so much.

"It's just a bug or something I've eaten. I'll be okay. I'm starting to feel a little better now." I try for a convincing smile, tilting my face toward him, but his face only hardens some more. He doesn't like what he sees; I know it's futile to hide this from him. I feel fragile, and my voice is exposing my little white lie.

"You're so white, and you're trembling. We're going home." He scoops me onto his lap, closes his legs beneath me, and holds me close. "If it's nothing, then it won't do any harm having a doctor look at you, will it?" He rests my head against his neck, holding me in.

"If it makes you happier, but I can promise you, this is nothing." I'm too tired to argue with him and too faint to care. I'm not even protesting when he lifts me and carries me to the car, sliding me in to avoid the puddle I left beside the door. He clips my belt over me and closes the door before getting to the other side and starting up.

"Home and bed," he commands, reversing, resting a hand on my cheek again, testing my temperature to see if I'm hot. I lay my head on him for a moment before pulling away as the emotional confusion hits home again.

Maybe touching isn't such a good idea.

"Yes, sir," I say, closing my eyes and resting my head against the seat. If I block out the motion and try to relax, I'm sure I can keep the nausea at bay until we're back at the apartment. It isn't that far.

* * *

"We're here, *Miele.*" Jake lifts me from the car when I blink my eyes open. I'm sure it's only been seconds since I closed them. I'm in his arms, being lifted out of the car, and the garage around us looks exactly like underground parking at his apartment, and I'm completely thrown.

"We're home already?" I blink a few times, snuggling closer into his strength, still trying to get a grip on reality, confusion all over my face, severely disorientated.

"You fell asleep pretty quickly, *Bambina.* You don't look so white anymore, so I think it did you some good." Jake brushes his mouth against my forehead with a soft smile.

What the hell is with the sleeping lately?

I close my eyes and let Jake carry me into the elevator and home. He's right. I do feel better for having taken a nap. My nausea has subsided almost completely, and now I just feel hungry. I know I should be fighting him to let me walk, but my body and mind unanimously decide to let him do this.

I open my eyes when he lays me on the bed in his room. Nora has been in and cleaned up in that precise hotel-esque method of hers. The room is surprisingly comforting, and I take a breath feeling like I've returned home. I'm more than aware of the surge of happy joy it gives me and frown at myself.

"I don't need to go to bed. I feel better, and I'm hungry." I smile as he slides down beside me on the neat sheets. I sit myself up a little, wary he might start wrapping himself around me and cross my arms over my chest defensively.

"You're staying here regardless. I'll get you some food if you're sure that's what you want." He frowns at me with a comical look on his face, his eyes take in my posture, and he moves away a little. Not that I blame him. Vomiting and then asking for food isn't exactly normal.

He lifts his fingers to my cheek, and I let them linger there. "You still feel hot, but you're not so pale anymore." The way his touch feels is more than enough proof that I should make it clear that I'm not ready for it.

"I guess the car just made me feel worse." I shrug with one shoulder, nestling onto the bed a little more comfortably. I watch how the sunshine comes into the room, lightening the color in his beautiful eyes to an almost transparent, gemstone green. One thing Jake will always be to me is gorgeous, despite how much he has hurt me.

"Maybe." Jake gets up and leaves the room, telling Nora to make me something light. Nora replies, saying something about homemade chicken soup, and I roll my eyes.

The two of them are acting like I have a terminal illness.

I swing my legs off the bed, standing quickly to tell him how ridiculous he's being, and instantly crumble. My vision blacks out, and my body loses all control, Jell-O legs, and complete disorientation as I stand far too quickly.

"Shit." I groan, feeling the cold wood floor connecting harshly with my limbs. I realize that I knocked my elbow sharply on the way down to my current crouching position.

"Emma? Emma ... Fuck!" Jake's panicked voice is followed by heavy boots running toward me, and I'm being dragged up from the floor into his strong embrace.

"Did you fall? Why were you up? Are you okay?" He's lifting me onto the bed with him, so I'm sitting in his lap, wrapped in him, aware my whole body has started to tremble and heat flushes across my face in a devastatingly horrible way; the rise of nausea strong again as dizziness gives way to coldness.

"I think it was a fainting spell," I mumble weakly. "I don't think I fainted, but I don't feel so good." I slump against his chest, knowing what's coming next, and I don't have the energy or inclination to argue. I'm out of whack and ready to lie down and stay in bed just like he ordered.

"That's it, this happened in the Hamptons, and now this, Emma ... I'm calling my doctor. Get into bed and do not move ... I swear if you so much as lift your head, there will be hell to pay." He's in snappy, bossy Carrero mode. He sweeps back the covers and lays me down in the open space, pulling my boots and sweater off before covering me up gingerly. He looks stressed and wired, and all I can do is smile weakly in return.

There he is ... That's my Carrero, a vision of domineering aggression in all his concerned beauty.

God, I've missed you.

"Yes, sir." I throw a mocked salute at him, still shaken, but lying down in the cool sheets helps. The overwhelming trembling is subsiding, and the nausea is calming down. He picks up the TV remote and presses it, the TV coming down from the concealed space in the ceiling, choosing a romantic chick flick for me from the menu. His body is stiff as he scrolls, but I can't help smiling at his choice.

"Here." He hands me the remote with a warning glint in his eye. "Stay put. Nora is making your food. I'm going to call the doctor. I'll be back soon, and I better not find you've moved out of this bed, even once," he commands. His eyes are fiery, and his face is completely serious. It makes my inner nerves jump slightly in a tug of heartfelt emotion. He bends, kissing me lightly on the forehead, then walks off, lifting his phone to his ear and heading to his office.

I can tell he's trying to act like he's in control, but that flicker of worry and the fact he's left the room to call his doctor makes my heart swell a little. Through all my crazy internal emotional mess, this part of him always wins me over.

Jake is really worried about me. It's so sweet it's almost funny, as is his movie choice for me.

Ten Things I Hate About You.

I guess he knows I'm emotionally all over the place with how I feel about him, and he's using movies the way he uses iTunes, except this film is for me to him. He knows I'm struggling to get past his actions to make me hate him. I can't help but sigh, feeling more than a little bit torn.

I don't hate you, Jake. I'm hurt, and I hate her. I'm just confused.

I know I'm physically fine, maybe needing bed rest and sleep. I've caught a little bug, but I'm positive there's nothing for him to worry about ... nothing physically anyway. My mind, on the other hand, is a completely different ballpark.

Chapter 8

I wake up to Nora placing a tray of homemade soup on a table beside the bed and realize I fell asleep again, another sign that I have a virus. The movie is still playing, so I mustn't have been out for too long. I move to sit up as Jake's hands come from beside me, lifting the cushions and helping me to sit.

He's on the bed next to me on top of the covers in sweats and a T-shirt with a mountain of files scattered beside him. It almost feels normal, like before any of this mess came between us. I guess while I slept, he's been keeping me company and working. Jake is doing what he does while he lets me relax and enjoy the peace.

"Thank you, Nora." I smile, looking down at the bowl of soup and plate of crusty bread served with a glass of fresh orange juice. The woman is a saint. She knows how to melt her way into my heart.

"How're you feeling?" Jake smooths back my hair as I pull the tray toward me. His fingers grazing my cheek as though checking my temperature, I can feel his eyes on me.

"Too fuzzy from sleeping to know." I smile at him over my shoulder quickly, halted by how gorgeous he looks. It makes my insides clench, part of me longing for a time before any of this happened when I could turn and curl into him without any of this emotional turmoil inside.

"How long was I out?" I turn my attention back to the bowl, leaning out of bed and taking a spoonful. The soup tastes amazing like I've been starved for a week.

"About an hour and a half." He picks up the files on his lap and shuffles them around. "The doctor said she'd be here about two hours after my call. So, eat up. She should be here soon."

He shifts and chucks a bunch of files onto the floor from his side of the bed. I hear them scatter as some slide across the surface. I have zero inclination to ask about work right now. If anything, this separation has highlighted how detached and non-interested in the Carrero Corporation I've become, and I know deep down I'll never go back to that job.

"I don't think I need to see a doctor, you know." I try to start reasoning with him, but the dark look on his face quietens me. He has that no-nonsense verging on yelling kind of scary look that I have no energy to handle right now.

Oh, hello, Boss Carrero; nice to see you still exist.

"Emma, whether you want to see her or not, she's coming." He watches me eat with his penetrating gaze, causing me to lose my confidence. "You're looking pale again." He leans over to feel my cheek and frowns. I don't feel hot, just tired and hungry, in fact, more than hungry. This soup is the best I've eaten in my life. Jake sighs and leans back, pulling his warm hands away; a mixed tingling of relief and disappointment runs through me.

* * *

Jake is right. Less than half an hour later, the lovely Doctor Rachael Brown is shown into the room to examine me. I tell her there's no point evicting Jake as he'll only linger, asking questions at the closed door every two minutes distracting her from her job. He has an air of command oozing from him, and he's in a no-nonsense mood. He's already hanging at the side of the bed with a grim expression as though he wants to beat someone.

"Doctor." He nods her way and watches her like a hawk.

She smiles indulgently and gives me a sympathetic look. I guess she's met a few overprotective men in her career, and it looks like she can handle the Carreros of this world.

"So, now, how can I help here?" She smiles sweetly, her voice as smooth as honey; with one perfectly manicured hand, she runs a stray copper hair back into her neat French roll. She looks more like one of Jake's top executives than a doctor.

"She's passed out more than once recently, this morning being the latest, and she vomited when we were out earlier. Something is just off with her. I can feel it. She never gets sick." Jake's husky tone and narrowed gaze are almost impaling her hands. He's watching intently as she moves a stethoscope toward me.

"You know she's not going to stab me with it, right?" I giggle at him and watch his facial expression soften slightly. He gives me half a smile, and the doctor smirks from the corner of her mouth as she encourages me to pull down the sheets so she can get to my chest and abdomen.

Jake walks over to his wardrobe and comes back with a T-shirt. I'm just wearing underwear right now, so he holds it out to me as the doctor moves behind me to listen to my back, and I slide it on over my head awkwardly.

"Do you have any other symptoms or concerns?" She's gazing at me intensely, checking my throat and glands, generally fluttering around my body while she listens to me. Despite being all over me, her hands are surprisingly soft, warm, and completely non-intrusive.

"I want to sleep an awful lot, constantly feel exhausted, a little weak, I guess, and I've noticed I'm hungrier than normal." I sigh and catch Jake's eyes narrowing even further. I know he's accusing me of not telling him something important. It's not like wanting more food, and being crazy tired is a symptom of anything but emotional exhaustion and insomnia. So he can take that glare elsewhere! I narrow my eyes back at him, and I'm met with that stubborn furrow on his brow.

"Hmm, mmm, hmmm." The doctor pulls something from her bag and a book and jots some things down.

"Anything else? Tender anywhere? Unusual behaviors or cravings?" She's not looking at me but rummaging in her bag, pulling out some bottles and vials, then moving to stand.

"Um ... not that I can think of." I hate being put on the spot when I haven't been paying attention to my own body. "I've been distracted with other things lately, so I've not taken much notice of anything like that," I explain, smiling. But then I catch Jake's glare dissipating. He looks completely guilt-ridden and hangs his head a little. The effect is devastating, and a surge of aches hits me hard. I want to reach out and cuddle him and make it go away. He looks so forlorn.

"I think some urine and bloods might be a good idea. Then, some more questions and a more thorough workup. Are you okay with that?" She blinks at me with a professional smile, and I nod. I catch Jake in the corner of my eye, hands in pockets, leaning back against the flat gray paintwork with the air of a guy who has no will to do anything but wait and watch. He's obviously mulling things over in his head, lost in his regrets and guilt. I want to pull him out of it and wrap myself around him. But the doctor's hands jolt me back to what she needs to do right now.

During the next half hour, she examines me thoroughly, questioning me endlessly about my daily routines and other things that don't seem to have much relation to tiredness and extreme hunger. She takes blood and asks me to urinate in a cup which is awkward, given that the act of standing makes me feel too lightheaded. Jake tries to come to my rescue, but there's no way I want him to watch me peeing in a cup. I hold him back with a raised palm, hating the look of pain that flashes across his face. He must think I'm refusing his help because of what has happened this last week. He moves back to his deflated posturing against the wall, sinking into a quiet, somber mood; I hate him this way.

The doctor takes away everything she has collected, all cups and samples, and moves to the oak unit that sits against the bedroom wall. She spends a long time pouring, dipping, and using other chemicals and powders in her chemistry kit. Watching her is fascinating, and it reminds me of the scientists in *CSI.*

She has a very serious expression while she dips and tests and writes down notes, then picks it up and takes things to the bathroom to clear them up. No one has said a word in what feels like an eternity, there are long, tense silences, and the apartment is eerily quiet, despite Nora being out there somewhere. We wait patiently while she disposes of things in the trash and washes her hands in the sink for at least five agonizing minutes.

Jake pushes off the wall and sits on the bedside, helping me fix his T-shirt so I can remove my uncomfortable bra from underneath. He pulls up my sheets, kissing me lightly on the forehead as though I am a simple sick child who needs mothering. He plumps the cushions for me wordlessly, guarding his emotions, his face is set in a blank expression, but his body language betrays his worried demeanor.

"What's the verdict, doc?" He watches the doctor as she strolls back into view. She writes something studiously on a medical pad left on the side unit and turns to look at us with a smile. He tenses, then take a long deep breath very slowly, emanating all kinds of fear. It makes me want to wrap my arms around his neck to make him feel better. He's the boyish young version of himself right now, and I'm incapable of withstanding that side of him.

"Emma, are you okay with discussing a diagnosis in front of Mr. Carrero?" She eyes me kindly, with a no-nonsense attitude and raised brow that tells me she intends to evict him if necessary. Jake stiffens. He either doesn't like her question, and it's grating on his infamous ego, most likely bristling with an attitude ready to take her on, or he's worried that the diagnosis is something to be truly scared about.

"It's fine. You can tell Jake anything you have to tell me." I graciously smile, knowing full well the drama that would ensue if I dared to make him leave. It would be horrific.

Jake cuts in instantly.

"So, what is it? What's wrong with her?" His low growl indicates he's stressed over the diagnosis, his caveman aggressive demeanor a show of the scared Jake, who her attitude has riled. I know him too well. He's clasping my hands, playing with my fingers in his *I'm nervous as hell* way, but to anyone else, he looks terrifyingly pumped and ready to beat someone down.

The doctor isn't fazed at all. She starts sliding her tools back into her open case, smoothing down her jacket, in a show of control and poise that PA Emma would have admired, and smiles widely, turning her full attention to my face.

"Nothing eight months of TLC won't cure, and I'll have your blood tests checked for low iron." She smiles, seemingly pleased with herself. She doesn't falter at her hidden joke and moves to close the front part of her case.

"Eight ... Months ...?" Jake's face blanks. He repeats it almost numbly, something registering in his head that I'm not getting, but his whole demeanor is stunned. His voice is suddenly breathy, and all the aggression evaporates.

"Give or take ... Here." She hands me a slip of paper. "It's a prescription for some folic acid and some vitamins." Another bright smile, an air of confidence at thinking I know what she means, but I truly don't.

"Doctor Brown ... Why eight months? What's wrong?" I blink up at her, confused by her manner and answers. Perplexed at Jake's instant zombie-like state. It's like I've entered the twilight zone.

Why do I need vitamins? What's wrong with me? Shit ... I really am sick. I don't feel sick, and eight months to recover is not good at all.

She smiles at us and sits on the edge of the bed. Jake is being scarily silent, staring blankly at her and her apparent two heads. His hands have clamped on mine firmly, and there's a good chance he's stopped breathing. My stomach is tightening in fear, my senses are going haywire, and my fingers are turning a little blue at Jake's deathly grip.

What the hell?

"I'm guessing I should be more direct, Emma. I'm saying you're pregnant. Given the answers to my questions, I would say you're roughly under a month gone. Your contraception failed, I'm afraid." She beams at me as though this is the most wonderful news in the world, but my throat tightens, and my stomach flips out. The room tips as the bubbling surge of panic hits me hard.

What?

Jake doesn't move. I'm not sure he even heard her. He's acting like he's in a trance. The complete opposite of what my inner mind is doing.

"Pregnant?" He finally says before his shoulders flex, and his fingers loosen the death grip on mine. He seems to sag a little, still staring but now down at his lap. His mind must be running through the possibility and the realization of what is happening, but I'm just freaking out. My mind is racing, my palms are sweating, and my throat is closing.

Oh, my God. Oh, my God. Oh, my God.

"You're going to be a father." She smiles at him and pats his arm gently before getting up. "I should leave you two to it, let it sink in. Congratulations to you both." She pulls her bag up onto her shoulder. "You have my number. Call when you want to discuss details about having her transferred to a specialist, Mr. Carrero. I can recommend a few. Emma, good luck." She gets up to go, and the panic surges over me in a terrifying wave of ice, loosening my tongue at last.

"Wait. I can't be. I mean, I really can't. I'm on the pill, and we, I mean, I ... haven't missed one. It's not possible. This isn't what was supposed to happen. I mean, I should know. I would have known, wouldn't I? Oh, my God. I can't ... I can't be pregnant; how can you be sure? You can make a mistake, right?" I'm rambling, voice bubbling out in sheer freak-out mode and about two tones higher than normal. My hands are flapping crazily in front of me. She pauses and gently lays a calming hand on my shoulder, leaning in close enough to make me sit still with bated breath.

"They pay me the big bucks because I'm never wrong, sweetie. Contraception isn't one hundred percent, and you're probably a little in shock right now. Take time to think it through and contact me with any questions until I sort you out a referral." She pats me gently. Then without any sign of me responding due to being completely speechless, she gets up with a goodbye to Jake, who is, quite frankly, freaking me out with his unearthly quietness. She moves off, smiling gently and waving, then walks out without another word as we both sit silent, still staring at the spot she vacated.

I turn my head to look to him for some help, willing him to say something ... Anything ... To make this better, take it away, or help me stop floundering and freaking out. My body is ready to self-combust with the sheer amount of panic coursing through my veins, and I want to shake him hard.

Fucking snap out of it.

A strange sense of disbelief washes over me, some inner voice trying to get me to calm down. I don't think I'm awake. If I stay still, then I almost feel like I'm dreaming. I can try not to think about what she's just said as the cold fear washes over me, over and over, like an all-consuming black hole. I'm sure doctors get it wrong all the time.

Even the $10,000 a pop variety that Jake employs?

"Emma?" Jake's gravelly tone cuts into my thoughts, his grip on my hand has almost fallen away, and now he's looking at me with an odd expression, a faraway spooky look in his eyes. He breaks into a slow, steady smile as though realization has crept up from somewhere low down, and he jerks forward in a flash, kissing me on the mouth ungracefully, hauling me into his arms for a hug. His reaction completely shakes me, the wind is knocked out of me, and I'm still reeling from this new development. Jake's face radiates sheer joy, from zombie to hyperactive crazy man in one swift move, and it only makes me want to throat punch him even more right now.

"Jake, she has to be wrong. I'm on the pill! I haven't missed any." The tears in my eyes are threatening to spill down my face, my body is like Jell-O, and I'm shaking. The shock is changing into some sort of soul-gnawing reality that this is not a dream. Jake holds me close, wrapping me in his arms slowly and carefully, as though he's expecting me to turn hellcat and fight him, his eyes on me warily.

"It's going to be okay, *Bambina.*" His soothing tone holds my panic in place and stops it from escalating into the full-blown hysteria that has been simmering inside me. His embrace unleashes the overwhelming emotion hiding behind the fear in the recesses of my confuddled brain, and it comes springing out, causing me to burst into tears.

I can't be ... I'm not ready for this. I don't even know if I want to be a mother. Ever. I have no plan in place for this, no real expectation of ever doing this.

"Hey, baby, it's not what we expected, but it's not awful. Don't cry. I know you're scared, Emma, but I'll always look after you. I'm right here." His tone almost sounds ... pleased! I sit back, glaring at him in complete disbelief, wiping my hand across my sodden face, blinking at him as though he's lost the plot. I'm sure he's had some mental breakdown. Am I the only one seeing complete sense of how ridiculous this is?

"How is this not awful? How is this not fucking craziness personified? This is a life, a real human life between us that we never even talked about, let alone planned." I choke on the tears forcing their way out, and Jake wipes them away, receiving a hand slap in the process. It seems anger was close behind my emotional outburst, and I'm suddenly ragingly aggressive and want to smash things.

Barely five minutes ago, we were contemplating a life apart and whether I can ever let you kiss me again, and now we're having a ... Oh, my God, I can't even say it.

Anger gives way to choking fear. My head is a mass of confusing emotions and feelings swirling dangerously close to consuming me. I think I'm having some sort of heart attack.

"I know you're scared, *Miele.* I know this is a shock, but Emma, we're going to be okay. It changes nothing about how much I will fight to make you trust me. It just gives me more reason to pull out all the stops." He looks down at my abdomen and smiles. I have a serious urge to punch him in the face. Jake Carrero has left the building, and some doppelgänger crazy weirdo is sitting in his place. There's no way in goddamn hell he can seriously think this is a good thing.

What the hell is wrong with him?

"Jake, it's easy for you to say ... You don't have to be pregnant, or give birth, or do whatever a mother does! Or be a mother!" I flap my hands at him, and he has the sense to lean back, so his face is out of range, but he looks just the same. Happiness is bubbling under the straight and serious expression he's trying to keep up for my sake only. "How the fuck can I be a mother?! I don't know how a mother is supposed to be! I haven't even touched a baby; I've never met one up close. Do you have any idea how stupid this is? How messed up we are, and how bad would bringing a life into this situation be?! Oh, my God, I think I'm going to be sick."

I flail my arms around, trying to grasp the sheets of the bed to get out, but Jake is quick. He scoops me up and hauls ass to the bathroom just in time to get my head aimed at the toilet bowl.

I give up my chicken soup in an unladylike projectile manner before slumping back into his arms and start crying again. Emotional train wreck Emma is making a grand comeback in remarkable fashion. I literally have no control over the emotions I possess. I can't even begin to dissect them or get them into any real order or control.

So much for a timeout!

"And how many more months of this?" I yell at him. I cry, hopelessly waving my hands at the toilet, grabbing the flusher in repulsion, and sniffing back new tears. "And the fucking crying ... I'm so done with all this crying!"

"Listen to me." He pulls me into his lap on the floor and cradles my face close to his, trying to calm down the freak-out I'm in the middle of having. He battles with my hands so I'm not quite so viciously poised for attack and smooths his fingertips across my mouth, softly and slowly. He knows how to bring my focus to him. It slows down my crazy, my temper taking a moment to pause, drawn into his touch. Despite the whirlwind inside of me, he's grounding me as effortlessly as he always does.

Breathe, Emma, and get control. Watch those endless eyes and take some calm from him.

"Take a breath slowly with me ... Try to calm down. Breathe with me, *Bambina.*" Jake moves so our noses are touching and inhales slowly, those wicked fingers tenderly stroking my bottom lip, encouraging me to do it too. I follow his steady breathing in and out as those captivating green eyes keep me locked in place. Slow, even, steady deep breathing and exhaling until I feel less psychotic. He's bringing some sense of control back to my body, even if my emotions are still out of whack.

"You need to let this sink in, okay? If you really don't want to do this, Emma, there are other options. I wouldn't ever force this upon you." The heartbreak on his face makes me feel physically sick, and I think back to when he told me about asking Marissa to terminate her baby. I doubt he looked at her the same way he does me at the idea of a termination. The look on his face has the same gut-wrenching effect on me as seeing him cry did.

No, I couldn't do that to him ... to us.

I shake my head, catching the sweep of instant relief washing over him, removing any doubt about whether he wants this. I wish I could feel the same way, but at least I know part of me, somewhere inside, refuses to consider termination. I've never been someone to have an opinion over pro-choice. I've always believed everyone should have their own choice in life and follow a path that makes them happy in all things.

"I'm not going to get rid of our baby, Jake. I wouldn't hurt you that way." I sob as the words hit me.

Our baby.

It's like a slap. Saying the words without even thinking about them somehow makes this more real.

We're going to have a child together, our own little bundle of Jake and Emma mixed up together for eternity, a creation inside of me that we put there.

I don't know how to feel. Fear and panic are consuming me, and I can't process anything beyond the next thirty seconds. I can barely breathe ... again. I've never had a full-blown panic attack before, but I know instinctively that's what this is. Jake catches my hands and brings them to his chest, pulling me to look at him, slowing my erratic breathing as it matches his. I let him bring me back from the verge again.

"We are in this together. I won't sit back and let you deal with all this alone, *Bambina*. I'll take care of you every step of the way. I'll be the guy who gets up and feeds the baby while you sleep, and I'll change the nappies and take care of mom the best I can. Trust me with this. Trust that I would never leave you to do this alone, even if you decide you don't want me back." He kisses me on the nose, and my heart melts at the way he always grounds me; a thought creeps, and I instantly go cold.

"But this won't be your first child, Jake. Marissa will give birth before I do and ruin another thing in my life. Your time will be split ... between us, between the children, so you can't promise me anything." Tears run down my cheeks, and I pull away from him, anger rising again at the thought of him and her, that horrible stomach-churning vision of his mouth on hers, always lingering to make me ache physically. I slide away from him and cross my arms across my chest, glaring at him, daring him to try to come near me because his touch is abhorrent, and I'm spring-loaded for an attack. Having that bitch in my head makes sure of it, and this feeling here is as close to hate as I could ever feel for him.

He watches intensely for a moment before sliding back against the tub and resting himself against it. He knows when to choose his battles. He's annoyingly good at reading me sometimes, yet other times as brain-dead an idiot as you could possibly get to what I'm thinking.

"I need to say this, Emma. You can look at me like that the whole time if you want, but I'm still saying it." He looks down at my abdomen between us and then back up at my face, his expression serious. I scowl at him more hatefully.

"Marissa may have got in there first, but it doesn't mean shit. The difference is, this one I want more than anything, and hers, I never did ... I guess that makes me an absolute shithead for saying it." He sighs and runs a hand through his hair, flexing his shoulders, resting both palms on the back of his head. His expression is that of fatigue, more than anything, "You will always be my priority, despite having two kids. I already know which baby will hold my heart more." He glances across at me apologetically, as though he does realize how horrible a person that might make him.

"You are a shithead." I spit out childishly, lowering my glare to the floor, and a new wave of tears hits hard. I can't begin thinking about this now, or I'll fall to bits. It's a complete mess, her, me, babies, Jake.

How the hell did it even come to this horrible fucked-up situation?

Jake ignores my comment and watches me closely, keeping his distance while I flounder in emotional turmoil. I have no clue what to do with all the excessive energy coursing through me.

"Emma, when Marissa told me about the baby, I felt like jumping off the building or hopping on a flight to Australia and never coming back. I still feel sick every time I think about it, even after weeks of knowing it's happening. But this ... US ..." He slides up onto his knees, shimmying across the floor toward me, awkwardly, yet extremely appealing somehow. He leans down, lifting my chin to look at him. He leans his forehead against mine. The urge to lash out and fight has once again dive-bombed into my feet; fatigue and sadness well up, drowning me instead.

"It feels completely different with you. I want this. I want it more than I ever knew I wanted it." He grins, that sweet little boy smile spreading across his face. "The second I realized what the doc was telling us, I felt this crazy joy building up inside me, *Bambina*, like straight from my toes and slowly up and over me. This is how it's supposed to feel when you find out you're going to be a father; the desire to shout it out from the rooftops and instant love ... I love you so much, and I won't let you down." He grazes his mouth against mine, but I only stiffen at the touch. Marissa is too close to the forefront of my mind right now for his touch. Everything he's saying has stopped computing. I need space to think and fresh air. I need to get off this bathroom floor and eat. We need sustenance because I just threw it up, which can't be healthy.

"I can't process this right now." I pull away from him, leaning out, telling him clearly to give me space. He sighs and moves back but doesn't go far. I think he's starting to realize the turmoil I'm in over him touching me, thankfully, without me having to verbalize it.

"You're moving back in as of today." A command, and there's an edge to his tone I instantly don't like. I snap up to glare at him.

"What the fuck? You don't even know if I'm even willing to take you back, and you're issuing orders to me?" I slam my hands on the cold tile floor angrily, shoving myself to stand. He knows how to ignite my fury button. I'm instantly seething. My skin is prickling with rage at his nerve. I'm already on my feet, ready to march out, but he catches my wrist and comes up to tower above me.

"If you think I'm going to let you stay anywhere but here when you're this fragile, then you can forget it. This isn't just about you anymore. It's my baby too. You get no say in this." He has his stubborn face plastered on, a mild amount of aggression radiating from him. I know when a huge fight is about to erupt, and I have no energy for this. I lift my chin, defiantly meeting the fire in his glare with a fire of my own.

"You will back the fuck off and let me decide what I'm doing. Right now, you're the last person I want to live with." I snap, angered at the turn in this situation, and yank my arm free. He clenches his teeth and glares over the top of me at something above my head, thoughts circling around his mind. We are standing feet apart, stubborn, meeting stubborn. His expression changes as he tries to figure out the best way to handle me, but I will not back down from him. He lost the right to cajole me the second he kissed that bitch; having a baby in this now only makes me more determined to stomp the shit out of his commanding tone.

His face softens unexpectedly, a gentle hand coming to stroke down my jawline and throat tenderly, his voice soothing. I slap his hand away. I know he's changing tactics.

Manipulative asshole.

"Look, I know I have no right. But you're still here after everything, which tells me that maybe I have more than a small chance of getting you back. That I have something to hope for. This isn't about trying to trap you here with me, Emma; it's about protecting who I love, and there are two of you now. I need to be able to take care of you and not go out of my mind worrying when you're in Queens. I wouldn't be able to function knowing that I'm not protecting you and caring for you in the way you need to."

When he puts it like that ...?

My anger simmers, my emotions tug a little, and how he's

looking at me breaks down my defenses. His eyes drilling straight into my heart with an annoyingly irresistible face. My breathing calms, and I try like crazy to ease the irrational mess in my head. He has no idea of the intoxicating effect he can have over me, and despite wanting to fight him on this, I know I want him to take care of me. I don't want to be a strong, capable mess back in Queens who fights herself to get up and eat or get up to do something to distract herself from the pain. Being here with him and having him close to me has been far more bearable than the last week of my life, despite the gulf between us.

"One day at a time ... I'm not bringing my stuff back until I decide if I can live with you again. You'll have to send Jefferson for clothes as I need them or crack out your credit card because I'm not making any long-term plans to be here." I stick my chin up defiantly and turn on my heel. I catch the slight smirk on his face out of the corner of my eye and storm through to the bedroom, yanking off his T-shirt and reaching for my clothes. I try to ignore the satisfaction he thinks he feels because he has not won this battle. I'm in charge, and I intend to make that clear. Jake has a lot of making up to do, and I'm not a girl who will let him stomp over her heart so easily and get back in.

"What are you doing?" Jake comes out after me and stands lazily against the door frame, one hand on the jam, almost reaching the top effortlessly. His eyes trail down my body, so I turn my back on him.

"I'm obviously not sick or dying, so there's no need to be bed bound. It's morning sickness, so I need to get over it." I grind my teeth. "I need to eat, seeing as I lost my lunch, and I'm starving." I sound angrier than I am. My brain automatically tries to push all of this into a contained space, so I can take little bits out at a time to analyze, process, and get my head around.

"And you need clothes to eat?" He's watching me, a little amused at my obvious bad mood. His whole demeanor has dramatically relaxed, knowing I'm staying.

Asshole.

"Yes, because you're taking me out to eat. I want barbecue

chicken wings, a side of fries, a huge tub of banoffee ice cream, and coffee donuts with caramel sauce." I lift my face to him as though saying, *"got a problem with that?"*

I'm freakin hungry.

"You think you can handle a car ride and not throw up?" His gaze doesn't back down from my intimidating glare. My menu request does not even phase him.

"We're walking. I need the air and the exercise," I snap out and wait for his protest. He shifts uneasily, his desire to argue with me crossing his beautiful brow before he thinks better of it. I will not back down on this. I know what I need right now, and it's not lazing in bed swanning about like some weak, sick person.

Maybe he's finally remembering that he should be groveling right now and not making demands.

"Fine." He pushes off the door frame and turns to his wardrobe, opening a door and yanking out a shirt. "We walk there, but we drive back. Jefferson can come get us later."

We'll see!

* * *

We sit across from each other in the busy little barbecue restaurant, the used plates between us, and I feel a hundred times better, if not a little too stuffed. I sort of regret the pie and donuts, but I had a point to make to him, and I was in no backing-down mood.

The walk here, the food, and the time to silently ponder it all have brought me down to a more even level of insanity. He's kept his distance, not touched me or talked, but let me think until I had some sense of calm, outwardly at least. The food has almost annihilated my thoughts of anything else. My hunger was so ravenous that I focused completely on demolishing the food he bought me, trying to ignore his surprised yet affectionate expression while watching me eat. He hasn't dared to touch anything on the plates I requested but has stuck to his own as though he knows I'll most likely turn feral. This place is one of my favorites for take-out.

This hunger is rather worrying. I hope it doesn't stay this way for the next eight months!

Being surrounded by normal people doing normal things is easing the chaos in my head. If I can pretend things are not as bad as they seem, I can act like none of it is happening to me right now.

"You look better." Jake cuts into my train of thought, and I glance up at him. He's lounging in the wooden seat, watching me while folding a napkin into a tiny square. The fidgeting tell-tale sign that he's not as laid back and comfortable as he appears but is mulling over the emotional turmoil in his head.

"I just needed to let everything sink in. It's been a lot to deal with the last few days. Honestly, I have no way of coping with it all at once." I push away my plate, full, and no longer want the smell wafting at me. It's no wonder I'm having some mid-life breakdown with all of this. I'm the girl who used to shun all emotions, locking them away so they couldn't touch her. I've never really learned how to handle my feelings from my younger life, yet Jake has forced a change in me over all of that. I was still playing catch-up, even before all this mess hit me.

"Look, if you want to stay in Queens, I know I can't stop you. I'm finding all this hard, Emma, not just because of the baby but because I miss you. I don't want you anywhere but with me. I can't think straight when you're not around me." He looks away and frowns across the café, and my heart constricts a little at the sad expression on his face. He's been thinking about how unreasonable his request was, given our current circumstances, mulling over his actions long after his crazy impulsive brain kicked the idea out there - typical of Jake. I can't help the little warmth of love spreading out from the pit of my stomach as I watch the lost look on his expression.

"Jake, I want to move on and forgive you, I do, but it's going to take time. It's not that I don't miss you, I'm just in so much pain, and this ... today ... well, it just adds to the mess inside my head. I'm hardly singing from the rooftops about it, am I?" I sigh, flicking at pieces of food on the table, attempting not to stare at his pensive face and cry. He makes me want to erase it all and hold him.

"Do you really hate being pregnant that much?" The pain on his face makes me wince. He can't conceal that level of hurt, even in public.

"I don't hate it. I don't know how to react. I have no idea how to be a mother or even deal with kids. It's not like I had a good example ... When have you ever seen me near a child? Please don't say Sophie because she's almost an adult. I'm scared, and this ... It couldn't have come at a worse time than what's happening between us right now." I sigh, rubbing my fingers into my scalp, and twirling a strand of my hair. I look out the window at the far end of the bistro, closing my eyes, wishing I could go back to a week ago.

"I know ... I'm sorry, baby. I'm sorry for all this; you must believe me when I say we will be okay. All this right now it's a lot, but we can get through it together. If you let me in, just a little, let me help you get through this. I want all of this with you." He leans forward, taking my hand in his, focusing on my eyes, bringing my gaze to him far too easily.

Damn you and your persuasive, pretty face. Why do you make me so stupidly weak?

"Trusting me, forgiving me ... It's not something you need to do right now to move on, Emma. That's something I'll earn over time when I prove to you that you can. I'm just asking for a chance to do this right, for you to take a chance on us again. We were good together. We *are* good together, and I won't lose you over a dumb mistake I made impulsively. We can be happy, Emma. I know I can make you happy." With that intense, serious face, and the love in his eyes, I sigh at it all and feel a little less broken somehow.

"But a baby, Jake?" The word hits me in the gut every time I say it. It's terrifying and a black hole of confusion in my head. I have no idea how I'm ever going to get used to this. I need time to let it sink in.

"You'll have to have a little faith that this will be amazing. You're a natural, Emma. I do not doubt that you'll know exactly how to be a mother when it comes. I know you're more than capable, and I'll be there every step of the way to help you." He turns my hand in his and starts circling my palm with his fingertips. It would be almost mesmerizing if it weren't for the internal battle over whether I want his touch. I must admit that it soothes me. I still ache for it, yet it hurts when I see her. I can't keep confusing the boundaries this way.

"What about her?" I can't bear to say her name. It catches in my throat like a spiked apple, she isn't going away anytime soon, and neither is the bundle she carries.

"What about her?" Jake asks carelessly, pausing and looking at me a little too intensely. My heart is thundering with an achingly familiar pain, and he seems deadly serious.

"Well ... She probably thinks she has a chance with you since you kissed her, and she's already carrying your kid. She isn't going to like finding out about mine." I yank my hand away, the inner wave of tears hitting hard. Either hormones are making me crazy, or bouts of anger and pain at Jake are taking turns to show face when I least expect them. I have no control over this at all; one second, I adore his face, and the next, I want to throw my mug at it. He sighs, pulling over the tray with our check on it, sliding a note from his wallet, and leaving it on the table. He's dismissing my outburst and being patient, which may be wise. He knows he has no grounds for protest on my behavior in any of this.

"For all I care right now, Marissa could emigrate to the moon. Come on, feisty; I think you need a nap." He smiles at me knowingly, and it makes me more pissed.

"Don't patronize me. I'm not tired!" I snap as I clamber out of my chair, knocking away his offering hand. I have no control over the crazy up-and-down moods I seem to be harboring toward him. "I'm pregnant, not a child!" I haughtily stalk past him and yank open the door before he can get close. He's still pulling our coats up from the chairs, silently and calmly, and I can feel his eyes on me with every step I take.

Catching up with me outside, he drapes my coat over my shoulders wordlessly, sliding his shades over my eyes, and I stop dead on my heels, an old forgotten Jake-ism knocking the wind out of my sails a little. His constant tender care is enough to make my crazy anger simmer back down to a defeated hum. He's keeping a pace or two behind me. My insides are pricklier than a cactus right now, and that bitch's face is beaming at me from inside my head.

* * *

I try to ignore Jake's smug look when I stroll into the open-plan living space, finally awake from my two-hour nap on his bed. I had a tantrum on the way home, making him walk with me while I refused to get in the car as Jefferson drove alongside me at the pace of a snail. It was utterly ridiculous, but I was adamant that Jake wouldn't tell me what to do, and he walked alongside me with hands in his pockets, daring not to argue.

I've woken up feeling a hundred times angrier and more emotional. I have no clue whether it's delayed shock or my brain unraveling slowly. I only know that I feel like breaking down and sobbing about everything and eating a lot of ice cream ... with chips ... and hot sauce ... And maybe a bowl of pistachios too. I suddenly want food more than anything; again. Food and some damn mental rest. This is completely exhausting like I am going through some sort of grief that I can't understand.

He's standing in the kitchen with a very smiley Daniel Hunter sitting across from him at the breakfast bar, and it only makes me tense up. The causal way Jake is sitting his butt against the sink sipping coffee and Daniel's relaxed posture on the stool facing him looks so normal, unaffected, and "every day."

Assholes.

"What are you doing here?" I snort at Daniel with an expression of utter disgust. I know it's completely none of my business, this is Jake's apartment and Jake's friendship, after all, and honestly, I can't imagine Jake inviting him here while things between us are an absolute hot mess. Plus, until Daniel grovels at Leila's feet, he's no longer on my *'I almost like you'* list. I'm not entirely sure when he got on that list, but he's certainly off it again now. I wander into the kitchen past Jake without meeting his smug look and yank open the fridge in search of food, ignoring the smirk or whatever cutesy look he's trying to give me.

Piss off. Asshole. Know it all. Will this hunger ever calm the hell down? I swear I know what vampires must feel like now.

"Hi to you too. Now is that the heartbroken Emma biting or the hormonal one? I hear congrats are in order."

I spin and scowl at Daniel, then Jake, for even daring to let that idiot in on our personal matters.

So, he told his bestie, and now they're out here having some little womanly chat over fatherhood and broken-hearted girls!

Dickheads.

"Both." I turn back to the fridge, rummaging through the tubs and trays Nora has stocked it with, finding a tub of cold chicken salad and digging in with my fingers. My eyes are still searching for something more satisfying ... preferably something greasy.

"I love her just as much when she's being this adorable," Jake smirks, and I catch Daniel frowning.

"You're totally under the thumb, dude. Your life is going to be a living hell if she gives you a girl. You'll have no chance two to one, and with that attitude."

I slam the bowl down, my inner emotion hitting hard, a lump catching in my throat; irrational feelings bruised so bloody easily.

"I'm sure Marissa will even up the odds by giving him a boy." I snap, slamming the refrigerator door before turning to walk off with tears in my eye.

"Hey..." Jake catches me mid-storm and pulls me into his arms, cradling me against his chest, smoothing a hand down the back of my neck. Bringing some calm to my outburst with his gentle touching relaxed tone. I don't fight him, just sag against him, but I refuse to put my arms around him or my hands on him. I close my eyes, pushing my face against his chest instead.

Is this a compromise on the touching thing?

"Nap didn't help, huh?" He soothes me, and my fire dies. I shake my head and press my face against him, turning my cheek, letting a little of my tears run free before trying to sniff them back. His hand travels down my back, and he slowly circles the base of my spine with light caressing, bringing some calm to my inner chaos and taut frayed emotions. I wish I could get a handle on things for five minutes.

"Chicks are cra—" Daniel is frowning at me.

"You finish that, and I won't have to hurt you. Emma might snap your head off your neck, the way she's feeling," Jake warns as he tightens his hold a little. He emanates a little irritation, and I know it's aimed at Daniel; he is always protective, even if it's just over my feelings.

"Guess I better get used to crazy women if I'm going to go ahead with my plan, right, Jake?" Daniel doesn't sound so smug anymore, his voice uneasy and a little nervous. I twist in Jake's arms to glare at him suspiciously under furrowed brows.

"What plan? What's he talking about?" I look up at Jake accusingly. Whatever Daniel is up to, I know Jake will surely be involved. He doesn't look phased at all. He just sips more coffee and gazes at Daniel for a moment.

"You going to tell her, or am I?" Jake smiles over the top of my head and then looks down at me when I don't hear Daniel respond.

"Danny has put himself into therapy ... The goal is not to run screaming for the hills when he convinces Leila to give him another shot."

Chapter 9

"Hey," I say to Sarah when she answers the phone. Her sweet hello makes me smile. I miss her like crazy, even though it's only been two weeks since Jake brought me here. I've been hiding, mulling things over, trying to get my head around everything that is my life before reaching out to her or anyone else. I swore Jake to secrecy about the baby until I could let it sink in and see how things went between us. I need time, and he's giving it to me.

"Hey, you. How's it all going? I didn't want to call after your text in case you two needed some time alone." She responds with a gentle tone, the one she uses when she thinks I'm fragile.

Oh, are you about to find out how fragile I am?

"I'm getting there. It's been a bit up and down. I'm still taking crazy angry turns at Jake, but he's been the model of absolute patience." I sigh and think back over the last couple of weeks, cringing. Jake has been understanding. He's keeping his distance unless I initiate rare touch. Still no kissing and no sex. He's enduring my cyclone of moods like a champ. I can't fault him at all. Jake has been everything he promised; patient, understanding, calm, non-demanding, and gentle, sometimes a little too gentle.

He is letting me behave appallingly towards him, not yelling back when I need to shout at him. Not reacting when I slap his hands away or avoid his touch. Instead, surprising me with take-out whenever he has to go out. He brings me everything I crave at any hour, night, or day, even when he has to drive thirty minutes to fetch it. He moved to another bedroom for the first two nights of my being here until I woke from another night terror and crawled in beside him, sobbing my heart out. After that, he refused to sleep apart again, so on that front, I relented. Sleeping apart was miserable anyway, not only because of the dreams but because I missed having him nearby, even when I wanted to throw things at him. Even in bed, though, he's kept his distance for the most part.

"He should be, seeing as he's the one who did this to you." She soothes.

Oh, the irony.

"Sarah ... talking of things Jake's done to me...." I break off and inhale slowly. I still haven't got my head around this little detail. Petrified by the idea, I'm still unsure if I've absorbed it.

"Please tell me he hasn't done anything else that stupid?" Sarah gasps, suddenly in ferocious mode, her tone almost a growl. I can picture that sweet face twisting in rage and over-protectiveness.

Well actually...

"I'm pregnant," I blurt out, breathing out so it comes out like a whooshing noise. I figure using the whole ripping off a Band-Aid method is probably best; say it quickly, and it won't be as bad.

"Say again?" Sarah halts with a sharp intake of breath.

"I'm going to have Jake's baby." Another quick whoosh of breath in a zombie-like monotone.

God, even the way I say it sounds like I'm in complete disbelief, trying the words out for the first time after two weeks of mulling this over.

There's an eerie silence for a moment, and I'm not sure if Sarah's there anymore; maybe she's passed out, but I didn't hear a thud. The inner swirl of fear I've been harboring for the last two weeks rises, getting ready to spill over.

"You know ... ordinarily, anyone else saying this to me, especially with all you two have going on, would make me feel a bit...well, upset. But I have this weird sense of happiness right now that I can't explain." Her tone's slow swell of joy as she lets my news sink in. She sounds almost as confused at her reaction as I have been in the past weeks here.

"You're happy?" I question flatly, not sure of what response I wanted from her. Now I'm confused and suddenly a little irritated. Sarah was always the word of reason and wisdom. Now she's being a Jake.

"I think you need this, Ems." She encourages softly, with a gentle tone.

I am beyond stupefied right now.

"I need an unplanned pregnancy?" I repeat like a completely brainless dimwit who can't absorb anything she's saying, with an edgy tone to my voice. I am trying to figure out how her brain works.

"No. I mean, I used to think you needed someone like Jake to bring out the inner you, but now I think this here is what's going to bridge that last gap. Motherhood Emma. I think you need motherhood." She sounds enlightened like she's just had the most amazing epiphany.

I don't think so!

I have no words; my brain is whirring and whizzing at my friend's idiotic logic.

"We're not in the nineteen fifties. I won't have a fulfilling life if I just get married and pop out babies," I snap a little too aggressively, trying to reel in the anger I've been going through a lot lately, annoyed at myself for getting snippy with her. But really, she has the most idiotic logic ever. It wouldn't surprise me if, in her next breath, she tried to marry me off to him!

"No, that's not what I mean. Look, stop getting upset. I just mean that part of you, maybe, needs unconditional love and the nurturing maternal stuff that comes with being a mom. That with Jake and a baby, you'll maybe find that place you've been looking for. What he can't give you himself, he can give you by making you a mother." She leaves me dumbfounded, so sure of her crazy ideology.

I run a hand over my face in agitation and rub at my closed eyes. Sarah has lost her mind.

"I have no idea what you're on, but send some my way. I could do with that kind of special this morning," I snap grumpily, hostility in full flow, only she giggles at the other end.

"Oh, my God, poor Jake. Emma, really? In less than five minutes, I can only imagine the crazy mess he's dealing with. All those versions of you colliding dramatically with hormonal imbalance thrown in, and you've probably no idea how to handle it at all. No wonder you're being so pissy." Her tone seems to quell my anger, and despite myself, I smile. Sarah, of all people, knows me well, and she's right.

My life has been turned on its head, and every version of who I was or am has me so upside down and back to front I've no idea who I am anymore. All I know is graceful and cold PA Emma would never be in the crazy mess I'm in now. I haven't worn any of her clothes in weeks, let alone those stilettos, which I've kept with me almost like a protective talisman. I wear flats now ... flats! Girly clothes, cute jumpers, and goddamn summer dresses in romantic fabrics. Hell must have frozen over, surely.

"I've been a nightmare, Sarah. It's a wonder he's still here." I cast my mind back to the tearful sobbing, angry shouting, and smashing plates of crazy Emma, who has been occupying the apartment with him. The woman who woke from a nap on the couch to find Jake had set up the bathroom with candles, music, rose petals, and a gorgeous bubble bath for me and told him I hated him before breaking down in sobs.

I am a mess. Jake is in pain too, but I'm selfishly stomping all over him, ignoring what he's feeling, marking it as invalid because he hurt me and ruined things because he took my trust and ripped it into tiny shreds.

The stuff with Marissa still claws at my brain every day. It's completely unhealthy, hanging over me like some doom and gloom cloud of tension. I've spent the last two weeks knowing he's been avoiding her contact, and it only adds to the build-up inside me; that somehow, the moment he sees her will make me break. It intensifies my anger when it hits, and I know a time will come when I'll blow up at him, an outlet for all the crazy inside me.

"Jake loves you, and he's repenting for his sins. If he can't handle all you're throwing at him now, babe, he's not the man for you." Sarah laughs and jokes, but I know she's being serious.

Jake *is* handling all I am throwing at him, bringing home my favorite foods when he goes out to meetings and pampering me with gifts and love notes to find whenever I open a drawer or use the bathroom. He leaves little surprises for me to find whenever he goes out. He's trying so hard to show me that I am loved and wanted, yet all he's getting in return is an unhinged emotional psychopath who occasionally shows hints of the girl he loves. I need to stop pushing him away and acting so hostile, or I'll be chasing Jake to win him back. But I can't help it. Something in me in the last two weeks has grown overly uncontrollable, with an emotion bubbling inside of me that I can't pick out, an aching cavern of emptiness that I have no way of dealing with or know how to deal with.

"I think he might get sick of how I'm being," I verbalize my inner doubt without thinking. Shivering at the thought.

"No, he won't, Emma. You're pregnant, and you're grieving over what he did. I'm sure even Jake has the intelligence to see that, and he's sure as hell got the sense to let you do it. Are you back? I mean, are you ... intimate again?" Her question surprises me, but with Sarah, she does like the juicy details.

"I let him touch me; occasionally. We share a bed, and sometimes he reaches for me in his sleep but other than that, we don't go near each other. I can't let him kiss me or get too touchy-feely just yet, and definitely no sex." I can't even begin to explain the heartbreak I get whenever I contemplate kissing him. She's always there in my mind, pushed up against him. It's all bound up with my trust in him and my inner need to inflict punishment on him. I can't even dissect it myself, and I haven't let him try in weeks. I've been too scared to let him if I'm being honest, because that bitch being in my head causes so much pain.

"It's normal, Ems. He betrayed you. All that stuff isn't owed to him ... it's earned. He needs to earn back the trust to let him go there again. I completely understand." She sighs.

I'm glad she does, as I have no idea.

I catch the noise of Jake coming into the apartment and the shuffle of bags as he strolls in; he and Mathews are laughing over something. He sounds happy, tugging at my heart and lightening my mood. The voice and laugh that has so much power over me. I miss that laugh lately; it hasn't been around much.

He had an early meeting at his father's building and was gone for hours. There's a rise in my stomach, the lightening of the heavy pit, and the urge to go to him overwhelms me. At least a part of me still wants him just as much as I did before; it reminds me every time he's been away. I miss him when he's not here, even if I am being a complete bitch to him when he is.

"Sarah, I need to go. I'll text you later, okay? Jake's home." I suddenly have an unyielding urge to see him.

We say our goodbyes, and as I hang up, Jake sweeps past, carrying many shopping bags with various brands and designer names emblazoned across them. I sigh and hope he's not brought home another mountain of gifts like he did last time he was in the city. I don't want gifts and trinkets; I want my head to stop with all its confusing crap.

He heads into the bedroom with a smile my way, and I get that surge of disappointment that I've been getting a lot lately. Sometimes I miss the forceful Jake who says, *Fuck this shit*, and pushes me to a wall kissing the hell out of me. I miss him that way, and part of me wonders how I would react if he did just that, if he took away my choice to kiss him and just did it. If he took away my choice and just forced physical contact again.

Would I push him away?

You chose to keep him at a distance until you can handle this Marissa shit!

I stare down at my phone to distract my thoughts, contemplating calling Leila, swiping to her face among my contacts, and telling her when I'm suddenly hoisted up mid-air off the couch with a squeal. Jake doing his best ' bride-to-be' hold, plants a kiss on my cheek with the most gorgeous smile I've ever seen. I melt a little inside and can't help but smile back at this forbidden contact. My inner stomach flutters crazily, and a tiny sparkle of something else, something warm and tingly.

"Did you miss me? I missed you." He's obviously in a very good mood; this spontaneous grabbing has been lacking lately.

Severely lacking.

"Maybe," I reply softly, looking away shyly. I'm suddenly nervous and awkward like I used to be before I knew he loved me. It feels weird to be nose to nose again. It feels like an age has passed since we were this close while awake.

"I come bearing gifts." He grins, trying to tilt his head around to get me to look at him. His cuteness has me shaking my head and giving in to his intoxicating mood.

"Stop spending money on gifts. I told you I don't need them," I huff lightly. But the inner swell of joy I'm getting from being in his arms is nudging away the anger so I don't sound mad. I sound like the old me.

"Technically, they're not for you, *Bambina.*" He winks cheekily and plants another kiss on me, this time on the corner of my mouth, his eyes focusing a little too long on my lips. I can feel myself urging him just to do it. I can't think straight as I take in those perfectly chiseled kissable lips so close to me. I clear my throat and bring my attention back to his eyes.

Oh, those eyes.

"Who are they for?" I sound childish, and he only smiles harder, a look of adoration evident on his face. He's chipping away at me, melting some of my ice with his current behavior and mood.

"I'll show you." He turns and carries me to the bedroom, gently laying me on the bed beside the bags. Yet as he does, I instantly return to cold and upset, that inner swell of warmth dissipating fast, my mood trickling away, and I realize what it is almost immediately; a clarity or epiphany like a lightning bolt out of the darkness.

I miss Jake's affection! His touch, his caresses, his hugs. I miss us! That's what this constant anger is.

I miss him touching me freely, without permission or needing to ask for it. I miss the spontaneous, arrogant, *'I can touch you because you're mine'* Jake. I miss being picked up, hauled around, and grabbed. I miss the way he would kiss me a million times a day just because he had to, and I miss that body molded to mine, making me feel complete. I miss that I belonged to him, and he never sought my permission to possess me. I owned him, and he owned me, and neither ever needed any urging to take what we needed from one another.

This space between us is what's killing me, knocking me off kilter because Jake is the one who always grounded me. Always brought my sanity back with his affectionate, touchy, '*hands-on Carrero*' approach. And he isn't giving it to me anymore.

I watch as he lifts a corner of a bag and ungraciously dumps stuff all over the bed while I try to get a handle on my thoughts and the realization I've come to and what to do about it.

A sudden catch in my throat almost chokes me as a bundle of tiny white baby clothes unfurls before me, shocking me with the unexpectedness of it, completely tearing my thoughts from anything else.

"Jake ... You shouldn't. It's too soon." I blurt out in hushed tones. My hands betray me as they automatically pick up a tiny white Babygro in soft velvet fabric. I pick it up to hold it against my abdomen without realizing what I'm doing. It's so tiny and fragile, so real and symbolic. A surge of something wells up inside me, and the urge to cry overwhelms me. It's precious and small, making me think of the little life growing inside me with every breath I take. My heart catches in my throat.

"I ... kinda got a bit carried away." He tips up another two bags, pouring out a bundle of blue, a bundle of pink, and one of lemon, plus one fluffy giraffe sitting proudly among them with a goofy grin on its adorable face. It strangely reminds me of Jake, but I can't fathom why.

For the first time in weeks, I get a stupid spontaneous smile spreading across my face, and I stare at him in a completely new light. It's as though I've just woken up, and blinking in the sunlight, I gaze at him as he comes into focus. He looks happy, idling through the stuff on the bed, his green eyes almost luminescent. I've never seen him as gorgeous as he is right now, beaming over his baby's things, looking every bit irresistible to me.

I couldn't fill my heart with more love than this moment. Everything that has happened, everything we've done to one another, yet this little moment here seems to wipe it all out. Just looking at him like this, knowing I've been falling apart without his touch, has me aching. I want him, and I need him so badly. This is making me crazy.

"Kiss me," I say so directly and spontaneously that I even take myself by surprise. His eyes snap to mine, and he seems to take a moment to realize what I've asked. A flash of something in his eyes, hesitation, and something else ... apprehension. The tension rises in my stomach with every delayed second.

We seem to stay motionless, looking at one another, while I wait for some verbal response, every moment becoming agony as the pit of self-doubt grows inside me. It's almost like he no longer wants to kiss me.

Shit ... I'm losing him. Crazy Emma pushed him too far away. Stupid Emma, you've been pushing him away for weeks despite everything he has done to show you he loves you.

Jake sweeps forward, pinning me to the cushions, his mouth meeting mine in almost a flicker of a second. I don't see the reaction coming, so I'm bowled backward, and before I know what's happening, our mouths are locked, and his hands are cradling my face. That soft, warm mouth, the feelings it rips up to the surface, consumes me, gently molding our movements in perfect unison. His mouth was always made for kissing mine. My toes tingle right up to my pelvis, and my heart aches for him.

He kisses the breath right out of me, moving on top of me on the bed so he can lie over me, yet holding his weight up. He gently slides his tongue into my mouth, a soft yet firm motion, as we get used to one another again. This is so right. I get lost in his feel and what he's doing to me. It feels like he hasn't kissed me in eternity, and it physically pains me. It makes me want to cry.

He tastes as I remember, smells, and feels like my dreams, and with every second of this unity, a part of me starts healing. I groan almost instantly, a thousand butterflies fluttering up inside my stomach, warmth spreading through my veins. My fingers find their way up around his neck and across those muscular shoulders, hair, and jaw. I'm roaming, devouring what I've been lacking for so long.

I wait for the vision of her to break in, wrenching us apart, but I'm too absorbed in the sensations and overwhelming tug of desire building up inside of me to let her in. I push myself into him firmly, intensifying the passion of the kiss, letting our tongues caress, breathing hard and heavily. His intoxicating touch drives my body into a frenzy now that his mouth is locked with mine.

Hormones kick in, and I lose control; arms sliding around his neck fully, I yank him down on top of me; forcefully. I want to wrap every inch of him around me, within me, devour him with a need so overwhelming that I'm going to self-implode. All those pent-up desires unleashed; hormones and heartbreak; anger and lust; I've been denied, love-starved for agonizing weeks; and they come crashing down with a passion that has me yanking his tie off, ripping open his shirt buttons aggressively like a crazed wild cat. Jake pulls away, a hand coming to my wrist, stopping the snaking motion of my nails running down his exposed torso.

"Emma, slow down," he pants, trying to untangle me, but I only dive back in, sucking his lower lip into my mouth and biting him, deprived for too long and turning feral with need. My inner body is combusting with fiery heat, and my lower body is aching with a pang of hunger so intense I want to scream. He automatically releases my wrist and moves down over my breast through the sheer satin of my dress, soaring heat from the sensitivity of it. He moves back into this, losing himself in the lust for a moment, deepening the kiss, his hardness against my pelvis. He wants me just as much as I want him, but he pulls away fast with no warning, lifting his hands in defense.

"Okay, this stops." He kneels back and lifts me up under the arms, pulling me into a sitting position before releasing me, standing back on the floor, expression wild and heaving in the air. "I'm trying so hard to be good, Emma ... I can't if you keep doing that." He takes several deep breaths trying to calm his body down. He's completely irresistible like this, standing there with an open shirt and raging hormones clouding any rational thought. His muscles and tanned skin are on show, with ruffled hair, kiss-swollen lips, and lust-fueled hazy eyes trying to control his emotions.

"Maybe I don't want *good Jake*. Maybe I want normal Jake." I pout angrily. My inner core almost twisting itself into a frenzy of horniness just looking at him.

I want authoritative, no-nonsense Casanova Jake. I need him. I need this. I need sex. I'm so crazy for him right now.

"Emma, please. I told you I won't touch you or do anything until you're ready." His tense body turns me on, and I bite my lip, fixated on his muscles moving under the form-fitting shirt, exposed toned abdomen, and tailored pants. A sex-crazed haze comes over me fiercely.

Throwing all thoughts except sex out the window, I stand up and yank his shirt out at the waist. I slide my hands under the hem of the smooth fabric and up the sculptured muscles across his abdomen, reveling in the feel of the body I missed so much. I bite my lip and focus on the body in front of me. A body built to make women go completely weak at the knees and their panties self-combust. He groans and slumps toward me slightly, tensing at my touch and empowering me.

"You know how much restraint I'm exercising right now?" His low husky voice and shallow breathing confirm it. I can feel the energy pulsing from him, making me feel desirable, knowing he's fighting the lust driving through him, knowing I could break his will with a mere touch. Knowing I have this much control over him only drives my need to have him joined to me even more.

I reach up on tiptoes, kiss his neck, nibble, and lick the skin I have been denied, as he stiffens in response. The tension is oozing from him, yet he doesn't move out of my grasp or move to touch me. My hand slowly traces the soft, hard muscles down his chest, across his sculpted stomach, around past his hips, and finally over his ass.

Every stroke makes the burning ache inside me notch up until I'm almost melting from within for him. I reach down, grabbing his hand, not satisfied with his self-control, pulling him into me, almost groaning at the look in his eyes as we come nose to nose. He may not be initiating anything, but he isn't stopping me from doing it.

He's just as weak as I am, and no matter how much willpower he's trying to dredge up, it's failing him.

Jake has many levels of lust. I've seen them all, from flirty starts to complete lust-driven sex, and right now, this look crowns them all. His pupils almost take over the green of his eyes, his face set in complete longing, and his mouth ready to kiss. I maneuver his hand under my dress to my waiting lace underwear and let go of him as it touches the flimsy fabric. I bite my lip and use his wrist to turn his hand to cup me fully and groan as the mere touch ignites sensations that can consume me. We both groan at the contact as his hand flexes slightly, and he fully connects to me. Neither of us looks away, eyes intensely locked.

"Emma. Don't," he whispers so softly it almost makes me break. I shake my head and lean up, brushing my lips across his, and he bends down further to accommodate me, kissing me softly and enjoying me. He's savoring me while his hand stays between my thighs, gently cupping my heat, making me throb with the mere touch. His thumb travels slowly to the front of me, hitting the exact spot I need him to be at, and he gently moves slightly. A sign of his weakening resolve.

God, I missed the way he kisses me, so badly. I forgot how he felt down there, how his touch could rip me apart so easily.

I glimpse her shadow inside my head, moving into view, and I push it away. I won't let her keep taking him from me. I need him too much. I'm not ready to completely forgive and forget, but I desperately want to start moving on to stop the overemotional angst of the last couple of weeks.

He's mine, she can't have him, and she has absolutely no chance of getting near him if I have any say.

He pulls back suddenly, his face a picture of confusion and agony, and rests his forehead against mine, sighing heavily. He removes his hand, much to my complete disappointment, and runs his fingertips across my lips, his eyes filled with conflicting thoughts and regret.

"Who's the over-thinker now?" I smirk, the tension still sparking between us. He smiles softly and runs fingers from his other hand lightly across my abdomen before looking back up at me, a sliver of emotion flickering through my stomach where his mind is. It quiets my combustion a little.

"I want you... Badly. I just can't ... Not this way. You're not yourself right now, baby. It wouldn't be right." He kisses me on the temple, pulls me with him to the bed, and sits me down like a child. His whole manner has returned to the gentle Jake of the last few weeks and the soft, caring mellow mood he's been in.

I'm not ready to back down yet. I know him too well. He's trying to be the good guy, probably worried I'm too fragile. Or that he'll hurt the baby, that maybe I'm doing this because I'm crazy horny with hormones, or that it will mess us up even more.

Maybe I am.

Maybe it will. I'm so confused about so many things, but not this. I know what I need. I need assertive, confident lover, Jake, who dominates me. He's the missing piece of this puzzle. The anger and frustration that snaps out of me are a direct result of missing him so badly that I can't function. I need the intimacy back, above everything else, the kissing, touching, and yes, even the sex to feel whole again. I need to be owned by him fully to feel like I can move on again.

I watch him resist, but he wants me. It's singing out from every pore of his body. I know he has very little will when it comes to me. I reach up and wrap my arms around his neck as he leans in to go for another soft kiss, catching him by surprise, and he tumbles on top of me gloriously.

"Fuck's sake, Emma!" He snaps in sparking anger, rolling off me onto the bed with a furious glare, and jumps up onto his feet like a panther. "I could've hurt you or the baby." His lust replaced with sheer annoyance. I instantly bristle and scowl at him, spurned on by his overreaction and the rejection of what I really need.

"Is this what I have to endure for eight months? Being treated like fine china and pandered to? Regardless of my behavior?!" I snap, frustration turning me into that crazy monster he once denied an orgasm to in his mother's gardens, my good old trusty anger bouncing up out of nowhere to devour me again.

"Yes!" His retort is nowhere near as anger-fueled, but it still pisses me off majorly.

"No fucking way." I haul myself off the bed and start slamming through cupboards looking for clothes. I have some here that Jefferson collected and the new things Jake ordered for me. Rage is coursing through me that he would deny me this, that he, of all people, would be annoyed at ME about this.

"What are you doing?" He follows me and tries to haul me back with a hand on my upper arm, but I shove him off aggressively.

"I'll leave you and go back to Queens if you're going to start being like this." I huff and stamp around, knowing I'm being crazy and irrational. Jake's just trying to be the good guy, and I'm acting like the bitch that I have been for weeks, acting this way because he doesn't touch me anymore.

Your choice, Emma!

"You don't want me to take care of you?" He croaks, dumbfounded and more than a little hurt. I glance up and catch the expression on his face, his little lost boy look, and it physically hurts me, a sharp pain in my stomach fueling my temper tantrum.

"I want you to rip my goddamn dress off and remind me of the guy I fell crazily in love with! The one who didn't take no for an answer or me pushing him away as a hindrance!" I snap and turn on him with tears in my eyes. "I miss you ... The real you, not this *over gentle and walking on eggshells keeping his distance* you. I miss us, Jake, and it's torturing me."

"It's what you asked for, Emma, and it's what you need. Do you think rushing back into sex will fix how you feel? Well, it's not, and I don't want it that way." He runs a hand through his hair in complete frustration and starts pacing around the side of the bed to avoid being too close to me. He's agitated and angry and something else; hopeless. He's out of his depth with this, just as I am, neither of us knowing what we should be doing to fix this.

"I've spent the last two weeks confused with what I need from you and holding you at arms-length, but it isn't working. Do you know why? Because you're not you either. I need you, not this half-assed version of you! I need the Jake who came after me in Chicago, who pushed me into a hotel wall and kissed me, the Jake who stormed across a dance floor to find me. I need him to come get me because I'm so damned lost right now." I cry, a sudden wave of emotion hitting like a ton of bricks as tears spill down my cheeks. That wave of heartbreak overtakes me as everything I've been holding back, deep inside, works its way free.

"You need time, Emma. I will not risk losing you by rushing things and pushing you further from me. I would die without you." He implores me pleadingly. Stopping his frantic walking and comes close to me, his hands pausing on my face, brushing away my hair and tears.

"How can you know what I need when I don't even know what I need?" I almost wail at him, emotions soaring, as I wave my hands around angrily between us.

"Because I know you, like it or not, and sometimes I know what you need more than you do, yet you're too damn stubborn to trust me on it!" He barks back and then frowns, instantly remorseful for losing his temper.

"No! You're just arrogant, always thinking you know what I need, but most of the time, you don't know what I need or want." I rant, storming and pacing, every ounce of me burning with heated fire. I'm angry at him and myself, for God knows what. An all-consuming fury that needs to be released. These past few weeks, I haven't let all this pour out, not this way, anyway. All my outbursts and tantrums have been aimed at other issues and lots of misdirection from the real topics, doing what I always did, avoiding the painful roots and letting them fester inside.

"You never tell me what you need or feel, Emma, so I've had to learn to second guess you. You're always so damn scared of truly letting it all out! Tell me what you need ... Say it to me and fuck the consequences ... Scream it at me if you have to because right now, I need to hear it. Hear once and for all that you fucking love me enough to let me see every fucking thing that goes on in your head!" he yells at me, losing his cool, fueled by my temper, and I snap. Enraged that he would even yell at me like this, uncontrolled anger at one another brings back the memory of him walking out on me that night. My mind spews out via my mouth hysterically.

"I need you to have not done what you did!" I wail out loud, my voice fracturing, the harshness of my temper breaking free. "I need her to not be pregnant with your baby because I hate them both, and I don't care if you're disgusted at me for it. I want us to be normal, for none of this to hurt this way because it all hurts so damn much, and I did not need an unplanned pregnancy thrown in the mix to royally fuck my head up more than it already is.... I don't even know how to feel about this baby other than I don't want to get rid of it, and that has me crazy as hell ... You want to know why I didn't want the house, Jake? Because I'm scared, I'm so goddamn fucking scared of all of this because it's real and frightening. All I've ever had in life to show me what relationships are is a fucked-up, selfish bitch of a mother who let men abuse me and a father who let himself get paid off to never fucking come near me again after years of acting like I didn't exist! I don't believe that anyone can ever truly love me the way you say you do or that you'll stay with me and protect me when no one else has.... Why would you?... You alone have the power to destroy me and leave me broken without effort, and giving myself over to you fully is utterly terrifying!... What I *do* fucking need, Jake, is just one piece of frickin normal, for one day, to stop me going out of my freaking mind.... I need the Jake Carrero, CEO, bossy, arrogant, cocky shit, who liked to get me naked and screw me on top of fucking cars and desks, and any damned place he pleased because he liked to point out every fucking second of every day that I was *his*, and only *his*. He owned that shit without even trying!... I *need him* because he's the one who found me once before and pulled me out of this shit with everything that he was ... *is* ... *so*... YOU... can you fuck off and go find him? Because he's the one who I need in this room with me, right now, not you!... *He's* the one I love with every piece of my messed up soul, the one I would follow to the ends of the Earth, it's his baby in here, and we both need no one else but him!" I explode at him, letting all the anger, rage, and aching pain come out in a rush of crazy sobs before I slump down onto the floor and start weeping violently, letting it all seep out.

I feel completely free with my rambling, uncensored, emotional, verbal outburst over. Like a weight has been lifted. The building heaviness and pain of the past few weeks have just exited the building, and all that's left is emotional exhaustion and a lot of light-headedness. I don't even know if what I've screamed, rather psychotically, at him made any sense. I just got lost in the outpouring of every emotion that's been bubbling inside me, rather manically.

Jake's arms come around me slowly and tightly, and he lifts me into him. Cradling me as he slides us both onto the bed to sit entangled. His mouth comes close to my cheek, his breath tickles my face, and his whole body is completely still, calm beneath me despite seeing the woman he loves turn into some crazy, ranting mental person.

"I never left you, baby. I'm still here, but I'm just so scared of losing you that I don't know how else to be. I'm trying to give you time and understanding, Emma, trying to undo what I've done and not make this worse for you." He strokes back my hair as I whimper and cry, curled in his lap, hopelessly overcome with extreme fatigue. Finding the strength inside of me to pull myself together and calm down the flood of pain to listen to the voice that seems to run through me with every word. I sigh and sag into him fully. "I'm scared ... I love you so much, and I know I'm messing it all up despite trying so fucking hard. I need you, Emma, more than air, more than anything, and I can't lose you. It would end me. I have no idea how to navigate this because I've never been here before. I'm just hoping I know you well enough to guide you when you're struggling." The painful break in his tone pushes me to look up to connect with two beautiful green eyes filled with moisture, studying me with the rawest pain I've ever seen, mirroring my own.

"I want to let it all go. I want to be us again." I cry and push my face into the crook of his neck, feeding from the warmth around me, just drawing everything I can from him. I can't go back to not being held by him after this. It's healing me in ways I so badly need, returning to some sense of reality, grounding me in the way only he ever could, the way only his touch ever could. I don't want to go back to not having him around me.

"I want that too. I miss us. I miss this ... Just being able to touch you and kiss you whenever I want to, being able to be close to you again is everything; this is my reason for breathing, baby." He rests his chin on top of my head and sighs heavily.

"I miss this too ... I want this back Jake; give it back to me." My tears have turned to silent droplets trickling down my face, and he tightens his strong arms protectively, a silent promise to keep me safe and always take away my pain if he can.

I love him so much.

"You can have this back, Emma, all of it. There is nothing in the world I want more right now than this. Just not sex, not yet trust me on this baby." He lifts a hand, running it across his face and rubbing hard at the spot between his eyebrows. "I can't believe I'm even saying this ... I won't touch you that way until I know you're ready for us to go there again. You'll know when, Emma, and you'll thank me for not doing this as much as it's killing me. I need your forgiveness first and to forgive myself before we can ever go there. I need to accept what I did to you, too. I need to be able to look in the mirror, not hating what I see staring back before I can allow myself to give you every part of me again."

He sighs and kisses me on the forehead. Each touch and caress makes me curl into him more and more, trying to take from this what I need right now; more than anything, I need Jake wrapped around me and loving me in the way only he can.

Chapter 10

"We need to go out today, Emma." Jake wakes me from my nap with a gentle kiss on my mouth. I'm on the couch where I fell asleep with a book. Kissing has made a definite comeback, although Jake never lets it move into a full-on passion. I know it's because he doesn't want to escalate things, but he has returned to kissing me softly, tenderly, and sometimes erotically. I've managed to gain control of the Demon Bitch appearing in my head, with the kissing at least; she doesn't pop in there as easily anymore.

"Where?" I stretch out and yawn. This last week I haven't felt like doing anything or going out; morning sickness and tiredness are currently ruling my life. I guess I'm finally starting to accept the idea of a baby growing inside me; appointments with doctors have been arranged for a week. I'm not exactly jumping around with excitement, but at least I'm not trying to ignore that this child exists anymore. I'm slowly coming to terms with it; whether that acceptance has found happiness yet is another issue entirely, but I'm no longer fretting every time I think about it.

I've been lazing around the rooms, watching movies, eating a lot, reading, curling up with him, or watching him work out at the gym while I laze on a lounger with a smoothie or a book. Jake has been working from home a lot more and generally letting me get away with extreme laziness since that day in our bedroom.

My anger is calming with his constant affections, and I have found myself in more level moods if still a little touchy at times. I'm more in control and at peace with myself, sort of. Jake's touch and his intimacy are what I needed all along. We're still healing. I still need to forgive him fully, and I'm not sure where I am with trusting him yet because we haven't gotten to a point where it has been tested.

Demon Bitch is still a situation he hasn't even begun to approach yet, still not facing the fact he needs to contact her regarding the child she's carrying, pushing that issue aside in favor of focusing on me. I have the impression that he avoids her because of how it makes me feel and what he did. It's a mess in his mind, and it's obvious his guilt is right up there beside my heartbreak.

"The Hamptons." He smiles, leaning down and kissing me on the cheek before helping me to my feet. He smooths down my dress and hauls my cardigan around me to button it up in a very paternal way.

"Why are we going there?" I lazily watch his fingers at their task and ignore the urge to have them on my naked skin, the desire to be with him fully still aching inside me. But I trusted him; to know that sex wouldn't help how I am thinking or feeling. He asked me to give him a little faith in knowing what I need, and so I am.

"First, we need to tell my family about this." He smooths a hand down my flat stomach affectionately, making me smile warmly. He's been waiting to see his mother face-to-face and had wanted things between us to be more stable before telling them. "Secondly, I set up a house viewing." He pauses warily, that flicker of doubt crossing his eyes and furrowing his brows as he waits for my reaction ... Tenses for my response, more like. I am still at the subtle change in his demeanor and can't help but eye roll that only he could bring us back around full circle to the reason we'd ever hurt one another in the first place.

"A what?" I ogle him with narrowed eyes, but he only kisses me quickly, with a fleeting look of apprehension, and continues straightening out my appearance for me, acting like he's in full control and not nervous in the slightest.

Hmmm.

I rub the tiredness from my eyes and try to get my foggy brain together. I'm not sure if I even have any real reaction to this.

"We're going to look at a house ... Our possible future home." He at least has the grace to seem uncomfortable and straightens up to lock eyes with mine. "You wanted commanding bossy asshole back? Here he is. Now, if you want to tell me you still don't want it, then fine, I won't be an asshole about it, but at least let me show you first." The confidence doesn't quite reach his tone, but I sigh and realize I'm not even mad. I'm not anything. No fear, no panic, no irritation. He is exactly who I wanted him to be, and I should accept that a future with him involves a new house.

"Okay." I run my fingers through my hair and try to fluff it out.

"Okay, you'll let me show you the house?" He queries, with a severe look of trepidation on his face. The cute youthfulness he sometimes gets when he doubts himself makes him more adorable.

"Somewhere with a garden and maybe less bachelor pad décor might be nice." I sigh, waving around the apartment. It's modern, sleek, and male, and even though I am happy here with Jake, most of the time, it's not exactly child friendly or homely, and the city is never somewhere I've loved living. It was convenient for work, but I've never bonded with it.

Jake's grin widens, and he throws a toe-curling kiss on me, taking my breath away and upping the hormones in my blood as he wraps his arms around my waist and thoroughly ravages my mouth. I'm almost panting with horniness when he pulls away. As kisses go, this is one of the *pre-fucked up relationship* varieties. He sits me back on my feet but stays close, nose to nose, as I try in vain to catch my breath and cool the heat creeping up over my skin. This no-sex thing better not be something we need for much longer.

"We're driving, not flying, so it's going to be a long trip, *Bambina*, pack some books. Nora is fixing you some snacks for the road." He turns and walks off toward his office, a place he's frequently using nowadays.

"Why driving? The flight is only an hour." I watch his strong back and shoulders dip as he picks up his cell from the charging dock on the way past. I'm a little too enamored with his butt and its lack of nakedness lately.

"You can't fly in the first trimester of pregnancy; it's too risky, *Bambina*." He throws me a smile and walks into the open door, leaving me to watch him depart and shake my head.

Jake, the attentive daddy-to-be. Who knew?

It makes me smile despite myself; this is another side to the Carrero playboy I met long ago. I never in a million years imagined that the smooth Casanova with a sexy smile and hunky body would be the guy pampering me to insanity over his unborn child. I swear one of the books I've seen him read lately is a pregnancy book.

I stare after him blankly as my head swims with how different he's being with me over this, compared to Demon Bitch. He seems to want this a whole lot but never seemed to care with Marissa about any of this and never seemed to take any real interest in her pregnancy.

I know he's kept in contact with the lawyers since their kiss, and she's fighting the DNA request; it seems after getting her hopes up with a kiss, she's now digging her claws in to make things difficult. He told the lawyers a few days ago that he won't attend maternity classes with her as planned and doesn't intend to be at the birth. He said he saw no need to complicate things further, not that he won't be attending those things with me anyway. I gaze down at my normal flat stomach and sigh. We'll be needing those things soon enough, and the idea doesn't appeal at all.

You have a lot to answer for, tadpole.

Going to tell his family is nerve-racking, and neither of us knows what the reaction is going to be, considering he already has another baby on the way with another woman.

I haven't even contemplated telling my mother. That's a whole other ball game I don't want to approach just yet; something in me knows she wouldn't exactly be a doting or happy grandmother, either.

* * *

"Ready?" Jake appears at the door as I zip up my case, placing it beside his. He's already done his, finishing before coming to get me off the couch. I'm playing catch-up under his watchful eye.

"Yup." I smile and squeal as he scoops me into his arms for a kiss and tells me he loves me. I have missed this kind of spontaneity from him; the last couple of days have been filled with never-ending touching and giggles. He's still being gentlemanly with where he places his hands, and it reminds me a little of the man he was before I was properly his, that boundary of what is appropriate touching but still hands-on in every way.

"I love you too." I breathe him in before he puts me back on my feet, biting my lip in painful adoration as he bends and kisses my abdomen softly and mutters, "I love you too" to my dress before hauling me with him to the living room. I can't stop the gush of complete infatuation coming over me at that little thoughtless moment, just instinctual, to tell his child he loves them. I know he will be the kind of father I can only dream of.

He directs Mathews to our bags and asks for the Mercedes keys.

"Mercedes? What about your bat-mobile?" I quiz, watching him take keys from one of the other men being handed my case by Mathews.

"It's a long trip, *Bambina*. If you want to nap, you can't in the P1. Its seats don't move and aren't built for long-distance travel. You need to be able to stretch out and get comfy. The Mercedes is that car unless you want me to take one of the SUVs? They're bigger and spacious."

I gawp at him in complete jaw-dropping awe.

Where did I find him? What has he done with Jake Carrero? The super-hot playboy who dropped women by the wayside weekly? Here he is sacrificing driving his pride and joy, so his girlfriend can take some pregnancy naps and be comfier.

I couldn't love him more if I tried.

"I love you," I say with so much conviction that he turns around and looks at me like I've never said it before. A grin breaks over his face, and he closes the gap between us, kissing me softly right in front of the waiting men; a wave of sheer emotion runs through me, my stomach tingling with butterflies. I can't imagine a life in which Jake didn't kiss me anymore. It doesn't bear thinking about. That gorgeous face, masculine jawline, teasing lips, and the pearly white Hollywood smile he always casually throws my way. He has no idea how devastating he is to me.

I am finally starting to leave the pain behind to make space to appreciate what he still is to me. I will never leave him. We will get through this. We have to; life without Jake doesn't bear thinking about ever again.

"Feelings mutual." He smiles with his most seductive *'I'm hot'* twinkle, leading me by the hand to the waiting elevator.

* * *

Two hours later, I regret the road trip as we stop for the fiftieth time so I can get some air. Nausea seems to take over anytime we get on the road, and I've had to stop and throw up a few times already; it seems my morning sickness likes to rear its head badly the second a vehicle is involved.

"I'm sorry." I grimace as the waves of nausea roll over me. He holds my hair away, gently rubbing my back while I grip my bottle of water. I've already been sick a few times and am no longer embarrassed at Jake seeing it. I need him with me to hold me and hold back my hair.

"No, baby; I'm sorry. I didn't know it would make you sick like this, we should've just asked Mamma to fly to New York for a visit." He helps me up from my perch in the grass and holds me tight against him, my body trembling at the effort of throwing up, not relishing the thought of getting back into the car. I feel like hell, as badly as the first few days of knowing I was pregnant.

"We're only an hour's drive away from Manhattan; we could head back?" Jake seems to read me, as he usually does, but I'm adamant he gets to tell his mother face-to-face. I know how much it'll mean to him to see her reaction first-hand. I owe that to him, at least.

"No ... I'll take some of the anti-sick pills Nora gave me and try to sleep; that might help. I'll manage. I want to go, Jake." I lean against his chest, closing my eyes, inhaling his smell, and enjoying the moment of calm before I get back in the car and let the nausea build again. I've managed twenty minutes, maximum, before getting him to stop again, secretly hoping for a lot longer before we need to do it again.

"I don't know, Emma. This was a bad idea; I'll take you home." He sounds dubious, and concern is etched all over his handsome face.

"No, I can't stay locked up in the apartment for the next few months, or I'll go stir-crazy. I want to see your family, and I really want to see the house." I smile up at him and flutter my lashes, instantly knowing he's folding. The lure of showing me the house and the look on my face; Jake is so whipped he has no clue, making me grin. I can literally see him caving in.

"Okay, but if we need to stop, then we stop, even if it takes three days to get to my mamma's, okay? I don't mind stopping for breaks and letting you get air or even finding a hotel and staggering the trip." He helps me back into the car, putting my seat belt on, and coming back from the trunk, he hands me a pillow and blanket, helping me get comfy before kissing me on the forehead and closing the door.

"You know ... you're nothing like the Jake Carrero I met in his office on day one." I giggle at him as he settles himself back in the driver's seat and pulls on his belt. His wide shoulders make me long to strip that shirt off him and see them in all their glory.

"I'm one and the same." He winks at me cheekily, pulling his seat belt out from his shoulder to untwist it, starting the car and revving the gas as he fiddles with some buttons on the dash.

"Sure, you are," I smirk. "That Jake wouldn't have entertained the idea of a girlfriend, let alone a baby and a house. I can't see him stopping to prop a cushion under his moaning girlfriend's head on a boring four-hour drive either."

"I guess you broke me, *Bambina*, not that I'm complaining ... In breaking me, I got to break you too, and that reward is worth it all."

He grins and ruffles my hair affectionately. "You're nothing like the Emma who walked into my office in stilettos and the tightest gray skirt I have ever seen, staring at me like I was the enemy. Oh, and for the record, I thought about taking that damn skirt off and bending you over my desk in those first few seconds. I wanted to fuck you the second I laid eyes on you." I turn my head to gape at him in outright surprise.

"You did not ... You barely looked me up and down." I protest, laughing, as he tries to tickle me in the ribs. Playful Jake has been slowly seeping back in these last couple of days, relaxing in a way. Our relationship is starting to return slowly and surely. The change in both of us had been a lie. We are still in there, trying to find our way back to each other, back to how it was before.

"*Bambina*, I'm a seasoned pro. I could check out any woman without even looking in her direction." He flexes his eyebrows. "You gave me hot dirty dreams from day one, Emma. Those skirts seriously ruined my concentration."

"Liar." I move in the seat, getting comfy with my cushion and blanket, snuggling down so I can watch him drive; he's too adorable not to watch...

"Trust me; I'm a guy. I thought about having sex with you at least once a day, sometimes once an hour. Even back when you tried your hardest to keep me at arms-length." He has us out on the road, smoothly sailing along the tarmac. It's sunny out, and the scenery is pretty and soothing. I can't imagine that back then. Jake was looking at me that way; I guess he really was a seasoned pro, after all.

"Okay, well, maybe you did. I admit I checked you out way more than I allowed myself to deny." I smile when I catch his satisfied grin.

"I knew you had the hots for me." He smirks, and I shake my head indulgently. His ego does not need any encouragement, then or now.

"I had to take a ticket and get in line," I respond with a lowered eyebrow.

We haven't had this easy, amusing flow with our conversation in a while. Experiencing an inner swell of happiness because I'm starting to feel this way with him again, easing into this, signs that maybe things could be okay again; perhaps we might be how we were in time.

"You must've had the golden ticket, *Bambina*." His cheesiness and wink set me off giggling, and I tell him to shut up. My face meets that annoying palm of his as he slides his hand across it, squishing my nose in the process.

"Stop it. Jerk." I slap it away.

"Make me, Sexy." He throws me an air kiss and a wink, then tugs the corner of my blanket up. "Now go to sleep before you feel like you're going to throw up again, and let me drive. You're too distracting with that beautiful face." He beams at me genuinely. I can't help but smile as I snuggle down at his command, closing my eyes.

* * *

"Jake. I need to get out." I wake with a start, my head spinning and nausea coming at me as soon as my sleep-addled brain comes around. It's close, and I'm going to hurl badly.

"We're here, baby. Hold on, let me help you." Jake jumps out and comes around the car, pulling me out fast. Just as my stomach throws up the bottle of water, I drank mid-journey all over the gravel driveway of his mother's house. Jake jumps back, making sure his trainers don't take a direct hit but keeps me in the crook of his arm.

"I swear that time you were aiming." His mouth comes to my forehead, and he holds me against him as the retching subsides. He sweeps back my hair instinctively.

"Payback for waking me up with a bottle of water an hour ago," I grimace, my stomach aching from the effort, and I'm rewarded with a smile. He picks me up in his arms like a child and walks me toward the house. He has no qualms about picking me up anyway, not that I am complaining.

"I can walk, you know. Your mom's going to think something's wrong," I protest weakly. The feeling of extreme warmth in my cheeks and forehead from vomiting is rising again. I hope this passes soon. Feeling this way is the worst thing ever. I never was good with being sick or having an illness, even as a child.

"Something is wrong, *Miele* ... You're very pregnant and look like you're probably running a temperature again." He scrutinizes me as he carries me up to the front door and up the wide sweeping steps. He makes carrying me seem effortless; nothing is showing on his face or body, and his walk is seemingly unaffected.

"It's the car. It seems to make this so much worse." I sigh, burying my face into his neck. This is not how I expected to greet Sylvana Carrero when seeing her again. "I should walk, Jake."

"You're fine like this," he responds with a no-nonsense tone, and I know arguing is futile. Jake has become that scary, overprotective, '*loss of a sense of humor*' father-to-be, and I'm too tired for another battle of wills.

He opens the front door without letting go and carries me inside, calling out that we're here. My face colors at literally being carried over the threshold, and I wonder if Sylvana will get the wrong idea. I try not to think about how it makes me feel. I'm just getting used to thinking we have a chance at forever again; marriage is not even an idea I'm thinking about right now.

Sylvana appears from a room down the hall, looking completely flustered. Her eyes go wide with relief and absolute stress; she doesn't seem to be phased or even acknowledge how Jake and I have entered. Her cheeks have a high spot of red on them, and she's manically squeezing a cordless phone in her hands.

"Jacob! I've been trying to call you!" She strains in hushed tones. Using his full name is never a good sign, quietening her voice as her eyes dart around behind her. She ushers us toward the kitchen in haste. Sylvana is normally the picture of cool and controlled, like her son, so I already have a rising sense of apprehension at her odd behavior.

"Mamma, what the ...?"

"Shhhh." She waves her hands at him to shut him up, pushing us into the kitchen, hauling the door shut behind us when we're standing in the cool, neat interior. "Answer your goddamn phone in the future, Jacob! She scowls at him accusingly.

"I was driving. It's on silent. I wasn't expecting anyone to call me. I was letting Emma sleep, Mamma. She's not too well.... What the hell has gotten into you?" He huffs childishly at his mother, and it's not hard to picture little Jacob as a kid being told off. I imagine he was a handful and can only hope he has the necessary wisdom and training to handle a mini him.

"Can you two stop arguing, and can you put me down?!" I frown up at Jake, with an eye of bewilderment and awkwardness, at being held aloft between a squabbling mother and son. Jake frowns, then tips my feet to the floor, standing me upright, pulling me into him, and wrapping his arms around my shoulders to nestle me in front of him.

I feel better out of the car, recovering quickly, and it seems I'm not allowed out of an inch of his reach.

"What's the problem? Is it Dad?" Jake almost growls: Still, no love lost between father and son. When we were last here, he barely acknowledged him at all and still doesn't seem interested in ever giving Giovanni another chance. I wonder if having a child will make a difference in the relationship.

"No, it's so much worse. Oh, and before I forget." She leans forward and smacks Jake hard in the upper arm near his shoulder. The noise echoes loudly, making him jerk to the side with the connection. Sylvana has a mean swing arm, another trait for Tadpole to inherit.

"Ouch, what the hell was that for?" He tenses, flexing his shoulder, and I can only guess at the look he's giving her over my head, especially if the anger radiating from him is anything to go by.

"For being an idiot. You know exactly what!" She looks at him, then down at me with a softening smile and a softening of sympathy.

Oh, God. Jake told his mother about our breakup.

"She's here, isn't she? I got her back. I'm not going to be that dumb again, I swear." He huffs and squeezes me a little tighter. Sylvana scowls at him, then her face drops, and she heaves a sudden sigh, remembering her dilemma.

"This is what the *so much worse* is." She flaps her hands with a dramatic sigh. "Marissa is here. In the sitting room." She grimaces, and both Jake and I tense up instantly. My breath catches painfully, but Jake is the first to speak.

"What the hell for?" He sounds angry. No, he sounds pissed as hell. Meanwhile, I feel sick, emotional, and ready to cry and storm away. This is turning into a day from hell for me.

"She's staying with her family for the weekend and just showed up asking to see me and talk about things ... She's carrying my grandchild remember? I couldn't turn her away!" Sylvana slaps her hands on her hips and glowers at her son.

Great. Of course, she lives near here or is from here. When Jake met her, he was only fifteen! Why didn't I realize this before agreeing to a house here?

"For the love of fucking God!" Jake curses and moves me to a seat nearby, helping me slide down into it. He strokes me across the shoulder and plants a kiss on my cheek despite his obvious agitation. He moves off and gets me a glass of iced water before coming back to stand behind me, resting his hands on the back of my chair. He's pacing to control the war of emotions in his head. I know his tells almost as well as he knows mine nowadays. "Fuck." He grinds through gritted teeth.

I drink the water slowly, glad of the small task to focus on and the cool liquid to quell my nausea, my head spinning out of control with a million emotions and crazy thoughts. The bitter pit of anxiety in my stomach expands at speed.

I wonder if you can blame murder on pregnancy hormones? Some sort of mental breakdown and loss of faculties?

"Language, Jacob!" Sylvana glares at him, then pats me on the shoulder and walks to the fridge, hauling out a bottle of wine.

"We need something stronger," she exclaims, waving the bottle toward us with a wicked smile.

"Umm. No alcohol for Emma, Mamma." It's out before Jake even thinks about what he's saying, and Sylvana spins. In an instant, I see it, and so does he. The clicking mind of a sharp woman who has just registered that he carried me in looking sick. He's been clucking around me ever since, more so than normal, and now, he's refusing alcohol on my behalf in a tone that suggests ... well, suggests I'm pregnant. Her eyes widen, and her hand covers her mouth in a swift gasp.

"Really?" Tears prick her eyes, and she visibly shakes herself.

"Depends on what you're asking?" Jake turns sheepish, trying to gauge his mother's reaction and figure out if she's shocked, happy, or pissed. I'm not counting on one more than the other, as I don't know. Marissa's baby puts a different spin on what would normally be a grandmother's dream.

I, meanwhile, am still sitting thinking about the fact that Demon Bitch is sitting a few rooms away. The woman carrying my boyfriend's baby. The woman he kissed not so long ago. She's right here in his family home, looking to talk to Sylvana about her future as the mother of Sylvana's grandchild. The ironic timing of this situation is not lost on me. My stomach thumps hard, and my heart aches with shattering pain. Even if I am learning to forgive Jake, I still hate the bitch with a vengeance.

"Are you pregnant?" She watches Jake closely, poised and still, barely breathing. Her voice is almost a whisper as though she daren't believe it.

"Well, not me personally, Mamma, but yeah, Emma and I are having a lil' Carrero." Jake sounds pleased and proud; for a tiny moment, I forget about *her* and gaze at him with sheer love. It never ceases to surprise me to see his reaction to our baby. The genuine happiness in his tone and no doubts whatsoever despite how crazy in turmoil I still feel every day. Any time he says it, he always looks fit to burst with sheer joy. I can forgive him anything when he looks like this.

"Oh, my God." Sylvana runs to her son, throwing her arms around his big frame dramatically, hauling him down to her height and kissing him on both cheeks in a very Italian manner before bursting into fluent Italian dialog. Jake answers her in a mix of English and Italian and I have zero clue what is being said other than she cries and grins a lot. It's emotional to watch, and it's obvious she's ecstatic. I can't help but wonder how she reacted when he told her about Marissa's child. I try to push away that lump of pain in my chest.

She turns to me, wrapping her arms around my shoulders, kissing me on the cheek from her position above me. Gushing and tweaking my cheeks with another bout of fluent Italian. I blink back with a smile and have no idea what to respond with. Jake always seems oblivious to the fact that I need a translator sometimes. I'm not sure he's aware of when they switch between languages.

"There's more, Mamma. Emma and I are here to see a house this weekend. A house I might want to buy for us." He can barely contain the beaming happiness bouncing off him in giant waves.

I think it's the first time I've seen a beautifully composed, graceful woman like Sylvana burst into a happy dance and sob simultaneously. He just made her wildest dreams come true, which goes a long way to making me feel better instantly, forgetting about Demon Bitch for a few needed minutes.

"Is it close by?" She chirps ecstatically.

Jake glances at me for a second. I note the little flutter of doubt, then he smiles slowly and cautiously and looks back at her.

"You can see it from here." He nods toward the refrigerator wall facing him, indicating the direction, and Sylvana breaks into a huge grin.

"The Wilsons? They haven't even told anyone it's on the market yet ... Jake, it's practically next door!" Sylvana is back calling him Jake, so I'm sure he's just made her month. She is the happiest woman alive, and I also feel a little buzz about his confession. The Wilson house is next door, close enough to be a part of his family, and a small piece of me is warming to this idea.

Okay, maybe not next door in the New York sense; I mean, they are far apart with grounds in between and a huge massive line of trees and security fencing ... But next door as in a five-minute walk across the backgrounds if you didn't have any fences to climb.

"You know I can't leave her chatting with Clara in the sitting room forever, Jacob?" Sylvana finally points out when the excitement and chatter about the house die down. She's still holding a hand to her heart as though it's fluttering. Her beautiful face radiates sheer motherly bliss. Clara is Sylvana's charity office assistant and a close friend who lives nearby.

Jake glances at me, and I catch the flicker run across his face. He has no clue how to play this. If it were just a case of it being Marissa and the baby, he would go and speak to her; but now it's a case of Jake having kissed Marissa, knowing his actions can affect me tremendously, affect what he's trying to fix. I don't want to tell him what to do. I want him to decide for himself. I want to trust him. If I'm ever going to move on, I need to learn to trust him, especially regarding her.

I remain impassive, with no expression or messages, just a blank look, so he gets nothing from me. He frowns, watching my face, then finally sighs.

"I'm going to take Emma upstairs for a while, Mamma. Let her lie down and have some time to recover. Just get Marissa to leave." He kisses her on the cheek before coming to me and pulling my chair out. He catches my hand, kissing my palm before enveloping it in his and pulling me up, tugging me into his arms and toward the kitchen door. I don't know how to feel, so I allow him to control and guide me.

"Jacob ... Ordinarily, I would agree, but this isn't about any of you ... It's about a child. Now, more than ever, you should understand that importance." Sylvana's comment hits home. Jake stalls in front of me, his body stiffening, and he sighs hard. She obviously knows how to get under his skin with very few words.

"What do you want me to do? I'm standing here with the love of my life, very aware of how close I came to fucking it all up with the girl in the next room, Mamma ... There is a baby involved, but I'm not going to ignore how this affects Emma and our baby, and our future together."

He's upset. I can feel the despair emanating from him and can only give him a sympathetic look. I hug close to him as his arm tightens around my shoulder.

Complication at its best.

"You're all adults, Jake. Let the past stay in the past. Emma is here with you. You have all got to get it together for the sake of these babies. They will be siblings, after all."

Her comment hits me this time, and I swallow hard, tears threatening. She's right. As much as this is killing me, she's so very right; my baby has a sibling already, and as much as I hate the girl in the next room, I can't hate the part growing inside of her that belongs to Jake. His eyes are on me as I stare at my stomach and a tear rolls down my cheek involuntarily.

"Go see her, Jake. I'll be upstairs." I pull out of his arms and head away, but he catches me and hauls me back against him, lifting my face to his with that no-nonsense expression set in.

"Hell. No." He kisses me gently on the nose and wipes my face with his thumb, keeping me close and reassuring me with his hold. "I'm sorry, Mamma, but I'm not changing my mind. Emma is my priority. Let Marissa hang around or come back later if she wants to talk. But right now, I'm taking Emma upstairs, and I won't be down until she's ready to come with me. The pregnancy is making her ill, and she needs rest. She needs me beside her to care for her like I promised I would always do." His eyes are steady on mine, so much transpiring in those green depths. He's making a stand, showing me that no matter what, it's always me first, and whether I knew it, it's what I needed, and I'm grateful for the way the pain in my heart lets go a little.

"I knew I raised you right." Sylvana smiles, patting his shoulder. "Marissa can come back for dinner, and you'll talk to her before she leaves. I'll send food to your room if you prefer not to eat with her, but at some point, you'll sit down and be adults. Enough of all this foolishness now." Jake grits his teeth and narrows his eyes before he finally nods.

"Fine. I'm sure we can all handle dinner without anyone throwing a few steak knives." His jaw is still rigid, and his body is still solid. He may be agreeing, but he's not happy in the slightest.

I hope the glance at me was not in any way related to his comment.

Although come to think of it, I better make sure he removes anything sharp if I'm to sit at dinner with her.

I don't have a clue about how I'm going to handle this.

"Good. Now go. I'm being extremely ignorant, leaving her this long. Go to your room. It's all made up." She smiles, waving us off, then bustles away toward the long wide marble corridor leading to the family room. Jake leads me up the long sweeping stair before pulling me into our room and into his arms.

"Are you okay? About all of this, I mean?" He looks worried. No. He looks scared, and it only makes me love him more.

"No ... Not really, but your mom's right, Jake. This isn't about any of us anymore." I hate that I even agree to it, the agreement doesn't mean it doesn't hurt like hell, but here we are. Being pregnant has changed my outlook so much in such a short time despite not knowing how to accept it. Maybe it's an internal maternal change, but I'm thinking about Marissa's child, and suddenly I don't want to be the bad guy in this. I don't want to be the bitch that shuns a child because she can't handle the relationship between her boyfriend and his ex.

Jake is pensive, his fingers tangling in my hair and his forehead resting against mine, sighing as he finds solace in me.

"I love you. I don't want you upset." He sighs. "I don't want you looking at her and thinking about ..." He closes his eyes, the regret shining all over his face. I can't say I'm not thinking the same thing, but this is how it is.

"I'm not going to leave you again if that's what you're worried about," I reassure him, and he opens one eye to look at me and then the other.

"Promise?" His boyish smile followed by a tentative kiss on the lips, soft and gentle, everything I needed right now. I sigh against him and let him pull me out of my head.

"I promise." I try a smile and fail. I may say the right thing, but I'm not feeling it. I'm overemotional and just a slight bit insecure. Nerves are getting the better of me, yet all that aside, I do mean what I say. He's stuck with me. Whether he still wants it or not, I'm never going anywhere without him again.

Chapter 11

"Breathe, *Bambina*." Jake's mouth comes to my cheek in a soft peck from behind; his hands are on my shoulders as I stand, smoothing down my dress in the mirror. It's late; we've been up here for a couple of hours. I slept a lot, and we lay together, talking about everything and nothing while watching daytime TV. Idle chit-chat and jokes, Jake tried his hardest to make this feel normal. Neither of us wants to acknowledge that she will be under the same roof soon enough. Neither of us wanted to talk about anything to do with her. I would be happy with never talking about what he did ever again.

I am so ravenous for food, but I know she's down there somewhere; I'm about to look at her for the first time since he touched her. I gulp softly and quell the nerves running through my stomach, causing a swirling ache of nausea.

"I'm okay." I try to reassure him, even though I'm far from it. I smile back at him from our reflection.

I'm looking better, less pale, and have no more rosy cheeks from the high temperature. My black shift dress clinging in all the right places, and my flat pumps making me a little less formal. I look right for dinner in a family home, just not right to face the woman who is crazy in love with my Jake. The woman he betrayed me with not so long ago, and my stomach lurches with a stab of pain.

"You look beautiful. Sexy ... Fuckable." Jake grins, kissing me on the neck, burying his face against me, and smelling me. I close my eyes.

He always knows what to say and how to touch me.

That familiar ache in my lower abdomen stirs that I frequently get, any mention of sex or gentle kisses or caresses, especially my neck, and I yearn for him. It's been too long, and I am salivating over him with every passing day. He's too damn masculine and utterly devastating not to want to be nakedly entwined with him. Just looking at him walk across a room in casual or formal clothes could send any woman's heart racing, let alone someone who knows what those hands and that body are capable of. I am craving everything he could do to me right now while watching him in the mirror.

Jake is right, though; something inside me isn't ready, and I'm not there yet. He never gives any signs of getting beyond kissing and cuddling. My lower body seems completely off-limits to him. When he touches me anywhere below my waistline, hips are all he will put his hands on, except my abdomen, where our baby lies.

"Ditto." I smile, devouring him visibly in his fitted navy shirt under a dark gray tailored suit, collar open as always, lacking a tie. He looks dressed for more business dinner than a family meal, but I know he's conveying a message. This dinner will be all business while Marissa is at his mother's table. He told me his mother wants to be involved in mediating the situation he's been failing to get on top of for weeks. In a way, I feel better knowing she'll be there for support. With her flawless grace, Sylvana will bring a presence to the table that will, maybe, finally, get Marissa to agree to set terms and stop the emotional tug-of-war and manipulative moves.

The problem is simple. Marissa is still in love with Jake, so she will not stop trying to maneuver this situation her way. She figures that baby means leverage, and after Jake kissed her, she thinks she has a chance of getting him back. She has no clue about the meaning behind his kiss. To her, it was a glimpse into the problems in our relationship and maybe a hint that he still wanted her. I do not doubt her showing up here because she thinks she can push Jake's mother to her side again. I know she was a regular in this house as a teen, and she's angling to get back in.

I watch him move back to fix his hair, his gaze over my head in the mirror as he expertly styles it with his fingertips. He looks adorable when he's doing simple things like this. Young and effortlessly sexy. I can't deny that with every passing day, I'm starting to learn how to forgive him, a tiny bit at a time, and it's starting to hurt a little less intensely. Looking at him now, there's none of the carnage I felt in those first few days or the confusion I used to feel when I stood close to him.

I know he doesn't still have feelings for her. Finally, in the last few weeks, that inner insecurity somehow has shaken itself free; in every look he turns my way, with every touch and word out of his mouth.

Jake loves me, really, really loves me. In the way that I love him. A fully encompassing and world-changing, blow-your-mind kind of love. Marissa never stood a chance with him. That kiss meant nothing, and I will not let it hurt me, or us, anymore.

His attention to our unborn baby is like a final sign that I am everything to him, and our life together will always be his sole focus.

He catches my eye in the mirror and smiles at me, that sexy natural slight flex he throws me every time we look at each other. My heart lurches a little and skips a beat. Jake could always say so much with a look, maybe because I know him so well and am tuned into him on another level. In one glance, he's telling me everything I ever need to know, and he means it: I look beautiful, and he's completely in love with me. He's giving me courage.

* * *

As much as I try to prepare myself by pulling on my most efficient *PA Emma* face, none truly prepares me for the blast of sickening pain when I am finally faced with one Marissa Hartley.

Walking down the stairs and into the dining room, I don't take in the beautiful space, elegant settings, or wonderful smells of food. I just see the girl with the long, curled, brown, highlighted hair. The seductive, tanned, Latino-looking face with sensual lips, wearing an overly tight floor-length animal print dress, fully emphasizing her bust, curvy figure, and undeniably compact baby bump protruding at her front. I also can't ignore how her eyes devour Jake hungrily as he walks in behind me with a guiding hand.

She exudes pure sexual energy, every movement calculated for maximum impact, hips swinging, and cleavage swaying. Her pouting and hair-flicking mannerisms all made for pure seduction.

I hate you so much I want to smash that centerpiece right into your face.

I glare at her icily, our eyes meeting for a moment, and I catch a glimmer of smugness. She has no qualms about meeting me dead on and even licks her lips in the process. I feel nothing but disgust and soul-scratching hatred for her.

"Jake ... Emma." Her low husky voice purrs our names as she slips effortlessly into a seat ushered by Sylvana, sliding down gracefully and never once taking her eyes from Jake as he settles me into my chair. I glance at the steak knives in front of me and wonder if Jake would mind if I stabbed her in the face with one.

The waiting staff nearby are laying glasses of wine down on the table. I note that both the glass before her and I are full of fresh orange instead, an inner smugness washes over me, and I wonder if she will even notice.

See, you think you have something over me, Marissa, but I have a secret you will hate more.

I catch Jake watching me carefully as he slides in beside me. Neither of us has said a word since walking in here. I catch his eyes going to the ridiculously sharp cutlery, and a slight hint of a smirk draws across his face. He knows where my brain has been heading, and I raise an eyebrow at him as if to say, *What?* He shakes his head with a smile and leans in to kiss me behind the ear.

"I love you, but please don't stab her while we have witnesses." The low husky tone, followed by his chuckle, sets a smile on my face, and I'm even smugger at catching Marissa scowling our way. Her eyes narrow at Jake's affection, and she twists a fork in agitation.

Arrick appears casually, with a new, non-descriptive girl in tow, a mirror image of the little thing that annoyed me so much last time we were here. He says his hellos, passing smiles and introductions when Giovanni Carrero saunters in, greeting us all unemotionally. I suddenly feel a little more uncomfortable when he's here. That steady, sharp gaze seems to devour this scene, the polite greetings as though he's walking into a business meeting and not seeing his own flesh and blood. Everyone sits, including Sylvana, and there is almost fake politeness in the atmosphere as quiet chatter and light, idle conversation begin.

I glare at Marissa as we're served. This is a family dinner, and she's been allowed to join. Sylvana is trying to bring her into the family's fold to send Jake a clear message. She wants him to fix this and ensure her grandchild is not kept from her. She wants Marissa to feel like she's a part of this and belongs here too, so she will want to bring her child here in the future.

My heart plummets at how much I hate her presence in this home with these people who are supposed to be my family one day. The realization that this is how it will be, that this isn't just about her, Jake, and I, but it's about all of us and what these people will be in her child's life. That tug of emotion rises, hitting me hard, swallowing down the pain that threatens to consume me suddenly.

Jake slides his hand over mine and pulls it to his mouth, kissing my knuckles softly and pulling me toward him a little. He bridges the gap and pecks me softly on the cheek, whispering, "I love you," as he pulls back. He senses the change in me that I'm feeling emotional; like always, he's there to ground me. I can't help but smile at him adoringly. Green eyes locked onto mine, so many messages translating in one tender look. My heart is rising a little that I have him, and she never will, not how she wants him.

I catch Marissa watching us with a glare of sheer hatred in her eye as the death grip on the fork she's holding turns her knuckles white. It only strengthens that inner triumph, and I smile at her almost salaciously.

"So, I hear there's some news you have for me, Jacob?" Giovanni cuts in smoothly across the chatter as the starter plates are slid before us by efficient house staff. I flicker up, catching both men's eyes locked across the table, with no emotion or message on either face. They are acting like they always do, like two men in a standoff, trying to be polite. Try as I might, I have never understood how they can stand this relationship. Jake never seems to want to try to fix things, and Giovanni never seems to make an attempt, either.

"I have a couple of things I need to tell you, just not here right now." Jake's voice betrays a slight edge in his tone, and his father instantly smirks. The irritating Carrero smirk shows they are undeniably related despite their very different appearances, neither looking away, the air almost sizzling with tension. I catch a nervous flinch in the corner of Sylvana's eye and feel a little uncomfortable.

Giovanni is one of the most unreadable people I have ever met. He gives no clue to what he's thinking or feeling, ever. An amazing poker face and never seems to have any other moods apart from this one or yelling at staff. Even in his family's presence, there is his usual air of authority and emotional distance. It's a little chilling.

"Yes, later, when we don't have guests," Sylvana warns with a tone of authority and throws a smile at Marissa, sitting to her right. It's a reassuring smile. Giovanni is at the head of the table and doesn't acknowledge Marissa at all. He doesn't even look her way, keeping his dark eyes focused on me, and I begin to tremble.

"Emma? I hear congratulations are in order." Giovanni raises an eyebrow at me, and I choke hard on the piece of broccoli I put in my mouth. My eyes dart around the faces at the table, and Jake tenses. The ripples of anger from him surging instantly because I've been put on the spot by a man who rarely acknowledged my presence the last time I was here. I can feel Jake's whole body change like lightning.

"Ummm." I falter. Stammering because I have no idea what to say.

"Jake told us you're his VP now because you have a good business head and could do a lot of good in the future of our company." Arrick cuts in with a knowing smile, and I get the same edgy tone from Jake's voice. I notice the same cool look he gives his father for the first time. Arrick is obviously the family mediator in this volatile relationship, moving in to diffuse whatever this is easily. I smile at him gratefully, warmed to him instantly.

"I'm undecided if that's what I want anymore. I need to take some time to evaluate my career." I return quickly. Jake seems happy with the answer, Arrick smiles encouragingly, and everyone sets about the food in front of them.

Jake relaxes and starts digging into his food with his fork. I can't help but glance at Marissa directly across the table, and she's watching him under her lashes as she digs into her food. The whole atmosphere is tense and weird, unlike the last time I was with these people. All that friendly, energetic chatter and cozy banter are severely lacking.

"Actually. No. I meant that he's buying you a house next door." Giovanni drops the bombshell, and Marissa's head almost snaps off with the speed she spins toward him. Jake stiffens. His fingers tighten around his glass mid-way to his mouth. Sylvana gapes at her husband in anger and throws him a look that can only mean she's got some serious words for him when they're alone.

"Why wouldn't I? I intend to marry her one day, so of course, I'm going to buy *us* a house where we can raise a family and settle down." Jake's tone gives nothing away. I could almost kiss him when I see that bitch's lower lip wobble. Jake is used to dealing with Giovanni and plays his part effortlessly, never giving his father a hint of being rattled. The constant power struggle between father and son that I have witnessed a million times at work.

I try to swallow down the ravioli I've jammed into my mouth, but the ability has deserted me. I gulp orange juice to dislodge the lump in my throat, trying to calm my pounding heart and clammy palms. This dinner is tense, and I need to get through it before the dramatics with Marissa commence. I wish we had eaten upstairs after all.

"Well ... seeing as you've already made a start with reproducing, I think it's a great idea, especially so close to home." This is obviously a remark to hurt me. Giovanni smiles toward him with an evil glint in his eyes. My heart rate quickens, and my stomach drops. I really do wonder why Giovanni hates me so much. Maybe he dislikes Jake looking to make a future with me. Giovanni obviously disproves Jake marrying his ex-PA.

Oh my God. Ground, please open and take me now.

"Yes. I'm sure when he gets weekend access to our child, a house here will be great, seeing as I intend to move back home for the first few years." Marissa flutters her lashes, deviously throwing Jake a sexy smile, hiding nothing of her malicious jibe. All I can do is gawp at her and what she's saying, the fact she intends to become a more permanent, closer thorn in my side by moving back here. Consumed with an inner rise of anger and heartbreak, dueling to get on top of one another. This is not how a new home is supposed to be received in our lives. I catch Jake frowning at her from the corner of my eye and know he's thinking the same thing.

Marissa moving here was never part of the plan at all.

"Actually ... I was talking about Emma's baby." Giovanni leans back with a wolfish grin and a satisfied glint in his eye. The clatter of cutlery as Marissa drops her fork and gapes at me with open-mouthed shock. I realize she's not the only one, Arrick's girlfriend is practically bug-eyed, gawping my way, and no one is holding cutlery now except me.

"Fuck's sake...." Jake snaps, raising a hand to pinch his brow, his elbow hitting the table to hold his arm up. He knows the shit is about to hit the fan, and he's waiting on it.

"Dad, you're an asshole." Arrick cuts in instantly, and Marissa erupts.

"What the actual fuck?! Since fucking when?!" She throws her napkin down on top of her food, glaring at him, then me, focusing on one after the other with sheer fury across her pouted mouth. She doesn't look quite so attractive now, and yet all I can do is lower my head and stare at my lap to try to control the surge of complete tension running through me. Giovanni certainly knows how to ruin dinner.

"Arrick. Please take Gloria to the front room, and I'll have your plates sent through ... Giovanni. I suggest you go eat in your office!" Sylvana snaps, taking control, and stands up. She puts a hand on Marissa's shoulder, sharply sitting her down since Marissa has risen from her seat in anger.

"How did you find out?" Jake glares at Giovanni furiously. The waves of rage can almost be seen rippling across the table. Everyone looks at the older man sitting smugly, sipping his glass of wine, as though he's completely unaware of the scene he's just caused.

"You underestimate me, Jacob. Two women at this table with a pregnancy glow and drinking fresh orange instead of my $2000 a bottle Chardonnay. You forget I'm a father who knows when a lady is carrying, and I'm fully aware you set up a viewing for the Wilson house. He's my golfing partner, after all. I'm just disappointed you felt you could tell your mother and brother, the only two who did not react to this news and still hadn't told me." He slides up, lifts his glass, and walks coolly toward the door while Jake visually throws daggers into his back. All I can think of is how keen-eyed Senior Carrero is. He is a smart cookie, after all. I can't help but be a little impressed with his scarily keen observations.

I want the ground to open and devour me. The seething hatred emanating my way from Demon Bitch is making my skin prickle, and inner-*Teen-Emma* rage is looming inside. Arrick and his girlfriend are practically high-tailing it out of the room, and Sylvana glares at everyone with a sheer *angry momma bear* look. This is not how I envisioned this would go. I had no idea we'd even be telling Marissa about the baby just yet, so I guess, in a way, Giovanni has done us a favor.

"So, this is why you keep fucking stalling and pissing me about?!" Marissa spits with venom across the table as Sylvana moves toward her. I'm unsure what her intentions are, but the kind maternal expression is gone. Now she's angry mamma ready to tackle a crazy pregnant woman down if she dares get up.

"Shut up, Marissa, and calm the fuck down." Jake glares at her. I catch the simmering of something between them; fury on his part and possibly the same from her. I wonder if this was how the meetings in LA went in the past.

"Mamma. I think the three of us need to do this without you here." Jake turns to Sylvana, and a flash of stubbornness flicks across her attractive face. She lifts her chin for a moment, narrows her gaze on him, and then sighs in defeat.

"Behave like adults. I'll be dealing with your father." She turns, walks around the table, and leaves, picking up Arrick and Gloria's plates in passing, ushering the last of her house staff with her, including the poor girl who was caught like a deer in headlamps in the corner and pulling the door closed behind them.

We're left, just the three of us, fused together with heightened emotion emanating across the dining room, air filled with the oppressive atmosphere and a moment of deafening silence. I look to Jake for any sign of how to act or what to say and notice he's looking down at the table, pushing around his wine glass, steadying his anger with slow even breaths. He's thinking about what he wants to say before he erupts too. I know this version of him. I've seen it in boardroom meetings when someone is pushing his buttons, and he's about to go all *'Alpha Boss'* mode and take them down. I shiver in anticipation and suddenly don't want to be here and doing this. I want to be upstairs or anywhere else but here between these two.

"Well?" Marissa snaps impatiently.

"Marissa, yes, Emma is pregnant. It wasn't planned, but I'm happy. We're happy about it. It doesn't concern you in the slightest." Jake's steady even tone is laced with aggression. He's trying so hard to get control of this conversation before it erupts again.

"How the fuck does this not concern me exactly?! Everything I have asked for with our baby, Jake, every request has been fucking denied me, and now I know why! You're setting up happy families with her, and my child is being tossed aside like it doesn't fucking matter!" She spits and slams her palms onto the table wildly, setting cups and glasses rattling unsteadily. I jump with the impact, and Jake immediately brings a hand to my lap to comfort me.

"This is recent, Marissa. It has nothing to do with any of that. Your demands are ridiculous. Parenting classes, running to LA every time you click your fingers. We're not in a relationship, and I don't want to spend more time than necessary with you." Jake growls back at her, tempers rising, and I grasp his fingers to urge him to calm down. Jake's so much better than this. He deals with negotiations and hard-headed business tycoons daily. He shouldn't lower himself to her standards. He squeezes back, and I throw him a subtle supportive smile. He takes a calming breath and sits back, lifting his wine, taking slow, deliberate sips, and giving himself a moment.

"So, tell me, Jake ... You say you're happy? Funny ... Because I remember the word abortion coming up when I told you that you would be a father! You said you didn't even want kids! Yet here you are now playing *Mr. Daddy-to-be* of the year, buying her a fucking house!" Marissa is sitting back with arms crossed across her cleavage, every word like venom on her tongue, glaring at me and not him, with highly intoxicated hatred.

"Why wouldn't I feel differently? You came to me after one drunk night that I can't even fucking remember and told me there was a baby. I am in love with Emma, had been for so long, and your appearance almost screwed up the chance I had with her." Jake stands up and walks off toward the unit behind us. Grabbing the bottle of wine, he steps back, filling his glass to the top. "When Emma found out she was pregnant, it was different. It changed everything, Marissa, because I love her and want a life with her because she's my world." He picks it up and downs the whole thing in one go.

Oh, this is not good.

Jake drinking is Jake sliding into a more impulsive, more aggressive mode, where he can be unpredictable and harder to control. I throw him a wary look, and when he goes to top it up again, I swipe his glass away quickly, giving him a pleading 'please don't' glance. He frowns at me and sighs before planking the bottle on the table, sitting down instead. I inhale heavily, trying to relax as much as possible while this crap continues.

"So where does that leave me?! Our baby?!" She spits.

"Same place it already is. Visitation, access. I'm just not jumping through hoops for you. There's no reason to be a part of your life before the baby is here. I don't need a relationship with you because, to be honest, it would always be like this; it has always been like this." Jake waves a hand between them, gesturing at each other, locking his green no-nonsense focus on her and willing her to back down the way I've seen him make many a man crumble.

"Fuck *no*! ... You want to see your baby, then you sure as hell accept that I'll be here and in your life. No relationship with me, then no fucking visitation!" She slaps her hand on the table again, and I can't contain it anymore.

"Is that what it's all been about? Having him in any way on your terms? Whether he wants it or not?" I sound angry, maybe even as vicious as her, but I don't care. I'm seeing through her bullshit. This isn't about the baby. This is about being close to him, having control over him like he's her possession, and somehow needing to bow to her will. It's about forcing Jake to have her in his life.

"Is that what your jealous little head tells you? That I want him? That I'm trying to take him from you?" Marissa laughs nastily. "Sweetie, please, he's the one who fucked me senseless that night and got me pregnant. He was the one who was all over me, asking for me to go home with him. If I wanted Jake back, I only need to ask." She smirks, but I only narrow my eyes and frown. Even I know that's wrong. Jake isn't someone who lets what he wants slip away. He's someone who goes after it, and if he wanted her all along, then I wouldn't be sitting beside him now. I saw her texts telling him she still loves him, and he never bothered to reply. The woman is deranged if she believes what she's saying.

"Marissa. I haven't wanted you in any way since I was about fifteen, and even back then, I'm pretty damn sure it wasn't even real love." Jake sighs, even he's exhausted with this conversation, and I can feel the vibes coming from him. He wants her to leave, as do I since he doesn't see this going anywhere.

"He's never wanted you, Marissa. I know him better than you ever will," I say flatly, focusing on my hands and the napkin I've been twisting the life out of instead of those fierce dark eyes emanating all sorts of hate my way.

"You know your fucking boyfriend cheated on you, right? With me ... about four weeks ago," Marissa spits at me across the table, shoving her plate out of the way and knocking over some empty water glasses.

"If you mean he kissed you, then yes, he told me." I glare back at her, lifting my chin defiantly. I lock my gaze onto those dark brown, almost black dangerous eyes glaring back at me. My face is completely devoid of emotion, even though it feels like a punch in the stomach to say it, just like it used to. There's a look in her eyes of surprise at me knowing about the kiss before she narrows them viciously.

"Kiss? Ha fucking ha! He had his tongue down my throat and his hand up my fucking dress, almost making me cum, inches away from fucking me if I hadn't stopped it. He wanted me just as much as he did the night he stuck a baby inside me." She tosses her hair back over her shoulder, and I jump when the table is slammed by Jake's palm disrupting everything and scaring the hell out of me.

"That's not what fucking happened, and you know it." He yells at her, and I cringe in fright, pulling myself back in my seat, my heart rate going crazy, my mind swirling with images of him and her. I don't even know what to believe in. She seems to find pleasure in sitting up straighter, meeting his fire head-on, and I seriously start to wonder if there was more between them that night. My doubts and insecurities filter in as I try to get a handle on the pain in my chest.

"I'm surprised you can even remember, Jake darling, seeing as you were obviously high on God knows what and probably can't remember exactly what happened. You were an absolute mess if I remember rightly." She purrs and flutters at him. I feel sick to my stomach, my head a mass of confusion. I look at him and her and back again in painful panic. I don't want to believe her, and I shouldn't.

I can trust him. He's been proving that to me all along, hasn't he?

"Why? You think because fucking you once had been so unmemorable that I wouldn't remember four weeks ago? I remember every single moment, Marissa, right down to the second you launched yourself at me, and I rejected you because I realized the only girl I ever wanted was Emma." Jake is seething. I know him. I watch him and read his body language. He's not lying.

He's angry that she would imply there was more. He's enraged that she has the gall to try to do this to me, to hurt us, and I'm not going to let her do it to him or me. I have one hundred percent faith that what Jake told me was the truth, and this manipulative bitch is just trying to make me leave him again. Making a pathway for her to try to get her claws into him, and I sure as hell will never let that happen.

"You have no clue. I saw the state of you. There's no way you remember accurately what you did with me, and I can assure you that you definitely remember how to finger fuck me to an orgasm, Jake." She smiles and evilly licks her lips, looking directly at his crotch now that he's on his feet, and I flinch. The urge to use one of these steak knives has never been so appealing.

"You're a liar." I lift my chin, eyes pouring tears that I wasn't even aware were falling, and face her full-on. "You're a disgusting, pathetic tramp and a liar. Do you really think I would believe you? Over him?!" I stand and slowly start folding my napkin neatly, lying it on the table, old PA Emma taking control, pushing my erratic emotions down.

"Then you're a fucking idiot because once a cheat, always a cheat. Whether he kissed me or fucked me, he still cheated! Believe me. He will again!" Everyone is standing and glaring at one another. Well, Jake and I at her, and her at both of us.

"You would know." Jake cuts in with a snide comment and a snarl. "You are the queen of fucking cheating, Marissa, right?!" I catch that spark of fury, bracing myself for another onslaught of nastiness, but she cackles, laughing like a crazy witch.

"All these years, Jacob. You're still so sore about all that because you're in denial. You feel like you do about me because it still hurts, baby. You still love me. You never forget your first love, and you never get over them. Do you remember telling me you loved me, *Bambina?* When you used to fuck me over and over. You could never get enough of me, could you? Seems you still can't." She's purring at him, using his pet name, which makes me pale, my fists clenching, and my nails biting into my palms. Jake shakes his head at her and snarls again. My fury is building to epic proportions at the thought of the two of them, back then and now when they made a baby. It's all one giant mess of visions and agony, making me want to rip her head off.

"I don't want you. I have everything standing right next to me that I could ever want. You're just that irritating nail in my shoe that I can't get rid of." Jake delivers it with a sneer, but she doesn't falter, just more bedroom eyes and lip licking.

"He did more than kiss me, Emma. He was unzipped and ready to go if only I'd stopped resisting. Pushed up against the wall in a dark smoky club. I bet you were the last thing on his mind, baby cakes." She meets his eyes full-on, challenging him defiantly, a glimmer of calculation in that face, and I know without a doubt she's lying. Jake may be all about kinky sex and hot-blooded even when drunk, but I know he wouldn't screw someone in a public bar, especially not her.

I don't even have to think about it. Jake's whole posture, anger at what she's trying to do, and the tension in the room tell me that I know the truth. I know he wouldn't have done that to me. She kissed him, pushed herself onto him, and he didn't stop her immediately. He let it happen for seconds, and then his head snapped into place; his brain came around, pushing her away. I know him better. I know that he didn't do this to us. I know without question because every part of this unfolding scene tells me so. I don't know Marissa, but even I can see she's lying, pure, bare-faced manipulation.

"You know who else was there, Marissa? ... Daniel ... and Daniel's version will undoubtedly match what Jake remembers, so don't try to split us up with your rancid bullshit because, *yes*! I am pregnant, and we're not only buying a house right next door but Jake's asked me to marry him more than once. So, please, a guy who is so quick to run off to his ex will surely not ask me to marry him and mean it." I rant at her.

Enough is enough. It's time I made a stand. I need to show her exactly how this is going to go. Jake and I are untouchable; some manipulative little bitch full of lies will not come between us in this way. I trust him, know what he's done, and am ready to forgive him completely. I'm not going to let some narcissistic tramp come between us. All the pain and anger and the weeks of going without sex, not only because of my broken heart but also his guilt, and this slut is at the center of it. Enough is enough. I throw my napkin aside and hoist myself in sheer fury.

"And I say *yes* ... *Yes, fucking yes!*" I turn to Jake and grab his hand, pulling it to my stomach, ready to fight for what is rightfully mine, not about to let some cheap-ass fake tramp take it from me. Jake and I have a future to look forward to and a child but holding back and being afraid made all this happen in the first place. I rejected the world he wanted to give me and hurt him, and now I have him back. I'm not going to let some asshole woman come between us and get in the way of that.

Jake is mine, always mine. Now. Then and *forever*!

"Will you marry me, Jake?" I fixate on him with pure sincerity, my heart pounding crazily, every part of me thumping out of my chest with sheer adrenaline, meaning every freakin single word. Jake's dumbfounded and stalls for a moment before yanking me to him, so I'm facing him full-on. His eyes are searching my face in sheer confusion.

"I told you I would give you fireworks and a floor show, Emma, but if this is what you want, you know I'd marry you right now. Just say the word, and I'll marry you in a heartbeat." He can't conceal the sudden soft emotion in his eyes, which fuels what I'm doing, making my decision concrete. I love him. I need him, and I never want anything or anyone ever to pull us apart again.

"I just want you." I lean up and softly kiss him on the mouth, my eyes filling with emotions and tears, sniffing back the sudden surge of happiness.

"You're pathetic. Both of you. Screw you both!" Marissa throws her glass at the wall and storms toward the closed door, spitting venom at us, sheer hatred and disgust over her face. "You'll wake up one day and look at that miserable icy little bitch you married and think of me, Jake. I was your first love, and despite this bullshit show, you kissed me, still want me, and you're just too hung up on the past to see that." She turns to me with pure malice. "Good luck trying to trust him, Emma. I can assure you he will crawl into my bed repeatedly in years to come because we fit, him and I, we're the same, and it's only a matter of time before I get him back."

"Marissa, just get the fuck out." Jake throws her a look that screams *leave before I make you leave and* turns back to me, pulling me into his body a little forcefully.

The door slams, but neither of us looks her way, too locked in on one another, and I just gave myself to him completely and wholeheartedly. We both exhale almost in unison at the sudden silence of her exiting. The immediate calmness and serenity that washes over the whole room so quickly now she's not in it.

"I'm sorry, baby. None of what she said is true. I swear, Emma. That's not what happened." He pushes his forehead to mine and focuses on my mouth, my heart ripping into shreds at the look of devastation on his face. Despite my show of unity, he's worried that I still doubt him, but I shake my head.

"I believe you, Jake. I know you wouldn't do that to me." I cry again as I reach up and slowly kiss him on the mouth, tears of relief and maybe even joy. Possibly hormonal, seeing as crying has become second nature since he impregnated me. Jake closes his eyes and kisses me back, deepening it slightly, tongue flicking against mine deliciously, aiding the wounds from the confrontation from hell. He pulls back and runs his fingers through my hair, scooping it behind my ear, focusing those beautiful green calm eyes on me.

"I love you more than life, *Bambina* ... I know you said the stuff about marrying me in anger, Emma, to hurt her—"

"I didn't!" I cut in and cover his mouth with my fingers. My heart is soaring at the peace I feel right now. "I mean it, Jake ... You're my life, and I'm done with all this bullshit. I want our baby to be born a Carrero. I'm done being scared ... I love you so much, and I forgive you."

Chapter 12

Jake, Sylvana, and Giovanni are locked in the sitting room with a lot of yelling and banging as I sit in the kitchen with Arrick and try not to self-implode. Sitting so tensely, my body aches with the effort, and I'm on high alert. It's been only minutes since we left the dining room, and my nerves are completely done in.

"Here." He hands me a mug of cocoa and slides into the chair beside me at the kitchen table with a supportive smile.

"Thanks." I accept it gratefully, still picking at the plate of food he warmed for me, trying to ignore the noise echoing down the hall. All the house staff has retired for the night, and the place is eerily empty. Arrick's girlfriend is either in his room or gone, so here he is, babysitting me at his brother's request because Jake didn't want me left alone to ponder everything.

"I guess I should say welcome to my crazy family." He nods casually toward the direction of the noise, and I take a long slow breath. I am blowing it out to try to bring some calm to my chaotic inner body, so tired suddenly.

"Is this what it's like? I never really had a real family." I shrug and look down. "It was only my mother and me, and she's not exactly going to win any awards for mom of the year." I sigh a little in deflation.

"Sometimes it's like this, especially when Jake and my dad go head to head. They seem to be able to get to each other in the worst way." Arrick smiles and sips his mug of cocoa carefully. He has Giovanni's grace and smooth, quiet confidence and authoritative quality when he's sitting like this, contemplating things. Mature for his young age.

He looks more like Giovanni than Jake, yet somehow there is still enough of Sylvana in there for him to be attractive in a way not too dissimilar to Jake, as I used to think. It's a little odd given his lighter hair and soft brown eyes, although sitting this close, I can see he has a lot of green flecks through the color, giving them more of a hazel quality. The older he gets, the more I see tiny hints that when he fully grows out of his teen years, he may be more Jake Carrero-like than Giovanni Carrero.

"What was all that about with your dad?" I blink up at him with a face full of confusion, trying to work out the motive behind his father's behavior. Giovanni is one person I'm never going to figure out.

"My dad hates Marissa. He always has. Blames her for Jake going off the rails when he was younger and screwing his head up to the degree that he brought the family name shame for many years. My dad doesn't trust her and loves nothing more than to get a dig in at every opportunity." He watches me closely for a second and then smiles. "He called you Emma at dinner. Did you notice?"

"What?" I glance up at him as he pulls that half-smile that Jake does, the way his eyes light up when he thinks he knows something you haven't figured out yet, makes me well and truly confused. It makes me feel comfortable with Arrick because he's remarkably like his brother when you stop and dissect him. Strong genes.

"My dad ... He's only ever referred to Marissa as Miss. Hartley doesn't use her name at all. It's kind of his thing. He called you Emma, so he likes you, he sees you as something permanent in Jake's life, and if Jake hadn't been so busy trying to control that crazy aggressive rage of his, then he would've noticed it too. It's almost like dad's giving his consent." He winks at me and takes another drink.

"You're telling me your dad gave his approval simultaneously, causing a massive fight?" I laugh at the ridiculousness of it, breaking the tension in my stomach with giggling.

"My dad never does anything without reason, Emma. He approved and tried eradicating your competition in one fell swoop to protect his son. I know what Jake thinks of him but believe it or not, his intentions were only for Jake. My dad doesn't show affection the way we do. He's a man from another time and lifestyle, back when men didn't show love or affection openly." He raises an eyebrow, and I take a moment to analyze this. I remember the mafia rumors a while back about the Carrero family, and I wonder if this is what Arrick means.

Does Giovanni still have ties to the mafia?

The thought is a little disconcerting, but it would explain the man's terrifying demeanor, the quick sharp manipulation, and the way he keeps all his cards very close to his chest, so no one can ever read him.

"How does announcing a house and baby to Marissa get rid of her? She's still carrying Jake's kid. She's still going to be connected to him for an eternity." I scrutinize Arrick's face with an expression of sheer disbelief.

"She's refusing a DNA test despite my dad informing her that no proof means no relationship with the Carreros. He doesn't believe this baby is Jake's any more than I do. So in a way, he was calling her out, showing her she has competition with a baby that really is Jake's." He focuses on me intensely, with a hint of a frown and a look of complete belief in what he's saying.

"Why would she lie? She would obviously be found out eventually?" I sigh and push down the fatigue sweeping up my body. My fingertips pressed at my temples to try to dull the throbbing headache growing there. I think all the emotions of that little dinner scene are playing catch up, and I need to go lay down.

"Marissa has always been manipulative as hell; she used to play Ben and Jake off one another like crazy. She tried with Daniel too, but weirdly he's the one guy who saw through her shit and kept Jake sane and clear from her for the longest time, so he could start moving on. The girl is twisted as hell." Arrick shrugs, seemingly well versed in all that is Marissa, giving me more ground to not believe what she said about that night with Jake.

"It doesn't mean she's lying about that one night ... You saw her, right? Baby bump! And even Jake remembers waking up in a bed with her." I push my cocoa aside, unable to stomach anything more. I want to lie down and stop talking about that stupid Demon Bitch. I want Jake to come to bed and hold me tight and forget tonight ever happened.

"I don't know, Emma, it's just that she's refusing the DNA ... She should want to prove it just to shove it in my dad's face."

"From what I've seen, she's stubborn and difficult and only refuses because she can be stubborn and difficult." Demon Bitch does not like being told what to do or ultimatums. The dealings Jake's had with her so far have proven that she's someone who digs in her heels and fights hard, even when it's futile.

"That could be true too, I guess. Look ... I didn't say this before because Jake swore me to secrecy until my mom knew, but congratulations on the baby, Emma. I really mean it. I know you're kinda freaked out over the whole thing but Jake's crazy happy about this. He tells me everything, and from the day you found out, he's been gushing about it non-stop. I know he fucked things up, and I'm glad you're giving him a chance to put things right. You're good for him in so many ways. I've never seen him this happy."

He smiles and puts an arm around my shoulder, giving me a small awkward squeeze before pulling away again. Unlike his brother, Arrick isn't as handy and touchy-feely as Jake. Every time I've seen him with girlfriends, he isn't as publicly affectionate either. He's more like Giovanni in a reserved, less emotional way.

"He's good for me too ... When he's not fucking things up." I smile softly, noticing for the first time that it doesn't hurt quite as much to talk about this, and mentioning the baby seems a little less scary. I don't know when I stopped panicking about the baby and our future, I guess it's been gradual, and my mind is hopefully completely at peace with both. It feels good to realize it.

"You belong together, and every one of us is rooting for it. You have a bunch of Carrero family members talking of nothing else but when Jake is going to get his head out of his ass and get you walking down the aisle."

I blush and look down at my hands.

"After tonight, I'm guessing sooner than you think." I smile and can't help but let it grow across my face with a sudden rush of certainty that I am doing the right thing.

"You finally said yes?" He grins at me, a show of enthusiasm and genuine joy.

"I did one better ... I asked him to marry me, in an angry, loud way, in front of her." I giggle naughtily and then appraise him genuinely. "Funny thing is, though, I meant it. Something snapped while listening to her, and I realized that he's mine, for now, and forever, no matter what happens. Jake's mine, he always will be, and there's absolutely no reason for me to keep freaking out over all of this in my head anymore. Wasting time and holding back is only making us miserable." I sigh and start picking at my nail varnish, still blushing at this outpouring of my inner emotions and thoughts. Especially with this almost stranger.

"You're going to fit right in with this family, Emma Anderson! Or should I say Carrero ... Emma Carrero has a nice ring to it." Arrick has a beautiful smile when he's happy. He has variations of smiles he throws around, like Jake, but this one here, boyish and genuine, is the prettiest. He has that whole sparkly white Hollywood teeth thing too.

"Yeah, it kinda does." I giggle again and kiss Arrick on the cheek rather quickly and nervously. "I always wanted a sibling." I smile at him and stand up rather purposefully. I look him over and evaluate my feelings. I'm not awkward around him, and I don't recoil at his touch. Probably because he's just another version of Jake. But I have a growing affection for him. Having never known what sibling love feels like, I can hazard a guess that it feels somewhat like this.

"You can tell my fiancée that I've gone to bed. His child is very tiring and having a head-on with his psychotic ex took it out of me." I grin and throw him a little wave as I turn on my heel and head toward the stairs.

"I'm pretty sure when I interrupt them and tell them his wavering fiancée is teetering unsteadily up the grand stair all alone and overwhelmed with fatigue, he will be racing right along." Arrick smiles wickedly, master of manipulating his brother, and I can't help the little giggle that escapes my lips. Arrick is slowly becoming my second favorite Carrero.

I glance down at my stomach.

Okay, maybe my third!

* * *

Jake climbs into bed minutes after I do. I'm lying awake staring at the semi-dark ceiling, lost in thought when he comes in. He strips off without looking over and climbs into bed, sliding up against me and pulling me into his arm. I can't help but smile that he did come swiftly along when Arrick intervened in the drama with his father.

"I'm awake," I utter quietly, turning toward him so I can face him, melting into his body heat and feeling glorious against him. It's dull here but not pitch dark so that I can see him.

"You okay?" He leans in and kisses me soundly, mouth molding to mine, hand running up my spine delicately. I can't help the tingles he ignites or how my inner thighs tense at his touch.

"Surprisingly fine," I say when we finally break apart. I'm starting to forget why we're not having sex anymore. My desire is aching to strip off the rest of his clothes and start licking every inch of that taut, smooth tattooed skin.

"Really? We should talk about what happened. I want to know how you're feeling, baby." Jake sounds concerned, but I'm distracted by all that flesh on show. Maybe fighting with that bitch has upped my adrenaline or Maybe those naughty hormones are acting up again but at this very moment, I am glued to muscular pecks, and a slight masculine scatter of hair at his chest, tickling my nose.

I slowly run my fingers across Jake's naked torso and along his body up to his throat. Without saying anything, I inch myself up so we're at eye level and move in for a more seductive kiss, letting my tongue slip into his mouth, moving my body, so I mold against him in every way. An inner surge of satisfaction when a hardness starts to grow between us, and he pushes me back. Jake certainly has no problem with getting turned on. I think it's time we explored the next step to forgiveness.

"Emma, we ..." I silence him with my fingers on his lips.

"Jake, I'm ready. Don't keep this from me anymore, please. I need you so badly it hurts." My body is yearning for more, and this is the kind of more I need. Somehow facing her, marriage proposals, and acceptance of the baby coming has kick-started a stubbornness in me that we're going to fix us fully and finally.

I move back against him and sense the hesitation rippling through him as he contemplates whether we should do this. I don't give him any choice and slide my hand into the waistband of his boxers, moving down to encircle him with my fingers, feeling that jolt of surprise come through him. He wasn't expecting me to start forcefully seducing him so readily, especially after seeing Demon Bitch and everything she said.

I push my mouth to his and kiss him as passionately as possible, using my hand to arouse him in the best way I can fully. Jake catches me around the throat, loosely pushing my face back so he can stare intensely into my eyes in the almost pitch-black room.

Without warning, he flips me on my back and is instantly over the top of me, caging me in. His arms are straining at either side of my head. He leans in and kisses me, slowly and softly, my hands still pleasuring him with even strokes and getting impatient. I bite his lip, nipping it hard enough to get a smile from him before he devours me again. His kiss sends searing pleasure through every nerve ending in my body, notching up the fire within me a hundredfold.

He comes down low enough to rub against me and leaves me no choice but to remove my hand from between us. He pushes himself between my legs, now no longer obstructed, opening me up to him fully as he grinds into me seductively. Our bodies connect to match the way our mouths are, passion rising, and Jake is fully immersed in the action. His hands trail over my breasts and downwards. I groan at his touch, at the feelings and sensations I have been crying out for, and now that I'm finally getting what I need, I'm soaring with desire.

Passion ignites inside of me, heat pouring through me at an alarming rate, and I push Jake off me aggressively with much more strength than I knew I was capable of. I flip on top of him, straddling him fully, peeling off my nightdress and bra, and grinding down on top of him. His hands slide up my body across my abdomen, fingers grazing and exploring me sexually. His hands are itching to trace every part of me that has been denied him, and I can feel it in the way he caresses me, biting his lip, eyes locked on me with unadulterated lust. He covers my breasts, tweaking my nipples with harsh grasps, making me throw my head back and gyrate on top of him a little harder.

No shame or embarrassment because this is his body. He's seen every single inch of me before now, tasted every single piece of me. His hands skim my ribs and move to my hips, pulling me back and forth to get the routine of my grinding into him more fluidly, his hardness below me trying to force its way through the fabric between us. His hands skim upwards and come to a slow halt as they cover my abdomen. Jake's face changes from sex crazed to frowning in almost a second, and every part of that body physically recoils.

"Fuck." The instant change in him as his hands drop by his side, catching my legs, lifting me effortlessly off him gently, "Emma, I can't."

"What?" I don't understand. My body is brimming with desire and longing. I'm seconds away from self-combusting, and he's putting the brakes on?! He sits up, so his back is turned slightly toward me.

What the hell, Jake?

"I can't do this! Shit!" Jake slides away and gets out of bed, adjusting himself in his boxers and walking off toward the en suite at a fast pace.

"Jake, what the hell?!" I snap after him, suddenly self-conscious, hauling the bed sheets over my naked upper half, the shame of rejection coursing through me. A sob hits my throat as I'm filled with self-doubt, but Jake spins at the bathroom door.

"It's the baby, Emma ... It's weird. As soon as I touched your stomach, it was all I could think about, and I'd be fucking you while it was in there. Not to mention it can't be safe!" He sounds angry, tense, and annoyed at himself mostly. He switches on the bathroom light and flops back against the door frame, running an agitated hand through his hair, looking completely devastated. I gape at him in shock.

"You're kidding, right? You haven't touched me in a month, and now you don't want to because I'm pregnant?" I can't contain the hurt in my voice or the complete disbelief, and he stalks back to me immediately.

"Jesus, Emma. I want to have sex with you right now so badly. I just can't." He holds up despairing hands. That perfect muscular body is so ripe to be devoured by me, yet denying me what I really want and need. The anger inside of me spikes.

"Yes, you can." I grab his hand and haul it back to my breast, forcing him to cup it loosely, but he makes no effort to try and lets his arm flop back down. No effort whatsoever.

"I can't," he repeats in deflation, eyes downcast, and he looks miserable.

Well, that makes two of us!

"I'm sure pregnant women have sex every day, Jake. You're being ridiculous. It's not in the same place, and it's sure as hell not going to hurt something that's barely the size of a bean right now. We were having sex before we knew about it." I pout, close to frustrated tears and burning up with need, almost painfully. That inner crazy hormonal me, being denied sex, is back with a vengeance.

Jake leans in and kisses my temple slowly and surely. He's trying to smooth my ruffled feathers and balm my feelings, but it's not going to work.

"I can't touch you until we see your doctor, Emma, and hear it straight from her. All I can think about right now is how much I just can't." He frowns at me apologetically and tries to embrace me with a soft cuddle instead.

I pick up the cushion from the bed and shove it into his chest angrily so he moves away.

"You're an ass," I snap, sexual frustration hitting me hard, aware of how completely unreasonable I'm being. I don't care, though. I want him, I need him that way, and he isn't even trying to give it to me. After everything, this is like getting a massive slap in the face.

"Jesus, stroppy. Hormones so bad you're that pissed at me right now?" He tries to sound jokey and lighthearted, but I scowl at him.

"You have no fucking idea!" I turn away angrily, throwing myself down on the bed and slinging an arm across my face in complete frustration. Jake stills on the bed, then slides off and saunters to turn off the bathroom light.

Probably trying to figure out how to make this up to me without any fucking sex!

Un-goddamn believable. Where the hell is the sex-crazed Jake that I'm crazy over?! A whole month of nothing, and now I'm offering it on a plate, and he just can't?!

He slides into bed while I try to get my crazy mood under control, disappointment surging through me at an alarming rate.

"Did we really get engaged tonight, Emma?" Jake's husky voice comes close in the dark, and my anger dissipates a little at his question. I sigh and push the traces of my mood deep down.

He's trying misdirection. His favorite maneuver. I guess he's good at it because it's working. I blow out an agitated breath and slide my arm down, so I can stare at the ceiling for a few agonizing minutes to calm down.

I can't be mad at him over this.

"I know it wasn't exactly some romantic blow-your-mind moment, but I meant it. Something inside me stopped running and decided to stand and fight ... To fight for you." I turn on my side and watch him in the dark. His hand trails down my shoulder and arm, slowly and tenderly. I flinch because my skin is still burning with desire, and his touch isn't exactly helping right now, but I stay where I am and don't pull away.

"You know it was probably the best moment of my life, but I still want to ask you properly, Emma ... Can I do that? My way? I don't know. Somehow, it just doesn't feel official." He's watching his fingers trail my skin hypnotically. I can't help but give up on the rest of my anger when watching him. So still and beautiful and wholly irresistible, with that little boy lost look, asking me for permission. I sigh.

"You mean fireworks and a floor show?" I smirk, reaching out to run my nails across his chest lightly, the ache to have his body still coursing through me despite knowing there is nothing I can do about it.

"You'd expect nothing less from Jake Carrero, CEO, commandeering, bossy, cocky asshole! I need to put a ring on your finger anyway, might as well make the most of the moment I do." He beams at me, and I know I'm completely beaten.

Something changed within me tonight, some shift of the axis, some inner defining moment that I'm still not sure of, but I know one thing, this is it for me. No matter what he did, it doesn't matter anymore. I know he'll never hurt me like that again, and I need to stop hurting him. We have done this to each other, and it's time to stop. We have someone else to think about now, and it's growing inside of me, slowly but surely, already starting to affect our life and relationship with its mere presence. Our relationship has changed somehow. No more sexy games or misunderstandings, no more pandering around what we mean or feel. We are growing as a couple.

The other stuff will come back naturally. Maybe he needs that peace of mind that won't harm our child. I can't exactly be mad at the gentle, caring, protective side of Jake that most people don't even know exists.

How can I stay angry when at the heart of his inability to touch me is love for our unborn child?

I sigh and cuddle closer, resigning myself to the idea of this being temporary. He better damn well give me some crazy, hot, kinky sex as soon as someone puts his mind at ease.

Chapter 13

We're walking hand in hand, fingers entangled, along the sunny pavement in the crisp morning air toward the house Jake wants to buy. It's almost a replica of the Carrero family home, yet instead of warm sandy brown roughing on the outside, it's brilliant white with palm trees gracing the front of the manicured lawn in an arc. It's beyond gorgeous and a postcard picture-perfect.

Two stories high with modern, clean lines and large windows under a sloped tiled roof. It looks much bigger than the Carrero family home because of the bright colors and straight, manicured lines of the surrounding lawns. It's neat and modern looking in contrast to the flower beds and bushes of Sylvana's gardens.

It reminds me of Jake's apartment in small ways. His neat masculine style and bold, edgy taste, but this has a much homelier quality and a long sweeping drive up to a beautiful, dark wood, grand front door.

The agent meets us at the open door, a man in his late 30s sporting a side parting, smoothed-back hair, and an expensive suit. He ushers us inside proficiently with a huge grin. He has a tall slim frame and a very cheesy smile with wandering eyes as I approach behind Jake, still being pulled by that possessive hand.

"It's a blank canvas to put your stamp on." The man beams at us, leading the way through the white marble, neutrally painted hall, identical to Sylvana's, to a modern black granite kitchen with white units and steel appliances. He sweeps an arm around the expanse, encouraging us to look around.

"That's what we want ideally, a place to mold into our own." Jake's eyes flick to me with a smile, then he walks forward to properly look around the kitchen, letting me go so I can stand and admire it all. He likes to cook occasionally, and I can imagine him in here making pancakes on a Sunday morning for me like he normally does.

The thought warms me through my stomach and rises to my cheeks. I can see Jake happy in this room, It's his kind of taste, enough modern and high-tech to satisfy him yet still warm and welcoming into the heart of the home. I can imagine small chubby legged children sitting around the long low table near the huge wall of patio doors, looking out into a massive manicured garden with an outdoor pool.

In the distance, there is an outdoor garage in the same gleaming white and a row of steel doors, suggesting he could fit many cars in. I have no idea how many vehicles Jake owns, seeing as he keeps them all over the place; his apartment complex, the Carrero business buildings, parking under the apartment, and I know he has a car here as well at his mother's home.

"Any chance we can do a walk around alone first?" Jake throws back to the agent, who is standing close to me, smiling a little too charmingly. The normal urge to recoil at his attention has been replaced with an empty ignorance and lifted chin. I find his interest in me more of an irritation than an outright sense of repulsion.

You have no chance; you don't compare to Jake in any way.

I catch Jake frowning in that *I'll beat you* glare now that he's spotted where Mr. Agent's attention is placed, and I smile at my jealous boy with adoration.

Some things never change.

"Yes, of course. I'll wait right here if you want to wander. The owners are away for a few days, and all the staff are non-residential. The place is completely empty, so feel free." He beams and steps away when Jake comes back to my side, slipping his fingers into mine, leading the way with another unfriendly glare in the man's direction as he deliberately lays his claim to me.

"Asshole," he mutters under his breath as we move back out into the hall away from the agent, and I stifle the urge to giggle.

"Really, Jake? Are you always going to be browbeating other men just for looking at me?" As we walk, I slide my other hand around his arm and pull myself against him.

"Yes." He replies non-apologetically, and I shake my head at him.

At least he's honest. I guess never having to deal with jealousy in his life means he has no clue how to notch it down.

I sigh affectionately as he leads me through the downstairs rooms. The layout is almost identical to next door. Large spacious lounge, a second big open formal lounge, huge windows, and great fireplaces dominating one wall, decorated in neutrals and wooden flooring.

Downstairs holds a couple of offices or study rooms, depending on what use you have for them and a separate utility room; tucked far along the long corridor through the long hall. There are a couple of small bedrooms, possibly for house staff, and each has its own en suite.

He pulls me back along the large hall, and upstairs we find more of the same layout as the Carrero house; more than half a dozen large bedrooms with en suites and equally fabulous neutral décor. The house is grand and airy. It's more than big enough to house a very large family. There's so much space, rooms with walk-in closets and little nooks here and there. It's everything you would ever need, even if you planned on adopting a football team.

"What do you think?" Jake asks, turning to me in the last room of the house, another vast bedroom. This one houses an en suite with a large jacuzzi and a gorgeous view of the distant ocean. I can see a little private balcony through full-length glass doors.

"The house is huge, Jake. I mean, I knew your parents' house was big, but I've never actually had the tour. This is more rooms than we'll ever need." I blink around at the sheer size of this one room. Sarah's whole apartment in Queens could fit into this one room, and it's a little overwhelming, if not slightly intimidating.

"I'm sure we could occupy most of them." He smirks and runs a hand over my abdomen with his flat palm, and I gape at him in complete horror. He giggles at my reaction, yet I'm still standing open-mouthed in shock that he might intend to have an army of kids. Right now, I'm on one, and one is almost just bearable for now.

"It's a house to grow into, Emma, and enough room for people to stay over. I'm sure moving out here would mean Sarah and Marcus would want to come and see you occasionally. Plus, Leila lives in the city, and even though her folks are nearby, I'm sure she'd want to kick back here when she visits. Daniel too. I'd rather buy a house that has space to expand than up and move again down the line when we decide on more kids."

He's let me go, walking around the room, looking at the space pulling open a door onto a full walk-in closet as part of me jumps up and down inside with a happy dance that urges my feet toward the walk-in. I quell the urge to be swayed over by a momentous wardrobe.

Oh, my God, it has a built-in vanity and make-up lighting. So weak, Emma ... But look at how many shoes I could fit in here.

"More kids? Let me get my head around this one, Jake ... One right now!" I frown at him sternly, trying very hard to pull my head out of the vast space for lots of clothes, shoes, and wonderful accessories. He turns and walks back to me, placing his hands on my shoulders, and looks me directly in the eye.

"Do you want this house, Emma?" He's deadly serious. His intense focus doesn't falter.

I bite my lip and look past his numbing gaze around the room we're standing in, at the huge four-poster bed, modern, sleek furniture, plush carpets, and heavy drapes framing the most magnificent view I have ever seen. It's more than a little tempting if I can get my head around how much a house like this would cost.

"I could see you living here. It's totally your style." I sigh, trying not to think about the price tag attached to this vast amount of space.

"Could you see *you* living here?" He nudges me gently with a small half-smile on the corner of his mouth. His face is utterly devastating with that twinkle in his eye. He's going all 'Charming Carrero' on me, and my knees are already weakening.

God, don't do irresistibly cute right now.

"If it was made a little homelier? Maybe less modern and harsh? I love the view." I know I'm being evasive. Part of me is thumping like a maniac, ready to jump into full panic mode.

This is the forever house. The big leap. The 'letting myself go and fully trusting Jake to take care of things' house. Letting him go ahead and spend ridiculous amounts of money on 'our' house.

I take a slow, heavy inhale. He still hasn't uttered a word. He's watching me with his intense green gaze, deepening into my soul. My mind is whirring and clicking, trying to stay sane; life with Jake will always include money. Life with Jake is always going to involve trusting him to take control because he doesn't know who else or how else to be. I need to learn to give in a little and enjoy that about him. I need to trust him always to do what is right for us and let him make me happy. I must relinquish that part of me, scared of a new life, and have faith.

"On one condition." I finally blink at him and resign to the fact that I must be brave for once.

"What's that?" He smiles softly, eyes glued to my face with a little smug hint of triumph that I'm trying to ignore.

"I choose the décor," I respond boldly, and he throws me the widest happy grin I've ever seen, planting a kiss fully on my mouth in an over-eager fashion before picking me up into a crazy round swing.

"Wouldn't have it any other way, baby."

* * *

"So, when do you move in?" Leila lounges across the bed in Jake's old bedroom and takes a grape from the platter of food between us; snacks and sandwiches, including lots of fruit, courtesy of Mamma Carrero and her constant care.

Sylvana is the perfect host, and she's been doting over me when the house is empty during the week when the men are at work or doing whatever the Carrero men do when not glued to their women folk. She enjoys my company, and Leila flew to see me when I finally drummed up the courage to tell her about the baby.

To say she was ecstatic is an understatement. The five-foot teddy bear suspended on helium balloons in the middle of the bedroom floor over the massive hamper of baby products was her arriving gift, humped in by two very good-looking men.

It's been four days since the house viewing, and Jake had to go into the city to oversee some business details and deal with the house sale. He's been gone two days, and it feels like an eternity without him here. Still not able to fly and still getting car sick means Jake has put me on a travel ban for the time being, and now I'm stuck here living in his old bedroom in the Carrero family home and twiddling my thumbs in boredom.

"I think Jake's pushing for a quick sale. He has his lawyers tying things up already, and I know the Wilsons were ecstatic about him being interested in the house." I imagine that Giovanni is applying pressure on his golfing partner to ensure his son seals the deal, and according to Arrick, Sylvana having us next door will make her year.

I have given up on contemplating my job and career for the time being, but it's not something I will give up on completely to live the life of a kept woman. I intend to figure that out in time, but for now, being pregnant and enjoying being pampered no longer makes me feel guilty. Finally, resigning myself to the fact that this lifestyle is a part of being with him. My phone lights up across the bed, and I reach over, grabbing it to me impulsively.

Jake Carrero has sent you an iTunes gift.

I start grinning, and Leila shakes her head at me. She knows the face that implies Jake has texted me. Obvious glee because I miss him so much and have been acting like a teen girl with a mega crush the last few days. His back-to-back meetings mean he has only been able to text through the day and not call me much.

I flick it open and smile again, unable to conceal my joy and how my heart gets warm, gooey, and tingly.

Jake Carrero has sent you–Avril Lavigne's "I Miss You."

I chew on my lip as I waver whether I should reply with a song that once broke my heart or scroll for a new one. Maybe it's time to make that song mean something else to us now; take away the pain I feel anytime I hear it on the radio or in passing. I push down the doubt with a slow inhale and send it on its way to him.

You have sent Jake Carrero–Avril Lavigne's "When You're Gone."

Attached message – Erasing the past. Remember? E xx

I stare at my phone screen as my 'gift' slips away across the interweb to my awaiting love, hoping he remembers it. The special song I once sent in hopes of him figuring out how I felt and instead rejected me, and the words attached are his words at a new beginning so long ago.

Leila is completely immersed in a magazine while I'm focused on the love of my life, amusing herself while I'm distracted. Surprisingly patient for such a little firebomb of energy.

My phone flashes with a text, and this time it's a message instead of a song, and again I can't stop that heart-fluttering gooey response in me.

I'll never let you go, baby. I'll never let you walk away either. I would never be stupid enough ever to go down that route again. The past doesn't matter, only what the future holds. I love you xxx. J

My Jake, with his fast words that always sing to me, is so in tune with everything I need to hear. My heart aches with his response, and a tear catches in my throat. I reply with a text and a song. A bright little smile stuck clearly on my face.

Avril Lavigne "Keep Holding On" ... I love you more xxx."

"You two are sickeningly cute, you know?" Leila is watching the obvious happiness spread on my face, thanks to Jake's messages, and seems a little sad where love is concerned. I feel guilty for ignoring her and pull myself up to move closer to her, putting my phone face down on the bed so it won't distract me if he replies. "Jake and his pushy one hundred mile-an-hour self." Leila giggles, bringing us back to the conversation about the house and a quick sale now she has my full attention, and she pops another grape into her mouth. I beam as I think of him. I wouldn't change him anymore, not even that part of him now I know where it stems from. Jake will always be pushy, bossy, and sometimes overbearing, but I'm sure I have equally bad traits, and I'm learning to counteract him in my own way. I love him regardless, and sometimes I even love those things about him.

"Pushy, impulsive, and spontaneous while I'm cautious, over aware, and over analyze." I sigh and reach for a piece of fruit to pick at despite being full to bursting already.

"Perfect balance, babes ... You need each other to even things out." Leila grins at me knowingly, all hints of sadness now gone from that pretty face. I push more grapes into my mouth and smile at her observation.

I never thought of it that way.

"What about Daniel? Any word on that front?" Since Hunter started therapy, he's been keeping out of the way, only calling Jake every couple of days, and Leila hasn't mentioned him since her earlier arrival.

"One text ... Telling me he was trying to figure things out and to give him time." Leila shrugs and rolls on her back, avoiding my eye contact suddenly. "I told him I met someone else, so to push off." She adds quickly and avoids even looking at me, lifting the magazine above her face as though she's trying to read in that position.

"What? Why?" I sit upright a little too quickly, upsetting the tray on the comforter, sending grapes rolling everywhere, and eyeing her accusingly. She shrugs and pastes on the defiant furrow of her brows, which I can still see clearly from this angle.

"I told you I'm done waiting for him. Yeah, he's finally in therapy ... Bravo. But for how long? And how long before he doesn't run a mile at any hint of real affection, Emma?" Leila sits up with a single tear in her eye. "He hurt me for the last time. Really hurt me. Why would I sit around waiting for something that may never actually happen? Therapy is a start, but it doesn't mean it will change much."

I must admit I didn't see this coming at all. She has waited so long for some sort of real emotion from the guy, and now he's doing something about it, she's running the other way. I can't help but wonder if Leila is now scared about the change in him and the possibility of more.

"I think he loves you, Leila ... He's doing this for you," I try, but that stubborn lift of her chin and hardening of her soft face shuts me up.

"He should be doing it for himself. I don't want that pressure." A tear rolls down her cheek, and she brushes it away with an angry jut to her bottom lip. Inner Leila is always fighting to come out and push him away, pushing out the memory of heartbreak and any weakness concerning Daniel.

"Is there really someone else?" I push in a new direction. I know how she can be; the more you pry, the higher that defensive wall kicks in. Leila doesn't do victim at all. In fact, she rarely does any sort of weakness.

"Kurt Robson ... He's followed me around for years. He's like a little puppy dog, always trying to get my attention, and I figure maybe it's time to let him try. He'd never hurt me. He's safe, gentle, kind, and completely dotes on me." She can't look me in the eye, and I feel utter sadness for her. She's running to safety, running to a man she doesn't love because he can't and never will hurt her.

"How do you feel about him?" I reach out and touch her fingers when I see that distant daydreamy look in her eye as her head gets lost in thought. No doubt, thinking about the one man she's refusing to give any sort of chance to.

Oh, Leila!

"I'll learn to love him. I mean, he's sweet, handsome, and funny. He treats me nicely and never drops me like an infectious disease. He doesn't care about my past. He's calm and straightforward with no wild tendencies, the exact opposite of Daniel. It's what I need." She swallows the surge of emotion and pastes a bright smile on her face. Her eyes betray what's coming from her mouth, but I let it go.

An overwhelming sadness hits me in my stomach, and I can't stop the moisture from piercing my eyes. Here is a girl completely in love with a man who is completely in love with her, and yet neither can get it together and be happy. Daniel is what Leila needs.

Safe, dull, and kind will only last so long. She needs someone as hot and fiery as her to match her every mood and handle her at her worst. She needs someone who will stand up to her bullshit and sweep her off her feet, someone who keeps life fun, interesting, and just as impulsively wild as her. She needs a man who can embrace her wild side and not want to tame it, someone who won't let that pushy side of Leila dominate him and knows exactly how to handle her. She needs Hunter. Yet she's too damn scared to let him hurt her again.

I get that lump in my throat and think of Jake. I'll go out of my way to do anything to make sure we never go back there.

I'll never let us drift apart again.

It's the most heartbreaking thing I've ever witnessed.

"Enough about that asshole ... Have you heard anything more about that god-awful psycho slut?" Leila blinks at me, and I know immediately that she means Marissa. The images that brassy whore conjures up in my head from the dining room experience make me bristle in hate.

"Surprisingly not. She's been lying low and hiding out since that little scene. Jake keeps expecting some backlash, like a refusal to let him see the kid after it's born or something equally vindictive. He says silence is never good with her, and I get the sense he's on tenterhooks about it." I try for nonchalant and just sound snooty. Leila grins at me, seeing through my attempts at being mature and disconnected.

"Yeah, she's always been a devious whore with a calculated mind ... Watch that one, Emma. She's got absolutely no scruples; money, looks, and entitlement have made for a very deathly spoiled bitch. Barbie with a shotgun and a hunger for blood."

I laugh at Leila's description and sigh, lounging back to pick up the last grapes we retrieved from the bed. That pang of pain at the mere mention of her. Even though I forgave him, I still ponder it all, and it can still hurt me when I let it.

"Still no sex?" Leila butts into my gloomy demeanor. I sigh extra loudly, shaking my head and rolling my eyes in frustration, flopping back against the cushions of the bed beside her feet.

"Jake literally can't muster up the ability to do it. Anytime we get close, he has images of impaling a baby's head or other such nonsense about guilt or making me miscarry. You know what he's like about being forthcoming with his insecurities ... pretends that he's got none. He's completely freaking out about it, and no amount of reassurance from the doctor has changed that. He's treating me like fine china, and if I so much as dare to move an inch, he's all over me asking me what I need, if I want to lay down, or if I should even be moving around. He's suffocating me with over-protectiveness, and to be frank, I feel like strangling him to death." I let it out in a gush, then grin at the hilarity of it all; it appears playboy Casanova Carrero has done a massive U-turn.

Leila bursts into hysterical laughter and falls sideways on the bed, unable to control herself.

"Oh, my God." She wheezes, trying to gain control. "Who knew hot stud Carrero would go celibate and turn into such a fish wife?" She bursts into another fit of giggles, and I hit her with a cushion.

"It's not funny! Sex happens to be one of his most defining qualities." I laugh and throw another cushion when tears start pouring down her face. Uncontrollable laughter bubbles forth from that petite little blonde.

"It's kinda cute, though." She chokes, trying to get the laughter under control, hugging her ribs. "I mean, he loves his baby so much already that it's messing with his head as much as you do, Emma." She wipes her eyes and throws one of the cushions back at me. I can't help but enjoy the feeling of warmth it gives me and try to ignore the niggle of guilt I get when I think of Marissa's baby.

"But what do I do about it? He says it's partly to do with forgiving himself. But my hormones are crazy bad! I'm thinking of slipping Viagra in his coffee and raping him in his sleep!" I huff and flop back dejectedly. The inner frustration from aching for sex lately has brought back touchy and grouchy Emma. I need more than cuddles and caresses. Jake has shown me a whole world of kinky sexual fulfillment, and I need that back too."

"You wouldn't need to. Jake has that sleep thing ... Ummm sexo ... something." Leila points out distractedly while thumbing through the magazine still on the bed.

"Sexsomnia!" I sit upright, remembering our conversation in Chicago a while ago. He initiates sex while sleeping if he's overly stressed.

"Yeah, get him stressed to the max, then make the moves on him in the middle of the night, and he'll do the rest. If he does it once, he'll see there's no danger." Leila laughs, but I sigh and shake my head at her.

"I couldn't do that. It's too sordid and seems like I'd be taking advantage of him. He wouldn't be happy about it, and I couldn't do it. It would be wrong on so many levels." I can just imagine the amount of pissed off I would get from Jake if he thought he'd done the deed while not being aware of it. The anger at being unable to protect me from himself and me for deliberately pushing him to do it. I know only too well how that head works.

"So? You need to pull out all the stops and seduce him. Push out those crazy fears and doubts by whirling him into a lust-fueled frenzy he has no control over. You seemed to be more than capable of that before all this." Leila winks across at me with a smirk. I think about what she's saying for a long moment and smile.

"You're completely right. I've got so used to Jake running after me, pandering to my every need, and still basically kissing ass to make up for things that I haven't once thought about turning on the sex myself."

I have spent weeks being heartbroken and moody at having a version of Jake I'm not used to, pampering my every mood, and I haven't even thought about unleashing my own powers of persuasion. The Emma from our games and Emma from the night in this very house dressed in sexy lingerie and tight dresses that drove him wild. Emma who knew how to push Jake's buttons. I need to up the game and remind him how much he wanted me.

Where is that, Emma?

She has been mourning and sulking, hiding for fear of letting him back in, and now she has no reason not to. She wants him back in, needs him, and she sure as hell will show him that's what he needs too. I'll be damned if I spend the entirety of this pregnancy as a sex-starved, hormonal, crazy bitch with serious sexual frustration. I am sure as hell going to get Jake back to how he was when I had no baby bump on show and could make the most of sexy lingerie and kinky fun. He doesn't know what is about to hit him. I will seduce Jake Carrero and sweep him off his feet this time! I need that man back, the one who drove me crazy with lust and wasn't afraid to have sex in many compromising positions in various locations. He made me feel desired and sexy.

"You know you've ruined one of New York's most eligible bachelors now?" Leila eyes me up with a mischievous smile.

"How so?" I smile at her, furrowing my brow.

"Workaholic, jet-setting man-whore, a serious commitment-phobe with an adrenaline junkie lifestyle. Now he's a doting fiancée with a baby on the way, buying houses, avoiding work and dangerous hobbies like the plague. You know, even if you left him now, Emma, he wouldn't know what to do with himself. His old life has no appeal anymore. It wouldn't satisfy him the way it once did. Irreversible damage, little one. I'm so proud of you." She grins and squeezes the ankle of my outstretched foot affectionately, and I can only smile back at Leila's always refreshing view from the outside.

"I guess you're right." I ponder her words and gaze at my lap.

Is that what happened to me too? Is this why returning to the Carrero Corporation no longer holds appeal or tug?

That girl was so focused on her job as an assistant because it was what she needed. Focus, control, and details to oversee, a distraction from her own life and pain. She liked to immerse herself in someone else's realities and needs. It helped her push down any emotion needed to connect to a life. She had no life.

Now I'm struggling to go back because it no longer satisfies me or appeals in any way because Jake changed me too. Irreversible damage! And if he left me now, I could never return to who I was either. The girl I was no longer resembles the woman I have become. That life is so far in my past that it's no longer connected to me. I need a new tomorrow, a new purpose, and a focus in life. I need a new job.

Chapter 14

Sylvana watches me over the rim of her coffee mug as I eat breakfast. Jake is due today, and I'm starting to get serious withdrawals over his absence. The only good thing about him being gone for three whole days is that I seem to have built a bond with Sylvana: a lot of time together this past couple of days while chatting about everything and nothing. I'm more comfortable in this woman's presence than I ever was in my own mother's. She has a gentle way about her that makes you relax and never judges you.

"You look so much better today, *Miele*. So much more color in your face than the day you arrived with Jake." She regards me with an affectionate warmth in her eye.

"I don't feel as bad. The nausea is improving, and I'm no longer tired and emotional. I think my body is settling with the hormones." I drink my cup of cocoa and nestle my feet under myself on the couch beside her.

"It's that Carrero blood. Jake, especially, was a trying pregnancy. I was so up and down in the beginning and so very tired. It could be a sign you're carrying another hot-tempered *Italiano* ..." She smiles, placing a hand on my knee for a moment and squeezing gently, "...a mini hurricane." The sheer pride in her statement has me smiling too. I can imagine Jake must've been a handful as a child. He's a handful as an adult, and that's with maturing. I can't imagine what his offspring are going to be like.

"Sometimes it doesn't seem real, and then other times it's so real I find myself panicking." I sigh and realize at this moment it's heading toward the latter. I'm a little breathless at the thought of a junior Jake giving me a good run around as a mother.

"You'll be fine. Jake will be a doting father as much as he will be a doting husband. You're lucky to have such a strong relationship to work with, a strong man who isn't afraid to show the world he loves you." She smiles my way dreamily, a twinkle in her eye at the obvious adoration of her child.

We're sitting in the cozy lounge reserved for family and have a cheesy romance movie on the big screen. She had the breakfast served here this morning, bagels and cream cheese, and we're both sat in our fluffy robes curled up in the quiet, cozy room.

"Yes, he does. I didn't think I would ever be here. There was a time I believed Jake never saw anything other than a friend." I sigh at the memory; it seems light years ago that I was that closed-off version of myself, getting Jake's inner thoughts very wrong.

"Jake always was a little lost when it came to verbalizing his feelings. He had a bad time with that Marissa, and it caused him to be a little overprotective of his heart. He had no defenses for you, though. I still remember him coming to me so broken-hearted because he sent you away from his office, thinking he could never live up to what he thought you wanted him to be or ever had a chance at gaining your love." For a moment, she's so pained that I get tearful. The thought of Jake so hurt brings tears to my eyes and a deep ache to my heart.

"Please don't. I can't bear to think of Jake that way, knowing we were both hurting and too stupid to be honest with each other. If we'd been honest after we did get together, then the mess with Marissa would've never happened." I sigh, laying my cup on the low table in front of us.

"Honesty is very important ... as is communication, and still cherishing one another even after the first throws of passion and excitement have died." Sylvana focuses on me very seriously. "I know from first-hand experience that marriages can stray if you don't focus on what you mean to one another and if you stop telling each other how you feel." She pats me again, and I get the impression she's talking about Giovanni's affair.

I have no idea what to say or ask or even let on that I know what she's talking about. It's too forward to say a word, so I say nothing. Sylvana doesn't seem to notice my awkward silence, more intent on carrying on. "Giovanni had an affair with a woman I'd thought my friend." She states rather factually. No flicker of emotion at all, which completely surprises me. "We grew apart, no time for one another anymore, and sadly we'd forgotten to still love and cherish one another. He found solace in another's arms." She sighs at the memory.

"Oh, Sylvana, I don't know if I could ever forgive Jake for more than a kiss. I can't imagine." The tears start brimming in my eyes as I try not to think of the pain she must've endured. How much that would destroy me if I had been in her shoes, a kiss was hard enough to forgive.

"In a way, it saved our marriage. We'd grown so distant from one another, and this brought emotion and pain to the surface. I realized by the depth of my heartbreak that I still loved him, and by seeing me so heartbroken, he realized he still loved me. The guilt pained him so much that it eventually brought us back together; now, we're stronger than ever. The same will be said of you and Jake over this nonsense with that girl." She seems completely unfazed by this revelation about her marriage, yet I'm so gob-smacked that she could've ever forgiven something so utterly destructive. The thought of her husband having full-on sex with someone else doesn't even seem to flicker across her face.

"What happened with her? The other woman?" I sigh at the thought of an affair. My heart wrenched for this woman I adore so very much.

"I'm sure Jake told you that it was Daniel's mother? I know Jake tells you everything, *Miele.* It's okay. Unfortunately, his relationship with his father is very strained because of it, and I know Jake believes that Giovanni had more affairs, but I know the truth. Giovanni cut that woman from his life and has never had another dealing with her." Her expression holds only conviction, and I believe her.

I nod rather than deny the fact, sure that she won't be upset about my prior knowledge. I nod to show I'm listening because I don't have any actual words to say; I nod to agree that Jake does believe his father is some womanizing man-whore and still despises him for it ... Ironically. Whatever she took my nod to mean, I hope I covered all bases.

"Jake was already becoming more than a handful. He'd gone off the rails, with that hot blood and impulsive nature of his meeting teen hormones and then a broken heart, and Giovanni was having a very difficult time reeling him in. Jacob has always been a very big handful to deal with." She smiles affectionately for a second, wrinkling her nose with a sigh. "He had a chip on his shoulder about trust and love, so finding out his father hurt me that way sort of sealed his fate. Jake has never trusted him since, and he's so stubborn, like his father, that he wouldn't listen to reason." Sylvana looks so sad and broken that her son and husband are still at odds over something she has long forgiven.

"Maybe if he knew the finer details of the affair and knew for sure his father never did it again ... or even why he did?" I offer, trying to find a way to help. Really wanting my beloved to find a way to mend bridges with his dad.

"I've told Jake all of this. He even knows that the women in his father's employment are blonde and blue-eyed because I made him promise never to have another woman who resembled me close to him again. Marianne Hunter was almost like a sister in looks. Daniel takes after his father with his fair hair and blue eyes, while his mother and I are almost like twins. Giovanni has a very specific type of woman he finds attractive." Sylvana pats my knee almost to emphasize the point with a hint of a smile.

This piece of information stuns me. I once took note of the sea of small blondes that Giovanni kept as his own personal staff and assumed he had a type. It never occurred to me that respect for his wife had prompted him to never employ any small brunettes with green eyes and Italian beauty like his wife. In his own way, Giovanni was showing his love for her, and Jake completely misunderstood it or chose to ignore it.

Stubborn ass of mine!

Jake is so publicly attentive and demonstrative that his father's seemingly apathetic attitude must be completely abhorrent to him. Chalk and cheese with apparently absolutely no understanding of one another in the slightest.

"But you found a way through it? You learned to love him again? Surely in time, Jake can also forgive him?" I'm now so completely in awe at the inner working of Giovanni and how his head must work. The man is a total enigma.

"Yes, we're so very much in love." Sylvana smiles dreamily, looking very much like me at that moment. A woman devoted and completely in love with a hard-headed Carrero. "He comes home every night regardless of the time it takes to get here. We made a promise never to drift apart again. I know he's not an easy man on the surface, but our private moments are filled with affection and love and a lot of sex." She grins naughtily again and winks my way, part of me laughs, and another wants to cringe at the thought.

"I can only hope that one day Jake finds a way to have some sort of relationship with him; where they are now is heartbreaking." Sylvana positively glows as she talks of her newfound relationship with her husband, but the obvious pain about her child's connection with him is evident in her tear-filled eyes. It renders me speechless. A mother's love torn with that of a wife's heart.

Jake has no clue about the depth of care between his parents. I guess he probably avoided any communication on the matter purely because his stubborn mind decided his father was a villain no matter what. He would be damned to believe otherwise. If only Jake knew of the love that still runs between them and that his father still cherishes and respects Sylvana above all others. Giovanni obviously has the same capabilities of love Jake has, that same deep heart, but they display it very differently.

I sigh hopelessly and gaze at Sylvana affectionately.

"Maybe becoming a father will make Jake re-evaluate things with Giovanni." I smile with a small offering of hope.

"Maybe." Sylvana smiles back with a twinkle in her eye and a tiny little glint of possibility, knowing deep down it is highly unlikely.

* * *

"Like this, *Tesoro*." Sylvana's soothing voice is close to my ear as she molds my hands in the dough bowl. "Gentle and delicate, so the Gnocchi stays fluffy." She smiles and pulls away as I continue the motion she's shown me. I have a strange surge of emotion at her tender touch and how she brushed my hair from my face with a smile. My affection for Sylvana is unlike my affection for Margo or even Wilma. There is something more, something deeper. I feel like I can come to her with anything, even cry over Jake, and she would embrace me with those loving, deep green eyes with maternal security and love me no matter what. I know she would never pick sides between us in our silly arguments, and when he hurt me, she had been so angry with him on my behalf.

Sophie is making a mess on the large table with a lot of flour and a lot of hand flapping and energetic slapping sounds but smiling widely as Sylvana moves to calm the frantic pounding of her small delicate hands in her heavy bowl. Sylvana's guiding touch is not rejected by the young girl either, and I smile to myself.

It's incredible knowing that her touch, so effortlessly, seems to break through the force fields that Sophie and I have; two kindred souls who used to recoil at human contact in any form, yet here we both were.

Leila is leaning over, watching Sylvana, working through a bowl of shelled nuts with a magazine in one hand, lazing in the kitchen after showing up for lunch. It's obvious she's bored, mulling over something, and she hasn't been her chatting sparkling self, but neither does she seem upset. Leila is one of those people who lets you know when she wants to talk and is very good at saying nothing at all if she doesn't. She seems happy to watch us learn to cook Italian food and revel in the atmosphere.

It's all so very relaxed, and I cast my mind to where I would be right now if Jake and I had never embraced what we were to each other ... probably decked out in tight tailored clothing and a set of stilettos on the sixty-fifth no doubt; stressed over contract briefs or mundane issues with financing and listening to Jake going off like a boar on the phone to some incompetent person. The thought doesn't bring me any sense of regret or loss. I don't even feel a spark of missing the offices, just the people, which is odd. For the first five years I worked there, I made no long-term bonds with anyone in that building until Jake. He somehow infected me from the word go and changed my entire outlook on the people I worked beside.

"I think you're maybe killing it, Sophie, dear." Sylvana chides gently, bringing my thoughts back to the present, and I can't help but watch with adoration as the two of them stand side by side, bringing the bowl of mess to order. There's something so complete about the whole scene at this very moment, watching someone who is truly maternal working with a child she treats as her own, giving healing to a girl who needs it with such a simple domestic task. Simply giving her time and patient attention in safety, trusting that no one will hurt her here or let anyone else for that matter, and as I watch the same love in Leila's eyes. I see now that maybe Sylvana did that for Leila too.

I know Leila came through the same channels as Sophie did as a child. Sylvana's charity is completely embroiled in taking children from abusive pasts. I realize I am among kindred spirits in this kitchen and have never thought about it before. I'm not the only one with scars and memories that haunt my dreams sometimes. I'm in the fold of two other beautiful young women who have their own demons and came out the other side happier and hopeful because they let people in again and learned to trust. They both sit here now, mere reflections of who they once were, smiles and genuine laughter in the knowledge they found a better, safer loving place. I'm the outcast I used to be. I'm one of them.

The warmth of the kitchen and the peaceful, serene atmosphere. This is what I need. This is what I've missed out on my entire life; a mother, a real loving maternal mother who cared enough to show her children how to heal, cook, how to improve themselves, and it doesn't matter that she isn't related by blood. She somehow changed the lives of at least two of us, and her son has done the same for me.

I'm happy here with her and with him because I needed this somehow in my life. I needed that nurturing love and guidance to show me how to be nurturing and kind to myself so I could become whole again. Learning how to let others have a little piece of my heart. Jake found that little scared Emma locked down tight in the corner of that terrifying dark room, and he slid his arms around her softly, told her it was okay to trust him, to let him save her from the dark recesses of her life and lead her out to the light. To let him protect her, and he did, still does, and always will; in a way that I know he learned from her ... Sylvana, the woman who, without realizing it, nurtured the man of my dreams into a replica of herself.

With a tear in my eye, I watch the smiling happy faces in front of me, absorbed in such a simple task, aglow with life and genuine contentment. Emotion coursing through me for this family. Even if we're not all related by blood, that's what we are. Jake isn't just giving me a family by loving me and having a child. He's sharing his entire family with me, showing me I'm so effortlessly accepted. They are all my family too.

My heart expands achingly at the thought. This kind of unconditional love that so many take for granted, and here it is, a gift being given to me so selflessly. They have no idea what it means.

I want this kind of purpose. This kind of touch on the world. I want to find others like me instead of hiding from life and locking myself away, take them by the hand and draw them to the light, and show them their world doesn't need to be so cold and alone. I want to make Jake proud and do to others what he's done for me. He gave me courage and hope. He taught me to look at the person I have become and not the person I was cowering behind in the darkness. He taught me to let people in.

I want to be like her, Sylvana Carrero, a genuine heart that reaches in and pulls out the parts of children they've hidden away for fear of being hurt again. Smothering them with a mother's love and gentle touch. I want to be like Jake, refusing to see only the walls we put up, looking beyond at someone worth coaxing out.

Being strong enough to bypass all the barriers, shields, and anger to find that soul inside.

I saved Sophie from a life of pain. At that moment in Chicago, it was the first time I felt worthwhile in my existence. In some small way, being her protector and drawing her away to a better life was my one defining moment, and I want it again. I want to see more Sophies and more Leilas shining in the world, pushing through from the darkness, finding their way into kitchens like Sylvana's and the lives of parents like the Huntsbergers.

For too long, I've denied my past and let it consume me, ashamed and blaming myself for what was done to me. But I've realized that true release from the memories came when I let them out and shared them with Jake, shared them with someone capable of loving me without seeing any blame or disgust in what I had to tell him, and now, I want to do that for others too. I want to be a better person than the empty shell that existed for so long. I want to be the person who saves myself and continues to do so, now they have shown me the way.

I gaze down at my stomach and run a protective hand across it softly. I want to be someone nurturing and warm, whose children will be proud of them, someone children will run to and embrace in the knowledge that I'll always keep them safe and always put them first no matter what. I'll never let anyone, not even Jake, come between my children and me or inflict any pain on them in any way.

* * *

"God, I missed you." Jake leans in and kisses me passionately, our mouths connecting sensually. He makes sure I know exactly how much he's missed me in one breathless embrace, lingering momentarily, and runs a hand across my face before loosening his tie and pulling it off. I can't help but giggle and sag into that strong embrace weakly. He's just arrived home and went straight to our bedroom, skipping up here like a child to see me.

Finally putting me down, he slides his jacket off and throws it on the end of the bed. I'm lounging, watching him in adoration, magazines strewn, and TV on low in the late evening, just so glad to have him with me again.

He's been gone three whole days; work was demanding today, and his texts informed me there'd been three back-to-back meetings he needed to get out of the way before coming home. He has so much going on, and a little part of me feels guilty that I'm not helping anymore, in fact, I have no clue about any of the ventures he is overseeing nowadays.

It feels like we haven't seen each other in weeks, and devouring that face and body with my eyes makes my heart swell to enormous proportions.

God, I love him so much.

He strips off, hauling on a T-shirt, and sweats quickly as I watch in complete admiration. His tantalizing body still being held aloft from me. I need to put my seduction plan into high gear soon, but I have other plans right now. As much as I ache for him, I must follow through on what I decided, and he looks tired enough to be less of a stubborn boy tonight. He seems exhausted for once and ripe for a little Emma cajoling.

I slide off the bed in my sexy nightdress, padding over to the side unit and picking up the cream envelope, turning to him and holding it out delicately with a soft smile.

"Here." I try for a gentle tone, watching him closely for signs of how this may go. Jake can be unpredictable at the best of times, and when it's something like this, he can be very prickly.

"What's this?" He takes it warily, a small frown crossing that gorgeous face as he comes close, and leans in, kissing my temple, a hand running down my throat tenderly. I wait until he returns to the envelope in his hand, watching him turn it over to open, my stomach tightens with nerves, but I stand my ground and clench my hands to give myself courage. I need to do this if I want to carry out my plans.

"My resignation from the Carrero Corporation," I state calmly and slowly. Jake's eyes shoot up to mine with a little look of hurt that instantly pains me, but I remain impassive. He opens his mouth with a severely intimidating glare, and I hold up my hands quickly, my nerves most definitely skyrocketing at his obvious instant reaction.

"Listen, before exploding ... Let me talk," I blurt rapidly, hoping to God he's missed me enough to have more than a little patience over this. He closes his mouth and crosses his muscular arms over his chest in an almost menacing way, a very unamused expression on that face that goads me to carry on.

The unopened letter is still in his fingers in one hand. He isn't going to open it until he hears me out. I know him. He thinks he will rip it up if he doesn't like my explanation and that I can forget everything. I grit my teeth to find my inner steel. Jake doesn't scare me in the slightest anymore, these bad moods of his are mostly just noise and temper, and if I'm going to be married to him for a lifetime, then I'm going to have to learn to hold my own when Mr. Dominant. comes into play.

Undeterred, I lean on tiptoes, kissing him softly and tenderly on the mouth to show him that I am not doing this out of malice. He stays stock still. His eyes burning into me with no hint of amusement at all. He's probably over-analyzing every reason for me doing this and getting it all wrong. I walk to the bed and sit down, deliberately making a show of being calm, in control, and hopefully a little bit sexy. I'm not against showing a lot of leg and cleavage to get my grumpy bear distracted.

Use your female prowess to tame that man, Emma.

"I don't want to go back. That part of me is done, Jake. The girl I was, her focus on that job ... It's all in the past. The person I was, used her job to avoid any real emotion, any real life, to avoid relationships with people. There's nothing for me there anymore except you, and I have you here." I blink up at him innocently, my voice full of conviction.

He's watching me, a million emotions crossing his face, but he's waiting for me to finish now that I'm on a roll. He's holding his temper and desire to demand for once in his life, and I have to say I am a little impressed with his newfound willpower.

"I want to do something that means something to me. Something more fulfilling, where I can make a physical difference.

Something that lets me be this version of who I am and gives me the flexibility to be a mother and a wife. This version of me that you keep encouraging to come out, this version you love." I look up at him pointedly and adoringly, a small hint of a smile his way.

Yup, hit him emotionally and wear him down.

Jake sighs, his look of aggression dissipating fast, and walks toward me. His hand trails my hair, and he scoops down to kiss me solidly, a passionate kiss that knocks the breath out of me with much more steam than his first. When he leans back up, he appraises me closely. His whole demeanor softens as he thinks through what I've said.

"There's too many smarts in this beautiful little head to ever be fulfilled as just a wife and mother, Emma. You're a tough cookie. Whatever you want to pursue, you have my backup every step of the way. I just want you to be happy. I'll move mountains to help you achieve it." He sits beside me on the bed, his arm coming around my shoulders, pulling me close to him, and smiling at me in a completely infatuated way.

I'm shocked at how easy this was. He didn't even try to argue a point against it.

Who are you, and where is Jake Carrero?

Maybe Jake's come to the realization too, that going back to how it was just isn't going to be an option for me, for us. Jake is happier not bringing work between us, knowing the stress and arguments it could cause again. His taking over work and leaving me alone is almost a sign that, deep down, he doesn't want me to go back down that path either.

He's taken a back seat compared to how he used to work, allowing Margo and her team to do our jobs. I know she now has six people under her control, all taking various positions and responsibilities, allowing Jake to wander in and out freely and deal with only the most important things. Jake's head is no longer embroiled in the Carrero Corporation. It's here with me, most of the time, and our future family. He engineered his work routine to dissipate as it gets closer to the baby coming, and I know he fully intends to stay put and go nowhere in the last month of my pregnancy or the first six months of our baby's life. That's why he spends so much time sorting and organizing things in Manhattan. There would be no real place for me in that role, even if he wanted there to be.

"I want to do this on my own, Jake, whatever it is. I don't want you throwing money at me in a bid to make it happen for me. I don't need your money." I gaze up at that expressive face and sense the protest from the slight tension in his jawline. He shifts around to face me, bringing a knee between us on the bed, letting me go so he can sit full-on and lock eyes. Mr. Let's talk business. Mode.

"Emma, you need to do something for me if I'm to accept this." He holds up the letter and throws it onto the bed carelessly. He doesn't even look as he does it, just eyes on me.

"What?" I'm waiting for the negotiator and manipulator to move in, but he sighs instead. He has a look on his face that shows no fight at all, just my beautiful man and so much love shining back at me.

"Accept that the money is a part of who I am. It's what I've always known, how I was raised. It influenced my lifestyle, character, and abilities and seeped into every part of the person you love. I never knew any different and probably never will, so when you constantly push it away, you're pushing away a part of me. I've always known that money was never something you pursued, but you need to accept that it will always be a part of our lives and our kids' lives too. I can accept every part of you, Emma, scars and all, so you need to accept this part of me and maybe even enjoy it a little. I worked hard to make my own money away from my father. Not a penny I have has come from him since I was twenty-one years old. I wanted it that way, and now I want you to revel in it a little too." He looks at me so seriously that I find myself shifting closer to him, so I can feel our bodies touching for comfort. I slide my hand into his on his lap, entangling our fingers.

I regard him thoughtfully, absorbing everything he's saying, and I myself sag a little with the realization that he's right. I fell in love with that high-profile, rich CEO, his expensive clothes, suave cocky attitude, and overbearing demeanor. Truth be told, a part of me always liked his lifestyle because it did make him so much more powerful and sexy and had women swooning at his feet. I've had some seriously combusting panties for his car anyway, and it all somehow collided together to make the man sitting in front of me. As much as I always knew I would have him without it all, I can't deny he probably wouldn't be the same person if he'd had a different path in life.

Jake's confidence and authority come from this lifestyle. His public persona is molded from a life in the limelight. His attention to his body and attire has become second nature, looking hot all the time to meet the demands of the media.

His heart and soul didn't stem from wealth, but everything else around his personality has been molded by it, even his spoiled child attitude and inability to back down. He grew up never wanting anything and never having to wait or earn what he wanted in his younger life. He has a spoiled little boy spark inside of him because of all that, which created his impulsive nature.

I must accept that turning down his money because of some stupid moral pride is ridiculous. I sigh, knowing that if he were just a man with a normal bank balance, I would accept his financial support, so this is no different.

I need to get off my moral high ground and accept that I want to marry a billionaire with a default setting of generosity. I need to get used to it or leave him. If credit cards, overindulgent gifts, and trips are part of what Jake is offering me, then I'd better suck it up and stop being so goddamn stupid.

"I'll try." I smile, knowing I've already backed down, but he doesn't need to know that. Some fun is always to be had, turning Jake down occasionally. I can't let him get away with thinking $10,000 dresses thrown my way should ever be normal. I tingle as his hands slide up my arms to rest on my shoulders.

"Good. Because I brought you home a beautiful and slightly expensive dress to take you out to dinner tomorrow night, I would be gutted if I had to take it back."

Really? A dress! After what I was just thinking? He never changes ...

"If you're using the word expensive, then I don't even want to know how much it cost, Jake." I sigh with complete deflation. Jake is someone who considers a couple of thousand dollars as pocket change. Expensive to him makes my head ache.

This will be much harder to get used to than I thought. For a start, I already own way too many of Jake's *expensive* dresses. I swear he has some sort of compulsion in buying me one almost weekly.

Chapter 15

The dress is spectacular, as are the shoes he bought with it. Like a good little girl, I don't attempt any rejection when he brings the boxes in from the car with the sweetest expression on his face. He looks almost boyish and a little excited.

Jake's gone all out, bringing me home a complete outfit. I'm standing in a full-length, dark plum, figure-hugging dress studded with sheer Swarovski crystals across its full-length and fuller skirt. My shoulders are exposed from its crisscross bodice style, ending in low cap sleeves off the shoulder, and my cleavage is almost bursting forth. Lately, my bust has gotten a little larger, and I'm sure Jake won't mind one bit. My feet are encased in low-heeled satin plum shoes because since I found out I was pregnant, he refused to let me wear my sexy heels, which is another argument still not done with, and then, of course, there's the underwear. Sexy underwear; I am glad to see he at least thinks about sex, even if he's not giving it to me.

He's been very mysterious about the dinner plans all day and now trussed up like a red-carpet movie star, I'm starting to wonder why we need to be so formal. Jake's in a tux of all things, but I don't remember any mention of any sort of event or dance. Jake avoids tuxedos like the plague if he can help it.

* * *

The restaurant is gorgeous, as is the appearance of Sylvana on Giovanni's arm and Arrick with Sophie in tow, looking sweetly cute together; even Leila is with us as we all walk to the pre-booked table near the back of the grand room. I assume this may be related to the Carrero Corporation, but it's odd that Jake would be elusive about the details.

This place exudes money, every table delicately set with lily centerpieces and crisp white tablecloths under a ceiling of grand chandeliers and fairy light nets. The color scheme is opulent reds, mauves, and a lot of gold, with sparkling crystals everywhere. There are tables and tables of richly dressed diners with an orchestra playing soft music and a booth set up for a DJ in another corner. The floor in the middle is a dance floor; there must be some dancing or entertainment after dinner.

The old me would've felt so out of her depth in a place like this, even as Jake's PA, but I walk with my head held high on the arm of the most gorgeous man in here, with the handsome Carrero family, and I can't help but feel proud. I feel like I belong with them and am not out of place in the dress Jake chose for me. It isn't Donna's style of clothing to choose for me, so I'm sure Jake has chosen this himself, which is more than a little sweet. He always had good taste for a man.

When we're shown to our table, I realize there are more familiar faces from Carrero Corp dotted around. I spot Margo with her husband waving at me. I flush as an inner panic starts to creep up. I swear there's a red head of hair behind her that could possibly be Wilma. Even if this is a Carrero thing or some charity event, we're so far outside Manhattan that I wouldn't expect to see them here.

Why are we surrounded by people that shouldn't be here in the Hamptons?

I glance at Jake and spot veiled nervousness hinting across his face that he's so desperately trying to hide and that his sculpted body seems a little too rigid in his tux, even for him. Jake is never nervous at events, and a sickening lurch connects the dots almost instantly.

Out of the corner of my eye, I catch a couple trying to usher their way out of sight through the shadows and realize it's Sarah and Marcus. They're trying to hide from me, and I freeze.

Oh, my God. Sarah and Marcus? They wouldn't be at a Carrero event.

Oh, shit ... Oh shit!

I know what he's doing. It hits me like a lightning bolt out of the dark with rather painful ferocity. He bought me a pretty dress he chose by himself and assembled everyone in one of the most beautiful restaurants in this town. He's gathered together people I know, people that matter to him and me regardless of the costs. He has my best friend trying to hide before she lets the cat out of the bag, and I'm sure if I check the sea of faces, I'll recognize more and more people.

I catch sight of Daniel moving in from the side under cover of shadow, and he slides into a seat beside Margo, throwing her a smile, and I suddenly feel sick and breathless. Daniel most definitely doesn't show face at corporate things. He never has. He always says it's not his thing, and bores him to tears.

Warning bells are going off inside my head, and that flight or fight impulse has my feet itching to head for the nearest exit. I tighten my grip on Jake's arm for security and a sense of calm. My heart is pounding erratically through my chest, and my palms are clammy, my body is turning cold with fear. He covers my hand with his, a grounding sensation that I'm aching for, but I'm still in panic mode and can almost feel the tension radiating from him. That's why his touch isn't working right now because Jake's more scared than I am, and he's transferring it rather than taking mine away. My strong, calm, and in-control Carrero is now adjusting his collar as though it's choking him and tilting his neck from side to side in a massive show of uncharacteristic nerves.

Fuck!

"Are you okay?" He looks completely terrified as his eyes meet mine. His beautiful gorgeous face looking about fifteen years old and completely out of his depths. I swallow hard, willing him just to stop, stop whatever his head has planned, and whatever I think. The last thing I need is for him to look so goddamn out of his depth, making me feel like I'm suffocating.

Don't hurt him, Emma. Don't do this to him after everything. Just look at him and breathe. Steady breaths, and remember how much you love him.

The fear gripping me holds at his eye contact, and I find the inner courage to slowly slide it further down inside me, gripping with fingernails to keep control. I hold still, trying not to portray my feelings on my face in case he sees it, and paste a smile on my mouth, loosening my death grip on his arm.

I can't ruin this for him. I can't hurt him again after everything we've been through. I just need to pretend I don't know and pray I don't freak out when he finally gets on one knee.

"Yeah, just a little overwhelmed with all this grandeur." I smile, maintaining a steady voice with a stoic effort, and he relaxes a little. I draw on all my old *PA Emma* abilities to be emotionless, even under extreme pressure. He's studying me a little too closely, so I stretch up and kiss him quickly, making him kiss me properly and deeply, trying to remove any doubts about what I know. It seems to do the trick, and he relaxes a little, all flickers of question smoothing from that beautiful brow and back to just a rather bad case of nerves. I squeeze his arm to calm him and, really, to calm myself ... a lot.

Count to ten, and breathe. Focus on Jake, on just him, and how much he loves you.

When we're shown to our table, Jake suddenly seems listless, and his fidgeting demeanor hits full force, moving his glass from hand to hand and back to the table, avoiding eye contact when he has me seated beside him. He tenses and keeps looking out of the huge windows behind us as though checking for something. He impulsively picks up the drink they just laid beside him and downs it in one go, which is never a good sign or move for him. His hands raking through that immaculate hair, trying to sit still. He is all over the place and unraveling in front of me; this is not the version of him I have ever known. Jake is always so effortlessly in control publicly, so his behavior makes me even more uptight.

He smiles at me, but I know it's pasted on and

disingenuous. His eyes flicker to the side until he spots something, then excuses himself with a peck on my cheek in a hurried fashion. I watch as he almost drags Daniel out of his seat in passing, they disappear through a door near the side exit, which takes you further into this grand hotel restaurant. Leaving me alone only makes me a hundred times worse.

My heart is pounding through my chest. The people around me are chatting and smiling my way, even Sylvana is trying to draw me into a conversation, but my eyes are scouring the room for Sarah. She's obviously been told to stay out of sight until the big moment. I have no idea what to do with myself. I don't even know if I'm angry at what he's doing so publicly or if I want it this way, and I'm just terrified. I can't even voice my fear because I'm not supposed to know what this is. I can only sit here, curling up the napkin in front of me, counting as I breathe, trying to quell the panic that has every nerve ending on high alert.

I have no clue how to feel or why I even feel this way. All the old inner Emma instincts are to run and hide, but the new Emma is holding me in my seat, all battling inside of my head with fears and reasoning, weighing up pros and cons, making my head ache.

Shit, crap, fuck. Breathe. Breathe. I can do this. I already said yes. I asked him! This is just Jake needing to do it his way and give me a ring. You love him. Let it go. Let him take control in this, and trust him. Trust him, Emma. Trust that he'll always make you happy.

I find Giovanni's eyes on me across the table. He's watching me with a slight smirking expression, those dark, terrifying eyes unmoving as I meet his. He slowly lifts his tumbler of gin and raises it toward me, like a little toast, a hint of a smile on his face, and then in an instant, it's gone. He turns to his wife and places a kiss on her cheek, leaving me completely dumbfounded.

What was that?

A light flush of color creeps up Sylvana's face as he leans in to whisper in her ear, and her blush intensifies as she looks down at her hands. I'm almost shocked to see such an intimate private moment so publicly shown by him, given that I know he loathes public affection. I start to watch a little too intensely, distracting myself from my inner panic, as she slides a hand from the table down and across his flat stomach. It's so discreet and slow, disappearing out of sight, and I can only imagine her hand in his lap. I look away quickly, almost embarrassed.

Holy crap. Sexless marriage? I think not! Jake has no clue that his parents are still having sex and naughty sex, by the looks of it. I cringe in disgust when I realize Jake takes after his father in more ways than he knows. Ughhh.

Jake has the demonstrative affection of his mother and the public loving nature. But his kinky naughty side is from his father. I wonder, seeing it now, if that cool demeanor and uncaring attitude hides a man with a lot more going on in his heart than anyone ever sees, and it dawns on me. I'm more like Giovanni than Jake is!

I have the same outwardly cool persona, a reserved side with a cool demeanor, and Jake is Sylvana. Jake has greatly brought me out of myself, but he's still the one who always initiates public displays of affection like hand-holding and kissing. I am happy to be pulled along by him, but if he'd been like his father, I would've been okay with that too, because I'm that way.

I clear my throat and down the glass of fresh fruit juice I've been served, pushing all thoughts of what my in-laws to be are doing under the table, trying to cast it very far away from my mind. Sylvana feigns innocence, but her hand hasn't reappeared, and Giovanni looks slightly smug now.

Ewwww.

I notice Leila wandering around like a maniac across the currently empty dance floor. She doesn't look so calm and controlled now, more of the aggressive and pissed variety in her short black dress, she grabs a random man in the most aggressive manner as he approaches her.

What the hell?

The man isn't very tall, around five-foot-eight at most, and sort of stocky with dark brown hair and brown eyes. Leila is hauling him this way, like a dominatrix leading a gimp, and as they approach, I realize this must be Kurt. The delicate features and adoring way he's gazing at her as she bullies him toward our table says it all. The guy has smitten written all over him and is in no way even attempting to battle down the wild Leila peeking out.

So not good for her at all.

She orders him to sit down icily, taking the seat next to his and slumps in her chair, downing three drinks in a row in the most alarming way. He tries to talk to her and she totally blanks him, far too intent on waving down the passing waitress for another drink by holding her empty one in the air. I'm too far across the table to warn her to slow down or throw her any kind of message, and I have no clue why she's trying to get so drunk so quickly. At least they've removed my focus from the near-overwhelming panic attack I was close to.

The waitress is rambling on in my ear about the courses and specials. I'm not even sure if she's asking me about ordering food or talking to someone else as I home in on the reappearance of Jake across the room. I'm always drawn to that masculine sexiness whenever he enters a room, like a moth to a flame. But then I am pretty sure about a dozen other female sets of eyes do the same thing.

Jake is here, minus Daniel, and looks on edge. His whole manner is uptight, his hair is a little messy, the tell-tale sign he's been running his hand through it, and his jacket has been unbuttoned with his tie loosened. He's disheveled, to say the least, and not the immaculate guy who was present a couple of minutes ago. He looks a lot like the Jake, who came home and told me he'd hurt me, and my heart tightens in response.

He would never do anything like that again. Trust him.

Sylvana snaps around at his approach guiltily and immediately jumps up to meet him. She's saying something under her breath, fixing his bow tie and jacket hurriedly. His hands go to his hair to calm it down, suggesting she's pointed out that he looks a little less groomed than before, and I can't help but watch the expression on his face as he does what he's told to, with zero arguments. He's completely out of his depth and nothing like the Jake Carrero I know and love. His eyes are raking in the faces of the people around the room as though taking some mental checklist.

My stomach tightens, and my hands get clammy again. Only one thing could make Jake this scared out of his mind even his appearance is something he's oblivious of. His behavior is all I need to see to know I'm right about what he has planned.

Fuck. He's really going to do this, isn't he? He's going to do this, and they all know! It's why They're all here and why she's fussing over his clothes. It's not that I don't want it. It's just so public and so ... Oh my God! It hits me suddenly ...

Fireworks and a floor show!

His words. His promise. He really is going to do this after all.

Tonight.

Here!

My insides lurch up in a terrifying need to throw up. I stare down at my cold, trembling, clammy hands and take steady, long, low, and calm breaths. Deliberately holding them longer and counting them out.

I won't run. I won't freak. I can do this.

I have hurt him so many times, and it always ended up hurting me as well. I need to relax and trust him on this, go with the flow just like he would. Don't ruin something so obviously special.

I glance up as he moves toward me, catching his eyes instantly, and somehow that small contact changes his demeanor. He grounds me the way he always seems to. Those endless eyes and his handsome face bringing me out of my own head. I seem to be calming him too, and he's returning the favor. If we keep looking at one another, then maybe I can get through this without turning into a crazy loon who high-tails it out of the door in a ridiculously long dress.

I love him. He's all I need. His heart is just as fragile as mine, don't bruise it, Emma.

"Dance with me?" he asks, holding out a trembling hand as he gets to my side. Adoringly, I smile at him and brace for what is about to happen, resigning to let him take the lead. I take one last steadying breath to push it down as far as possible and try to find my inner bravery.

You won't fuck this up, Emma.

Jake is nervous, and he's making me even more so. He moves against me on the dance floor as the orchestra plays a smooth ballad, soft and romantic, and others join us on the floor. His eyes are on mine, and even though he's smiling, I can feel his heart beating at a hundred miles an hour through his chest. The tension radiating from him is alarming. Even locking eyes is starting to fail as his inner emotions begin to get the better of him, and suddenly I don't want to let him fall apart. I want to calm him down, so he can do this for us.

"I love you." I smile at him and lay my head against his chest, trying to soothe him without giving the game away. I hope that I radiate some reassurance that I'm here with him, that I'm not running, and that there is no doubt about my answer. I always knew what my answer would be from the moment I figured this out. It was never about saying no to him because I never would.

"I love you, baby ... maybe too much." He smiles at me, and this time as I tilt my face back up to him, I can see it's genuine. I notice a small squaring of his jaw, reminding me that he's still coiled up like a spring about to erupt.

I catch sight of the outer patio doors in the grand room being opened by waiting staff and lift my head to look, slightly confused. It's not an overly warm night, and it's not nearly warm enough to open every door wide this way.

Jake takes a loud breath slowly, so close to my ear, and I face back up at him questioningly. His body is hitting an all-time high tension, and my heart starts hammering again, knowing it's close. He blows it out over the top of my head and avoids my gaze.

Breathe ... Don't freak out.

I stare up at that handsome face to ground myself once more. His eyes are focused on the orchestra, and he's so tense he's almost rigid. Our dancing has slowed to a partial halt, and the couples around us seem to be moving away as though they've been given some signal that they should do so. I'm not sure that I like the fact we seem to be in the center of the room with a widening gap happening all around us, so very public among a sea of faces. I just need to keep reminding myself, whose strong arms are around me, that he will always keep me safe.

Jake has a silent trance-like look on his face, the same one as the day we found out I was pregnant, and suddenly I don't feel so brave anymore. Even in his arms, I'm submerged in the icy coldness of fear engulfing me. He's not with me right now, his head elsewhere, and I'm left adrift.

Looking around in a panic, I realize people are staring this way, terror is rising inside me, and hysteria grips hold until it's like I'm almost choking. My body starts to tense with the first signs of an all-out panic attack. I'm starting to freak out, the tension starting in my toes, sliding up my body slowly in a horrible, sickening cold wave that I know will black out my mind and devour me. My feet are ready to run far, far, away from something terrifying, and I have no control.

And then I hear it.

The beautiful words of the singer floating our way across the crowded room. These words that will be ingrained in my brain for a lifetime. It completely stills me, like a calming balm, and somehow, he's already figured out the one thing to halt my fear, focusing me back on him. His arms come around me gently, and he pulls my chin to face him with one hand. I can feel him begin to calm too, as our eyes meet again, and he mouths along with the song, swaying me gently to dance with me in his embrace.

"Say you love me...."

The woman sings the song that makes my heart break wide open, and, at this moment, I forget about everything else. Every person, every terrifying feeling, and anything that isn't him. Emotions flood me and push every single fear away, my stomach aching, and my heart fills with love.

This song started it all between us, the real relationship and the beginning of feeling his love for me. The one he sent me across a crowded dance floor in an opulent setting, much like this one, and I suddenly get it.

He's re-enacting that dance floor, wiping out the memory of me running from him, and he's using the same song to ask me the same thing, only this time, he wants to know if I'll be his forever. He's offering me himself the way he did that night, a chance to clear everything that has happened between us since that dance and start again. To forget about her and hurting me and everything else. To let him love me the way he promised he would.

Jake, you're killing me with your ability to sweep me off my feet.

Tears fill my eyes while my soul is aching, watching him sing to me with that beautiful husky rock star voice. I gaze up at him with complete adoration. It seems like hours lost in those green eyes and that face, dampness hitting my skin as he brushes my cheek with his thumb and moves me slightly in his arms. He moves further away again, holding me at arm's length but never breaking eye contact, and slides down to one knee mid-song.

I catch the sob in my throat as it hits me deep in my chest, and I hold onto his shoulder when the urge to crumble overtakes me, almost turning my body to mush. I steady myself, focusing on the way he's looking at me so intensely. Those emerald eyes hold me so readily in their strong gaze, grounding me in the way only he can, despite everything around us, bringing my focus to what is happening between us.

I forget about everyone, the faces, the sea of people, even the noise, and I see only him. Always ... only him.

The sounds of fireworks echo from an outside set of a chorus of 'oohs and aahs' from other diners, but I don't turn to look. I'm caught with him in his gaze, he has me captured, and I'm completely mesmerized. All fear, panic, and doubt fluttered away on the breeze as though it was never there, locked together, just the two of us. So, when he opens a box containing the most beautiful delicate ring I've ever seen, my hand flies to my mouth, and I let the tears fall freely. No longer ashamed of people seeing my vulnerability or emotions.

"Marry me, Emma? Make me the luckiest guy that ever lived. I'm yours. Always yours, and I'll spend a lifetime worshiping and cherishing every single part of you, *Bambina* ... You're my heart, baby." Jake holds the box out toward me. His hands are trembling, and his gaze is focused on my face as I take deep, calming breaths to find my voice. Completely overwhelmed with emotion and love for him, with the perfection of what he has done for me.

This cocky CEO who infiltrated my heart every second of every day since the moment I laid eyes on him, and here he is, kneeling in front of me, in front of everyone in the world who matters to the both of us, asking me to trust him. Giving himself to me fully, not caring about being on his knees before a woman, and wholeheartedly letting me take the lead. Hanging up his Casanova crown rather spectacularly.

"Yes, Jake. Yes!" I cry silently, and my hand shakes as he slides that cool piece of metal and sparkle onto my finger. He is every bit as overwhelmed as me, and the happiness all over his face is radiant. I'm swept up in the arms of the strongest, sexiest man I have ever met, and when his mouth comes crashing to mine in a toe-curling assault of love, I know I am completely and hopelessly lost to him for an eternity.

Chapter 16

The song choice from me to Jake plays across the floor, surrounding us as we sway. We're still wrapped up in each other, our eyes focused intently. The swell of happiness between us is infectious, and I don't think either of us has stopped smiling since his dance-floor proposal an hour ago. I truly know joy beyond all bounds. I wanted to reply to his song. After all, it was our tradition, and in a grand fashion to match his, the DJ was more than happy to oblige when the orchestra finally took their leave.

Ella Henderson's "Yours" plays beautifully across the room, telling him everything I want to say right now.

He sways me around the dance floor for the hundredth time, wrapped in his arms and smiling like crazy. Feeling like I could die from contentment. People congratulated us the whole way through the meal, and neither of us has managed to stop touching the other, smiling brightly with only eyes for each other. I can't stop glancing at my hand over his wide shoulder to the understated, delicate diamond ring, showing me he'd thought about what I would like. Non-showy, vintage, and perfectly me. He chose something I would've chosen for myself, elegant and meaningful, rather than a display of wealth. Jake knows me better than I think he gives himself credit for.

Sarah appeared and enveloped me in kisses and tears as soon as

I had that ring on my finger. She's now swaying with Marcus, feet away on the floor, looking merry, drunk, and very much like a girl in love. Marcus looks quite groomed and a little different, eyes aglow with infatuation for Sarah, evident on the face of a man I've never warmed to. Maybe I've always been too harsh on him, seeing them together with new eyes, the love evident between them, and the way they seem to fit so effortlessly together, like Jake and I do, but in their own way.

I can't help but look back at the man of my dreams and take in every part of that face. Someone has his attention to the left of me, and he's smiling and answering with an amused, furrowed brow. His low sultry voice always makes my blood pump faster. His arms around my waist tightly, mine around his neck, bow tie now undone and hanging loose at each side of his collar. The jacket is gone, and his shirt is open at the top. He looks exactly like he should, sexually casual and a little rough around the edges, yet confidently tailored to perfection even when his tie is discarded. The boyish bad boy Carrero always dominates every part of him, and it's exactly who I always want him to be.

The night is a blur of smiles, giddiness, and floaty memories of people I know hugging me and lots of kissing. Jake has kissed my lipstick off until my cheeks are permanently blushed and my mouth puffy. Yet that doesn't seem to stave off the craving to kiss me more, not that I'm complaining. Kissing Jake is my all-time favorite thing in the world. That seductive mouth locked onto mine, bringing our hearts together as one. No one makes me feel like he does with something so simple as a gentle brush of lips. Just his proximity to me, eyes locked and noses touching, makes every part of me surrender to his will.

Jake stops talking to whoever has his attention and turns back to give it all to me; another kiss and soft grazing of noses make my body tingle for him. He knows no bounds when it comes to being tender and gentle with me, and I love that it's a part of him reserved only for our unborn child and me. The side of him that the world never sees and probably couldn't associate with the 'Playboy Carrero Casanova' public figure that women still drool over. He was never that way with his endless meaningless women, never so touchy and adoring with them at all, and it only highlights what I mean to him.

"You thought I was going to say no, didn't you? Even though we were technically engaged." I sway with him, now completely relaxed, with so much heart swelling love. Moving to the music emphasizes his powerful body, and he positions my feet to stand on the shoes of his toes so he can dance me around, reaching my lips a little better. I feel

like a child, but with his arms encircling me tightly, I don't want to be anywhere else. He always has a way of making me feel protected and cared for, even if it's just propping sunglasses on my face in bright light or taking off my shoes in the car home after a dance, or swirling me around on his feet so I can stand and relax as he takes control of my movements.

"The thought crossed my mind about a million times once we got here. I'm not going to lie; I started to panic that I was going about this the wrong way, *Bambina*." He grimaces at the memory and scoops down to kiss me again. His face is one of confidence, showing no hint of doubt now. Cameras flash nearby, but Jake is oblivious to the paparazzi's attention. I, on the other hand, am still adjusting.

"I love you, Mr. Carrero. This was beyond perfect." I smile lovingly.

The fireworks display lasted forty-five minutes and were beyond spectacular. After the emotion of the moment calmed down, we crowded outside in droves and saw the last half of the most magnificent fireworks display ever. Jake draped his jacket around me and held me in his arms for warmth while we watched in awed silence. He certainly supplied, as promised, 'Fireworks and a floor show,' and in true Jake Carrero style, it was go big or go home.

He smiles back.

"Mrs. Carrero ... Emma Carrero. God, I love how that sounds." He moves his forehead to mine and continues to drive our feet in time to the ballad. "I can't imagine anything more perfect than this." He brings a hand to my face and trails his fingertips across my bottom lip, oblivious to the flashes of cameras nearby going off repeatedly. Unfortunately, the press appeared at some point. I'm not sure if they caught the moment he proposed, but they were here for the fireworks and seem to like the tender moments we were having a little too much.

We're moving around, lost in each other's eyes, when we become aware of a commotion behind us; raised voices and glass smashing. I turn to see what's going on, and I'm completely unsurprised to see it coming from Daniel and Leila off to one side of the floor amid a group of gaping bystanders ...

"Why are you here with him?" Daniel has Leila by the wrist, and she's struggling to wrench it free; fiery fury latched onto fiery fury. Daniel looks poised and ready to beat someone with a death glare across that handsome face. His grip on Leila only accentuates how muscular he is.

I never really notice it when he's with Jake since Jake is much broader. He is equally tall, with sandy blonde hair and piercing blue eyes, and right now, he's terrifying; aggression rippling through him the same way it seems to ignite Jake. I wouldn't want to get on the wrong side of them as a pair.

"Shit," Jake mutters and lets me go, lifting me from his shoes and pulling me with him. He heads their way in a rather brisk fashion.

"It's nothing to do with you who I date." Leila spits back, eyes flaring at him from her much smaller height, arm wrenching and attempting to kick him with her killer pointed heels, just as Jake intervenes.

"Daniel, take this outside. Come on. It's too public here, and the press is lurking because of my engagement." Jake nods toward the men mulling around with cameras, aiming this way. Jake keeps my hand in his and draws me closer to shield the pair from probing lenses. Daniel looks around as though realizing where we are, his face softens a little, and I can't help but feel a twinge of heartache at the utter devastation on his face. Kurt is lurking nearby, but even I can tell he knows he's no match for Daniel Hunter, not in the slightest; that dominant alpha male thing that Jake exudes is a Hunter trait too.

Leila snatches her hand away and turns to Jake imploringly, raising her hands in complete frustration.

"There's nothing to take outside ... I'm. Not. Interested!" She throws her hands on her hips in defiance, but Daniel scoops her up in his arms in a flash, ignoring any attempts from her to refuse him, and turns on his heel to march out toward the pitch-black gardens with a look of sheer rage. There's a flash of cameras, and Jake grimaces and grabs my hand a little more firmly, pulling me to follow the bickering pair into the night air.

We stop a few times to thank well-wishers in passing as if it's the most surreal thing ever. I can see Hunter's back with a struggling pair of legs sticking out to one side. They disappear behind a swaying velvet curtain, and I am urged to follow them in a hurry.

"Put me down ... NOW!" there's an unmistakable yell as we get into the cooler night air and dim lights. Jake pulls the doors behind us, and a waiter inside instinctively draws the curtains. I blink back at the movement and catch a tight look on Jake's face. It makes me wonder if he issued the command for privacy. Or maybe the staff of this establishment is used to safeguarding its high-profile clientele from the media. I don't think I'll ever get used to their intruding presence.

Jake pulls me in front of him, wrapping his arms around my shoulders now we're about seven feet away from the pair.

Leila sits as stiff and as straight as she can in his hold. Her legs taught and knees together, arms folded across her chest, staring straight ahead to avoid his glare. It would be almost comical if it weren't for that hopeless look on Hunter's face as he gazes at the rigid little woman in his arms. I can see his love for her pouring out like a waterfall.

"Not until you tell me you're going to break up with that asshole, Leila." Daniel is beyond livid, speaking through gritted teeth and sounding like the jealous boyfriend. I glance at Jake, aware of another similarity, and catch him smirking back at me.

At least he knows it.

Daniel has an air of aggression that Jake usually emanates, and for a moment, I think he might chuck Leila on the ground. The way he's taking in her stubborn face and closed-off posture, I wouldn't blame him right now. The girl is more stubborn than me and has less ability to give any leeway.

"He wants to marry me. Why would I dump a guy who actually wants love and commitment from me?" She spits at him sarcastically, wriggling instead, realizing neither of them will back down with this odd standoff.

Daniel drops Leila down onto her feet and yanks her around to face him with too much fury. He's holding her by the upper arms, so they are inches apart, ducking his head to try to bridge their height difference.

I tense up, ready to wade in at his volatile behavior, but Jake's arms on me tighten. He knows Daniel would never physically hurt her, or I would be behind him.

"I'm not there yet, Leila. Okay? I've only just started getting my fucking head together, but I'm doing this for you. Can't you see that? I'm trying to sort my shit out, so I can be that guy who gives you love and commitment. I asked you to give me time, and I fucking meant it. I wanted you just to give me a chance and wait for me. I fucking love you!" Daniel sounds ravaged, and Leila's stance crumbles a little. I open my mouth in shock at what he's just said, but Leila turns on him accusingly, sheer anger in her little body as she tries to bring her height up to his by stretching.

"So, I'm supposed to hold my fucking breath and wait? For how long? Put my life on hold while you figure out if you really can give a shit about one woman? In the meantime, we do what, exactly? You still fucking around and me twiddling my thumbs?" She starts to cry as her words tumble out of her mouth, her body sagging in defeat, and Daniel softens too, his grasp on her arms loosening, and he slides both hands down to bring her palms to his chest.

"I don't know how to navigate this. You know I've never been here before! I've never wanted to fix this or go down this route, Leila. All I know is that when we get close to something real, I freak out and run. I'm terrified that I will do it again if I try to date you right now. I don't want to keep hurting you that way." There's sheer fear in his eyes, pleading, and his body is almost all but curled around her.

At least he's honest. Another Jake trait.

"You don't know if you don't try." Jake cuts in flatly from his position behind me. His arms are around my shoulders, and his back is to the closed patio door. "Just saying." He shrugs, and I can feel his smirk as Daniel eyes him up, and Leila stays intensely focused on Daniel's profile. I can feel her willing him to make a choice—a real one.

"I don't want to keep hurting you." He looks at Leila, and even from his tall, over six-foot height, to her tiny, five-foot odd, they still manage to lock eyes. No one can deny the electrical surge sparking all around them, an ever-present hum whenever these two get close. I wonder if Jake and I exude the same thing, and he instinctively pulls his arms up around me a little more firmly.

"You're hurting me now. By doing this. This nothing. This waiting thing." She cries quietly, and he slowly lifts a hand to tenderly brush away the tears on her cheeks. She slaps it away, and he raises his hand back up to try again, ignoring the furious little wildness in the girl he loves. His lack of reaction shows how used to Leila's outbursts Hunter really is and how tolerant he is.

I wonder if the other man could so easily brush off her violent tendencies and true passionate self quite so effortlessly. Daniel seems to be taking moments to think, and his eyes never leave that little blonde head as she stares at their feet on the ground between them. Her body is emanating all kinds of aggressive self-defense, but he holds tight.

"Tell Kurt it's over and give me a chance Leila. I'm willing to swallow my fear and try if that's what you want. I can't promise I'm not going to fuck things up and make mistakes, but I can't stand the thought of you being with anyone else anymore. Too many years we've done this and come around in circles. I just want you and no one else. It's never been anyone else." It's barely a whisper, but we all hear it loud and clear, oozing complete sincerity.

"By trying, you mean stop fucking around with other women and me? Stop acting like some man-whore on a mission to bed everyone in the northern hemisphere?!" Leila lifts her chin and glares at him fully. She's not for backing down; I wouldn't expect anything less of her. She is a spitting little fireball, even with love declarations and promises of more, still not quite ready to trust him.

"I mean by dating you, Leila, exclusively and seeing where this goes. No fucking other women if you swear you'll stop fucking other men. Stop seeing other men altogether." Now he sounds deadly serious. That jealous tone is back in full fury, his intense gaze boring into her eyes. He tilts his head, so she can't escape it.

They are obviously more alike than I thought.

"What? You didn't bring a date?" Leila is still holding out, still being a defiant little pest, and still meeting his eyes with a huge amount of attitude. I sigh at her. Jake's soft chuckle under his breath from behind shows me he's thinking the same thing.

Leila is a fighter until the very end, but you've got to admire that about her, and I'm sure by his patient demeanor, it's one of the many things Hunter loves about her. Daniel isn't even remotely intimidated by the wild little hellcat before him or the hateful tone she's throwing his way. He smooths her hair behind her ear, not flinching when another slap comes his way, and the sound echoes around us.

I knew you two were a match.

"No dates and no women. None since the night we picked you up from that bar, and you told me you hated me. That hit me more than any slap in the face. You have to believe me on this, Leila." He's leaning in, trying to get her to look back at him, but she's intent on looking elsewhere. I notice when she flashes her eyes our way that she's crying. Leila doesn't do vulnerable very often, and she doesn't want him to see the effect he's having on her. She's fighting him to the last.

Leila looks this way again and chews her lip, swallowing hard, as she tries to gain control of her emotions. She catches Jake's eye over my head, and I've no idea what look he returns, but she pulls her head down to face her feet in complete defeat. She thinks long and hard, leaning into long agonizing moments of silence.

"You must be suffering a lot right now, then? It's not like you to go five minutes without a woman and sex." She glances our way, a look on her face I don't understand, as Jake chuckles under his breath. I don't know what I'm missing, but something seems funny.

"I don't want anyone else, Leila. Sex is great, yeah, but with you, it's mind-blowing, and nothing compares. Why would I want anything else?" Daniel uses his fingers to tip her chin back to his; this time, she doesn't resist. His eyes find hers, drawing her close with an arm around her waist. He begs, "Give me a chance, Leila. Please."

"Maybe I need a reminder." Leila sniffs quietly, that little defiant chin stuck up, a glare on her face too cute to be intimidating. Daniel smiles as Jake shifts behind me and leans closer to my ear.

"Come on. They don't need us here for what's going to happen next." I look dumbfounded at the two, still standing feet apart in some quiet standoff, silently regarding one another, but Jake pulls me with him.

We shouldn't leave those two to self-implode.

I'm slow on the uptake because I don't know what he thinks will happen. He turns me away, guiding us toward the glass doors, and opens them into the overly bright room. I squint my eyes as they adjust, and I glance at him as confused as I can be.

"What do you think they're going to do?" I blink, trying to adjust to the brightness; his arm loops casually around my neck, and he draws me against him with a kiss on the temple.

"Isn't it obvious?" Jake winks down at me. But I still can't gain any sense from how we left the two of them out there. He forgets I'm not as wise in the acts of sex, love, and relationships as the rest of the population. I didn't see any foregone conclusion to that little scene we just abandoned. I shake my head in complete blank-mind mode.

"Something I seriously wish I could do right now," he sighs and frowns at me with a spark of sheer regret, a flicker of pain, replying, "Much-needed reunion sex, Emma."

Oh. That ...

Chapter 17

It's been days since the restaurant, and here I am, sitting in the huge, empty garden of Sylvana's home, agonizing over what to do. I stare at the cell in my hands for the hundredth time and sigh. My mother's name is on the screen staring at me, and I've contemplated pressing the dial a million times. I should tell her about the baby and our engagement. She's my mother, yet something inside me is holding me back.

Jake comes strolling out to me, carrying a blanket and a hot drink, coming level to my face with a look of adoration in his eyes. He carefully drapes the blanket around my shoulders and slides the mug in front of me, kissing me on the temple.

"Still undecided?" he asks gently, slipping onto the bench beside me and sitting between his legs so he can face me and pull me close between them, nuzzling me against him, cradling my head with his palm. His fingers thread themselves into my hair in the way he always does. I close my eyes at the feel of him, surrounded by his unique smell, driving away anything but a feeling of serenity.

"How we left things. What I feel about her now. It's all so confusing." I sigh against his chest, completely confused.

"I can't make this choice for you, baby." Jake pulls my head up while he angles down to look at me, my head nestling into the crook of his neck. Automatically, his hand smooths over my abdomen, and I get that inner swell of warm emotion. I've been thinking about little tadpole more as of late, more frequently and affectionately, no longer hit with the tremors of despair I had in the beginning.

We had an appointment with the *OBGYN* yesterday, making everything real. Jake was his usual domineering self and tried to intimidate the poor doctor when he realized my specialist was a male. His posture grew by about a foot, and Boss Carrero appeared in full fury in all his glory. The unamused look on Jake's face at finding out Dr. Sandy Jones wasn't the female he'd expected was hilarious, for me, anyway.

Jake went into feral jealous mode and glowered whenever the poor man put his hands on me. Temper bristling as he held my hand in a deathly grip and watched with gritted teeth as the doctor listened to my heart and took my blood pressure. Jake still has this no-touching rule when it comes to men, and as much as I wanted to be mad and tell him it was ridiculous, I found myself giggling instead, which only made his brow furrow more prominently and therefore gave me more amusement in the process. He was trying hard to be good, sit still, and say nothing, but his face said it all.

When the doctor suggested an *internal test, called a sonogram*, I thought Jake would rip his head off his shoulders.

"No. No fucking way is anyone sticking anything anywhere near Emma until that baby comes out!" Jake was in full aggressive mode, and the poor guy could only raise his hands in defense, trying to soothe Jake's very angry feathers. *No sonogram* and *no more touching* of any kind. I was rapidly pulled into his lap and encircled protectively like a wolf guarding its kill with an expression that clearly said, *if you touch her again, I'll kill you with my bare hands.*

Poor Jake. I couldn't answer any questions without tears filling my eyes whenever I saw Jake's violent glare. I didn't help make anything better, falling into a giggling fit, finding the whole situation hilarious, the poor doctor. Ultimately, my demeanor softened Jake enough for the doctor to get within five feet of me and finish our appointment.

I know I'll probably never see that poor man again. Jake was on the phone as soon as he ushered me out of the office in his tight embrace. He barked orders at whatever poor soul was on the other end of the phone, bidding them to find a list of the top female obstetricians in New York.

* * *

It reminds me of the Jake I miss like crazy. The one I have yet to seduce. If only I could get my head to calm down over these confusing emotions about my mother so I can concentrate on seducing Jake back to his former glorious self. The lack of sex is starting to show on both of us. He isn't himself without it, and I'm not myself without him being that way. His over-sexed and kinky nature is a huge part of the man I fell in love with, and it's starting to take its toll on my emotions.

He's mean and short with everyone except me, acting like a bear with a sore head most of the time. He jogs like a maniac daily, hitting the gym, and has a new trainer putting him through boxing training three times a week, trying to kill the excess frustration not being able to have sex has given him. He's burying his head in work, and when he's frustrated, the poor employees on the phone are often yelled at.

He has tried to pleasure me in other ways. Jake's got many tricks and methods in his armory that don't require full-on sex, but I stopped him. Until he fully gives me himself, I don't want any substitutes. It's not the same. This means I am also severely grouchy and sexually frustrated while living with a man who is the walking, breathing epitome of sexiness, and it's killing me.

I bring my head back to my cell, and my mother, in hopes of finding some solution to at least one of my problems today.

"If I don't tell her, this will just keep bugging me every day until I do." I sigh heavily, curling up into him, wishing life could be as simple as it feels anytime I snuggle up in his embrace. Jake is my home in every way. Nothing can touch me here and infiltrate those arms and that aggressive demeanor when he's in protector mode. I want to stay inside my Jake bubble.

"How do you think she'll react? Are you afraid she won't take the news well?" Jake is trying to figure out what's holding me back. It's hard for him to understand a mother who wouldn't want to know that her only child is engaged and pregnant, but then, his mother is Sylvana, and he has no way to compare. His mother is the walking definition of motherhood, no wonder she produced such amazing sons.

"I honestly don't think there will be a reaction. Maybe she won't acknowledge it at all." I shrug, and his arm moves further around me, planting a kiss on the top of my head to soothe me. How can anyone not feel loved when they have someone like Jake? He's the walking and breathing perfection of my life. He knows what I need as effortlessly as breathing and never fails to deliver.

"It's her grandchild. Surely that will push some kind of emotion?" Jake sounds unsure, but I'm not. My mother only cares about things that pertain to her and her life. Getting married and having a child cemented the fact that I'm never coming home to take care of her again; this is not something she'd want to hear. These revelations won't enhance her life, so I don't have any hope of stirring up some long-forgotten maternal warmth from her. Once and for all, I need to realize I'm chasing the love of a woman incapable of giving it. For whatever reason, my mother has never been able to provide me with what I deserved, and I'm certainly not going to get it now. Maybe some women miss that essential gene, and I hope I'm not going to be one of them. The fierceness of that thought has me cradling my stomach protectively.

Maybe there's some deeper cause that created Jocelyn Anderson, but I know for certain that I am not going to be the mother she is. My mother's never spoken of her own childhood, her parents died before I was born, and I never knew them. Her past is a closed book, and I only know the life she put me through.

I stare down at my stomach, a swelling sensation in my chest and an ache in my throat as I trail my fingertips across the flat expanse. I will be a mother who gives a shit, a mother who cuddles her child, kisses them, and tells them that she loves them. A mother who picks up her child and walks out of Jake's life if he ever dares to hurt either of us, no matter how much I love him. Because that's what a mother is supposed to do; put her child above anyone and everything and fight like hell to protect it. That's the mother Sylvana is, and the type Leila's adoptive mother is too.

A surge inside me swells at an alarming rate, a fit of anger bubbling forth at the thought of what has been denied me my whole life; a given right to any child. I sit up suddenly and lift my chin defiantly, immediately so sure about what I need to do.

"I want to look her in the eye when I tell her, Jake. I want to see how she reacts because when I tell her, I'll also say goodbye once and for all. No child of mine will ever know the pain of rejection that woman can inflict, and I won't give her a chance to try with our baby. I want her to know but not give her a chance to change because she never will, but to give myself some closure and know that she found out from me." My revelation comes from nowhere, the dots connecting in my mind, and now the words are there between us. It's as clear as day to me.

There's no doubt in my decision, and as Jake's eyes scrutinize me, I know one thing for sure. If I let that woman linger in my life the way I always did, this to-and-fro thing I used to allow, I will be inflicting her on my baby. I will be hurting my child by letting that kind of poison linger in their life, and I'm not about to do that. I am the protector now, the nurturer and the mother, and I'll be damned if that woman, with her toxic love, is going to poison my baby's life.

"Jake, I need to do this on my own. You can come to Chicago with me, but I must face her alone for one last time." It's just something I need to do; this has always been between her and me. I'm going back to see her in the way that I left her so long ago, with my mind made up about the direction of my life without her in it.

* * *

Jake holds the keys out in front of me, swinging his hand just out of reach like a torturous plaything, and I lean up to swipe them. He lifts them higher and hits my mouth with a kiss when I try for a second time. He has a happy, playful smirk, and his sexy stubbly jaw looks delicious this morning to match his very good mood.

"Stop tormenting me and open the damn door." I giggle and step back, folding my arms across my chest in a no-nonsense Carrero pose. I try to appear authoritative, but he frowns and annoyingly tweaks my nose.

"Ask me nicely." He grins and lifts them higher above his head with a wicked look in his eye. He's been like this since he got up, and I'm enjoying the return of playful Jake. It's been almost non-existent lately, and I can only sigh at him.

"Please, Jake ... loving, gorgeous, beautiful man of mine. Can I have the keys to our new home? Thank you very much!" I pout at him with a sickly-sweet voice, oozing sarcasm. My hands on his magnificent chest, imploringly, in a very sexy black sweater.

"Nope." He turns in front of me, walking toward the front door we've been standing a few feet from, and I scowl viciously, jokingly at his back.

Asshole.

He wants me to beg. He seems to get a kick out of it lately, torturing me over these last few days with sexual gratitude. Not that I mind. Jake in fun and playful mode is almost as good as Jake in sex mode.

OK, not even a close almost.

I walk up behind him, sliding my hands into the butt pockets of his jeans as he unlocks the door. My hands are flat against his pert ass, enjoying the way I can grope every movement of his body. It makes me ache for him more, and my temperature climbs as my eyes devour that muscular set of shoulders straining under his black smooth, knitted sweater.

He opens the door and pulls me in with him, pressing numbers into a keypad on the wall beside the door, shutting off the infernal beeping that started the second the door opened. I gaze around the grand entrance at the white marble floor and sweeping staircase, almost a mirror image of the Carrero house next door, with a surge of complete excitement.

This is ours. Jake and I have a home together, a new start. We really are home.

He reaches behind and pulls my hands out of his pockets,

turning to face me and bending down to scoop me up in his arms. I squeal with the sudden motion, and I'm met with a full-on passionate kiss. Tongues, teeth, and smiles.

"Get a room." Leila's voice cuts into our intense meeting of mouths, and I lift my head as she lazily saunters in. Jake told her we were getting the keys today, and she assured him she would come over as soon as possible to get the first dibs on a guest room. Her timing is impeccable.

"I thought that's what we were here to do?" Daniel walks in behind her, and I can't help but throw her a smile with raised eyebrows. He places a hand on her shoulder, and she pulls away, throwing him a defiant look, met with a sigh from Hunter.

Still torturing the boy then. Oh, Leila, give him a break, even a little one. He's really trying.

Since our engagement party, Jake told me that Leila has been making life as difficult for Hunter as possible. At least he's clinging on, so far, anyway. He needs to break through her wall of hostility and prove himself worthy to her. She has so much to guard, considering their history.

"Go ahead. I'm taking Emma on a tour to refresh our memories." Jake smiles at Daniel encouragingly, and we watch as he wanders off after his little hellcat, trying to get a hold of her, being met with little slaps on the hand each time and quiet, *I don't think so's*. It's obvious that Leila has no intention of letting Daniel in just yet, and it amazes me that he's following her around so tolerantly.

"What's going on with them?" I ask.

"A lot of angry sex and Leila trying like hell to push him away ... That girl is hell-bent on making him hurt her because it's what she's expecting." He shrugs and carries me toward the large downstairs formal lounge, sliding me to my feet when we walk into the huge blank room. All the furniture is gone, despite the owners leaving some included in the sale. Jake wanted us to start from scratch and choose everything together.

"And Daniel?" I look back through the door, but they've disappeared.

"Has been well and truly forewarned that he only gets one shot at this. Honestly, I think he kinda likes her behavior. He's always been a warped kind of guy." Jake grins, and I can't tell if he's joking or serious. I try not to wonder too much. I know one thing for sure ... Hunter needs to play this right because Leila is done with being hurt by him; there will be no second chance this time. She wants him to prove he has what it takes to be with her, and she will put him through a lot worse before he gets past that wall. I just hope he has what it takes to persevere.

I turn my attention back to the room as Jake wanders to pull the drapes wide open, letting the sunshine in and dazzle me momentarily.

Somehow, without furniture, the place seems monumentally bigger. The huge floor-to-ceiling windows frame the view, taking my breath away instantly. I turn slowly and scan around; this room has one large open fireplace and a distinct marble mantle on a far wall. It's hard not to imagine this room filled with comfy furniture, expensive Christmas trees, and trimmings by a roaring log fire.

"Dime for your thoughts?" Jake cuts into my daydream of children opening presents on a warm furry rug on a snowy day, and I break into a smile.

"Just imagining this room with furniture." I blush, a happy surge at where my mind was.

"I was imagining this room with a huge roaring fire and serious plush rug down there." Jake smiles and nods at the floor where I'd imagined the same thing. I wonder if we had the same thoughts on the rug. "Great place to fuck." He winks cheekily.

Yeah, I guess not.

"I don't know what that is." I smile sassily, and he sighs, bopping me on the nose with a fingertip. We've been making jokes about the lack of sex lately. I guess to try to get our heads around the emotional barrier that Jake still has, one I can no longer understand. We've come so far, yet he still doesn't attempt to touch me that way. I've never pushed because I don't want to be rejected again.

"Well, play your cards right, shorty, and I might be talked into trying again. I can't keep beating the shit out of boxing bags for the next few months. I can't handle looking at you and not doing anything about it." His pained gaze tells me he's been thinking about this a whole lot more recently than he lets on.

My ears prick up, and I pass him my wanton look below lowered lashes with more than a little hope simmering.

"Keep looking at me like that, and it'll convince me to try right now." He groans and walks off toward the doorway as though reeling himself back in. Jake is walking off again as he does anytime it looks remotely like something will happen with us, and again that huge surge of disappointment hits me painfully.

"I'm not stopping you from trying right now." I retort huskily, throwing him my best seductive look, mustering all the sexual prowess I can, willing him to come back to me. He pauses in the doorway, appraising me for a moment. I can tell he's arguing with himself over whether he should or shouldn't. A bang above our heads breaks the moment, and we both look toward the ceiling in surprise.

There's another thud, not as loud this time, followed by some smaller noises and then the unmistakable noise of Leila moaning.

Oh, my fucking God. Really.

"For the love of God, the wrong fucking people are christening this damned house." Jake snarls, bristling at another man marking his territory, and without warning, he storms toward me, lifts me around his waist, pulls my legs around him, and backs me against the wall a little too aggressively for how he's been lately.

His mouth hits mine with force, and he braces all my weight on his hips. His hands come to undo my wool cardigan and push it back over my shoulders rapidly. He's obviously got his mind hell-bent on his purpose, fueled by the couple upstairs taking away what is his right in our new house. Or Hunter, as this is probably more of a male pissing on another's territory kind of thing, and it's doing the trick. I mentally tell myself to thank Leila later.

Right now, though, I'm too zoned in on what his mouth is doing to mine, sudden exhilarating heat coursing through me with the fact that Jake is attempting sex again finally after so freaking long. He stopped trying to initiate it after the first few times, and judging by the intense way his hands are roaming over me, he's managed to build himself into a lust-filled fury without help from me.

Okay, maybe a tiny little bit of persuasion ... and a lot of help from upstairs.

His tongue slides into my mouth as I grasp my arms around his neck, our bodies pressed close, and I can't help but grind against him mercilessly. Jake feels better than good, so much so that I almost forgot what this feels like. It's like realizing a fantasy all over again. I slide one hand down to the hem of his T-shirt and yank it up. Rewarded with his helping hand as his top is soon lying on the floor behind us, exposing all that chiseled muscle and tattooed sexiness that has me panting. He pulls my dress up, slowly moving his hands up my thighs, his mouth trailing to my neck as I buck and arch at the way he feels. There is no sign of wavering libido or his confusing and conflicting thoughts.

I missed every second of this, wanted every single one of his erotic touches so badly that I've dreamed of him around me and inside of me and woke many a time after experiencing the craziest sleep orgasms known to womanhood that I didn't even know existed. The surge of pregnancy hormones has only made all those feelings more intense.

He cups me from underneath, his thumb pulling my lace panties to one side, and I gasp in pleasure at the connection. I slide my hand to his waistband and yank open the buttons of his jeans with little effort ... given that he's pushed against me so hard. I slide and wiggle my fingers into his jeans, finding the source of what they ache for, and I'm practically singing in happiness. I'm so ready for this kind of reunion. Long awaited.

This is really happening, God.

Chapter 18

Jake groans against my neck as my hand closes around him inside his boxers. I almost jerk out of his hands with pleasure as his fingers find what I've wanted from him for weeks. Lack of touch down there has me at my most sensitive, and I can already tell that I'll cum the second he is inside of me, not just those wickedly good fingers. Jake's mouth captures mine again as he slides his hand in a rhythmic motion, and I start the familiar internal building of hot waves and clenching pleasure. It's happening too fast. Weeks of not being touched are making my body long to climax. I'm over-sensitive; at this rate, it will be over before it's started. I don't want it that way. I want to savor this and enjoy it. I have him back in his entirety, and I want it to be everything I've been dreaming of.

"Jake, wait." I pant as my legs start trembling. I don't want it this way. I want us to get past his emotional barrier and have him inside me, all his hot hardness. If he makes me finish before he starts, he might not follow through, and I need him more than air right now. I need his body and mine as one. He buries his face in my neck again, kissing me and pushing further into the rhythm our grinding has created with subtle moans.

"Jake? Emma?" A voice rings through the house rather loudly. The familiar song of a woman you don't want catching you up against a wall with her son, semi-naked and about to screw you. Jake immediately snaps his head up and looks at me in sheer surprise.

"Fuck, it's my mom." Jake pulls his fingers out of me, slides me down to my feet, and hauls down my dress, throwing a quick kiss on the corner of my mouth before retrieving his T-shirt from the floor and yanking it on crazily in one fell swoop; a move suggesting this isn't the first time he's almost been caught red-handed by her.

Noooooooooooooo!

I huff and pick up my cardigan, previously discarded on the floor next to me. Jake adjusts himself and buttons his jeans in almost lightning-flash speed, already walking toward the door to see Sylvana while I sort myself back from the frazzled horny mess we've gotten ourselves into. My face is on fire, and my body is screaming for release, tingling in a crazy motion, making me as cranky as sin. I want to cry or kick something ... really, really, hard. We were so goddamn close!

Jake was so close to getting over whatever this bloody stupid fucking thing is.

I stomp around in a circle, buttoning up my cardigan and straightening my dress, trying hard to bring some calm to the fury of hormones ravaging me.

Maybe smashing something will help.

We were so close to him trying again, but now, with the interruption from his mother, I'm not sure he will do that anymore, especially if cooling off while talking to Sylvana gives him time to re-think all this, make him go back to not wanting to try at all. It was unplanned and completely fueled by the thought of Daniel and Leila marking his territory. I could scream right now!

How on Earth am I going to find a way to get that spark back in him to where we'd almost been?

My skin is still tingling with the memory of his touch, and I am sure as hell not going back to its absence. That sizzling sensation on my body has me aching with longing, a pain so intense that I am not, in any way, going to let this go. I need Jake to have sex with me, or I will go insane.

I wander into the hall and am greeted by the sight of mother and son talking. Jake looks unruffled and normal, not that it surprises me. Even after full-blown, mind-numbing sex, he has a knack for looking completely fine. Sylvana, on the other hand, looks flustered and completely uncomfortable.

There's an embarrassingly loud wailing sound echoing from upstairs, much louder out here than in the room I just left, traveling due to having no furniture or floor coverings in the empty echoing house. Sylvana's face turns beetroot as the noise pitches higher.

Yes, we're standing here listening to Leila having what sounds like an earth-shattering orgasm right now ... Lovely.

"So, yeah, I'll bring Emma over soon, Mamma. We won't be long." Jake kisses her on the cheek and walks her to the door talking loudly to cover the moans still happening overhead, trying his hardest to get her out the door fast. Jake is still an old-fashioned boy at heart, and subjecting his mother to any kind of sexual noise is almost as painful for him as it is for her. He looks positively agitated. I'm trying not to count how many seconds it's lasting, annoyed with green-eyed jealousy as I glare at Jake's back a little moodily and curse internally at our interruption.

It should be me making all that noise.

I don't know why Sylvana was here or if her departure is because of the obviously cringe-worthy noises upstairs, but I can't help but sigh with disappointment. The noise upstairs reaches its pinnacle with a rather embarrassing long, drawn-out scream and then deafening silence.

Thank God for that.

Jake shuts the front door and looks toward the ceiling with a hint of the Carrero Death Glare before slowly walking back to me. He takes a long breath and glances back at the door, checking if his mother is completely out of earshot.

"Remind me later to beat the shit out of Danny." He grumbles and takes my hand loosely. Again, he has that whole aura of distance with a calm and gentlemanly touch that screams celibate. I immediately get the vibe that what started between us will not continue at all.

"Why'd your mom leave so soon?" I ask with more than a little attitude. Jake looks at me with a frown and raised eyebrow combo, pointing out the obvious.

Ah okay. So maybe I would've run off too, if I hadn't been in the middle of trying to achieve the same noises myself.

"About before, Emma, maybe we should leave it for a bit." Jake avoids looking at me. That urge to bash him on the head takes me over, disappointed rage, and crazy hormones rise, hitting me hard.

I goddamn knew it.

"Not a fucking chance." I snap in complete tantrum mode and yank my hand out of his. "I've had enough of this. You're more than capable, as you've just proven, and if you don't make good on what you started in there at some point today ... then I'm going back to Queens until you fucking well do!" I spit harshly, lifting my chin toward him in complete frustration, weeks of pent-up sexual desire kicking in. Jake gawps, totally taken aback by this sudden and very loud verbal defiance, and raises his hands in defense.

"Emma ..." Jake puts a hand to my face, and I slap it away, a Leila-type maneuver coming in handy. I am so beyond angry right now, and the lack of sex between us has finally come to a head. I can't handle this anymore. It's torture.

"Don't goddamn "Emma" me!" Tears prick at my eyes through sheer exasperation. This situation is getting beyond ridiculous, and if I'm being honest, it's not just about the lack of sex either.

"You don't want me, do you?" I spit as tears start falling hard. "You don't get the same lust I used to make you feel?" His face crumbles as he steps toward me, but I step back. He looks devastated, which only upsets me more but makes me think that maybe, finally, I've hit a nerve.

"Baby?" He tries to reach out for me again, but I hit his hand away harder than before, fueled by heartbreak and emotions cruising through me at speed, pain aching inside.

"No. Don't touch me unless you're going to have sex with me! Do you have any idea how it feels having you go from being unable to keep your hands off me to this?" I wipe the tear away from my chin angrily, moving anytime he tries to catch hold of me. Every frustration of the past few weeks is bubbling to the surface in an extreme emotional breakdown and raging insecurity, raising an ugly, tortured head.

"It's not like that, Emma ... You know I still want you that way." He's trying, but I'm not interested in hearing it, so fueled by hormones and frustration, my irrational mood is moving back in. His actions of late haven't shown me that he still feels that way, and now it's no longer good enough to just hope.

"I want the Jake Carrero with zero ability to stop lust and love consuming him. Where is he? The guy who screwed me in the back of a limo and the guy who pushed me against a hotel wall. Because that's who I fucking need!" I'm stomping around, waving my hands, letting all fury loose, Teen Emma throwing her ponytail back in defiance.

"Emma, I don't know what else to say." Jake's face is a mix of panic and pain, holding up his hands in a defensive manner, and he has no clue how to handle my sudden outburst or this version of me. This was supposed to be a happy day, getting the keys to our first home and coming to see it now that it's all ours. It's ruined because our friends were too horny to get out of this house before having a quickie, and it makes me aware that they are behaving exactly like we used to.

"You haven't touched me that way since you kissed her!" I snap loudly, and his expression instantly turns sheepish. I swear I see the blood drain from his face, and I falter for a moment as a tiny flash of doubt comes back to haunt me from that bitch's words. Maybe he did do more than kiss her? I shake it away as stupid.

"I know." He drops his gaze to the floor and closes his eyes. "I know how this looks, *Bambina,* but it's not like that. Hurting you, breaking up, and then the baby fucked my head up more than I know how to explain, and I'm scared to have sex with you." His voice is low and sincere, stopping my rampant storming around almost instantly. I calmly turn to him, holding the crazy still for an explanation.

"Because of the baby? Talk to me, Jake, because this is killing me." I beg him, moving toward him, holding onto the hem of his jumper like a vulnerable child, trying to understand.

"Every time I get close, Emma, all I can see is how you looked at me that night. It's not just about the baby. It's about how much I hurt you!" His eyes come to meet mine and flit down to my mouth, unable to rest on one feature, from eyes to mouth and back, as though all he's thinking about is kissing me. I'm shocked into silence by this unexpected confession.

"What do you mean?" I breathe softly. He slides his hands over my shoulders and pulls me closer so we're nose to nose.

"I told you I needed to learn to forgive myself too and that's what's stopping me. I haven't forgiven myself for hurting you. It doesn't matter that you seem to be able to forgive me and love me. I still feel like a completely shitty asshole for what I did to you. I don't deserve every part of you back, Emma. When I look at you, it kills me that I hurt you. This perfect, angelic, trusting face that looks at me like I'm her everything. Don't you see how much it hurts to know the sadness you carried in these beautiful eyes for the past few months is because of me? Not some bastard from your past but me ... That I hurt you, baby.... I never wanted to be that guy to you. When you told me what happened to you, I swore to myself, right there and then, that I'd never do that to you. I'd never do anything to put that look of devastation there again, but I did, and I saw it, and no matter how hard I've tried, I can't get your broken face out of my head anytime I think of touching you that way." Jake's voice breaks.

His hands tighten on my shoulders, and he clears his throat to dislodge the intense emotions caught there. I am stupefied into silence. My head is racing around in circles, unable to formulate one sentence with the mish-mash of thoughts brimming through my brain. My heart is aching between love at what he's saying, how deeply scarred it has made him, and by sadness that he can't overcome in the way I have.

"Jake ... If I can forgive you, then all of this is stupid." I blink up at him and see nothing but guilt and self-hatred looking back. This is never what I wanted for him; this is not how I want him to still feel about what he did. I need to fix this because this is not the Jake I want or the one I know he can be.

I lift my hand to his on my shoulder and clutch it, pulling it down, then turn with complete determination and yank him with me. He follows obediently like a child as though he somehow knows I'm in no mood to be questioned or refused. I storm straight for the front hall, hauling him with me at speed before he can protest. I turn at the stair and pull him after me. He's being compliant, letting me, for the first time in existence, be the one to take charge without argument; a part of me tells me he wants this as much as I do. I'm empowered and not in the mood for any resistance.

Daniel and Leila appear at the top of the stairs as we level them, looking a little disheveled. Daniel is sporting a bloody nose and a grin like the Cheshire Cat; I don't want to know. They obviously have some severely kinky preferences, and Daniel can handle Leila at her absolute worst. She seems to look a little less aggressive, at least, and as his hand is on her ass without any refusal from her, I assume it's all good.

"Let yourself out. We will resume whatever later ... Don't wait for us." I command and give Jake another demanding yank behind me. He follows obediently with absolutely no expression on his face. He's probably mulling over everything he said in the kitchen and wondering if I am having some sort of psychotic break that he should indulge in because I am fragile and pregnant ... I wouldn't put it past him.

I catch Daniel throwing a cautious look over my head at Jake. He seems confused but sees some sort of sign on Jake's face that satisfies him, so they both slide past us and head down the stairs. Leila giggles as she mumbles, "about time." The sound of a slapped ass echoes our way, and they disappear out the door.

I lead Jake in a very commanding manner to the biggest bedroom of the house. The one that previously held the huge four-poster bed, the one I've already chosen as our bedroom. It's the master suite of the whole house with the best view, and I'll make a goddamn start on claiming my home! Bedroom first.

It has thick plush carpets and drapes left hanging on the windows. I let go of Jake at the door and walk into the room toward the windows, grabbing the curtains and drawing them hastily. My mind is completely set on what I will do to fix this little situation.

Jake has spent the past couple of months fixing my emotional issues for me, and I am sure as hell going to do it to him in true grand Carrero style. Never take no for an answer; don't back down when what you want shows resistance. I'm going to earn my future surname.

Turning to the middle of the room, I march forward and immediately start taking off all my clothes in a confident non-caring manner. Completely unbashful and not giving an actual fuck that the door is still open. I watch him stand a little taller, raising an eyebrow as he watches me.

"You have thirty seconds to get in here, shut that door, and get naked or this." I hold up my hand with the engagement ring on. "Gets posted to you from Queens when I dump your ass. No fiancée of mine will let guilt destroy our relationship ... I'm no fucking nun, and if you want a celibate girlfriend, it won't be me!" I snap and throw one of my shoes off, letting it fly across the room at the wall beside him aggressively. It hits it with a thud, sliding down the wall, and I wonder for a moment if this is what Leila did too.

Jake watches the descent of the shoe silently before turning his eyes back to me. There's a look of humor and a tiny upward crease to the corner of his mouth as though a smile is not far behind, yet he's frowning.

He still hasn't uttered a word. He moves in wordlessly and shuts the door carefully and deliberately, looking very much like a guy contemplating running away from his crazy girlfriend or fiancée or whatever. With furious intent, I continue pulling off every item of clothing I have on and throw each item at the wall by his feet very pointedly, each time with a raised eyebrow.

"Well?" I stand naked and face him with my hands on my hips. Completely unashamed at being nude with a guy who can't seem to get over his emotional impotence. Jake runs a hand through his hair nervously and takes a deep breath. All hint of humor is gone, and he seems torn and scared, yet little hints of lust are in there. The darkening of his eyes and the way he can't stop trailing up and down my naked body with them. He stands staring at me as I am in front of him, completely stark naked for the first time in God knows how long.

"I fucking love you." He stalks toward me and pushes me backward at speed, walking me the full distance of the room with eyes locked on mine. His green depths growing more lust fueled with every step. His expression changing from dubious and scared to dominating and sure. As my back hits the wall, Jake bends into me and lifts me around his waist, pushing against me and grinding into me as his mouth meets mine. He slides his tongue into my mouth, and I can already feel the difference in his kiss, a hint of old passion and burning desire switching on his more aggressive Carrero Casanova mode.

Thank the stars ... Finally!

"I said naked, Carrero." I push his face away so that I can give him my best haughtiest glare. He smirks and lets me loose from the wall, sliding me down to my feet and stepping back. His sweater is off in one easy movement over his head, making him strain every one of his delicious muscles. My body is heating up in readiness as I watch him. I can't tear my eyes off that magnificent frame.

He looks down and unbuttons his jeans easily, sliding them and his boxers down in one go as he quickly pulls his trainers off, discarding them all in a heap. There is no hesitation in his glorious face anymore, just the look of the guy who carried me into his room the first night he ever took me as his. He wants and needs me, and nothing will stop him. My heart soars that I finally have all of him back.

Within moments he's completely naked, and I can't stop my eyes from wandering over that hunky body, hungrily devouring every inch he's kept from me, my eyes almost glued to the part of him that will bring me the most pleasure.

"Looking at me like that definitely helps." His hoarse husky tone sounds exactly like the Jake I need, and he grabs my hand, yanking me toward him forcefully. He catches me behind my neck and the small of my back and flips me onto the plush carpet in one fast stroke, making me catch my breath. I squeal in delight at the obvious return of his manhandling at its finest, the grand return of Carrero. He maneuvers on top of me with a firm stroke between us, along my abdomen and thigh.

"No hands," I murmur breathlessly, "I'm too close, and I just want you." I lock eyes with his and suddenly catch the flicker of doubt across his face. His focus moves across my body between us as his brain starts to take over. "Look right here at me." I urge him. His eyes come back to my face. "Look at me, Jake, don't stop looking at how much I love you and how much I need you in this way. I forgave you and need you to forgive yourself too if this will ever work." I silently plead, hoping my expression translates all that he needs to see.

He gazes at me with the slow change of his eyes, from darkest green to pale, as every doubt and thought consumes him. I push my head up and kiss him slowly and gently to stop the onslaught. He opens his mouth enough so I can slide my tongue in, and he follows me back down to the floor so that I can lie my head back. His touch raises the heat inside me once more to a soaring temperature effortlessly, and I start to let my hands roam him sexily. My kiss devours him how he always consumes me, and he starts to respond. His body hardens against mine as his hands move down over my exposed breasts.

I slide a hand between us and find him, urging him with strokes and caresses as he groans into my mouth, and I know I'm winning. I'm pushing away his doubts and indecisiveness, bringing him back to me again. I slide my legs apart so he comes to nestle between them and wrap my thighs around his hips suggestively, securely, so he has no way to escape from me. Our bodies naturally start to move against one another. He breathes in heavily and breaks from my kiss.

"I don't want to hurt the baby." He murmurs against my mouth, and I shake my head.

"There's more chance of you hurting me by not doing this. The doctor told you that this is perfectly fine and even healthy for us to have sex." I soothe and stare straight into his eyes lovingly, open trust all over my face.

He takes another deep breath, locking his focus fully onto my face, roaming over my eyes, nose, and mouth slowly as though imprinting it to memory.

"You're so beautiful, Emma. I don't know what I did to deserve perfection like you," he croons softly, staring at me without fully connecting our bodies yet.

"You have no idea how often I tell myself the same thing about you. You rescued me from myself, Jake. I owe you everything. I belong with you. I belong to you, and I always will. Stop fighting yourself and show me how much you love me instead of telling me. I need to feel it again because I miss it so much more than you can ever imagine." I kiss him, feeling the change in him as his body relaxes into me. His hands find my wrists, sliding them above my head and pinning them to the soft floor, a move that only my sexually competent man would make without thinking about it.

Yes, come back to me, Jake. I need you. The real you.

His body moves slowly against mine. That furious arousal in me heightens and hitches. He devours my mouth and then my neck and back again. His tongue caresses mine, helping me get lost in pleasure as his body slowly slides with mine. I wriggle a hand free and once again find him hard and ready. I maneuver myself and use my grip on him to find our way together, lifting my hips, sliding him into me very slowly, pensively, waiting for him to halt all of this and hold my breath. He tenses and pauses as his kiss stops for a mere second.

Stay with me, Jake, don't give up on us, please.

He exhales and screws his eyes closed tight. Our bodies adjust to the sensation of being joined again, my body stretching as he inches slowly inside of me. We're fully connected, yet neither of us is moving. Jake lifts himself over me, using his hand by my wrist to steady his weight, and catches my free hand returning it to the same position beside the other. I let out a slow sigh of relief. Him holding me down and gazing directly into my eyes is a sure sign that he isn't going to try to stop this.

He slowly moves back and then forward, easing in and out of me, letting us both get used to the feeling of each other again. I groan as the sensation floods through me, keeping my eyes wide open, never breaking our connection so I don't lose him in his own head. I want how I look now to be what he sees when we make love, not the memory of that girl he broke in two. I want to erase his guilt and see only where we are now—that's all that matters anymore.

He does it again, and some tension softens in his furrowed brow and gorgeous narrowed eyes. This time he groans softly under his breath as my body tingles and soars.

"You feel so good." He moans softly. My answer doesn't make it out of my mouth as he moves again, quickly, with a few gentler thrusts. All I can do is inhale and arch my back as my body jumps into high pleasure mode. Being held down this way, he has full access to my breasts and tips his head, catching a nipple between his teeth softly.

"Harder," I command, in a husky tone, as he moves into me again in the same painfully slow motion. He sucks my nipple, and a shooting wave of pleasure sparks straight from there to my core, causing me to groan far more loudly than I realize. It spurs him on. The next thrusts are firmer and more intense. Jake lets go of my wrists and cages my head with his hands, so he can push his body higher above me, giving him better leverage. He thrusts again with more passion and intent, his eyes never leaving mine.

"Oh, my God." I start whimpering as the rolling waves of hotness tingle at my toes, moving slowly up with his every push inside me. My hands come to his arms, snaking around his muscles, my nails dragging on his skin. I'm rolling around in ecstasy, and when he begins to push into me more rhythmically, with harder thrusts, I start to lose all control. "Oh, God! Yes! God ... Jake." I cry out as I scream internally with extreme divine pleasure. Every single moment of being joined with him takes away the last pains or regrets in my heart; being reunited this way is the final healing balm I need.

"Wait for me, baby. I'm really close." He groans with a devilishly low tone that is as sexy as sin. It's been so long for both of us that neither of our bodies can contain the pleasure, brimming close to conclusion without effort. The tidal waves and ripples growing are coursing up from my legs and over my pelvis. He thrusts harder with more intent.

I'm trying so hard to let him find his release with me, but I'm being taken over by them, crying out and groaning, panting, and clawing at his shoulders in ecstasy. I can't contain it much longer as it consumes every fiber of my body, and my vision turns to the tingling sparks of an orgasm coming close enough to engulf me.

"Now, baby. Fuck." Jake groans out, and we both explode together, stars and sensations crashing through my body, making me convulse and arch into him, losing all sight of the blackness that consumes me while each wave and racking spasm runs its course. It lasts for what seems like forever, bursting fireworks and satisfying ripples, then convulsions before I'm finally still.

We lie motionless, entangled in the aftermath of our release for a few moments, my fingers in his hair, and I run my nails lightly through it as he rests his head in the crook of my neck.

"I love you so much, Emma, more than I can ever tell you, baby." His voice is raspy and deep, and I start smiling against his head.

"I'm pretty sure what you just did more than tells me." I grin as he levers himself up to plant a firm kiss on my mouth; the look of hesitation he had is now gone, that haunting faint look in his eye that was lingering for weeks, always brimming under the surface like a tiny insecurity is completely gone.

"We just christened our house ... Now we just have to do that in every room before we can officially move in." He grins at me boyishly, his face returning to the man I missed so much, a hint of cheeky and sexual innuendo lurking in its depths.

You're finally back. God, I missed you.

"Well, seeing as I have crazy ravaging hormones that make me sex mad, and I'm already hoping for a second round, I wouldn't say it's a chore." I grin at him, seeing his body heave with a huge relaxed sigh.

"I'm game if you are," he winks sexily, the gorgeous dark lust-filled depths of those eyes already returning.

"Completely!"

Chapter 19

Jake is nibbling my neck, and his hands are all over my breasts as we walk back to the Carrero family home. He's walking behind me, making it impossible to get on at a decent pace while groping the life out of me. I can't stop giggling with every suck and nibble, and when his mouth finds my ear lobe, I sink back against him, halting us in the street again. The pleasure overtakes me at being back in a world where Jake can't keep his hands off me.

We spent an alarmingly long time making up for wasted hormones by christening every room and almost every cupboard in our new home, and now I'm tingling from every pore with the biggest radiant grin on my face. Jake has well and truly found his long-lost libido, and by the last two rooms, he was over his previous concerns about hurting babies or feeling guilty. The sex in those two rooms was hard, hot, and taken from behind. I'm sure my skin is marked from the ferocity we finally built up to in the last screaming stages of christening the house. There is no way I'm allowing him to go back to a sexless relationship now.

"Put her down, will you." Daniel's voice cuts into the extremely naughty thoughts running through my head, and Jake and I look up simultaneously. We forgot about our so-called guests, who I guess were waiting for us at Sylvana's.

"You two were a very long time." Leila winks at us, sliding into

Daniel's bright red sports car parked in the Carrero drive, she looks happy for once, and Daniel's bloody nose is clean, except now I notice faint bruising along his jawline starting to develop.

"What did she do to your face?" I ask Daniel as Jake wraps his arms around my waist and pulls me against his torso to stand beside the driver's door in front of Hunter.

"I'm dating a crazy little hellcat who likes to play rough." Daniel shrugs as though it's completely normal behavior.

"I can imagine you two featuring in a BDSM article for sure." Jake laughs, and Daniel's raised eyebrow and smirk make me think that maybe Jake isn't that far wrong. I really don't want to think of the weird crazy things these two get up to; knowing Hunter's reputation in the past, I'm guessing Leila must be equally wild to keep him on his toes.

"I need to punish him for all his wrongs," Leila cuts in, clicking her fingers, "Daniel come." She glares at him from the passenger seat, and he inclines his head at her.

"Sorry, dude, can we maybe come back for the grand house tour and shit later?" He checks his watch. "I have a session to go to, and the little woman is coming with." He smiles when he calls her that, and his sheer adoration for her is obvious. Daniel is hopeless for my girl.

"I heard that. I ain't no little woman, Daniel 'bastarding' Hunter. I'm *thee* fucking woman." Leila snorts at the eye roll Hunter throws her way. Leila is still trying to exert her dominance over him for sure.

"Calm your sexy, lacy panties, baby cakes. You're thee fucking woman that's going to get fucked black and blue in the car if she doesn't stop with the attitude." Daniel throws Jake an indulgent look, and I can only shake my head at the pair; at least things in that relationship will never be dull.

"You sure as hell pick the most challenging things to do in life, Danny." Jake laughs and bends to throw Leila a cute little wave. She sticks her fingers up at him and her tongue out. I laugh at her, my heart brimming with love. The girl is too adorable for words, even when being a little psychotic.

"She keeps things interesting. How else is a guy like me supposed to stick with one chick for the rest of his life? Leila has enough personalities to keep me amused for a very long time ... and enough sass to keep me horny for an eternity." Daniel winks at us and, with a grin, bangs the top of his car over her head.

"And enough violence to make you suffer if you screw this up ... I'm pretty sure this version of her is not against cutting the family jewels off if you fuck it up again." Jake cuts in. He's still watching Leila in the passenger seat, and Jake's warning tone is evident. He's reminding Daniel that he only gets this chance once.

"Must be fucking love then, eh?" Daniel shrugs and turns to open his door nonchalantly, making me giggle.

"That is almost romantic in an extremely vague way." I point out with a smile and blow Leila a kiss, seeing her smile and return one at me.

"I'm not Jake, honey. He's the smooth talker and Mr. Hands-on-cuddly-feely and all that crap." He slides into his seat and puts down the window before shutting his door. Leila switches on the radio and starts scrolling until she finds a song she likes, turning it up loud.

Taylor Swift – "Blank Space"

It fills the air, and Daniel sticks his head out the window, throwing Jake a deadpan look.

"This is Leila's theme tune. If I ever go missing, check her basement for my body." There's such a serious look in his eye that I burst out laughing, and Leila slaps him hard on the shoulder. He doesn't flinch at her assault.

"Are you trying to say I'm insane?" She balks at him angrily, leaning forward in her seat so he's close enough to lick.

"If the shoe fits, princess." He smirks back at her, starting the car, revving the engine, and adjusting his seat belt, seemingly ignoring her proximity and threatening expression.

"Fuck ... you!" She says slowly and deliberately, leaning toward the side of his face, dangerously close, with a look of pure hatred. Daniel turns to catch her chin and kisses her full force on the mouth with startling speed. I can't help but watch how cute they look kissing. They make for an attractive, if not slightly crazy, couple.

"I love the fucking crazy in you, Leila. It happens to be the most adorable part." He sits back, leaving her blinking at him, and waves at us as he screeches out of the drive at speed. Leila is undoubtedly being thrown back in her seat violently with the force of his maneuver.

Well, They're certainly interesting together anyway.

"Normally, I would say that a girl has no clue what she's getting into with Danny, but in this case, I'm more worried about him." Jake watches the car screech out into the street and turn at a junction at an alarming speed. Daniel drives like a maniac, his red Lamborghini ringing through the air even long minutes after we can't see it.

"I think they're perfectly matched, but they need to calm the hostility before someone gets scarred for life." I giggle as Jake comes to wrap his arms around me once more possessively and dives back into my body.

"Honestly, I think Danny is the only one in danger of receiving wounds, and the pervert in him will probably love it." Jake leans in and bites my neck again, making me squeal. "Now, where were we, *Bambina?*"

* * *

Splayed out like a star on the bed with Jake's palms pressed to mine, our fingers interlaced and pinned down on the mattress. He's panting on top of me and finally finds the strength to move, rolling off gently and lying beside me after an energetic couple of hours in an empty house. I'm lying in the afterglow of the best morning of my life.

Yesterday we endured a day of meetings, one with an interior designer, then the local press for the announcement of our engagement in the paper. Finally, we had Sylvana clucking around for the remainder of the day, treating me like fragile glass, just like Jake does. Leila and Daniel never returned for the tour, so Sylvana finally got hers, minus the sexual moaning from upstairs. We hadn't had another moment all day to be alone until we came to bed when his parents left for a dinner date. The day had been busy and unstoppable, and by the time we got to bed, Jake was tearing my clothes off in a frenzy to get our bodies back together now his mental block is gone.

It's safe to say he's returned to his former glory. All the emotional crap in his head was finally dealt with. This morning he woke me in the most spectacularly sexy way, which led to the hottest morning sex of my life, and I'm hopelessly falling in love with him all over again. He's finally the man I loved, all domineering, bossy and sexy, and now that every part of him is as it should be, I am glowing inside and out. Basking in an afterglow of multiple orgasms.

Anyone who thinks sex isn't important in a relationship is crazy.

"You up for trying a car journey today?" Jake leans in, kissing me on the temple, my body still tingling and vibrating from our recent energetic session like I've had a serious workout and my body could do with a shower. Irritatingly, he looks immaculate, like always, and smells exactly as he always does. Fresh and citrusy.

How the hell he does that, I'll never know. It's annoyingly seductive.

"Depends on where we're going." I turn to him, snuggling into his broad chest, dragging those strong arms around me satisfyingly. These arms are still the best place in the world, and luckily for me, Jake gives me them whenever I want, night or day.

"We need to go back to the city and sort out what we want from the apartment. I've got three days" worth of crap to deal with at work over the Hunter contract, and I'd rather you were close by so I can see you at night." Jake releases me and slides out of bed. He obviously has his bossy brain in gear this morning and a look on his face that says *we have plans*, not that I mind. I've been getting bored with lazing around in the Carrero family home while he dashes back and forth from the city. I'd rather be back in our private space until our house is ready, then after that, I'll just have to get used to his disappearing acts when he goes to and fro from work.

"I haven't been as sick lately, so I should be okay." I stretch out and yawn like the cat who got the cream and then some. It's early, but I'm restless and want to do something beyond a day of reading books, lying around, and cooking lessons. I need to sort out other parts of my life before I can come here and start a new chapter. Other parts being my mother, work, and seeing Sarah properly.

"Sophie's supposed to be coming over later today, after school, to see the house." I watch him move around the bedroom, lifting towels for the shower, that magnificent naked ass and body on full show. He's never been shy about wandering about in front of me naked, not that I can blame him; with his body, I would've taken up nude modeling to show it all off.

Not that I want him to, I think I'd scratch the eyes out of any girl who ogled his body these days.

"I'll leave keys and alarm code with Mamma and tell her to show Sophie around. The designer has all your preferences for our bedroom and the lounge, so if she gets that in motion quickly, we can move in while the rest of the house gets done." He throws me a panty-melting happy face. I start smiling, biting my lip, aching for his body to be entangled with mine again already. It's alarming how my lust has returned tenfold with a reminder of his skills. I have to drag my eyes forcefully back to his.

"When do we leave?" I roll onto my stomach to watch him. He yanks on sweatpants and throws a T-shirt over his head, covering up that gorgeous expanse of tattooed lusciousness. He's obviously changed his mind about having the shower right now.

"After you eat, baby. I'll have the housekeeper pack up food for the trip, still can't have you flying, so it's a long drive back. Jefferson is coming with the Lexus so that I can sit with you in the back." He picks up a gray bathrobe and throws it beside me with a raised, suggestive eyebrow.

Hmmm, sexy backseat time. I like this idea.

"You're very bossy this morning Mr. Carrero. I like seeing some of the old you kicking in." I giggle as he crawls quickly across the bed to haul me onto my back, kissing me passionately. Caging me in with those glorious muscles assaulting me with his very sexy essence, like a strong aftershave folding around me.

"Amazing what a lot of sex with the woman I'm crazy about can do." He grins and takes a shot at devouring my neck playfully.

Amazing what a lot of sex with Jake Carrero can do.

"No more guilt and crazy thoughts about hurting the baby?" I push him up to see his face, smiling at how lust-filled those eyes are again.

"Still lingering a little but no longer crippling me into celibacy. I needed yesterday more than you could ever know, Emma. I needed to get back to this to us. I love you so much." He runs a finger over my mouth before scooping to replace it with his lips. I moan at the contact, so ready for more. He sits back up, looking at me adoringly.

"I love you too, although yesterday I contemplated triggering your sleeping disorder if my plan didn't work. I even googled it." I laugh as he shakes his head at me.

"I would've probably liked it." He laughs, biting my neck playfully again, sending me into squirming giggles. He slides up and flips me over to my front, smacking my butt a little hard, but I like it. I've missed all forms of Casanova Carrero. It's like he's reappeared from being away for a long time, our honeymoon period in full force once again.

"Get up. We have shit to do today." He jumps to his feet over my body on the bed, balances walking over me carefully, then drops to the floor before stalking to the bathroom. I sigh obediently and slide out of bed to retrieve the fluffy robe he's left there and haul it on.

I've got so used to living in this house that breakfast is normally eaten dressed this way, curled up in the cozy main room on the couch in a fluffy robe. Sylvana comes to breakfast dressed the same way and always with a huge grin on her happy morning face.

I've seen Giovanni briefly. He's always impeccably dressed; never caught him wearing anything less than a shirt, waistcoat, pants, and shoes. The man must rise at dawn and always have that cool, controlled demeanor, never a hint of relaxed softness or harshness, just being Giovanni.

I can see why Jake and he collide. Giovanni is never demonstrative or outwardly emotional. He's not touchy or affectionate. Arrick has more of Giovanni's traits than Jake does, that same cool mature manner, and even when girlfriends are here, Arrick doesn't overly pander to them. The odd hand-holding, but no real public displays of affection that Jake is always happy to throw around, and no open flirting or cuddly feelings.

Even with his mother, Arrick is more reserved than Jake. Jake kisses her on the cheek and hugs her in passing or walks with her arm in arm. Arrick is like his father, with hands in his pockets as he stands in a domineering manner among people, those eyes never miss a beat. Arrick understands his father a lot more than Jake. That much is obvious, and I believe it's because he's far more like Giovanni than Jake is.

Giovanni works in the city, so he flies back and forth a lot to be home every night just as he promised his wife, another display of respect and love for Sylvana that Jake doesn't notice either.

Arrick's still in education. I'm not sure if that means college or some high-priced university or business school, but he seems to come home sporadically, always with a new girl in tow, much like the Jake of old. Carrero blood has a lot to answer for, and I'll be damned if this little Carrero gets up to such things ... if he's a boy, that is.

Sylvana splits her days between here and her charity, so sometimes she's home for days and sometimes gone for days depending on her commitments.

She has gushed at me on occasion at how much she's looking forward to having little feet running around again and a little face to spoil with kisses. I can imagine her as a grandmother, giving so much love to a new generation of little Carreros. She's a woman built to love and to keep loving every child who comes her way, and I know she'll love both mine and Marissa's child equally.

I have tried to ignore the pain in that statement. Once again, realizing that everyone will bond with Marissa's baby months before mine comes. Ours won't be the first tiny feet, the first grandchild, or even Jake's first child, which still hurts me to the core. My baby will be second in everything, second to arrive, second to be loved, second to be pampered, but in Jake's eyes, my baby will always be first. My baby will be first to him in every way, and I should use that thought to be okay with this. That's all that matters to me. He will love his other child, but I know his bond with me and living with this child will make a difference in the relationship. Something Marissa hasn't thought of.

"Come on, sexy." Jake reappears from the bathroom and catches my hand in his, dragging me off the bed and through the door in that infuriating, bossy manner of his.

* * *

For once, we're sitting at the table eating breakfast together. I'm on toast and fruit salad with fresh orange juice, Jake's got a mountain of pancakes and bacon, and Sylvana is on some healthy granola stuff piled high in a bowl with yogurt and fruit. The two of them have been amusing to watch.

They have the same mannerisms as they read the morning paper and then switch pages, shifting in their chairs, rounding their shoulders, and tilting their heads to one side. Both talk with full mouths when they point out something interesting in the paper. The same way they cradle their mugs, not using the handles, and hold their cutlery when eating, propping a fork in the air when engrossed in reading a column or news story. It's beyond adorable, and they are like mirror images.

The housekeeper wanders around, picking up used dishes and replenishing the coffee mugs, and I can't help but feel completely relaxed sitting here this way. Smiling at the two bowed dark heads, noticing from this angle they have the same nose profile and eyebrows, makes me giggle impulsively.

Jake looks up at me with a cute smiling frown.

"Something funny?"

"You two are like book ends ... Just wondering if this one will have the same Carrero good looks and quirks as you two do." I tip my head to one side and smile at him, his face breaking into a grin.

"With my genes, *Bambina* ... more than likely." He sits back in his chair and appreciatively looks me over.

"Oh no. I hope this little one looks like Emma." Sylvana chirps in with a dreamy expression. "Can you imagine a little curly blonde-haired cherub with soft blue eyes and little pouty lips just like his mother? Face of an angel but, of course, the little devil child that you were, Jacob." Sylvana is beaming, and Jake gazes at me intensely.

"When you put it that way, I'd love nothing more than a mini Emma ... It Would be the most beautiful baby on the planet." He sighs, and his look grows intense, eyes locking onto mine in a devastatingly attractive way.

He knows exactly what to say. Gold star to you, Carrero.

"I want a mini Carrero." I sigh, loving how Jake looks at me, a focused, warm caress, because, before today, I haven't expressed much about our baby other than being unsure of how I felt. I guess part of me is starting to get used to what this is, what we have coming, and I can feel the joy radiating from him at this sudden change in me. I should tell him more often that I'm not entirely unhappy about a little Jake growing inside me. He looks like he needs the reassurance.

"Either way, it'll be a mini Carrero, in looks or charm; there's enough of my genes in there to make sure of it, not like we haven't had enough attempts." He winks naughtily, and I blush. Sylvana throws a piece of fruit at him, and it bounces off his head.

"Your mother is sitting right here, young man." She lifts an eyebrow at him. "Don't make me put you over my knee." The warning tone is deathly, but the insincere way she smirks ruins the whole effect.

"Mamma ..." He raises his hands at her, shrugging in defense, but she only shakes her head.

"I wish I could blame that high sex drive and mischief on his father alone. Sadly I think Italian blood is naturally rich in it. I'm just as bad." Sylvana winks my way, and it's Jake's turn to cringe at her.

"Jesus, Mamma, what the hell? I swear I need to poke my ears out with something sharp now." He glares at her with an utter look of disgust on his face. I can't help but giggle at them. Jake catches my hand, leans in, pulls it up to his mouth, and kisses my palm. He lets me go and continues with his coffee.

"Well, since we're talking about libido, you should know that kid has no chance of boyfriends if it's a girl. I'm buying a shotgun and a really big dog for the dating age." He frowns, and the hunch of his shoulders gives me the impression he's not kidding.

"You're going to be a nightmare as a father. I can see it already." I sigh and watch him studiously.

"Yeah, well, guess you better keep me in a steady supply of kids, so I get lots of practice at getting better." He winks at me and laughs when my face drops to a stone-cold blank deadpan. My heart doing a sudden drop in sheer panic.

"Oh, Emma." Sylvana bursts out laughing as she clocks my expression. "You're marrying a Carrero, honey. If Giovanni had his way, we would've had fifty kids. Sadly my body wasn't too happy about that." She croons at me.

"I'm not that bad. Fifty is maybe a bit much ... maybe five or six?" Jake winks at me with a mischievous smile, and I scowl at him. I hope to God he's kidding right now for a reaction from me.

"When you start popping them out, you can have five or six. Until then, I'm not making any promises beyond this one." I pout at him huffily, only to be met with a look I know all too well. The one that says, 'you know I'll have it my way by any means.' I stick my chin up and raise my eyebrows at him.

"Baby, wait until this little one comes out and melts what's left of PA Emma's heart." He grins at me with wickedness, and the urge to throw my fork at him is not lost on me. "You'll be begging me to keep you barefoot and pregnant."

"I think not." I stare at him steadily. "I have decided that when this baby comes, I want to study." I divert down at the table, suddenly losing courage. I've thought about this a lot, considering it when Jake's been gone long hours, and even though I'm not sure how I will form a future with what I have planned, I know it's what I want to do.

"Study what?" Jake regards me with interest, a small quirk of a smile on the corner of his mouth, and Sylvana is watching me with an equally warm expression. Encouraging is the word that comes to mind when I look at them both.

Is this what family does when you have some hair-brained idea you want to try?

"I was thinking I could, maybe, possibly try becoming a counselor of sorts... You know to work with kids who Ummm ..." I lose the courage again and focus on my fingers as they make their way to my hair, the nervous fidgeting habit coming back to haunt me; saying it aloud sounds dumb.

What do I know about helping other kids?

"... came from abused backgrounds and broken families?" Jake finishes my sentence, taking my hand away from my hair, calming me like he always does. I glance up at him and nod shyly as he focuses on me with an encouraging smile.

"I think that would be pretty amazing, and not just for the kids you could help, Emma, but I think for you too." He gets up and slides his chair back, walking around the table behind me, leans down, wraps his arms around my shoulders, kisses me on the neck, and buries his face in my soft hair to nuzzle me. Telling me that he's fully on board with my plan and making me feel a hundred times surer.

"I think that is a spectacularly selfless plan, Emma." Sylvana beams at me. "I'm pretty sure with my connections, I could help you along the way, help you find your feet and direction. If helping kids from the same abusive situation you were in is what you want to do?" She shines at me, and my courage returns tenfold.

And there it is ... Sylvana says it so effortlessly like it's not some shameful, horrible, ugly secret, just a common piece of knowledge between the people close to one another in the room, and I don't feel anything like I used to.

No shame, no pain, no anything. Just Jake's arms around me, and when he straightens and runs a hand down my hair, igniting the usual thrill of shivers and heat, it comes to me in a flash.

My past doesn't hurt me anymore. I'm not ashamed of it. I gaze adoringly at the man I love as he moves back to his seat, glancing at me with equal infatuation, and I feel different. I'm sitting taller, my chin held higher, and my expression migrates to a bright smile.

That kid from Chicago who separated herself into different versions and locked boxes has somehow come crashing back together again into one complete person. Her past is no longer a deep dark secret she hides from those who she thought would run from her if they knew ... because here they are, sitting facing her, with love and care despite knowing about it all. They don't look at her as though she's some broken or dirty shell. They don't look at her like her own flesh and blood did. They accept her and love her even more for the scars she bares ... a real family with real love.

I'm not broken anymore; I am whole, and only one piece of my puzzle remains out of place. I will have to face my mother and the fact that she will never give me what I've been trying to get from her my entire life.

Her love.

The difference now is I no longer need it.

Chapter 20

"Baby, wait until I'm back to do this?" Jake is trying to tug the case out of my hands. We're back in the Manhattan apartment and have been overseeing the packing of some of his favorite items and our clothes to be shipped to the Hamptons for a couple of days. The journey home was sickness-free, and I'm starting to feel much better these days. I am beginning to feel great, especially now that I have the full undivided attention of my lover once more, and he's only too willing to keep me satisfied.

"No, I told you. I'll take Mathews if you're so damned hell-bent on me having an escort. I'm sure he's a major in karate, kill whatsits or some other nonsense. I know you sometimes spar with him in the gym downstairs, so he must be a deathly ninja of some kind to put up with your crazy martial art commando ways." I huff back, trying to wrestle the handle free from his annoyingly strong grip.

"Emma, I said *no!*" Jake yanks the case out of my hands, throwing it behind him on the floor. The contents splay everywhere in a crazy dramatic fashion. I square up and glare at him angrily. So seriously not in the mood for immature bossy dickhead Carrero right now.

"Are you telling me what to do?" I stick out my chin defiantly. My rage bubbling forth at the return of one stroppy domineering asshole I thought I stupidly missed.

Ha fucking ha.

"I am the guy you're marrying and the father of that fucking baby. If you dare step foot in Chicago without me, I'll seriously lose my shit." He's scary right now with his blazing green eyes and tense stubbly jaw. Scary in a sexy male model 'who could possibly use his top coming off to cool him down' sort of way.

Really, Emma, sex while you're raging at him?

Hormones!

"I lived there my whole life, Jake. I'm sure I can handle Chicago, and stop yelling at me ... I don't particularly appreciate the swearing either." I stomp and pull my height up to meet his, unsuccessfully, seeing as he's six feet two and I'm barely scraping five-foot-four. He's glaring down at me, anger emanating from every pore. His aggressive psycho mode that does absolutely nothing to me.

"Last time you went alone, some guy hurt you in the fucking stairwell. You're never going there alone again, and your mother ... Don't even get me started on her because last time she fucking crushed you." He is radiating pure aggressive dominance, an alpha male asshole, but I am not backing down on this.

"I'm not the same anymore, Jake. I'm stronger, and stop it." I slap him in the abdomen churlishly. "Stop talking down to me like I'm your PA." He doesn't even flinch when my palm connects with his hard six-pack.

Or is it eight? Hard to count as when I'm usually on that body, I'm preoccupied.

"Emma!" He has his gritted teeth voice on and the bunching muscles of a severely pissed-off Carrero. "I have to go for two days, that's all, two fucking days to oversee this crap, and then I'll take you myself. *I'll* drive there and back. Until then, I'll lock you in this apartment and tell Mathews I'll fucking fire him if you step one foot in his car." He seethes at me; pretty sure breathing fire would be one of his things if it were physically possible.

I step back at the wave of his rage and lift my chin slightly higher, inner Emma refusing to be railroaded by this cocky, arrogant ass.

"Jake, if you dare try to intimidate me right now, I'll not only get a fucking train to Chicago, carrying my case by myself, but I'll go as soon as it's dark and you're gone and not even take a goddamn phone, so you can't track my cell or call me." I threaten smugly. Not phased one bit by his show of scare.

There's nothing Jake would hate more than that! He'd go into worried protective overload and maybe blow a brain cell ... or three thousand.

We have a monumental angry stare-off, rage bubbling between us, but I don't care. I'm not scared of Jake's little moods anymore or him storming off with hurt feelings, and I'm sure as hell not frightened of any little consequences. Somewhere along the way, I've realized that I have nothing to worry about when it comes to Jake, and if anyone is going to be leaving anyone, it will be me. This right here is not the behavior I am about to put up with for the rest of my married life, and he should learn that fast!

"You wouldn't dare, Emma." That nasty growl does nothing for me. If anything, it makes me want to unbutton his pants, but we're so not doing sex right now.

Maybe later!

"Try me." I bite back, my defiant, hormonal mood in full swing, and he straightens up, that tiny smirk twitching to his mouth breaking his scowling intimidation in a second. He rubs a hand across his face and scrubs it for a second. I guess all his posturing is just a very convincing act if he's so quick to chuck it aside.

Hmmmmmm.

"You, woman, are going to be the absolute death of me." He sighs heavily and reaches out, tugging me toward him, planting a kiss on my mouth, cupping my jaw with both hands, and burying his fingers in my hair. Sighing in defeat because he knows there is not a thing he can possibly do to me.

You're so whipped, Jake.

"I don't want you to go." His tone is softer and gentler, and he's obviously changing tactics, but my mind's made up. I know all his devious little manipulations, he's going in for soft and tender, but if that fails, he'll pull out the sex strategy.

And, well, sex I can never resist, especially his kind, so I better get this stopped now since my head has been heading that way for the last twenty minutes.

"Jake, please don't make me beg you to do this. Let me do what I need to do to move on in life." I flutter my lashes at him and give him my sincerest wide-eyed look of adoration.

There's a flicker of doubt in his eye, and I know I have him over a barrel. Two can play that emotional card, Jake.

"Arghhhh." He raises his palms in agitation and paces away from me and back again.

"I'll fucking beg. Do you want me on my knees right now?" He pleads in an annoyed tone. Maybe not ready to let this go just yet.

Depends on what you're planning on doing down there.

"Stop being so melodramatic." I sigh and turn away, leaning down to pick up my case, but Jake grabs my wrist to stop me from bending. He scoops instead, throwing everything on the bed, and I can't help but smile. I stand watching him with folded arms. He's a stroppy ass, but even in a mood, he's still taking care of his pregnant woman.

"I'm not happy about this at all." He's back to brimming with sourness, but I pinch his butt as I walk past him to the bed and smile. He throws me a look of indulgence, and I sigh.

"So, I see." I flip the case over and start folding my clothes again, sliding things in neatly and slowly, bringing some order back to the mess he made. Un-phased by the amount of death-ray looks aimed my way as he watches me painfully.

"Fuck's sake!" Jake snaps, and my case is yanked off the bed and thrown behind him again like a child having a meltdown. It will be a very long night if things carry on at this rate. I should check his birth certificate sometime and ensure he is not actually a five-year-old in a man's body.

"Are you really going to keep doing that?" I'm not angry anymore, just amused by the temper and childishness of my husband-to-be. The massive man-child I used to love working for has returned in full fury. If it weren't frustrating to keep refolding the same clothes, I would be laughing at him right now.

"Yes." He sulks and glares at me, knowing he's not winning this argument one iota, so he's stropping about instead.

Sulky Jake—Oh lord.

I walk up to him, slide my hand into his back pocket, pull out his wallet effortlessly, and flip it open. He narrows his eyes, watching as I slide out his sexy black credit card without attempting to stop me and wave it in front of him.

"If I'm not allowed to pack or take anything to wear, I'll buy what I need, and that'll resolve that little issue." I tease with a naughty smug smile. Jake takes hold of my wrist with one hand and yanks the card out of my hand with the other, throwing that behind him on top of the scattered case too. His expression completely serious, and I can't help but burst into giggles. He still has my wrist in his hand, and it's obvious he's not about to let go.

"You're impossible," I poke him in the chest accusingly but can't stop the giggling.

"That's why you love me, and that's why I'll cancel my fucking trip and stay right here if you keep this up." He moves toward me menacingly, and I spring back, yanking my hand free and waving my hips at him playfully, goading him childishly. His mood is simmering, but that twinkle in his eye hints at a desire to stop arguing and do something far more fun; that never-ending heat between us is never far away nowadays.

There's a small knock on the open bedroom door, and Mathews appears, graciously clearing his throat to alert us of his presence.

"Mr. Carrero, Mr. Hunter is here to see you." He nods and then waits for Jake's response. Jake looks immediately irritated and sighs, resigning himself to the fact that this is going nowhere.

"Show him to the lounge. I'll be there in a minute." Jake smiles, and Mathews turns and leaves us to it. Jake goes to walk forward, then stops and glances over his shoulder at the case on the floor. His eyes narrow suspiciously as he knows I'll pick it up and keep packing as soon as he leaves.

He stalks toward me in two easy strides and, without warning, bends down to flip me over his shoulder with a sharp smack to my ass, making me squeal as he marches us through to the next room with determination. He thinks that if I'm with him, then I can't disobey him.

Asshole.

"Jake put me down." I protest, helplessly squirming on his wide shoulders in his vice-like grip, and he only sets me on my feet when we're beside the long, low white leather couch. Daniel is sitting far too rigidly on the far end, not even looking our way but studying his own hands. Jake catches my wrists and pulls me onto his lap as he sits down, catching me, so I don't fall, nestling me into his embrace. It seems I'm to be his prisoner in case I defy him and pack my case.

What am I going to do with him?

Seriously!

"What's up, Danny? You look a little stressed." Jake turns his steely face to Hunter. I struggle to get free but realize it's futile. Jake's grip is like that of a man on a mission to keep me here. I might as well give in for the time being and see what's going on with Daniel *Forlorn-Looking* Hunter. I must admit I am a little nosey, seeing as he looks rather ... well, sad.

I wrap my arms around Jake's neck and curl my legs on his lap. His arms are loose around me, and I turn, glancing at Daniel. Jake is right about him looking stressed, the boy is sitting straighter than a poker set, and those blue eyes, normally so calm and cheeky, are a little red-rimmed. His usually slightly ruffled hair is too flat and unkempt.

"I need your words of wisdom." He runs his fingers through his hair in agitation, and I notice his shirt is more than a little rumpled. His face isn't its usual clean-shaven self either, he's sporting Jake's designer stubble, and on Hunter, it looks odd. He's too blonde to pull it off.

"Leila?" Jake asks with his sharp instincts, and I immediately zone all attention on Hunter again. I have learned from watching Jake that only woman issues could make a man go to hell like this.

"She's dumped me." He sits back, flopping dejectedly, and slides his feet out wide, sighing heavily, bringing his gaze to the ceiling as though he's going to find some divine wisdom up there.

"Why?" I ask slowly and deliberately, with a hint of edge in my tone. My body bristles in Jake's embrace as he slides his hands down to my ass, pulling me closer to get comfy.

I'll kill him if he's hurt her again.

"She's bat shit crazy! That's why! Jealous as fucking hell, and nothing I said to her helped one bit. We fought over some stupid chick who came up to me in a club two nights ago, and Leila flipped the fuck out." He sounds exhausted, and all hints of smug Hunter are gone.

"Please tell me you haven't done anything, Danny?" Jake slides me off his lap onto the couch next to him, leaning forward to rest his elbows on his knees toward Daniel. It seems I'm no longer a flight risk now that his friend is genuinely in need, but I stay put anyway.

"No. I'm not stupid, Jake. The girl was someone I hadn't seen in a long time. She tried to get me to dance, and I told her to beat it. Leila just saw red." He sighs again. "I'm trying so fucking hard, Jake, trying to see her as often as possible, showing her that I'm not dating anyone else. Seeing my shrink every week despite the undying urge to take off at a hundred miles an hour. It doesn't mean I'm not struggling with all of this relationship shit, but I'm doing it for her." Daniel slides forward to mirror Jake's pose, so they're closer together.

"But what exactly happened?" I pull a fluffy cushion onto my lap and start stroking it as I stare at the poor guy's tight expression and tortured eyes. I can't help but feel a little sorry for him. He truly looks miserable, and I know only too well how that can feel.

"She threw her fucking drink at me, told me it was over, told me to go fuck the whore, stormed off, and went home. She won't answer my calls." A hint of anger in his tone seems to spark the same on his face.

"Have you thought about going around there and seeing her? Leila is majorly insecure, Daniel." I narrow my eyes on him, and he sighs again.

"And say what? No, Leila, I'm not fucking you about or touching other women publicly on a dance floor five feet away from you. She wouldn't let me near her front door. I know Leila too well.

She won't let me in if she's not answering calls." He sits up sharply. "What about some fucking trust? Some fucking benefit of the doubt?" He gets up and then immediately sits down again. "See this shit?" He throws a gesturing hand down the length of him. "She's got me so messed up I don't know if I'm coming or going ... Fuck's sake! Seriously. I'm all over the place. I don't think I can handle this anymore." He seems perplexed, slowly unraveling, and I can't help but wonder if this is how Jake was during our separation.

"What are you saying?" Jake doesn't look happy at all; his body tenses a little too sexily for my liking. I can't seem to get my head out of the gutter lately. All this rush of sexual longing has hit hard since getting our back intimacy, and now I can't seem to switch it off. I wonder if this is a pregnancy thing.

Damn, these hormones. I'm so horny for him right now.

"Maybe I'm not able to do this ... Maybe Leila and I are better off not together because I can't seem to keep that chick happy." Daniel looks defeated. He restlessly shifts position three times in a row, then resigns himself to returning to his first position, flopping on the couch with legs apart.

I go to snap at him in anger, but Jake stands, and his sudden motion silences me. I wait for his flash of anger, but nothing comes.

"Fine ... Leave it this way then. Finished." He shrugs and walks toward the kitchen rendering me utterly speechless. He sounds completely normal and, well, sort of accepting.

What the fuck?

I have no idea what he's playing at, but whatever it is, I don't like it at all. This isn't the Jake who loves Leila to death and puts Hunter in his place when he's being a moron. I'm unhappy about his lack of care for her and start glaring at his back.

"You agree I should give up?" Daniel seems equally shocked at the lack of lecture.

"If you can't do it, then don't. Walk away. Let her go back to that Kurt preppy boy asshole and have a happy life with Mr. *Squeaky Clean.*" Jake's level, even tone, is giving nothing away. Still, I know the manipulation tells in his sexy body how he's casually in control, setting out mugs for coffee nonchalantly, unemotional about the topic. Everything is a bit too precise, and because I know him, I see a very calculated famous Carrero maneuver from miles off. I smile internally at the cleverness of my man.

Reverse psychology. Well done Mr. Carrero.

"Just walk away from her? And then what? That guy won't make her happy ..." Daniel can't do anything but stare and question Jake's mental state.

"Go back to being a man-whore with parties and whatever else. Just forget about her." Jake shrugs, holding up a mug and waving it at me, asking if I want one too. I smirk and shake my head adoringly. He is playing Hunter so well.

My devious asshole of a man.

Daniel sits for a moment and stares at his hands quietly.

"I can't do that." He says it more to himself than to either of us, sounding sadly defeated, looking up at Jake as he says, "I love her too much."

"Well, man up, Danny, and stop acting like you weren't expecting any of this shit from her. Leila is acting out because she's waiting for you to fuck things up. She's pushing her damned hardest to make sure you do because she's expecting it, and sooner will hurt far less than later." Jake snaps at him, and I know exactly what he is doing. His insight into Leila's head warms me.

God, I love you.

Daniel contemplates this for a moment as I watch in absolute silence. Jake's ability to read people and situations has always impressed me. His ability to sometimes understand the female mind must be a rare gift for a guy. I'm sure not many men have his level of understanding. Although at times, he is denser than most, so maybe it's a sporadic gift.

"Why did I have to fall for the one who drives me so fucking crazy?" Daniel sighs, returning to picking at his thumbnail absently, staring at his hand with a complete utter lost boy look on his handsome face.

Jake gazes at me intensely from the kitchen.

"It's not love if she can't get under your skin and make you a whole lot of crazy." He smiles, winking at me, and I can't help but smile back, especially when he opens the fridge and starts fixing me a tropical alcohol-free cocktail that I've been craving like mad lately.

Now that's the man I love right there.

"Leila has always got under my skin, but dating her has made it so much worse," Daniel admits, seemingly confused that finally loving his girl would intensify what she does to him.

"Is the therapy helping?" I nudge in with a lighter, warmer tone, and Daniel turns to me, expression a little young and tired and more than a little bewildered.

"Yes, I guess, and no ... Well, it's bringing up a lot of shit I need to deal with, but Leila's been with me twice, and when she's there, I dunno, it doesn't mess me up as bad." He shrugs as though just the thought of her brings him some peace, and the sudden flicker of heartache that runs across his face is a giveaway of the fact he's just realized it as the words come out of his mouth.

"You know she won't always be this way. She just doesn't trust you not to run again." I soothe, a little more sympathetic at the real pain I'm seeing in his tropical blue eyes.

"The thing is, for the most part, I don't mind Leila's kind of crazy. She's feisty and wild and moody as shit. Man, she's got a temper and a hell of a right hook. I kinda dig it, though ... It's the silence and not letting me near her when we fight that's killing me. Not knowing what's going on in that head of hers and having her freeze me out of her life." He sighs again and looks tormented.

"She's hiding," Jake interjects. "She's probably just as messed up as you are right now." His soft, husky tone as he watches his best friend gives me all sorts of horny thoughts, and I shift to a sitting position crossing my legs. I catch Jake's smirk and realize he knows exactly what I'm thinking.

Jerk.

Daniel frowns, staring emptily down at his hands; he has a fidgeting tell as Jake has, and he starts picking at his other thumbnail.

"I don't know how to do this, Jake ... but I don't want to walk away. I've spent years trying to run from how I felt about her, but I can't outrun it anymore. I can't do it ... I need her ... But I know her. She won't see me or talk to me."

Both men fall silent as they contemplate the best way to deal with Leila, and an idea hits me, a self-serving, killing-two-birds-with-one-stone kind of idea.

"Sarah and I could take her out. Then casually run into you both. That way, she would have no choice but to see you, and she wouldn't suspect that I side with you and set her up." I smile innocently and flutter my lashes Jake's way with an innocent smile.

Jake frowns at me, and I know what *Mr. Protective-father-to-be* is thinking. I focus on him intently, seeing that frown deepening, and I don't think this is going down well at all.

"You could run into us almost as soon as we arrive and mollycoddle the shit out of me, Jake. So don't worry about my being out on the town in such a delicate condition." I smirk at him, and he has the nerve to smirk back, only confirming what is running through that beautiful head.

What am I going to do with him?

"It could work. Leila wouldn't suspect a setup at a club. If Jefferson drops you at the door, we could meet you at the other side." His intense look boring into me makes me sigh. He's trying to clarify that I am not allowed out of his sight.

We'll see.

"You're only going to get worse the bigger this gets, aren't you?" I point at my slightly fuller stomach, decidedly less flat these last few days.

"Count on it." Jake lifts his eyebrows at me as though challenging me on the subject before he turns back to Daniel.

"What do you say? You want to see her this way?" Jake gives up on making coffee and leans on the counter, those glorious biceps straining at the fabric on his arms.

Oh, man. Hot flushes.

"Any way is better than no way, man. I fucking miss her so much already." Daniel sighs and drops his head into his palms between his knees and scratches his head, then sitting back up, he looks at Jake, then at me with so much pain in his face.

"How soon can we do this? I can't stand the agony of waiting."

Chapter 21

Jake kisses me in the sitting room as Mathews takes his luggage past us toward the elevator outside the apartment door. I still haven't got a handle on this panty-combusting thing he causes. His hands cup my jaw, leaving me with a kiss that curls my toes. My hormones perking up to say hello, giving me the usual warm, tingling longing.

"I'll call you when I land, okay?" He brushes his nose against mine and lightly kisses me.

"I'll miss you." I sigh against him, my arms around his neck. I reach up to be wrapped around him tightly. He slides his hands down my sides and around my back, pulling me in further still. Nothing in this world feels like a full-on cuddle from Jake. Nothing will ever compare to this.

"No sneaking off to Chicago until I'm back. Promise me." He narrows his eyes at me, and I sigh.

Last night and again this morning, he predictably used his "sexpertize" against me and had me screaming out in agreement that I wouldn't go. I can't believe he can still maneuver me that way, yet here we are.

I really am pathetically submissive when he gets me naked.

"I'm only agreeing because you're agreeing to *Operation Leila* and taking me on a night out when you return," I smirk at him. His green glare hits me again. He isn't too enamored with the finer details yet.

"We could've just arranged for them to meet here, you know?" His voice hitting a slightly edgy tone.

"She wouldn't fall for that, and I wouldn't get my night out on the town that I need badly. All this lazing about and being housebound is getting old. I'm so bored." I sigh and give him my most appealing smile, fluttering my lashes and pouting my lip slightly.

"You do know I'm putting a curfew on this, right? No alcohol, minimal dancing, and home in bed by ten." He focuses on my mouth, making me think about kissing him again.

Yeah, I think not, Mr. Carrero. You sound like a father right now, not a fiancée!

"We'll see." I smile sweetly

"No, that's what's happening!" He narrows his gaze on me, and I kiss him quickly. Sometimes that mouth is too tempting, even when he's being difficult.

"We shall see," I shrug, slowly and deliberately, watching that twitch of a smirk start at the corner of his sexy mouth. Jake likes to be bossy and in command, but he also likes me defiant too. He's getting a kick out of my standing up to him lately, but he can't keep his temper when I do. I'm glad, though. Life would be dull and tiresome if he expected compliance from me. He never got much of it when I was his PA, so he sure as hell won't get any more of it just because we're together.

"I need to go, *Bambina*. When I call you tonight, we'll try some phone sex. We're definitely doing that if I have to leave you for work." He grins, and I roll my eyes at him and his typical guy-ness.

Well, you wanted this side of him back in full roaring glory.

"You know you're only going for forty-eight hours? You sound like it's going to be weeks." I laugh at him as he turns away, swiping a hand at that delicious ass.

"Forty-eight hours without you does feel like weeks." He catches my hand and uses his hold on it to twirl me around so he can deliver a hefty smack on my ass, showing me how to do it. I yelp at the contact, grinning.

Oh, Casanova, you are still very smooth, aren't you?

"Well, you better get going then so I have time to brush up on my most seductive chat up lines for your call, Mr. Carrero. I might start with what I'm wearing." I giggle, and he catches me in one final kiss that melts my bones. I wonder if all couples still kiss this way after the honeymoon period has worn off? I can't imagine him not doing this to me, even when we're old and crippled.

"I'll expect our kind of phone sex to be conducted naked, via Skype, on a video call, baby," and I get the Carrero wink that makes my knees go weak.

Of course, he does.

The naughty look he throws my way says he's serious, then he turns, and I walk with him to the door. He kisses me one last time before sauntering out, dressed to impress in an immaculate three-piece gray suit over a crisp white shirt. He doesn't often do waistcoats under his jackets, but this Saville Row number makes him hotter than hot. I sigh blissfully, watching that ass move out the door, then muse a little sadly when it shuts, and he's gone again all too soon. He is far too tempting nowadays, and I still can't get a handle on the craziness of my sex-crazed hormones.

Damn. Maybe video phone sex isn't such a bad idea after all?

Especially if I need to get through forty-eight hours alone.

Forty-eight hours to amuse myself, and I'm determined to find something more productive than sitting around twiddling my thumbs, feeling like a crazy horny pregnant woman. There's no denying it. That man has simply ruined me.

Tomorrow I am going to shop, maybe abuse that sexy gold card Jake always leaves in my purse, and buy some things for this little tadpole, seeing as I can't get around the fact of it coming. We've already picked the nursery in our new home. I'm sure spending money on Jake's offspring is acceptable, as I'm still getting used to this money thing. I did agree to accept this part of his lifestyle and indulge a little, so that's exactly what I'm going to do.

At least try to.

I flicker down at my slightly extended stomach and sigh. Its presence ignites a familiar tingling ache in my heart, running a hand over it soothingly. Shopping will be a good distraction.

We've heard nothing from Marissa directly, but the lawyers have informed Jake she is fighting the DNA tooth and nail. I'm not surprised since she seems to be hell-bent on making this a battle every step of the way. All her recent outburst has done is convince me she believes this baby is Jake's, so it must be. She wouldn't fight for it this hard and this much if it weren't.

I turn my thoughts back to our plans, and Hunter, in a bid to push the Demon Bitch back off the cliffs of my mind where she belongs. We're going to hit the club we went to on Arrick's birthday if I can talk Sarah and Leila into it. Daniel will get his chance to talk Leila out of her crazy decision, with all of us backing him up. I like this plan, and knowing how much of a party girl Leila is, I'm sure she won't say no to a girly night out with her two most favorite women.

* * *

Jake wasn't kidding when he said he wanted to try video sex! However, we've ended up laughing a lot on a Skype call while I sit in my underwear, and he lies in a hotel bed with a sexy naked torso making me ache. Sexy turned to funny; before we knew it, he had me crying tears of laughter. I sometimes forget that he can be quick-witted and sharp. His sense of humor is devastating; I can't remember ever laughing as much as this in my life, and my muscles ache with the effort.

"Soon as you're able to start flying again, I'm bringing you everywhere I go." He sighs at me through the iPad screen. I trace the shape of his mouth on the smooth surface, inner loneliness aching through me that I always get at his absence.

"You need to get used to this; soon enough, I won't be able to follow you around the world, Jake. We'll have a child to stay home for." I sigh at him, snuggle down in bed, matching his pose, and get comfortable.

"I'll bring you both." He raises a stubborn eyebrow, and I can only giggle.

"And what about when it starts pre-school or an actual school? You can't just demand we come with you anytime you need to go." I giggle at that boyish face.

"I like this you know?" Jake regards me seriously, and I frown.

"What? Our useless attempt at video kinky, and we're talking schools instead? How very sexy!" I giggle again, caught in the best mood because of him.

"You talking babies. I still wasn't sure you were warm on having it, and now you're acknowledging that a baby is coming." He chews his bottom lip, and I spot that little tell. He's thinking about what he's saying, choosing his words carefully, still walking on eggshells occasionally, especially when it's something that matters to him.

"I needed time to get used to it, to get used to everything. I guess I'm happy ... It still feels surreal and weird, but tadpole is in there, and it's coming no matter what we do." I sigh and glance down at my stomach under the thin sheet, experiencing that same tingle in my heart anytime I acknowledge its existence.

"Tadpole?" Jake raises an eyebrow at me.

"Yeah, you know ... Because I think of a tiny little sperm, and you know ... well, I don't know what it looks like this early!" I giggle, and Jake bursts out laughing. It's maybe about time I start reading pregnancy books.

"Jesus, baby, could you be any more goddamn adorable? God, I love you so much." He laughs in the deep husky way that he does, a little sensual but overall infectious. Jake can be irresistibly cute when in completely natural and relaxed mode. It sounds good to listen to him laugh this way. It sounds even better to hear him trying to curb his swearing. I felt like a broken record chastising him every time he swore; now, his chatter is filled with *goddamn* instead of *fuck*. I guess he must've realized that he doesn't want our child's first words to be *fuck* or *fucking* after all.

"So, what would you call it?" I pout mockingly at him, laughing at me.

"Seriously?"

"Yes." I laugh, watching how he furrows his brow and chews his lip, deep in thought, with a suddenly serious expression on his face.

"Mia or Lucas. I guess I would call it one of those." Jake suddenly seems so young and unsure, a lump catching my throat. It's not what I expected as an answer. I expected some cute inner womb nickname. The thought of a little Mia or Lucas Carrero suddenly overwhelms me, realization hitting me at how much thought Jake has put into this. He has thought about names for our child. I could cry.

"Where did you find those names?" I breathe softly, eyes glazing over with moisture.

"Mia just sort of sounds close to Emma, and as you know, it's my favorite name in the whole world." He winks cheekily, but my heart tells me he's not kidding. "And Lucas, well, I like it. It sounds like a good Carrero name." He watches me through the screen as I think through his choices, and I honestly can't find fault with either.

"I love them both. I especially love that you like Mia because it sounds like my name. Sometimes you're too cute for words, Mr. Carrero. You always surprise me." I sigh, touching the screen again, desperate for his mouth on mine, especially when we're talking like this. Suddenly he seems so very far away, and I miss his arms around me.

"Don't let people know how soft I actually am. It would totally ruin my reputation." He winks again, and I eyeroll.

"I'm pretty sure your reputation that preceded me will go on for a very long time. It's more famous than you are, baby. I'm sure, even with an engagement announcement, the world still assumes you have a row of scantily clad women in the back running around, getting drunk, and acting wild. I've seen the endless tabloid scandals about you, remember!" I narrow my eyes at him and smile.

"How do you know that isn't my backup plan for the next time you leave me?" He winks, and he's lucky he's thousands of miles away, as that remark deserves a dig to the ribs. I stick my chin up and raise a haughty eyebrow.

"Hmm ..." is my only reply, and Jake breaks into an adorable Hollywood hottest smile.

"You know I'd follow you to the end of the world, baby, chase you with everything I've got if I was ever stupid enough to lose you again. I don't plan on us ever being apart, Emma. I can't wait to get you down the aisle and have you as mine ... Mrs. Carrero." That smooth declaration and sexy smile calm down my inner bristled feathers.

"It does have a nice ring to it, I guess ... Emma Carrero ... Mr. and Mrs. Jake Carrero. I could get used to that," I ring off dreamily.

"You better get used to it as soon as the house is sorted. Our next plans will be wedding themed." He warns with a wink.

"You don't think I should maybe push a baby out first so I don't look like a whale on my wedding day?" I frown at him, then look down at my stomach, trying to figure out how long I have before I do start looking like a round Christmas tree ornament. I know nothing about pregnancy at all.

"Hell no. No child of mine is being born outside of this marriage, baby."

We both pause as Jake realizes what he's said, and I frown at him.

"Except ..." I sigh back at him with a rather sad expression, and Jake rubs a hand across his face as he realizes what he just said.

"I know. This shit with her ... I know. Fuck, baby. I'm sorry, I just totally ruined this." He sounds so gutted and remorseful that his swearing self has returned ...

Well, he can't always be perfect, can he? Although, the swearing makes him who he is, and that's perfect enough for me.

"Don't be silly. I need to get used to that part of our reality, that's all ... Is she still on radio silence?" I push down that lump of emotion and don't let him see it's hurt me.

"As far as I know. The DNA refusal was her only contact, and no one has seen her in New York since we left. If she's still in the Hamptons, no one there has seen her around either; she may have gone back to LA." He shrugs with one shoulder.

"Good riddance. I hope we don't have to deal with her until the baby is born." I huff out loud, and Jake grins at me again. "What?" I frown at him and can't help but smile back.

"Just ... You don't realize how much more you talk to me now. How open you are about telling me things, *Bambina*. You don't hide your feelings or those crazy internal insecurities like you used to. I love that it's changing." He's smiling as he speaks, full of genuine happiness.

"I hadn't even noticed, to be honest." While twisting the bed sheet between my fingers, I ponder it and realize he's right. I do verbalize more openly how I am feeling now. I no longer get that terrible fear or tightening throat when I try.

"Do you ever still think about the stuff that happened when you were a kid, Emma?" The question bowls me over, and I click Jake's probing to see how I'll react and respond. He wants to know if I'm going to open up to him or clamp down, and I sit for a moment and think, try to analyze how I'm feeling, yet realize there's nothing there.

"Sometimes, but not really anymore. The dreams are there when you go away but not as bad or as often. They're more like distant memories that aren't very clear. The memories of what those men did and tried to don't hurt me anymore. I'm not ashamed of it now." I shrug, and Jake watches me with an intense look of sheer emotion.

"And Vanquis?" He clears his throat. I can tell he's having a hard time expressing his feelings over my readily talking about this stuff, with zero reaction and zero hiding.

"A part of me still thinks he's out there somewhere, but I don't think of him much. Not since you told me you loved me, Jake. I know you wouldn't let him hurt me again, and to be honest, life is too consumed with you to dwell on the past." I try to lock my eyes through the screen and hate that it doesn't have the same effect. I miss him a little too much, especially when having this kind of conversation.

"Emma ..." Jake's voice breaks, and he sighs. "Jesus, I never thought you answering me straight about this shit would turn me into a fucking girl." He rubs a hand across his face, and it's then that I spot he got as close to tears as I think I could have coped with.

"You're such a man! Don't wuss out on me, Carrero. I happen to like your strong pushy self." I tap the screen as though warning him, pointing a waggling finger his way.

"Don't worry, baby. I'm all man when it counts. I'm allowed to shed a couple of tears over the fact that my girl has moved on, mon-u-fucking-mentally, in only a few months of being with me. You have no idea, baby." He settles his arm behind his head, and I watch with sheer delight how his muscles grow magically.

"You're very sweary tonight, Mr. Carrero." I yawn and stretch out, my eyes getting heavy with the late hour. I've been a total lightweight since getting pregnant, still sleeping way too much.

"Being away from you makes me sweary, *Bambina*. Go to sleep and dream of me. I'll be dreaming of you. You're tired, so that's an order." He gives me his bossy tone and serious look.

"Stay with me." I sigh and watch him via the screen lying on the pillow next to me, propping it as though he's right there.

"I'll always stay with you, *Bambina*. Now, go to sleep, and once you're out, I'll disconnect."

"I love you." I sigh gently, tired and already fading out quickly.

"I love you so much more. Sleep." Jake props up his laptop too, so both hands come into view behind his head as he gets comfy. I snuggle into the cushion and close my eyes.

"Talk to me until I sleep." I yawn again, hearing a small noise that sounds like he's laughing under his breath.

"Could you be any more adorable, baby? ... I'll read to you if you like? I have a Stephen King book with me." He sounds happy and amused; I could listen to that voice forever.

"Do that. I want to hear you as I fall asleep." I open one eye and look at him as he stretches across the bed away from the screen and comes back with his book, and I blow him a kiss, closing my eyes again, ready to listen to the only voice in the world that has so much power over me.

Chapter 22

I'm lying in the bath, resting my aching bones after dragging Sarah around the city with Jefferson in tow. I did it. I abused Jake's credit card shamelessly and bought a mountain of stuff for my growing tadpole and its swelling vessel in the form of cute maternity clothes. I was a woman on a mission, pushed and encouraged by Sarah and her undying enthusiasm, gushing over the cutest baby items ever. I don't have an ounce of guilt over it, either.

Okay, so maybe this baby thing is finally real. I'm starting to feel ... Dare I say it ... Excited. It's the bootee aisle in the baby shop that did it.

I skim my hands over my stomach, that little inner tingle expanding some more, only this time, I stop and analyze what this weird feeling is, the one that comes anytime I allow my thoughts to land on this little being suspended inside of me. The tingling, slight achy sensation in my heart and stomach, a strange fluttery breathless tightening.

Love.

I love my baby ... I love Jake's baby ... I love our baby.

I sigh and relax into the tub a little looser, a smile plastered on my face as I recognize and embrace this new feeling. Now that I can identify it, I can see how different it is from anything I've ever felt before, something deeper and instantly stronger, almost close to what I feel for Jake, yet different. I love this sweet unformed being, body, and soul in a way that is as all-consuming as how I feel for him.

I know if Jake ever did anything to hurt it or me, like my mother's lovers did, then I would take this child and run, run far as I can and lock us both in a safe little box that no one would ever get through. I would die to protect this tiny being inside of me.

This is what my mother lacks. The overwhelming protective desire to do anything within her power to protect me. Maybe not all women get that maternal surge, but Jake is right. I do, and it's so strong it's overwhelming me; from this instant, I know I'll never be anything like her. So sure of this fact and realizing it, I smile and slide down in the tub with a sense of happiness and self-assurance.

I have wireless headphones on, the iPad running through all the songs Jake has sent me, sighing at the memories, feeling more than a little euphoric with every melody. Shopping today was exhausting, and yet, I'm strangely energetic. My body is alert, tingling, and extremely happy; only one more day and he'll be back with me ... with us. I stroke down my stomach, comforting our little tadpole, missing its daddy as much as I am already.

I sit luxuriating in the hot bubbles, completely immersed in thought, eyes closed, when I'm shocked, blood-freezing, hearts stopping, terror induced to sudden attention. A hot mouth lands on mine, delivering a kiss that has me jerking back in shock, followed by an almighty slosh of water that drenches my face in a gasping wave and has me grappling for air. Strong hands yank my headphones off my head simultaneously as I attempt to rescue myself from drowning.

The urge to panic comes out full throttle, snapping my eyes open at the assault. I'm met with cheeky green eyes and the biggest grin I've ever seen. Jake is straddling me in the water, and he leans in for a second kiss without any apology.

"Surprise." He grins as our mouths meet again, his teeth colliding with my lips. I'm startled and floundering in his embrace, not sure if I should be happy at his sudden appearance or smack him for scaring the living soul out of me. My heart is pounding through my chest, and I'm heaving breaths to calm down. I slap his shoulder haughtily and only get a grin in response.

"You scared the shit out of me!" I scorn as he lifts me higher in the bath, stroking the damp hair off my face, nestling me into position so he can get closer.

"I saw you lying here looking fucking breathtakingly beautiful, and I just couldn't help it." He grins again, and I flick water at him as he leans over me, waist-high in the bath. I realize he still has his T-shirt and hoody on, and I can feel jeans ... maybe even trainers, down the sides of my legs. He's completely insane.

"You couldn't stop, and you know ... Undress?" I glance him up and down as he starts slowly and sexily unzipping his sodden hoody. My eyes welded to how his clothes molded themselves to every hunky muscle in his body, complimenting his appealing physique.

"Nope ... As I said, you looked too inviting. I rushed my meeting and got everything done in one day to get back to you, so I wasn't waiting for a second more."

That smile, though,... heart-stopping, to say the least.

Oh, God, that man. He melts my heart so effortlessly.

He peels off his upper layers, wringing them out, and tosses them toward the open shower floor in a basketball slam-dunk move.

Could you be any more of a guy?

"Planning on staying?" I look him up and down as he slides back to sit at the other end of the bath, fishing into the bubbly depths for trainers and socks, launching them toward his discarded clothes.

"Yup." He leans back against the tub and wriggles before producing the rest of his attire. The water is sloshing everywhere, so now the floor is soaked too.

"Nora will kick your ass when she sees this mess." I push my toes at his chest, and he catches my foot with a quick hand. He pulls me down the tub with a little tug, and I squeal in response, slapping my arms to the side to stop myself from submerging. He doesn't let go and starts kneading the ball of my foot expertly.

Really!

"Well, seeing as I'm the one paying her, then tough." He grins some more, and it's obvious he's happy to be home with me; his cheery, playful mood is majorly adorable.

"I'm glad your home." I gush at him, relaxing into his foot massage, that inner warmth swelling when I'm hit with his sexiest *I'm hot, and I know it'* smile.

"I'm glad too. I missed you more than is healthy." His massage stops, and fingers travel up my ankle slowly. His body seems to rise in the water, and he starts easing his way toward me, hands skimming my inner leg and up my inner thigh.

Oh ... hello.

"Want to help me get clean?" He winks as he approaches me, his nose grazing mine and our bodies delicately touching in the hot water.

"I'm pretty sure what you mean is giving you help in doing something dirty." I point out that wicked gleam is the last thing I see before he devours me. The floor will see a lot more water than this before we're done.

* * *

I sigh as I watch him empty bag after bag onto the bedroom floor, feeling more than a little guilty about my mountain of purchases. Seeing it all now in the daylight, I'm sure I've gone and lost my mind ... maybe I got a little credit card happy.

Yesterday it was easy to keep on buying, as each purchase was swiftly carried off to the car by Jefferson, and I didn't see the entirety of it until he laid it all together on the sitting room floor. I cringe and watch Jake's face for some reaction, but there isn't any. He doesn't seem to care that I probably maxed out the card he gave me.

He rifles through some of the tiny things I purchased, holding them up with a happy expression on his face, then eyes a couple of the dresses I bought myself. I watch him lift the leggings with the weird stretch stomach panel and giggle at the confused look on his face.

"I can't picture you this way yet." He says as a matter of fact and stretches out the panel with his hand to simulate a bulge.

"You've just been presented with your crazy fiancée's credit card, happy shopping, probably a rather obscenely large card bill, and all you're thinking about is me getting a baby bump?" I stare at him, completely bewildered. I'm sure any normal husband-to-be would be hitting the roof right now at the momentous mountain of stuff.

Jake just shrugs and picks up a tiny little pair of fluffy booties.

"I told you to start abusing my cards. God knows I do it often enough." He lifts a baby-grow in the tiniest size ever, holding it between us, closing one eye, squinting at me and the little suit simultaneously. Looking utterly devastating and making my inner thighs clench.

"Are you trying to envision me wearing that?" I raise an eyebrow at him and pull a hand to my hip.

I'm not sure what sorts of kinky run through his brain sometimes.

"I'm trying to figure out how something this size will fit inside something your size, and to be honest, I'm starting not to like myself very much." He drops it back down and picks up a tiny hat instead, fingers tracing it delicately, returning that little, tugging, happy smile.

You're so cute.

Jake is obviously one of those rare men who like babies, whether he's aware of it or not, and I can guarantee he will be a very 'hands-on' daddy. The thought warms me to my core.

"I'm sure I'll manage like every other pregnant woman on the planet, baby." I smile indulgently at his slightly cautious look before he goes back to snooping through my purchases. As soon as he knew I'd bought items for the baby, he'd been all over the bags searching for new tiny, cute treasures. He really is odd for a guy. I try not to think of that bitch when I say pregnant women or while watching the mountain of baby things on the floor.

Inner peace ... Breathe. She will not ruin this.

"You're not just another pregnant woman, though. You're my pregnant woman, and I must admit, baby, now I'm thinking about this whole birth thing ... I'm getting pretty fuck.. goddamn scared." Jake glances up suddenly, stopping mid-swear to correct himself, completely ashen-faced and white. I gulp in surprise, praying to God he didn't get his first flashes of doubt about being a father. I don't think I could handle it if he were changing his mind; after all, his happiness and being the first one excited about it. I've just realized how much I love and want this little bundle, and I don't know how I'd deal with Jake if he didn't. My heart sinks dramatically.

"You are?" My voice wobbles a little, and his eyebrows lower.

"Women still die giving birth." Jake looks utterly devastated, and I relax. He's so heart-destroying sometimes. I get off the bed and walk to him, sliding down into his waiting arms, finding my comfy place on his lap, and nuzzling close among the sea of pricey things ... now eating away at my inner morality.

"You'd never let me die. You're far too stubborn a man not to grip onto me for dear life." I joke, but his tense body tells me he's serious about this. Jake is overthinking, stressing the shit out of himself, while I'm barely two months gone. Yet another level to that quick brain and keen eye of his ... he's just too loveable for words.

"We should see your OB-GYN again. Work out all the birth details and start planning for a C-section early and...." It all comes out in a rush, and I silence him with a kiss.

"Stop and breathe." I gaze into his bottomless green eyes and smile, calm about this whole conversation, while he's the one doing an Emma.

Crazily turned tables.

"Shhhh," I kiss him for a second time, trying to nudge his narrowed frown away. "We will be okay. You told me so ... Remember?" I give him that *'you're never wrong'* face and hope it calms him.

"If I lost you...." His voice is breathy and afraid, his eyes decidedly damp, and I wrap my arms around his neck tightly, bringing us nose to nose so I can inhale his intoxicating smell. His sexy designer aftershave mingled with just Jake, that's devastating to me.

"I'm too stubborn to let that happen," I smile, catching a tiny glint of a grin hidden in those hazy greens, peeking through the fear. His arms come around my waist and to my back, pulling me close, bridging that tiny gap, so our noses touch, and I'm straddling him on the floor, bodies close ... Intimately close, seeing as I'm in a bathrobe that's now draped open revealing my naked body, and he's only in a pair of very sexy boxers. It's hard to stay on topic with so much bare skin-on-skin contact on the go.

"Maybe you could take my mind off it for the next few months?" He smiles, and I catch his eye flicker down between us; it seems being naked has its advantage of distracting him anyway. I can't help but giggle. With a shift of wariness hitting on a full sexual glint, he swings me around onto the floor on my back, lying over me, elbows and forearms at either side of me, holding his body taut over the top. I'm still wrapped around him, so I add my legs around his waist tightly and suggestively.

"Are you going to let me set a date anytime soon?" His eyes come to mine, fingers tangled in my hair fanned across the carpet.

"If you think I'm getting married with a bump, then you can forget it. I'm not having pictures of me hideously lumpy as our forever photos." I pout at him, but he only smiles at me in a way that screams, 'You're adorable.'

"I think it would be sexy to marry you while carrying our baby." He smirks.

"Not a chance. I want to look and feel gorgeous on that day, and seeing as you ooze that already ... I can't have you outshining the bride." I bring one hand down and poke him in the cheek gently.

"You will always outshine me. You are perfection in every way, not one woman in the world will ever be as beautiful as you. Bump or not, Emma, you're stunning." He's deadly serious as he gazes at me.

My heart aches deeply at what he's saying.

Could I love you anymore right now?

"I'm still not marrying you with a baby bump." I point out with a devilish smile; heart-wrenching romantic declarations don't sway me that easily, Mr. Carrero. I'm not completely under his spell, and I know in his head that he's still trying to manipulate me into what he wants. He just can't help himself.

"Fine, we'll wait until Junior comes, then get married. I'd rather it was the other way around, but I'm not in the mood for a fight over this. I don't want to fight about our wedding in any way, so I'm going to let you decide how it goes and how you want it." He smiles in that swoon-worthy way, and I narrow my eyes suspiciously.

"Why are you being so amenable suddenly?" It's not like him at all. He leans in and starts running a gentle lick up my neck, shivers tingling through my body, and his hot breath is making my inner core clench.

You're so easy, Emma. It's pathetic.

His stubble scratches me sensually before he goes for my exposed throat, planting kisses vertically down my neck, from my ear to my shoulder.

"I have other battles to deal with, and I don't want our happy day to be one of them." He's focused on making my body tingle with expert attention to the places he knows affect me most.

Good answer, Carrero.

"So, you're fine with waiting until the baby is here, and we're all set in the Hamptons then?" I tilt my head to catch his eye as he lifts his gaze to mine.

"Sure ... Just so you know, that tonight, when we go on your little *Leila Operation*, I'm bringing you home as soon as things look rosy for the two of them."

He smirks, and I eye roll.

God damn you, Carrero.

I've convinced both girls to have a night of celebratory 'I'm having a baby.' Jake should've been flying home today, so I arranged it for this evening. Sarah's fully on board and up to speed with all that is the 'Leila and Daniel' show. Marcus is even invited to tag along with the men. Fortunately, he works most evenings at a bar in Queens, so Jake and Daniel will be a duo tonight. When I called her at lunch while shopping, Leila didn't seem to suspect a thing.

"That is in no way some sort of verbal agreement or compromise, Mr. Carrero." I huff and get a little pouty as he smiles at me, his mouth lightly trailing my neck near my jawline. His hot, warm breath sends shivers in every direction, and his voice takes on the severe husky low tone that always drives me wild for him.

"We'll see."

Oh, no, you don't. My words. Not yours.

"No, we won't." I turn my face away from him as though I'm completely unaffected by how his mouth is seducing me; my body is brimming with horniness right now.

"Annoying ... isn't it? Those few little words?" He nibbles my ear lobe, and I sigh, relaxing into what he's doing because it feels good, the way he lowers his groin into me, slowly and gently rocking over me. My eyes snap open.

"Oh no, you don't. Mr. Sexpertize! You are not bending my will with this." I know exactly what he's doing, and he chuckles in the most annoyingly cheeky way like a young boy caught with his hand in the cookie jar.

Smart bastard!

"We both know I can," and he can. It's true, I can't think straight with the infernal body rubbing going on. I know I should stop what he's doing, but all my resolve is fading into nothing with his pressed to mine and those hands skimming me seductively.

Jesus.

"No. No. NO!" I try to push, my hands meeting his unmovable hard chest muscles, but he doesn't budge. I want this night out to relax and let my hair loose, Hunter and Leila drama aside.

I'm looking forward to doing something sociable and glamorous.

Okay, who are you? Where is Emma?

What the hell does he bench press? Freakin yaks or something?! For God's sake! Wow.

"You're pregnant." He says as though it's the only answer in the world that should matter.

"Yes. Pregnant, not disabled, or dying, or incapable." I point out, trying again with the pushing, getting nowhere.

"Fragile." He says a little more forcefully.

"Please. I'm not that goddamn fragile. It doesn't stop you from maneuvering me into kinky positions, pounding into me at your heart's content when the moment overtakes you." I point out.

"That's a hell of a lot different. I'm always conscious of how I lay my hands on you and how I'm fucking you." He frowns at me and shows me his deadly serious glare. He does remain aware of the little tadpole, even during sex. My heart flutters a little.

Okay, that is unbelievably sweet ... despite his use of that vulgar word.

I roll my eyes and sigh.

"I need you to loosen the reigns a little and stop saying 'fucking'. I'm not asking to go out without you, just stop smothering me so protectively. You're driving me insane with this. I mean, that poor doctor looked like he was afraid for his life." I attempt to get my arms into a chest fold, but he's too close, so I slump them down beside my head on each side.

"Good, he should've been. If he had the urge to touch you one more time, I was going to...." I cover his mouth with my hands.

"...That's what I mean! He felt my stomach like he was supposed to, not feeling me up. You never once noticed that I let an actual man touch me without wanting you to rip his throat out. I was very proud of myself that I could accept he was doing his job and not being some sleazy leech. If I can accept that, then you can too." I smile triumphantly, feeling a little courageous.

"I changed your doctor," he says in such a deadpan way that I choke in disbelief. I guess that's why I haven't received any follow-up appointments yet. Although, to be fair, I already knew this was coming because of his call straight after our appointment.

"Why?" I pretend to sound stern. I'm really not, though.

He narrows his eyes at me and sighs, rolling off me onto his back, staring at the ceiling, looking guilty as hell, arms bent at the elbow, crossed over at his forehead.

"Because I'm still a jealous dickhead. I got you a woman instead." He throws an arm over his face and looks a bit remorseful in a sexy '*bossy little shit*' kind of way.

I know I should be angry at him. I know I should be throwing all sorts of stroppy tantrums, but I just want to kiss him, so I start giggling. Giggling turns into laughter at the realization that I'm stuck with this man-child who can be so suave and confident one minute, then this insecure, impulsive little boy the next.

"I didn't think you would find it funny. I was sure you'd be pissed, so I was hoping to spring her on you."

I nudge him in the ribs. If he wanted to do that, he shouldn't have openly called for a list of female GYNs in front of me.

"She better not be prettier than me!" I laugh at the absurdity of the two of us, and he relaxes and then laughs too.

"Fuck, no, baby. No woman will ever take your beauty queen crown ... Are we always going to be like this?" He turns on his side and leans on his elbow, propping himself over me, his free hand coming to cup my abdomen possessively, splaying his palm out flat, covering our baby.

"Probably. I mean, maybe we won't be as bad the longer we're together, but I don't think I'm capable of not being a little bit jealous about other women lusting over you." I smile hopelessly as he leans in and kisses me softly.

"And I'll never want to stop beating the shit out of any man who dares to touch you, baby." He smirks at me, and I sigh.

"We're perfect for each other," I giggle as his hand trails my face, tracing my features slowly.

"I've been telling you that since you met me." He winks and leans down for another passion-fueling kiss. His mouth molded so deliciously to mine, tongue teasing me into complete submission.

"Want to spend the day in bed letting me show you all the ways in which we're perfect for one another?" He smirks wickedly, and my body heats up almost instantly. He should know by now that lately, I never turn that down.

"So long as I'm not late for meeting Leila tonight. We have a couple of friends to sort out." I giggle as that adoring hand moves from my abdomen to my inner thighs, sliding slowly up under my robe, arching as he connects with me divinely.

Chapter 23

"You look sexy as hell. I'm not sure about leaving you in that bar for an hour. This was dumb." He rakes a hand through my hair, catching it in his fist and giving it a little pull to bring my mouth to him for a gentle kiss.

"Leila will smell a rat if you're all there when we walk in. I want her to loosen up a little so give us time to talk before you two come crashing in." I'm trying to be patient with him tonight, his jealous and protective side wants to dominate, but his loving side is trying to give me a little space. He is visually struggling with himself.

"Then you should've let me arrange a quiet club. Fewer people, less chance of someone knocking into you and—"

"Stop." I lean up and kiss him. Jake's heart is thudding, and the way he keeps rubbing his hands on his jeans tells me he's on the verge of a panic attack. He's completely contradicted who he normally is over this, like our proposal night all over again, and it melts me. He's been sweating rivers since we arranged this little operation at the thought of me being out in the big old world without his constant protection, and I giggle at the thought.

"I'll be fine. We'll get a corner seat, ply her with cocktails, and just talk. It's a weekday. The place will be quiet, with no real party animals on a Tuesday night, Jake. Just people meeting for drinks." I'm trying to soothe the face that has come over him, a furrowed brow, the infamous Carrero glare, and a touch of childish pouting. My heart softens to goo.

"An hour, though? I'll go out of my mind. Maybe if Mathews sat ..." He's close to pacing again, like he was before, a frantic wild-eyed look draining over his face.

"No. Stop. Seriously." I take both of his hands and pull them to my waist. He follows obediently.

"Trust me to take care of myself. I was doing it long before I had you. You, on the other hand ... I'm not sure you can be trusted out with Daniel Hunter. There's a lot of things you two could get up to in an hour." I point out, and his face crumbles.

"You know I never would again, Emma ... You know..." Again, with the panic-stricken expression. I silence him with a kiss.

"Trust," I say slowly and deliberately with two raised eyebrows, and he sags with defeat. That green-eyed glare is turbulent, but he's resigned to the fact that this is happening. He realizes that trust is a two-way thing and wants me to trust him more than anything in the world.

"Keep your cell out. We're going to a bar that's close, really close, so if you need me sooner, I'll be there." He raises an eyebrow at me in finality.

I sigh at him and then kiss his cheek indulgently before moving off to finish getting ready. He sighs heavily as he goes to the wardrobe to fish out his usual black shirt and jeans for a night out. I know this isn't easy for him, the thought of not being there to look after me, but he needs to let this go. He trusts Nora and Mathews to take care of me here in the city, and he trusts Sylvana and her staff to tend to my every need when in the Hamptons, so now he needs to trust that I can take care of myself when out with my girls ... when out anywhere in general. He needs to learn this, or my life will be almost impossible with him in the future.

"Don't come until I text you. That's the deal. If Leila is still too hostile, it won't go well, so let us talk her around first. Promise me, Jake." I turn toward him with my most efficient PA, Emma tone, which used to get him to behave. He tenses his jaw as he stares into his wardrobe, mulling over his response.

"You have an hour, max. If there is no text after an hour, then we're coming." He grits his teeth, and I find myself eye-rolling. I'm not in the mood to keep this going. I'll have to play it by ear and hope I can deter the force that is Carrero from turning into a cyclone in that bar if he tries to enter before I need him.

"Stop glaring at your clothes and come over here and help me with my necklace." I smile at him, a tad happier, as I catch that naughty look wash over his face. I'm in for some serious groping before Jefferson takes me to meet the girls, no doubt of that.

* * *

"Whatever you have that's going to get me smashed in the shortest amount of time." Leila eyes the bartender, wildly tossing that choppy blonde hair back off her face. She's dressed to kill, wearing a strapless, short, tight, electric blue dress with killer spiked heels that look rather dangerous. Steel spikes sticking out the rears with a defiant look welded to her face. She's been this way since we picked her up at her apartment, and she's not our usual, bubbly, happy Leila.

"I'm not getting smashed tonight." Sarah cuts in. "I have work tomorrow and last time was brutal; we cooked seafood all day. Do you know how bad raw seafood is when you're hungover?" She grimaces at the memory.

"I obviously can't drink." I point down. "So, I suppose I'm on orange squash or something fruity and non-alcoholic." Both girls throw me a pitying look but then smile and rub my belly, almost in sync. They've already declared themselves aunties and argued over the godmother rights of my future Carrero offspring.

Back at our seats in the corner, I relax a little as I look around. The place is busy and full on a weekday, but there's a mellow atmosphere, and people are milling around chatting rather than hardcore partying. The DJ box in the corner is on low, playing chilled music, only adding to the calm atmosphere. I find myself aching for him to be here, despite myself, and push it aside.

"Get that dreamy look off your face already, and tell me when they're coming." Leila breaks in with a look that says *busted*. She doesn't sound happy but not angry either, just resigned, knowing this would happen at some point.

"What?" I blink at her rapidly, guilt coursing through me, and I wonder how the hell she worked it out from just one expression on my face.

"Oh, come on. I've known Jake practically my whole life, and I happen to know what he's like over you. This little phony freedom right here ..." she says pointedly, drawing a circle around me in the air, "...without armed security and a huge plastic bubble keeping you and his heir safe from people breathing on you ... God forbid ... I knew instantly you two had set me up." She looks rather pointedly at me and then at Sarah accusingly. I blush, and Sarah giggles.

"Gee, this one's sharp. Is that common with all of Jake's friends? Far too quick on the uptake!" Sarah takes a sip of her drink and watches us both with amusement. I should've known she would figure this out. She's completely right. My being out of Jake's sight for any length of time these days screams of huge red warning flags.

Dammit.

"Okay fine. But we did it out of love, and Daniel wants to see you, Leila. You dumping him is just plain absurd." I wave my hands guiltily. She throws back her drink and starts waving manically toward the bar with her glass in the air. The tender throws her an obvious *What?* shrug, informing her this is not a table serving service, but starts making her a new drink regardless.

Leila and her power of persuasion.

"I can't do it." Leila looks down at the table and sighs, the feisty girl I adore taking a moment to lower her angry guard. "He's going to crush me; the longer I see him, the more I fall for him, and he's going to fuck it all up." She flails at me in complete raw despair while Sarah reaches out a careful hand. Leila looks so broken somehow.

Sarah's always been good at giving touching, empathetic love.

"Leila, it's fear. You're not giving him a chance," she croons at her with her wide doe eyes in sympathy.

"You never saw him, some girl all over him trying to get in there, and he was just so ... blank." A single tear fills her eye, and she wipes it away angrily with the back of her hand. Her little face is crumbling, and her lip wobbling adorably.

"I'm lost. I don't get you?" I sit back, trying to analyze her face. Trying to put myself inside Leila's head and failing. The girl has as many complicated walls and levels as I used to have.

"He didn't exactly push her off the way Jake would for you. No, beat it or fuck off. He just stood there watching her gyrating at him with her hands on his chest. Then it hit me. He would've totally fucked her if I weren't there." She brings a red-rimmed set of heartbroken eyes to me, and I sigh. I know how soul-destroying that kind of insecurity can be. Hunter probably wasn't even aware of the effect his indifference to the girl had on Leila.

"I know he wouldn't have. You're not giving him a chance, Leila. You're so sure he will disappoint you and hurt you that you're looking for fault. Looking to push him away." I take her hand in mine, trying for maturity and directness. Sarah can be the soft one. I need Leila to see sense.

"Did you confront him?" Sarah is watching her with the same expression as me, and maybe she's decided logical is the best route too.

"Of course, in grand, *crazy bitch* fashion, the stupid me who has been giving him hell for weeks." she sighs and sinks even lower in her seat. "I told him to fuck off. We were done, and I threw my drink at him. Told him to take the whore if that's what he wanted." A blush of red surges over her delicate features as she cringes at the memory; at least she has the sense to realize she acted like an insane woman.

"Jealousy is a killer." I point out, knowing fine well I probably would've kicked Jake's ass if it'd been me. Jealousy makes us irrational, seeing red no matter how innocent the situation is.

"Well, aren't we little angelic bundles of insecurity?" Sarah chirps in with a smile, patting Leila's hand. "I once threw an entire plate of pasta at Marcus in a restaurant because some *ex-girlfriend* kissed him on the cheek when she came by to say hi." She shrugs as a matter of fact.

"I tried to convince Jake I was climbing into another guy's bed because I heard a girl in the background when he was on the phone to me." I also shrug. The three of us regard each other for a moment, then burst out laughing. Even Leila laughs and wipes her smudgy eyes.

"None of that is healthy at all." Leila looks deflated. "But it makes me feel less insane. I know I flew off the handle, but honestly, this is so hard. Daniel has made an art out of fucking my head up for the last ten years, and now he's doing it again. I'm so scared that one of these days, he will turn around and be like ... "This ain't for me, kitten." She does a very good Hunter impression, alarmingly so, even the way she tilts her head and raises a palm.

"Have you ever thought about not being so hostile and giving him a genuine chance? Letting him in a little so that maybe he won't want to turn and run?" Now it's my turn to pat Leila's hand, and she sighs as the bartender nudges in with a round of drinks, leaving his card in full view in front of Leila, cockily and a little too smoothly. A move Jake would've pulled off a hundred times more seductively.

"Call me." He winks at her before wandering back off back to the bar with a smile. All three of us watch him go with equally unamused expressions. He's tall like Hunter, overly muscular and blonde, but way less appealing. He has an *I'm in love with myself, so I bet you are too* aura about him, making him unattractive instantly.

"Asshole," Leila retorts, dumping the card over her shoulder toward the floor, not caring that he can still see her.

"So, if sexy barmen dropping their card on your lap are not going to cut it, then what next?" Sarah is now trying to decipher Leila's thoughts, appraising her intensely.

"Guess you better tell the assholes they can come in then and at least try to pretend to look surprised at seeing us here." She mumbles, sitting up straight, and taking a steadying breath. Fingers in her hair, tidying it up self-consciously.

* * *

As soon as Leila knew they were coming, she lost courage and high-tailed it to the ladies' room alone, telling us she needed a minute to breathe and fix her face. I know the men won't take long to get here. Knowing Jake, they are probably camped out on the bar's doorstep. He's probably wearing out a hole in the pavement from frantic pacing.

Sarah and I sip our drinks, watching the scenery, chatting non-descriptively in the few minutes it takes that sexy six-foot-two Adonis to come swaggering in, making my insides liquefy. He has the same effect on me every time I see him. He makes everyone else disappear, with just an appearance, like watching him course through the crowds at the Charity Ball all over again, and my heart soars.

He spots us with his eagle-eyed observation and immediately turns our way with Hunter behind him. Some little brunette appears, stopping their progress, waving her hands and hips at him, and a frown crosses Jake's face as he looks down at whatever she's saying. He gently and firmly puts a hand on her shoulder, pushing her aside without another glance, and he keeps coming toward me.

Suddenly, I get what Leila meant. She wanted some sign that Daniel was hers, not just weird, angry dating and sex. She wanted to see him show loving possession in subtle ways like Jake just did. The girl was a test in Leila's messed-up head, and he failed, whereas Jake just succeeded.

Hunter needs to start making obvious shows of his love for her, be demonstrative, and assure her that this is the real deal for him. I doubt he's had any chance of showing any form of softness while Leila's been in high-maintenance feisty mode. He needs to be the guy he was when she was sixteen, the gentle boy who made her first time beautiful if he's ever going to win her round.

Leila is the same insecure and terrified girl I was. She needs Daniel to cut through all her crap and see it too. He needs to romance her rather than handle her; under that crazy-spirited exterior, she's still a girl shielding a fragile heart.

When they approach, Jake swoops in and kisses me hard on the mouth, a hint of aggression telling me the last half hour has probably been torture for him, and now he needs to expel all his tension. I tilt my head back, straining my neck with the ferocity of his kiss, and lose my breath at the sheer passion in it.

"Steady on, Carrero." Sarah giggles, slapping him on his huge muscular shoulder. "Let the lady breathe. You might break her neck if you keep that up." Jake throws her a non-apologetic smirk, then comes back to kiss me gentler while still cupping my face and saving my neck from injury.

Daniel is holding back behind Jake, looking around sheepishly. He seems tired and stressed and, need I say, heartbroken. He looks nothing like the Daniel Hunter of old, the little lost soul inside of him in full view.

"Where is she?" He butts in, doing another eye sweep of the room. It's obvious he's on tenterhooks and can't seem to stand still. Jake stands and motions to the bar, almost ignoring his question.

"We're going to get drinks; we'll be a couple of minutes. You need top-ups?" He strokes a hand down my face, turning away when Sarah and I shake our heads.

"Bathroom." I raise my eyebrows at Hunter as Jake pulls him away, part of him so sure she wouldn't be here, and he relaxes a little.

Bless him.

"Wait," I say hurriedly. Jake halts, and both men look my way. "I know you're expecting fiery hell-cat and her usual shitty attitude, Daniel, but she needs some delicate handling. It's all an act; maybe if you try the gentle approach, it might make a difference. She needs the guy who made her first time the best time," I raise a brow subtly, seeing how his frown ripples across his face as he takes in what I'm saying. Jake throws an arm around Daniel's neck with a rather intrigued and mildly aggressive expression ...

Oops,... a reaction to finding out about Hunter's removal of Leila's virginity.

"In that case, seeing as I'm the 'pussy touchy one' that you're nothing like, we should compare notes, right?" Jake jibes Daniel's own words back at him and pokes at his ribs with his free hand dragging him off to the bar. I would love to be a fly on the wall in their next few minutes of conversation.

I watch the pair saunter to the bar, heads close, as Jake obviously imparts some much-needed wisdom or maybe drags Leila's first-time truth out with hostility. They're only just getting there when I spy Leila appear across the room. She instantly spots the most attractive pair here by a long shot, and she loses every ounce of Leila confidence and spark. She fumbles with her bag and turns, retreating to the ladies' room as though her ass is on fire.

This is not going well.

I go to get up, but Sarah catches my arm, sitting me back down, her eagle eyes having seen Leila too.

"Let her regroup and try again, she's only just laid eyes on him, and I'm guessing it threw her. Give her time to do this on her own." Sarah is always wise, and I nod as we watch impatiently for any sign of her return. I can't help catching the way Daniel's head tilts in the same direction, and I know he's watching for her coming out. He didn't see her the first time. His body language emanates all kinds of fear and tension. The boy is seriously desperate to see her, it's so touching. If Leila can't see how much he loves her, she's quite frankly a fool.

It feels like a long time of Sarah and me passing silent tense facial expressions before she nods toward the distance. I turn to see Leila walking out with her head held high, a look of pure defiance on her pretty little face, and the stride of a woman in complete bitch mode. She looks at us, locking onto her focus, before marching our way on a mission. She turns as she gets to the DJ box, swinging her hips sexily as she makes her way toward him, leaning in and touching the DJ on the shoulder, whispering something in his ear.

I catch Hunter out of the corner of my eye looking her way, and he moves out. Jake's hand on his chest stops him suddenly, and Jake leans in, saying something in his ear. Close and serious and Daniel nods without tearing his eyes from his prize.

The DJ nods at Leila and seems to put on whatever request she has made as she moves back with a satisfied fake smile on her little face.

The sound of Pink "So What!" starts flowing across the room, and I know Leila is trying to convey to Daniel that she doesn't care one iota about his presence. She's in full defensive mode, and the walls are up. Her song choice is one of attitude, and *I don't need you.*

So definitively, Leila. She's found her spark again, and Daniel better bring his backbone.

She turns to saunter away from the DJ booth saucily, and I'm drawn to the fact that Daniel is almost upon her. Catching her arm mid-stride, she recoils and tries to haul it from him. But he keeps a strong hold tugging her back with him by the wrist to the booth. His arm stretches out as she tries to go the opposite way, but he keeps a firm hold of her while leaning into the DJ and saying something. He holds out what looks like a hundred-dollar bill then the music is cut instantly. As soon as the softer notes of a new song start, Hunter turns back to the deathly still, glaring girl in his grip.

Ed Sheeran's "Thinking Out Loud" waves across the room, and I can't help but smile. Hunter is taking my advice, doing this the softly, softly way. I could almost applaud him now; instead of bringing his wild cat back to heel, he's sweeping her off her feet. He should have done it this way long ago.

The only thing on his face right now is fear, and I watch in fascination. Her little chin lifts and bristles with defensiveness, his body sags, and he becomes completely submissive to her, almost in response, reading her.

Daniel is not his usual dominant, cocky self with his little fury girl. He's reaching inside, showing her a part of him that obviously existed when she was sixteen when he'd made her first time with him memorable. A part of Daniel I'm guessing no one ever really gets to see.

Jake slides in next to me, places two beers on the table, slides an arm around me, and joins in on watching *The Hunter and Leila Show.*

"I told him to stop with the games and just talk to her, like a normal person; to stop acting like this was all some "casual see where it goes bullshit" and just be honest with her," he says huskily.

Games huh? Not so long ago, I knew a certain guy who was

rather partial to our little games. That guy seems to have calmed down nowadays, though.

I warmly smile at him, receiving a kiss on the forehead as a reward before my eyes snap back to the couple that I really want to sort things out.

Leila tries to tug herself away again, but Hunter won't let go. Her normal fire is absent despite her resistance, and she turns her body instead so that she can look away from him. He only steps closer, so he spoons her, his hand instantly moving to her hair, gently brushing it away as he leans in, saying something in her ear. His whole manner is soft and agonizingly sincere, and I can't help feeling like we're getting a glimpse into something deep and meaningful. The music flowing over the entire bar only adds to the heart-tugging scene before me, the song, somehow, crazily Daniel.

Whatever he's saying has some effect as Leila's lip starts to wobble, and she bites on it to stop herself from crying. The music gives a helping hand as her defenses start to crumble, lifting that chin again, tensing her body to try to resist. He lets go of her arm and runs a trail of fingers from her wrist to her shoulder, still bent low, talking directly into her ear. She physically trembles, and I smile, knowing exactly how Jake can make me feel by doing that, knowing Leila has zero chance with Hunter if she does love him. Brief tender touches have a way of going straight into your soul.

Daniel stands up straight, walking around her, so they're face-to-face. He tilts her chin up on gentle fingertips, softly. Leila stiffens and presses her lips together hard. She's trying to stop herself from crying and prevent herself from submitting, but Daniel is doing an amazing job with whatever words are flying from his mouth. He has an expression of sheer adoration on his face as he moves in, slowly lowering himself to her height. He looks nothing like the boy I met so long ago, smug and cocky, checking me out. Instead, there's the softness of a heart on show, desperation to win back the woman who makes him whole. It pulls a little tug of emotion from my chest.

It's obvious to the entire room that Daniel Hunter is well and truly deeply in love with Leila.

He delicately cups her jaw with one hand, brushing stray hairs from her face with the other. He's still saying something to her. The whole time they've been standing there, he hasn't stopped talking to her while she's been in defiant silence. Her body is slowly loosening its stiff resolve.

A tear rolls down her cheek, and he gently wipes it away with his thumb, kissing her where it was. There's a body flicker a little at the contact. He leans in lower, bringing his mouth achingly close. With bated breath, Sarah and I are locked on, watching and waiting. Captivated by every beautiful moment unfurling across the room, mentally pleading with Leila to let him in.

Jake's drinking his beer, casually stroking my shoulder, not as fascinated by this emotional scene as we women are. I nudge his thigh and point, urging him to look and take some interest in what's happening here.

Daniel and Leila are connecting.

I glare at him as he smirks and shakes his head at me. He's a typical man with no clue or care and looks moderately bored. Watching him means I'm missing them, so I flip my gaze back to the pair, feeling Jake's hand run across my head, petting me because I'm so devastatingly adorable to him. I sigh, eye-rolling at his typical guyness, and wait with bated breath.

Daniel is so close to her that their mouths are almost touching. He's still talking, still moving painfully closer. Edging in softly, keeping her eyes locked on his.

I wonder what the hell he's been saying all this time.

He's cradling her face, and slowly, the tension in her body disappears. He's breaking down the Leila defense system, and the walls are slowly lowering. Finally, agonizingly, he bridges the gap and kisses her painfully slowly, eyes fully locked. Their gaze, one of the gentlest and tender I have ever witnessed in my life, tugs right into my stomach, causing a huge pit of female emotion.

Sarah and I both clasp hands and gasp, "Aww ..." at that same moment, I catch Jake's eye-rolling dramatically, which earns him a smack on his thigh.

Unfeeling bastard.

As soon as Leila relaxes into Daniel's kiss, their eyes close, and he slides his arms around her waist and lifts her to his height. Her arms slide around his neck and press into him, so they mold together perfectly. They make a gorgeous blonde couple with cute little compact curves against tall, hard, athletic muscle.

Leila's heels pick up, and she bends her knees so any passing victim could be impaled on those shoes, but neither of them seems to care. They are oblivious to everything around them as they move into a deep passionate kiss with a lot of tongue, getting as close to one another as is humanly possible.

I know how that feels.

I shy away with an uncomfortable frown as their passion turns up a gear.

Okay, so cute when it's romantic. But now it's just a little pervy to watch them hit full-blown erotica.

Jake leans into me and kisses me on the cheek. I guess that's his little *'Oh, I'm happy for my mates'* gesture, and now he can get back to convincing me that I want to go home. He seems unaffected by this scene, and I wonder what he's done with my normally so-loving Adonis. I guess that side of him only comes into play when it's about us.

* * *

We've been here for hours, and everyone, except me, is moderately drunk. Leila is wrapped around Hunter on his lap, and the pair haven't stopped ogling and kissing one another since they sat down. We gave up trying to keep them in conversation ages ago. They only have eyes for each other tonight. The crazy aggressive nature of their relationship is completely missing, all gentle looks and caresses, and they seem so ridiculously in love. I guess there will be no bloody noses and bruised jaws when they finally get to a bed.

Jake has pulled me against him in a very possessive manner, arm looped casually around my neck, hand hanging loose in front of me. He's been this way since he got here, constantly close.

A few more of Jake's friends have joined us at the table, familiar faces from Arrick's birthday. Sarah's lost in conversation with two brunettes who keep ogling over Jake and Hunter, despite the men being very obviously attached to Leila and me.

Jake has spent the entire time looking at some guy to his right, and Daniel is too wrapped up in Leila to even notice. Luckily, or both of those bitches would have very sore faces. They're lucky I'm too tired to care.

I yawn, snuggling against Jake, bored with drunken chat and aching to sleep. Jake is merry and not as sober as he seems, which is why he's relaxed enough to let us stay. Jake wasn't interested in staying after his bro,' and Leila hooked up. I wanted to stay, and with some perfectly placed doe eyes and pouty lips aimed his way, I realized just how much I can wrap him around my little finger. Outright defiance bristles his domineering side, but sweet soft looks seem to melt all his resistance.

So much for marching me home before ten!

I won this little battle, not that there won't be many more in our future, knowing him. I think Jake is enjoying kicking back again. Drinking and being in a club is something he's avoided since the night with that bitch. I sigh adoringly at him, with no tug of pain from thinking about her.

Am I finally ready to accept what happened? All of it? Baby included?

Jake spots me yawning for the second time and slides his beer on the table. An instant expression change as full-on caregiver mode moves in.

"Come on, baby, let's get you home." He kisses me gently on the temple, and I'm not arguing for once. I'm exhausted and happy to go home to curl up with him. I can't imagine anything more tempting in the world.

He pulls me up with him and starts looking around for something.

"I didn't bring a coat if that's what you're looking for." I yawn again, ignoring the look of irritation passing over his brow. He picks up his leather jacket and puts it on me instead. I smile, especially when he tugs me forward to zip me up like a child. I get a tiny vision in my head of Jake doing this for his child. He's an absolute natural, and I can't help but notice the sheer envy on the two brunette's faces at the way he's tending to me.

"Danny? I'm taking Emma home." Daniel lifts his bottle in acknowledgment over Leila's head, then goes back to saying something close to her mouth that makes her smile, and she kisses him gently. Completely enamored, all signs of feisty Leila dissipated, and this tame, snugly version far more her somehow. Hunter has one hand on her ass and the other on his bottle, but his eyes are all for her.

Maybe they have a chance this time.

"Sarah, you can come now or let Jefferson come for you when you want to go? Danny has his number." Jake nods toward her, and she grins back at him, shamelessly drunk.

So much for going easy on the booze.

"This here is Delilah; she's taking me home as we're both from Queens." She beams a little too drunkenly, and Jake doesn't smile back. He takes his caretaking role very seriously.

"Then you won't mind if Jefferson takes both of you. It's non-negotiable." He's obviously in no-nonsense mode, thinking practically, looking after my friend, and dismissing her wishes.

I love him!

"Okay, okay, keep your hair on." Sarah laughs good-humoredly, and Jake relaxes. "I don't know how you put up with him being so bossy," Sarah smirks at me, but I curl myself around him and snuggle in.

"Because I like it for the most part," I mumble as his arm tightens around me appreciatively, and he lovingly kisses the top of my head.

Jake leads me out through the milling people, and we head toward the bar's main entrance. His hand is entangled with mine and his jacket, warm around me, smells of him in a very sexy manner that has my tiredness giving way to something naughtier.

Thoughts of Jake in the back of the car are sweeping through my head at a hundred miles an hour, and I'm suddenly so eager to get him alone. Drunk Jake is usually a lot of kinky fun and far less cautious of being gentle.

"Jake?" A male voice cuts into my thoughts, and the instant aggressive stiffening of Jake's entire body alerts me to him as we stop in the foyer. He turns and looks over his shoulder in the direction of the voice and scowls with a deathly glare I've only seen on him once before. I gulp and turn as I know who invokes that reaction. My stomach hits the floor, and instant apprehension prickles my skin.

Ben Huntsberger. Oh shit.

He's making his way toward us from across the room, looking anything but friendly. Jake tugs me behind him in a heartbeat and seems to grow about two feet as he rounds in front of me, putting himself between Ben and me like he's posturing for a fight, and the waves of sheer terror move in.

"What the fuck do you want?" Jake growls and snarls; it's the most unnerving sound in the world. His body bristles with sheer aggressive tension, and I start to feel afraid. The last time Ben appeared, Jake shoved me out of the way, not once but twice.

Am I in danger of being roughly handled again?

The coldness sweeps through me at the thought of what harm an innocent push could do to the child inside of me. My hand instantly comes up to cover my stomach protectively. I start to try to free my hand from his grip in panic, wriggling my fingers to be released and pulling back.

Feeling my attempts to disentangle, Jake senses my unease and looks back at me with a slight softening to the look he's throwing Ben's way. His eyes go to the hand on my belly and back to my face with an intense gaze.

"Emma, no! You know ... I'd never ..." He utters softly to me, a moment of tenderness in his eyes, reassurance during the cyclone rearing its ugly head.

Still, I'm scared.

"I need to talk to you." Ben finally comes level, seemingly more agitated than aggressive, despite Jake's posturing and bristling like an alpha male. He has none of the smug scowling behavior of the last time we saw him and looks directly into Jake's eyes confidently. They are matched in height, and being stuck in a corridor behind them is not exactly my idea of a good night.

"What the fuck would I have to say to you?" Jake's being charmingly Carrero. No fake politeness or friendliness, just direct and to the point.

"Look, I know we have a history, but I need you to put that aside because we have one big fucking thing in common, and I need to talk to you." Ben raises defensive palms raking his hand through overly neat hair, weirdly Jake-like. It's crazy how much more they resemble one another, especially now that Ben's hair is a little messier. I wonder how the hell that happens with two completely unrelated men.

Jake's grip on me loosens a little, and I sigh in relief when his body seems to return to its natural stance, losing that terrifying fighter's attitude.

"And what would that be?" He still sounds defiant and most definitely aggressive. No love lost and all that.

"We both fucked Marissa in the week she fell pregnant. Me more so than you." Ben states, as a matter of fact, with a raised eyebrow and a look that says, 'Yeah, exactly' ...

Fuck.

Wait ... What?

Chapter 24

"I just found out that she's pregnant." Ben is pushing fingers through his hair, rubbing his face in complete agitation. "I've been away for a while on business ... London. I only got back yesterday." He seems so overwhelmed and completely rattled. We're sitting in the quiet booth of a bar near the one we came from. It's almost deserted, and both men cradle neat gin while I hold a glass of coke. I'm too wired and awake to contemplate sleep now. Ben's revelation has all sorts of crazy plots swimming through my overemotional brain, and Jake seems far too calm and in control from this revelation, to be good for him.

"So ... The baby could be either of ours, yet she failed to mention it?" Jake appears pensive. He's been in closed-off thoughtful mode since Ben's disclosure, with his dark looks and scowling tone, and I want to know what's going on in his brain. He's not someone to hide a temper flare-up unless something more sinister is brewing in his clever head. This is very much business brain mode and usually means a lot of trouble brewing in its calculated depths.

"She came to me after the awards show. The after party you and her apparently hooked up at." Ben downs his gin and slides the glass away while Jake cradles and warms his. "Told me she wanted to give us another go and proceeded to fuck me stupid for three days with no protection because she was on the pill. Then I never heard from her again." Ben's face tightens, anger on show, now obvious to the game of manipulation he's been duped into.

There's a lurch in my stomach at the disgust of any woman being that vile, that conniving.

"But if she were on the pill, then she wouldn't have got pregnant, right?" Ben looks at me, expecting to confirm it, but Jake cuts in.

"Emma's pregnant, and she was most definitely on the pill." I nod. What else can I do in a conversation so over my capabilities right now? This bitch was riding Jake's back for months, and now he might not even be the father at all.

"Oh ... Congratulations, Emma." Ben frowns and gazes at his glass again, both men mulling things over, trying to decide if Marissa's pregnancy was planned or accidental.

"Thanks, Ben," I reply shyly, noticing Jake's unapproving glare toward Ben. I interrupt to break up whatever that look meant. "I think she got with you to ensure she would get pregnant and lied about the pill. She was making sure there would be a baby no matter what, and she probably has no idea which of you it belongs to, hence the resemblance." I carry on instead of silently listening. My brain is whirring in chaos, trying to figure out if one woman could be this cold and calculated.

Ben is as close to Jake in looks as earthly possible, so it would make sense to ensure that when she got pregnant, she would pick someone to resemble Jake. That way, when the baby came, he wouldn't question paternity and possibly drop the DNA request just on looks alone.

Was she that desperate to link herself to him for a lifetime that she would do this?

How could any woman have so very little morals or self-decency?

"She's turned down the DNA request enough times." Jake cuts in before Ben can answer, his mind slowly turning over my theory. I can see it in his face, the same one used to churn over business proposals that I thought might benefit his company.

Both men regard one another for a second, some strange look transpiring before them, and Ben sighs heavily. The atmosphere is weirdly calm, considering these two are at the same table, and the topic is Marissa.

"I'm sorry, Jake ... Not for this shit, but the past, for letting her get inside my head and making me believe she meant more to me than our friendship did." Ben looks defeated and remorseful, sitting with a bowed head and a sad expression.

My breath catches in my throat as a hit of emotion inside of me flashes at this sudden apology right out of the blue. Jake pauses and stiffens, exhaling loudly, before sitting back in his seat.

"You were in love with her ... I thought I was too." He shrugs quietly, looking at Ben with absolutely no emotion whatsoever.

Thought? Meaning he never really was?

I catch the way he's looking at me, and I get it. He thought he knew love until he found it with the right person, and my stomach somersault, a little jump of happiness, probably mildly inappropriate right now.

"I know, but I should've seen her what she was, the way she always twisted things, so she was the victim. For years, she had me hating you, believing that you broke her heart and she could never trust me because of it. Too stupid to realize it was all her, and you were just as much a part of the fallout as I was." He looks genuinely sorry. Despite what I know of him and the past, there's something decent coming through about Ben. Underneath all that anger and rivalry is a guy that once meant a lot to Jake.

"And now? ... You're obviously still in love with her if you wanted to try again?" Jake watches Ben intensely, and Ben shrugs.

"I was ... Maybe I still am. I don't know. I never could understand why she wanted you no matter what I did. But now I realize Marissa doesn't know love. She only does possession. She thinks you owe her; she hates that you walked away and won't accept that she can't have you. To her, I'm a sure bet she can pick up whenever she feels like it, so to her, I'm not any fun anymore." He sighs, knocking his glass against the table, emotions running across his face in a flash.

"She's cold and calculated, so none of this surprises me." Jake laces his fingers in mine and pulls my hand to his mouth, rubbing my knuckles across his lips. A gentle gesture to reassure me because of the topic, always caring about how I feel. Right now, with him and all this mess, I'm strangely detached and emotionally tired; Marissa and her antics exhaust me.

"So, what do we do now? ... How do we find out who the father is?" Ben is watching us closely, hints of envy glimmering on his pretty face.

"We can't find out for definite until it's here, but I'm not one to sit back and wait while she calls all the shots. We go see her now and let her know her little fucking game is up." Jake's tone has tightened considerably, and I think the anger is beginning to settle in. The fact that she's been deceiving us all for months has dawned on him. My chest tightens, and I turn to Jake with wide worried eyes.

"You want to confront her?" Suddenly, I sound childlike and vulnerable, every instinct telling me he shouldn't do this tonight.

"Why not?" Jake looks like a man severely pissed and not about to drop it. He's also more than a little drunk, and impulsive spontaneity is his worst trait when under the influence.

"Because it's stupid o'clock in the morning, and you're both drunk." I try for sense, but I do not get any. With a wolf-like snarl, they both nod in agreeance at Jake's plan.

"Can't imagine a better time." Ben quips in, and both men raise an eyebrow in solidarity. It's not hard to see that these two used to get along. They are annoyingly similar right now, reading each other's minds, already making moves to get up.

Oh crap, crap, shit.

"You don't even know where she is." I sound panicked, and I am. This has stupid written all over it, and a part of me wants Jake to take me home so we can talk alone and process all of this. I have no idea what confronting her right now will do.

"She's here in Manhattan, her father's apartment." Ben points out as Jake lifts his full glass from the table and downs it in one very quick glug.

That's not a good sign. Oh god.

"You sure?" Jake's even voice is simmering with rage. His no-nonsense posture and tense muscles make my heart pound through my chest.

"Positive. I was screwing her friend Amy last night. That's how I found out she was pregnant. Amy told me where she is." Ben shrugs into his jacket.

What is it with these Casanova men and random hookups?

"Why haven't you gone to see her then? Asked her before you saw Jake?" I wish he had, we could've avoided all of this, saved it for a time when Jake is sober, and this isn't so fresh. I can feel anger bubbling inside of him, and it's only spelling disaster.

"I needed space to think. Then when I saw you two at the club earlier, I figured some confirmation was a good idea. For all I knew, Amy was lying." Ben is seemingly more accepting of this situation than Jake, but it's most likely because he hasn't had months of Marissa badgering him, arguing, and digging her claws in.

There's something so ... Jake-like in Ben ... old Jake. It's in his mannerisms and alarmingly similar face something disconcerting about his presence and authority. Only Ben is less fiery and calmer, as Hunter appears to be. Jake always seems like he has something hot brimming under his surface, a sense that you know he's capable of pouncing. Changing from laid back to crazy aggressive in an instant, but Ben doesn't. He seems to be a calmer and more relaxed person than Jake.

"No better time than the present." Jake's already on his feet, pulling me with him, that spark simmering, highlighting what I was thinking. I wonder if it's the hot Italian blood Sylvana likes to boast about.

Uh oh.

"Jake. Wait until tomorrow, or maybe I should go home?" inner panic sets in, and a wash of fatigue. I don't want to get into an all-out screaming match with Marissa again. As much as the last one ended in happy tears, this one might not.

"No. I want you with me, baby. I swear we won't need to stay long. I'm sure Ben will want some time alone with her to talk when we're done, then I'll take you home. I want you to witness this too." Jake leans in, kissing me tenderly, his hand grazing my face softly, and I catch Ben's eyes on me. Jake doesn't want to be with Marissa without me being there. Always in the back of his head that I won't trust him. I would rather he went without me in this.

"This is a better fit," Ben says suddenly, nodding at me, "You and Emma. I see what Marissa always wanted with you and never got. It's obvious how much you love her; it was never obvious with Marissa." He drops his chin to his chest. "I don't have that with her either ... I don't think I ever will, even if the kid is mine. I can't trust the bitch anymore." He lets out another deflated breath.

Ouch.

Ben lifts his head and gets to his feet, showing seriousness on his face, and we all head out. Jake all but has to drag me out into the crisp dawn air on a mission I want to be no part of. Jefferson appears as though by magic, and I wonder where he's been hiding all night.

Surely that isn't what he has to do? Sit around and wait for us?

We slide into the car, and Jake pulls his phone out and dials it before sticking it to his ear with a look of sheer determination and a somewhat sardonic expression. It rings for a few minutes before she answers him. I can almost make out her sensual purring on the other end of the receiver, even from my distance.

"Marissa, it's Jake. I need to see you. Where are you?" He sounds deceivingly sexy as he tries to keep his tone even. I know he wants to make her think he's begging to see her for something she may actually like.

I shiver with jealousy but bite it down. He sounds like the guy from the office who used to call dates and arrange casual hookups back when I was his assistant. Casanova in full control.

"Stay there. I'm on my way." He slurs a little, trying to make sure she thinks he's coming to see her for a booty call in the middle of the night or early morning, whatever it is, believing that she's getting a drunken Jake and some sort of reunion. He's making sure she'll open the door to him alone. I know it's pretending, but it still hurts me emotionally. I look at my lap and instantly feel his mouth against my temple.

"I love you, baby," he whispers in my ear, brushing my hair back, his eyes finding mine reassuringly with a small tender smile.

Always so in tune with me.

I smile up into his adoring face and melt.

"Still a clever fucker." Ben smiles, and Jake pulls me closer, an arm around my shoulders between the two men, as he helps me get my seat belt on in the black Lexus. Ben is still on the pavement at the open door, leaning in.

"Much smarter than you ever were, Benny-boy." Jake smiles back, and a moment of friendly sparks suddenly fills the air. It's weird yet strangely comforting.

"That's true. You saw through her shit and got the fuck away ... I kept getting dragged back, repeatedly, it seems." Ben sighs and climbs in beside me. I notice that Jake has no qualms about sitting me between them. Jake of yesterday would've put me on one side away from Ben, guarding me possessively from the guy he hates so much. But, in the last hour, something has changed between the two men, some sort of truce and forgiveness in such a simple conversation.

* * *

Getting into her apartment is easy enough; all Jake needs to do is bark two words into the intercom.

"I'm here," and she lets us in without hesitation.

Whore.

She is shocked when she answers the door in nothing more than a lace bra and panties under a see-through robe and is faced with two angry men and a seething little blonde girlfriend. All I can do is balk and take in her slutty attire. She truly believed he was coming to fuck her.

What planet is she from?

Marissa visibly steps back, mouth gaping, before recovering her equilibrium, making no attempt at covering herself. She glances swiftly at Ben, noticing him seems to knock the wind out of her sails, and she pulls her robe across her protruding bump.

"What the fuck is this?!" She snaps. Jake pushes past her dragging me, quite confidently, by the hand into the large, expensive apartment. It's a loft apartment and is decorated in an almost industrial style. I don't want to know if he's ever been here with her, even when they were teens.

"What does it fucking look like, Marissa?" Jake growls, taking me to a low couch, sitting me down gently, plumping a couple of cushions up behind my back, and running a finger across my mouth as though to ground me, trying to help me relax. His attention is always on me.

"We came to party." Ben breaks in sarcastically. He wanders to the mini bar, and I notice how he starts fixing two drinks, acting equally as cocky as Jake. He seems a little too comfortable in here as well. I guess this is an apartment they've both known quite well, and it makes me feel a tad sick.

"I want you all to leave. I don't know what this is, but ..." She starts with hands on her hips, nastily pouting.

"Cut the shit, Marissa," Jake snaps and walks beside Ben to lift a glass, downing it in one go. I cringe at every drink he takes, knowing it'll fuel his less-than-reasonable side. Jake is more capable of ferociousness when he's consumed alcohol.

"Were you ever going to tell me that your baby has two possible fathers, Marissa?" He glares at her icily, all hostility on show.

Ben seems immersed in cracking ice for his drink and pours Jake another without question. He is irritatingly cool, laid back, and almost smiling. I wonder if this is why they used to get on so well. Jake was the hot head, and Ben was the calm one. Hunter is that for Jake now, sometimes.

It's weird to see them so buddy-buddy, side by side at the drinks bar while impressively intimidating the shit out of her. Both are scary in the full-blown scowling-alpha mode in entirely different ways. I can see why she has a hard time picking between the two when they're like this, so effortlessly alike, domineering in their own way. But to me, Jake is far more beautiful. I like his impulsive fire way more than Ben's cool mood.

"I don't know what you're talking about. I know which one of you is the father." She lifts her chin nastily, with no hint of remorse and no hesitation.

Interesting.

"Sorry ... How can you tell who the father is when you fucked two men within twenty-four hours of one another?" Ben remarks, snapping at her, and I catch a tiny flicker of something appearing on Marissa's face.

Not knowing her well, I assume it's a tiny flail in her perfected bitch stance. She's lost her confidence, but Jake's sharp eyes swoop right in.

"What the fuck was that?" Jake snarls viciously, and I jump at the temper only moments ago, I was admiring.

"Hmm?" Ben looks up, a little clueless, completely non-phased by Jake's outburst.

"That look ... That tiny little falter on her calculating face." Jake raises his empty glass like a pointing tool and Ben is now staring intently at her. She moves her hands to her hips.

"You can stop the double act and get the fuck out before I call security," She walks toward me, and Jake grows a little taller, bristling if she dares come anywhere near me. She sees it in the corner of her eye, halts, changes direction, and goes to the chair near the door. It seems like she knows enough about that Carrero temper not to be sure how he would react to her getting so close to me. At last, she realizes I mean more than life to him, giving me a sudden sense of calm and control, old Emma moving in, making me a little taller.

"You have thirty seconds to leave." She sounds confident and bolshie, but both men laugh at her almost manically.

"I'd love to see your fucking security try, sweetheart." Jake bubbles. His anger simmers as he downs another drink equally as fast as the last. I'm a little nervous. I'm starting to wonder if his fast alcohol consumption is wise. He knows how it can make him, and Marissa isn't someone he can take his fists to. He's bristling for a fight, and I pray to God she doesn't bring any men in here that he can inflict damage upon.

If I were her, I'd fear the psychotic sound of Jake's tone. He can be as scary as hell, and I can't imagine what he'd do to her security.

Ben isn't much of a fighter against Jake, but I'm sure he would give it a damn good go countering some heavy-handed bouncer. He has Jake's build and height and looks like he could inflict a great amount of damage, and, despite downing as much booze as Jake, he still appears to be the calmer of the two.

"What do you want? You want me to say yes, I fucked you both?" She laughs, and nothing but manic bubbling comes out, acting as if this amuses her. I'm starting to wonder if she's mentally all there.

"We already know that, sweetheart." Ben glares at her icily.

Yes, that's what it is, ice and fire, Ben and Jake. I can see it clearly now.

"So, what? You will try to force me to consent to DNA testing when it's born? You can both fuck off, and I'll see you in court! No one can do anything to this kid without my fucking consent, and as neither of you will get a chance to be alone with it ... good luck with that!" She gets up and goes to walk airily toward the phone sitting on the table beside me. I automatically pick it up, standing to meet her.

"Looking for this?" I hold it up. "Calling your security?" I raise an eyebrow at her and catch Jake moving nearer to me from the corner of my eye, always trying to protect me. He's ready to take her down, I have zero doubts about that, and I'm not sure how I would react if he did. Jake isn't someone who would hurt a woman, but if he felt I was in danger, maybe he would.

"Thank you." She sarcastically holds out her overly manicured hand, red talons, and swinging charms, but I slide her phone into my bag with a wicked smile. She isn't bringing any help that would put Jake into fight mode until he's finished with her.

I can protect him too.

"When we're done ... I wonder how many close friends you talk to about your pregnancy, Marissa? I know I have at least one female friend who knows everything intimately. You know? Every single tiny detail." There's that tiny ray of hope inside of me. The one Arrick planted a while back, the slithering of doubt that this baby is

313

Jake's. The way she seemed to suggest she knew exactly whose baby this was confidently... there's only one way a woman would know for sure.

There's that faltering flicker on her face again, and I sense Jake's warmth behind my shoulder. I'm a little more empowered as he seems to get what I'm hinting at. His hand on my waist lets me know he's right behind me, not that I need it. I can always feel his presence.

"I wonder how many texts you've sent about it?" I reach back into my bag slowly, wondering how easily I can make her fold, especially if I'm right about this.

"You can't access my fucking messages. I have a pin." She smirks, but Jake steps in front of me protectively, sliding a hand behind him to keep me close, telling me he doesn't trust her not to fly at me.

"I don't need one," he growls at her. "I'm pretty sure any of my tech guys could access your messages seeing as I managed to track my girlfriend's cell in less than five seconds when I needed to." He's back to that furious, snarling tone sending shivers down my spine.

So, that's how he did it?

"What do you hope to find?" She lifts her chin defiantly, smirking, but the look of smugness has evaporated from her dark eyes, replaced with a slight hint of apprehension.

"Maybe something fun and incriminating, maybe nothing." Ben slides in and seems to be enjoying this a little too much. I'm sure he has no idea what we're talking about, but he's playing along. Old friendship flickers between the two men who used to have each other's backs so closely.

"Did I actually fuck you?" Jake comes out with it, getting to the point, and I catch Ben's confusion flicker across his brow. He quickly regains his previous expression, blank-faced, and says nothing while turning to look at Marissa.

She snorts but doesn't answer. Her head shakes as though this is ridiculous. Her foot is tapping, and her hands are firmly on her hips as she pushes her bust out. She looks impressively feisty and ready to take them both on. I can see why she may have held some attraction to a fifteen-year-old Jake. He likes my feistiness and my ability to stand up to him. He always smiled when I bristled back at him and gave him attitude as his PA.

"Did. I. Lay. A. Single. Fucking. Hand. On. You?" Jake says it very slowly, so unbearable to hear. Every word precise, oozing with a hint of poison.

"It's not my fault you can't remember, baby. But you still fuck hard, even when you're drunk, and I more than loved it. You made me cum like a freight train." She throws me an evil look, her arched eyebrow and haughty smile trying to wound me. Ben clenches his jaw and looks away, still obviously affected by her. He has some feelings left for her, but Jake shows that there's nothing in there for her with him. Inner anger seethes and bubbles inside me, and I want to gouge her eyes out.

Fucking bitch!

"I never, did I?" Jake sounds shocked. My head snaps up to him, wondering what he sees close-up in that cocky whore's face that I can't. She hesitates and looks back at him like she's been caught, and she loses the mask for a millisecond. It quickly draws back up, but I think even Ben caught it, a tiny flicker of *shit he knows*.

"Yes, you did," she snaps a little too quickly. The flicker turns into a full-on twitch as she has trouble controlling her face.

"No, I didn't. I can tell when you're lying to my face ... I never had sex with you, did I?" Jake's tone has completely dispersed. Instead of rage, he sounds shocked, something in his brain whirring and clicking. Figuring it all out, trying to work through the drunken haze of a night he still can't remember.

"Marissa? Surely even you couldn't scrape as low as that?" Ben snorts in absolute disgust, and I see how she clenches her teeth, pure hatred emanating everywhere. Ben shakes his head, appalled, deciding that this is the truth right here. He walks off to get another drink.

"That night in the hotel ..." Jake's lost in memory and talking loudly, his voice a little soft, "... You never said *my* baby. You said you were having *a* baby." He seems to be trying to pull something out of his head, running fingers through his hair. "You knew I would see a lie when you faced me that way." His chin lifts again, and he glares at her angrily.

"You've got no clue of what you're saying." She throws her hair back over her shoulder and turns to storm off, but Jake's lightening quick reflexes mean he catches her wrist and pulls her back with serious aggression, yanking her to him with a hollow thud as she hits his chest with her arm, he draws her wrist up to his shoulder angrily. The grip is harsh, even from here.

"You said you were pregnant and having *a* baby. You asked me what I was going to do about it, but you never actually used the fucking words, *your* baby ... Not once ... In that whole conversation. Later, when lawyers and distance separated us, sure ... but up close like this ... Never fucking once!" He's standing, but his back is bent, nose to nose with her, voice seething, scarily intimidating, and I begin to wonder if he's capable of hurting a woman in this state. I recoil behind him, suddenly unsure of this person I've never seen before coming out.

My heart is pounding, and every part of me is fighting to intervene. I can't let Jake hurt her, even if I hate her. I would never look at him the same way. This isn't what I want. This isn't who I love. I can feel his hatred for her sweeping off him, around us, like smoke filling the room. So many memories of cruel men with power over me, and I can't let that happen to anyone else, even her.

"Stop it, you're hurting me," she snarls through gritted teeth, but there's fear in her eyes too. She doesn't know this version of him, and neither do I. I feel faint with the confusion tearing through me. My hands cover my mouth, and I have no idea what to do. Even Ben looks a little uneasy at this terrifying version of Jake in full-on viciousness, and he tenses as though ready to intervene.

"Did I fuck you?" His glare and nasty growl, through clenched teeth, show a man on the verge of so much rage it's sweeping off him in droves so powerful the air seems to be cracking around him. His knuckles are white with the grip of his fisted hand by his side, and the one on her wrist almost crushes her. This is a side to Jake I've never known, and he's terrifying.

Her eyes fill with tears, and she stops pulling at her wrist because it obviously hurts. The color drains from her face, her eyes losing a little of their confident arrogance, and her lip starts to wobble in the presence of this version of him. She feels the same fear I feel, but she's the object of his pure undivided attention, so I can only imagine how much worse it is. He's almost nose to nose with her in the most vicious scowl I have ever seen. I reach out to his back and touch him, a begging touch, to stop hurting her for me. I may hate her, but I can't bear to see her hurt like this, not by him or any man. No woman deserves to be treated this way, even if she has done the unthinkable.

His grip loosens enough for the color of the pale skin in her fingers to start warming again. He's responding to me even full of rage, and I calm down, knowing he's still in there and responsive to me. He hasn't succumbed to some red veil of rage and blanked me out. Marissa looks ashen-faced and scared.

I don't blame her; this isn't my Jake. This is a man with the potential of someone like Ray Vanquis, with enough strength and aggression to make a woman submit to the truth by any means. Someone who could beat a woman to the floor without a second thought if he wanted to.

The tears start pouring down my face, willing me anywhere but here, so I don't have to witness what he thinks is necessary. I couldn't forgive him if he did this. I don't want to see this, so many memories brimming to the surface of my brain and wounding me.

"You still want me," she whispers to distract him, aiming for some emotion inside of him that she's sure he still has for her, trying to manipulate and claw back some of the man she previously knew. But this time, she's pushed him too far.

"Marissa, I fucking hated you for years, but I don't hate you anymore because I don't care enough about you to feel a single fucking thing." He lets her go, with a voice as cold and empty as ice, and steps back, much to my absolute relief. I feel faint with it.

His words must sting as her eyes fill with moisture and tears come pouring down. I'd be dying right now knowing that Jake could be so brutally cold and cruel and emotionally dead inside if it were me. My body sags with relief that he's backed off, and I'm so confused with all the emotions hitting me over this scene.

I shiver and wrap my arms tightly around myself, willing my Jake to come back into this room. I hate being here without him. I need him to be the one dealing with this, not this crazy, rage-brimming Jake that Marissa seems to have pulled out of him. He's like a stranger to me.

He stands towering over her, every part of him poised and solid. Even Ben has moved away far enough for me to understand that this isn't over, and I start to tense again. That tingle in the air, a mix of dangerous and crazy, lingering, and I am on the verge of tears again. My body, heart, mind, and soul struggle to endure this.

She doesn't say anything and looks from one man to the other in desperation, like she knows she's losing and is floundering at what to do. Afraid of the man before her, her face softens, her tone changes, eyes widen to alarming Bambi-type levels. Her whole body seems to sag and turns submissive.

"Ben?" she whispers tearfully, reaching out for him, turning on the tears and victim eyes much like my mother used to do, trying to get some comfort or reaction. She's acting scared, hoping Ben will protect her from the obvious lunatic in the room.

She's completely nuts.

"I don't think so, sweetheart. I'm done being head-fucked by you. Just answer him." Ben downs another drink, clinking the glass down onto the counter without another look her way. Offering no help, he does shift closer, and I wonder if, deep down, he would still protect her, especially from this angry and raging man standing in front of her. Jake is possessed by something, by her and their past and how she nearly messed up our future; all his anger is focused on her, built up, ready to burst.

She raises her chin in one last show of pride, and then nastiness moves in, darkness taking over her face as she stands tall to meet Jake with matched venom. She's decided to stand and fight. A switch in her head goes off, and a new personality steps in; she knows she's lost, so she's going down in a blaze of fire.

"All your lame-ass drunk self could do was talk about her." She nods at me nastily, eyes never leaving him, defiantly. "Some fucking assistant you were hung up on, then you told me to fuck off before you passed out face down, fully dressed." She's decided that if the truth is to come out, she will do it in grand fashion, twisting the knife simultaneously. She's on a sinking ship and doing herself no favors.

A massive gust of relief rushes through me, my heart soaring, squealing, and aching that Jake loved me even back then. It makes me forget the past few minutes in elation. But I need to hear her say it. I need to be a hundred percent certain. I want the actual words to free us from all the anguish finally she's held over us these past few months.

"So, I never touched you in any way ... Nothing? Not once?" Jake is back to snarling as pieces of the puzzle click into place. The agony of these past few months and all the drama and hassle she's caused over a baby that wasn't even Jake's? All of that, and there was never even a tiny sliver of a chance at it being his. He is ripping her head off with his eyes, yet his ferocious, unpredictable poise has slowly dissipated. Her confession was all he wanted. It was all an act, a maneuver, another Carrero manipulation on his part.

"You were as much of a disappointment to me that night as you always have been, Jacob. You don't know what to do with a real woman like me, and you sure as hell couldn't get it up. Yeah, I fucked Ben to ensure I got pregnant because payback is a fucking bitch!" She slaps the glass out of Ben's hand since he'd sauntered over to hear every word from the lying whore's mouth. It smashes to the floor, and she turns on her heel, storming away.

Jake seems to be immobilized in rage and maybe relief, while Ben, with blinking disbelief, is still trying to take in the fact that he is one hundred percent the father. He's ashen-faced as though it's dawned on him that he's having a baby ... with her!

He has a look I must've had when I learned about tadpole and Marissa's baby.

"Marissa?" I call after her, and she stops, spinning her head to me with a look of complete hatred. I toss her phone onto the floor between us, not caring if I break it, and scowl right back.

"You're pathetic ... It's sad that you had to go to such lengths to get something he gave me so freely." I lift my chin and slide my hand into Jake's, anger tremoring through his body, vibrating with rage, as I tug him with me. I'm no longer afraid of that scary psycho look on his face. Jake would never hurt me that way, no matter how seething he is, and my touch seems to calm him. He never left me here at all. He needed to push her to break her barriers and confess, always the manipulator and never a Vanquis.

I was stupid ever to doubt him.

"Take me home, Jake. I want to go home." I turn my adoring eyes to the man who loves me, smug at the seething despise on her face as she watches us. Secure in just how little he must've ever felt for her to be able to scare her that way and now elated that her hold over him is gone.

Jake slides an arm around me, pulling me in, watching the sheer toxic rage in her eyes, and we leave Ben and Marissa to sort out the future *their* baby will have now. As we walk out, I niggle with a little remorse at poor Ben's crushed demeanor.

With every step away from that apartment, Jake seems to lose some soaring anger coursing through his body and starts to loosen up. Every footstep pulls him back to the man I know and love, and as we reach the stairwell, his palms slide over my stomach with a huge sigh of relief. He pulls me to a stop before hauling me into his arms and exhales slowly into my hair in an all-consuming full-body embrace.

"I'm sorry I scared you, *Bambina* ... Really, really sorry. I just needed to push her for the truth ... I needed her to be scared enough to admit it."

Chapter 25

"I can't get my head around it," Jake utters for the hundredth time as we lie in bed, our bodies entwined. My exhaustion has dissipated, giving way to mind-numbing silence after the events of the evening.

We finally have freedom ... from her.

We've been home for a few hours, yet mostly all we've done is lie together and talk. Hours spent regurgitating the fact that there is no other baby, wondering how his family will react and how different things will be from now on without it hanging over us. It's still too surreal to believe, and emotions between us have been swirling like crazy.

"I can't believe it's over," I exclaim out loud, hearing him sigh again. A happy heavy relief kind of noise.

"Me either. It feels like it's been consuming me ... us ... for months." He's lying on his back, staring at the ceiling while I rest my head on his firm abdomen, tracing the tattoos on his inner forearm of the arm across me casually.

"How did she think she would get away with it?" I blanch, thinking it through, and turn, shifting up to him, resting my head on the bicep of his arm nestled behind his head, and stare at his profile with inner bubbling happiness. Jake's naked torso is deliciously on show. The sheets pulled up to waist level.

"That level of crazy has no logic, Emma. I'm just glad Ben had the sense to come to see me and not let the festering past stop us." He sounds calm and stress-free for the first time in forever. It's only taken hours, though, for it to hit home.

"I can't believe it," I say again through the numb disbelief still hanging in the air; aftershock, anger, tears, and relief subsided. We have been through it all.

"Just you, me, and tadpole from now on." He beams, turning to face me. His arm shifting under my head, bending at the elbow to make himself into a better cushion.

Jake was angry when we came home, rage pouring out of him like a spewing sewer, and it took a lot for him to expel it. He disappeared into the gym for a while to recklessly punch and kick the crap out of his boxing bag with deadly precision. But lying here, calm and serene, I think it's finally sinking in that this is a good thing, a happy thing. I know a part of him will feel a sense of loss at the severing of the connection he built up emotionally with Marissa's baby, believing it was his. Some part of him accepted the child she was having; the anger is his way of grieving its loss, as well as Marissa's depth of betrayal and deceit.

"I guess it won't be a tadpole now. If you'd let that doctor look, I'm sure we would have a better idea of what size it is." I point out with a smirk. Jake touches his fingertip to my nose with an unapologetic smirk.

"I have an appointment for you this week, I forgot to tell you, and I'm still not letting anyone stick a wand up there to see. Male or female." His furrowed brow and smile tell me he doesn't care if it makes him look possessive, controlling, and slightly overprotective.

"I'm sure it's not long before they can scan my stomach instead. Plus, the thought of being impaled by some nasty-looking probe isn't giving me the greatest of thrills anyway." I cringe at remembering the weird medical implement the doctor was stupid enough to wave around near one very hostile Carrero and giggle at the memory. The probe, moments from being used in a very different way and leaving the doctor with an unusual walk if he kept waving it within Jake's reach.

"New obstetrician and many more appointments. I just wasn't

happy with the guy all over you." He grimaces at the memory as though I was somehow assaulted in front of him. I roll my eyes at him with an indulgent smile and stroke his face tenderly.

What can I do with him ... Honestly?

"You'll need to tell your family about this now, you know, this thing with Marissa? We need to tell our friends too." I focus on those soft green eyes and see nothing more than uncomplicated love shining back. Whatever demons he needed to expel were banished successfully in the gym. That version of him was a little too uncomfortable for my liking, reminding me of how easy it would be for someone Jake's size to hurt someone my size, highlighting how gentle he really is.

"I think it's a given that everyone will be happy for us; pity I can't say the same for Ben. I wish it weren't him that got left with the fallout, even after everything." He frowns and runs a hand across my mouth, a habit usually followed closely by kissing or sex. His mind moves from mundane topics to fun activities instead. My skin starts tingling in anticipation, and a small warmth appears low down in my stomach as I watch his green eyes darken.

"Maybe in a way it's retribution? They have each other now, whether either one wants it or not. Ben will have some hold over her with the baby, and seeing her for what she is has probably helped him a little." I inhale softly and nudge my face into his palm so his touch applies more pressure, longing for him like a never-ending craving, yearning for the extras that his hints usually lead to.

"Very philosophical for you, baby." Jake smiles and strokes my hair back from my face. "Maybe you're right. Karma has a way of coming around to bite you in the ass. God knows I've felt that set of teeth in the last few months." He shifts us closer with a hand around me, and in one swift maneuver, I'm suddenly pressed right up against him, hard body to my soft curves.

"Hmm, you must've repented successfully, seeing as you're living a very charmed life; everything is working in your favor nowadays." I giggle when his hands slide down below my waist, trying to push my thighs apart with a sexy naughty glint in his eye.

"Charmed is only one of the many ways to describe it." He

slides his knee between my legs, maneuvering them apart, a wicked glean in his eyes taking over.

"Right. I guess we're done talking about serious issues, and now you're angling for sex?" I giggle but don't resist, my body fully heated and ready for meaningful, energetic action.

"Pretty much ... I'm a man with needs, *neonata*." He leans in to devour my neck with tiny nibbles. I giggle and squeal as his hands turn playful, and he tickles me, pulling me into him. My happy, carefree Jake let loose.

"Jake!" I protest, which encourages him to flip me onto my back, covering me in one swift move.

"You're amazing, baby. Beautiful, sexy, smart, and so unbelievably perfect." He hovers above me tantalizingly, keeping his mouth from me that's crying out to be kissed.

"I'll be expecting to hear the same when I'm the size of a whale or a crazy hormonal mess again like I was in the beginning." I bite on my lip as I devour the way his eyes roam my face as he smirks in that lustful way of his.

"You'll always be sexy and beautiful and perfect to me; a baby just adds to what is so amazing about you." He leans in, kissing me softly, our mouths molding as he slowly brings his body weight down. His hands seek my hair and neck, coming to hold me close, a sign that Jake will blow my mind in ways only he can.

* * *

"Here." Jake hands me the small cooler bag Nora packed for me, crammed with food and snacks since I'm still eating like a starved animal, and he only encourages it with a constant food supply.

"Thank you, gorgeous." I wink at him, and I'm rewarded with a smack on the ass as he walks past me with our cases. I grin at him. He is still the sexiest man alive, possessing the ability to turn me to mush with one look.

"Grab my sunglasses," he calls, and I obediently pick them up, my beloved Jake's defining symbol, and slide them onto my head, smiling at myself as I do. He doesn't need them as much when he's driving now since the weather is getting colder and the sun is disappearing earlier from the sky. But I still carry them around whenever I get the chance, holding them close, reminding me of him in many ways, a constant item in our relationship of trials and tribulations. He's driving us to Chicago, and I'm in surprisingly high spirits, despite knowing what this journey is for. Since finding out Marissa never slept with Jake, I've felt on top of the world, and nothing can ruin my buzz. That high feeling and relaxed smile are ingrained on me, and Jake is in the same amazingly good mood. Our black cloud is gone.

When he told everyone about Marissa, there were mixed reactions; anger and outrage and even tears from Sylvana, shocked that Marissa could be that manipulative, but for the most part, everyone sighed with relief. Even Giovanni seemed pleased in his own way since he promptly sent a bottle of champagne and some fruit punch to our apartment, tied together in a blue and pink ribbon. Jake glowered at them and left them on the counter. I don't know what he imagines the symbolic value of the gift is, but I doubt it's the same one I interpreted it to be.

To me, the gift from Giovanni symbolizes his congratulations to us on the removal of Marissa and the building of a family between Jake and me. He's not so hard to figure out when you realize a good heart beats beneath his cool, tightened demeanor. It's that simple.

Leila told me she and Hunter are off to a remote island destination for a week, despite still being an emotional enigma, to start putting the past behind them. Daniel is holding in there, treating her tenderly now that she's not putting up such a fight. She sounds happier, less hostile, and not as angry bitchy, especially with his voice in the background cooing and telling her to come back to bed. It was noon when she called, so I take it things are still going well since they were still in bed, and I could hear him dotingly calling her his "princess" in the background.

"Baby, are you ready?" Jake's voice echoes through the apartment, and I look around for my handbag. This place seems decidedly less polished nowadays that Jake's favorite art and furniture have been sent to the Hamptons, along with many of our personal belongings. We've decided when we come home from Chicago, we're going straight up to follow our personal effects up there, then Jake is having this place redecorated and revamped as his pad to stay in when he comes over for work. He plans minor changes to the room layouts, making this apartment child friendly and moving our bedroom down to the hall with the guestrooms, bringing us closer to the nursery he wants to put there.

Nora is staying here as a housemaid since Jake's going to be here at least once a week, and Mathews is training the new security to be positioned here since we'll be taking him to the new house; their choice, of course, always so loyal to Jake.

Jefferson will be driving Jake around when he's here, and Mathews will be spending time chauffeuring and protecting me in the Hamptons and training the new security staff at the house. Jake has kept on the previous owner's house staff, and once we're moved in, they're all returning to work as they did before. Jake has this all effortlessly organized and everything smoothly in place.

I admit the thought of cooks, cleaners, and chauffeurs is no longer something I balk at; a life looking after my child without the stress that most mothers endure sounds like heaven to me. I know how lucky I am not to worry about mundane house tasks or troubles with money. I am finally accepting it all, seeing it as a perk of loving the most amazing man in the world, another gift he's effortlessly given me in this fairy-tale life.

I'll have the Carrero family nearby to support me, including Sylvana and her amazing cooking skills, Sophie, and Leila when she comes home to visit. Giovanni, in his own little way. Daniel ... and Arrick when he's around too. All people as important to me as Jake infiltrated into my life. Not to mention all the staff bending to help me at every beck and call. This move is the best way to start a new life with the perfect man of my dreams. I finally convinced myself daily that this isn't a dream I'll one day wake up from.

The one person I'll miss more than most when I leave is Sarah, but she's promised to head our way at least once a month for God-motherly visits and girly catch-ups, so I'm sure everything will work out perfectly.

Jake appears at the door and visually scans me. He comes over and smooths his hands down me appreciatively, my little bump barely on show, yet somehow the dress draws attention to it because of how the high waistline kicks out as it reaches the top of my bump.

"You changed your mind?" He rubs his nose against mine affectionally, and I shake my head.

"No, just thinking about how much I'll miss this place when we leave." I look around the open sitting room and stark modern décor, realizing that it's everything Jake used to be the epitome of a bachelor pad. Jake looks around and shrugs.

"I guess. Been here a while, *Bambina*." He pulls me into his arms, turning me to spoon him, wrapping his arms around my shoulders, and resting his head on mine as he looks at the four walls around us. "If these walls could talk." that dirty laugh pulls a frown from me, and I elbow him in the stomach, my green-eyed monster peeking through. "They would only say I've had some seriously amazing sex with one feisty little PA." He quickly replies and chuckles when I shove him again. There's no way I'm letting him ruin my beautiful moment of reflection and sentiment with his prissy wild ways and past seductions of other women.

"That's all they need to say," I warn with a half-smile, bursting into full-on giggles when he spins me around under his arm, planting a big sloppy kiss on me.

"That's all that matters, sexy." He smacks my butt again, pulling me with him and tugging me playfully. "Come on. This is a long ass painful drive, so we'd better get going."

I follow and grin widely at his sexy ass and broad shoulders.

* * *

The drive to Chicago is long but pleasant. Between listening to the radio and talking about everything and nothing, Jake has me giggling for more than half of the journey. It's like huge heavy darkness has lifted from us, and we're back to being who we used to be when I was his close friend and Personal Assistant. Although, back then, we didn't stop the car a million times to fumble in the back seat and get half naked as we have on this trip.

"You're getting too good at that, baby." Jake winks at me and zips up his pants with a smug look. I surprised him with a false nap in his lap with a naughty twist, something I've been bravely improving on, returning the pleasure that he so freely gives me ... many times over. I know it had to be good when he groaned loudly and pulled into the first lay-by he saw. Jake, the master of control, unraveled in under three minutes. I am feeling decidedly pleased with myself because of how quickly I brought him to completion with some masterful oral.

"Well, you're driving me back to the windy city, so you deserved a little reward." He sits back in his seat and stretches his legs before starting the car.

"I'm going to miss these high levels of horny when tadpole comes." He twists in his seat to check his blind spot before pulling us back into traffic, and my body heats up at his muscular frame and strong neck. His profile makes me drool, and watching him drive has me fluttering in panty-combusting heat.

"I don't think it's all pregnancy hormones." I flutter lashes at him as he turns to me, eyes running wide over my face with one of his amazing swoony smirks. I'm sure the high levels of horny I've been having are from the complete package of one Mr. Jake Carrero.

Hmmm. Swoon.

His hotness, muscular perfection, all-around sexy voice, and charm should be illegal. He has no idea of the effect he has on the hearts of the female population. Yes, he's good-looking, and I know he used to use that trait many times to his advantage, but his caring nature and beautiful heart win me over time and again.

"Bambina, keep looking at me like that, and we'll never get to Chicago. You make me want to find a motel, fast." He winks at me as his eyes roam my face. It makes me wonder exactly how much ogling I've been doing. I giggle and exhale slowly.

"I shall try to contain myself until we get there; you need to stop looking so sexy. It's ruining my calm." I moan as his fingers trail up my thigh lightly to under the hem of my dress, sliding into my inner thigh, so my body is instantly delirious with the tingles he ignites.

"Welcome to my world, *Miele*. It's called payback." His lust-filled gaze is distracting, and I'm surprised he's hard so quickly for me, given why we stopped the car a few minutes ago. I push his hand away as it gets seductively higher and shove his shoulder.

"Eyes on the road, Carrero. The last thing we need is a prang in your stupidly expensive car because your mind is between my legs." I pull my knees together in a bid to calm my devouring need. He is right, though. If we keep this up, we'll never get to Chicago. The conclusion to the Marissa debacle has sent our hormones on the crazy up and up lately. Not that it wasn't already, but still.

"*Our* stupidly expensive car! My mind is eternally between your thighs. It's all I think about, whether you're beside me or not." He winks my way, increasing the heat in my lower pelvis more so, making me squirm. "I was serious about getting you on the road." Jake flickers a look at me, both hands on the wheel, as an eye roll takes me over, instantly calming my fire. He's been on me to learn to drive so I can be more independent when we move to the Hamptons, but he's handing me a chauffeur, so I don't see the point. Plus, the thought of managing New York traffic terrifies me.

"For a guy obsessed with being overprotective, it's pretty contradictory of you to want me to drive." I poke a finger into the cute boy dimple on his face, and he catches my finger, kissing it before releasing me.

"I'm protective, baby ... not archaic. I do actually want a wife that has her own independence, a career, and something more than just me and babies." He throws me a sympathetic look and then systematically concentrates on the mirror and windscreen as he maneuvers us into a lane.

"You surprise me, Mr. Carrero. I figured, being the overbearing man you sometimes can be, you'd be happy for me to laze around being served and kept." I watch as his handsome profile picks up with a beaming smile.

"I would be happy with that if it made you happy, but I know it won't." He answers diplomatically, and we both know if I chose to be a kept woman, he would have absolutely no problem with it.

"No, I suppose it won't." I sigh, relaxing into my seat a little snuggly. I have no idea how long we've been driving; it feels longer because of the constant stopping and naughtiness on the journey so far. I stretch out and run a hand over my stomach absent-mindedly, a mannerism becoming second nature.

"My mom is pulling a few strings for you, gathering Info on ideas and directions you may be interested in. She thinks you could start by maybe seeing a counselor yourself ... and talking through the past?" He tenses as the words come out a little delicately. I know he's waiting for my overreaction or possibly just an angry reply, and I watch him go from relaxed and cocky to unsure and nervous, and my heart swells.

This suggestion met an icy and angry reply when he mentioned it while we were standing on the hills of the island overlooking his father's boat, right before he stormed off for a week. But the past is in the past, and I've already moved on from everything else. Maybe now is the time to try to shake it all for good.

"It might be an idea, seeing as I can't exactly encourage kids to talk if I haven't had the guts to do it myself." I shrug when he glances my way, surprised, then relief sweeps his face. "I mean, if Daniel, of all people, can handle therapy ..." I smile with a raised eyebrow, waiting for his reaction.

"You never cease to amaze me, you know? I never would've imagined this conversation going this way a year ago," His hand comes to my leg with an affectionate squeeze. He looks overjoyed with pride, and his smile is infectious.

"Yeah? Well, I never imagined, even a month ago, that we'd be coming back here or I'd want to see her alone and tell her what I need to say, but... things change." I sigh, trying to push it out of my head. The pit in my stomach about seeing her is starting to weigh heavily as the air around us stirs up unpleasant memories.

"You sure you don't want me to come with you?" He's watching me with wary eyes. He's been trying to convince me not to do this alone, afraid she'll hurt me as much as she did the last time we were here, but this time is different. I'm not going to give her the ability to keep hurting me. Coming here is a test since I'm not sure she even has that power over me anymore.

My mind, emotions, outlook, and whole life are very different from the last I saw her.

"I'm sure, Jake. Drop me at the door and come back for me, but I need to do this alone. I need to see her alone." It started with my mother and me, so it'll end the same way. I owe her that much. I want to show a modicum of respect despite her never having the decency to show me any.

"You should've told her we were coming." He's glancing in his mirrors, and I realize it's because we're cutting off, signs for Chicago are looming over us, and a dreaded weight settles in my stomach with a sickening lurch, my nerves jangling inside me.

"No, it's better this way; surprising her means she hasn't time to prepare or dress things up. I'll catch her off guard." I tap my leg with my fingertips and bring my hand up to play with my hair as the tension of familiar surroundings sweeps over me. Jake instinctively places his hand over mine, bringing it back down to my lap, grounding me effortlessly.

"I'm crazy about you. Just remember that ... no matter what she says." He smiles warmly, indicating a turn-off, eyes on the road, and hands on the wheel. Despite his assurances, I can't help but start chewing my lip as my insides churn.

"I know, trust me, it's different now. I'm different. It won't be like last time, Jake. I know what I want to say and why I've come." I sound surer than I am, but I know I'll find the strength to do this.

"I'd be lying if I said I won't be pacing like crazy while you're with her, and you know, *Bambina* ... one call, and I'll be there for you." The seriousness in his eyes warms me and helps ease the tightening despair growing up inside my body.

"I know. I love you. I just need to do this and get it over and done with."

Chapter 26

Gazing up at the crappy brown building that houses "The Haven" homeless shelter, an internal wave of anxiety builds up inside me, like an all-consuming black hole, now that I'm faced with old memories. Jake is standing behind me with hands on my shoulders, and a kiss on my neck brings me back to the present.

"Call me, and I'll come, okay?" His voice is a reminder that I can do this. I can be strong enough because of him.

"I know. Now leave before I change my mind about going to the hotel first." I giggle as his hand skims my ass; he's a tempting distraction to what I know I need to do.

"If I'd known you were this torn about it, I would've applied a little more pressure." He smirks wickedly, letting his hand trail lower under my dress. I laugh and shove him off playfully with my butt, which only serves to cheer him on because he pushes his hand further between my legs, and I fight the scalding surge of heat it causes.

For the love of God. Stay focused.

"Go! There's plenty of time for that later, a lot of that." I smile as he holds up his hands in defeat.

"I'm holding you to that, baby." He smacks my ass and turns back to the car, winking and waving as he slides in effortlessly. I stand watching him and sigh, a chaos of emotions churning up at the loss of his touch. He waits by the sidewalk until I swallow down the inner dread; when it passes, I turn with a wave and head inside.

Jake won't wander far, probably a nearby café or something within walking distance so he can get back to me in a hurry. Knowing he's close helps. Knowing I can call him and he'll be right here gives me strength. It gives me the peace that I desperately need. The man is too much for my heart to handle sometimes, but I wouldn't have him any other way.

I swallow down everything building up inside of me and push through the doors into the main foyer of the building; it's a lot nicer than the last time I stepped in here, and I remember my mother talking about refurbishments to this place the last time I saw her. It's airy and light but cozy and welcoming. I spot the familiar receptionist, Claire. Even after all these years, she looks the same but surprised to see me and beams at my entrance.

"Hello, Emma! Well, look at you! God, you look great. The vision of happiness with your glowing face and hair is adorable." I smile warmly, my composure slipping when faced with people from my past. The urge to lift my chin and force out those cold mannerisms and icy tone almost overwhelms me, but I don't. That instant compulsion died a while back in the glory of Jake's presence, and I won't slide into an old habit to deal with my discomfort around this poor woman.

"Hey. Thank you. I was wondering if my mother was here and if I could maybe go surprise her?" I take her in with a genuine smile hiding my inner waves of fear. My palms are already clamming up, and I can't ignore the faster thumping of my heart now I'm in here.

"You're in luck. She's in her office today doing the accounts. She'll be alone too, I imagine, holed up with her head in the books." She pats my shoulder gently and smiles. "Just go on up. She'll be so happy to see you."

Doubtful.

I smile gratefully at her before heading toward the far-right corner staircase, thanking Claire as I go, by-passing a couple of undesirable-looking teens loitering nearby, eyeing me up.

Wonderful.

I swerve around a little older woman, with a huge sense of sadness for her, as she drags carrier bags behind her containing all her worldly possessions.

I skip up the steps, two at a time, in a bid to get this over and done with before I lose my courage, then turn a corner to come face-to-face with the old familiar corridor leading to her office. The same pale cream walls and red carpet, no refurbishments up here to keep my memories at bay. Her pine office door is chipped and scraped, but her name is executively etched onto a brass sign screwed outside, looking so out of place against the old entrance.

I stand outside, fixing my hair, smoothing down my pink sundress, and take a deep calming breath before I steady myself to bring a sense of calm to my demeanor. I picture Jake's soft, caring face and breathe deeply, seeing him clearly, imagining him beside me with an encouraging hand in mine, a genuine smile lifting at the corners of my mouth.

I can do this.

I don't knock or hesitate to reach out. I turn the handle and walk in like it's the most natural thing in the world for me to do.

She's sat at her desk, glasses perched on the end of her nose and face inclined toward the papers she's looking at. Her tousled wavy hair, the same color as mine, is falling over her face. She looks up, hearing the door creak open, and I catch a moment of shock gape across her mouth as it quickly turns into a warm smile, a little wary but still warm, making my stomach ache. Doubt creeps in and makes this instantly harder. My mother is always capable of showing affection when she knows it's appropriate, but even now, I can't decipher whether it's genuine.

"Emma?" She stands and smiles, rolling a pen between her hands, elbows bent in front of her. We still, for a moment, neither is the type to initiate any sort of touching with the other.

"This is a lovely surprise." She gestures pointedly with her pen for me to sit down. "Please, have a seat." Her voice is steady, with no hint of anything other than minor surprise at my appearance.

"Mother." I swallow hard and move slowly, closing the door behind me to give us some privacy, deciding not to sit down, knowing I won't be here long enough to get 'comfortable' – if that's even the definition of this situation. I'm glad we're here and not at the apartment; this is easier, detached, and business-like, with a desk separating us and making me feel more capable. This is a place I rarely visited as a teen, so there aren't many lingering memories or heart-breaking thoughts here to distract me.

"I wasn't sure I'd ever see you back here after the way you both left last time ..." She raises a brow with a hint of attitude, and I bristle. She's clearly still angry about my behavior and accusations, no doubt irritated that Jake saw that side of her. This is the reaction I've been expecting, though, no hint of her own wrongdoing, just highlighting her disappointment in me and noting my failures according to her. Again.

You know her, Emma. This is what she's like, don't take the bait.

She wants an apology, wants me to admit I behaved badly, like always, and because I'm not playing her game, she's not giving me anything in return. She's turned on her cool demeanor and closed-off persona, a sight I've seen many times, withdrawing any form of affection, like she always did when I was a child. She's freezing me out, except this time, it's not because I've upset one of her lovers. It's just because I'm here, and she didn't know I was coming. She can't pretend with me this way.

Right now, she wants to punish me for daring to turn the finger back on her about my childhood. My mother is narcissistic, clear to me like a flash of light as I take in her familiar pose and expression, deadpan blankness.

"Actually, I'm here to tell you my news." I push down the chaotic feelings threatening to override my courage. A wave of nausea washes over me, tadpole's instincts at knowing something is wrong with me. I nod toward the chair in front of her desk, looking for permission to sit despite already having it. She frowns at me, annoyed by my ignorance of her request before, yet obliges and nods toward the chair opposite her desk with an exasperated look. I scold myself for my childish questioning to sit; PA Emma would've never sought her permission. An adult should be able to sit without needing consent, but she has a way of making me feel like a child all over again.

"Please." She sits back, removing her glasses and laying her palms on the table across one another. I cannot help but watch her stiff upright posture, careful mannerisms, and sigh. Jake is right, I used to behave exactly like her, but I didn't see it; every movement, carefully placed, always aware of her grace and gestures, cool and coldly poised. I look down at my hands, casually laid in my lap, and my sagging posture and smile. I'm sitting how Jake would sit, loose and relaxed, with no thought to how I'm perceived, and I can't help but feel his warmth run across me as though he's here with me, encouraging me even in his absence.

"Jake asked me to marry him." I smile at her, shining with inner joy at his face in my mind, thinking back to the night when he asked me to be his forever.

God, I love him so much.

She sits for a moment, and I scrutinize her every expression, a hint of surprise followed by a look of disappointment, and then a fake smile is plastered on to hide it all. Her façade is disrupted only momentarily, and then she's back in full control.

Why am I not surprised that she doesn't want me to be happy? She never has. She doesn't care if it's not something for her benefit.

"Congratulations. I'm assuming the wedding will be in New York?" She can't look me in the eye, but there's a new tone to her voice, a slight edge, and for the first time, I click to what it is. I've been completely oblivious before today, but now there's a bright, shining magnifying light forced over her for me to peer through.

She's jealous!! She is jealous of her own freaking child finding happiness. Her child finding love. What kind of mother is that?!

"There's more." I sit up straighter, old anger rising at her response to her only child getting married, Inner-Teen-Emma making a grand appearance, the girl pushed down repeatedly by the woman before her.

She hasn't even asked me if he makes me happy or how much I love him. She has never acknowledged my relationship with him before, so it's no surprise that she wouldn't now.

"Let me guess ... You've quit work to live the life of a billionaire's trophy wife? I'm so proud." She stares at me blankly, and I start stiffening. She isn't good at hiding her envy now since we're getting into it, forgetting herself and her outward demeanor because we have no audience. Hence needing to do this alone, for this persona right here. The woman who used to tower over me in passive emptiness when her boyfriend was upset or when one left because of me.

Breathe, don't let her get to you.

"No, actually, I'm currently looking toward a new career. One more fulfilling in which I can help children who have been abused like I was." I lift my chin proudly, meeting her eye, ready to take on her response in a non-emotional way. I am at peace with how I am going to handle this.

Her eyes glaze over, and her eyebrow rises as she sighs, acting as though 'little girl Emma' is at it again, being over-dramatic, making herself out to be the poor defenseless, innocent child.

She is no mother of mine. I can see it now. I'll never call her my mom again; she's never been deserving of the title. In the short time Sylvana has known me, she's been more of a mom to me than Jocelyn ever was.

She's pondering over how to respond, no doubt bringing memories of our last meeting fresh to her mind, afraid that raging and violent Emma may strop out again. That tiny trigger of annoyance builds higher at her silent pause.

Hold your temper, Emma. She's not worth this. I swallow it down; just say the words and get it over and done with.

"Oh," she finally says, sounding disinterested, with no reaction to what I said, as though she's already internally decided to dismiss it.

I used to stupidly think my achievements would make her proud, that if I did something worthwhile with my life somehow, she'd love me. I ran to New York to be free of her, but I spent years allowing her in, still trying to please her from afar. Excelling in my work and trying to show her I was worthy. I did expect some reaction about my chosen path or why, but I was wrong. So very wrong. It's not me who has to prove my worth anymore, it's her, and honestly ... She's not worthy of my love, affection, or time.

"We're having a baby," I state flatly, not expecting the same response that Jake and I received from Sylvana. "You're going to be a grandmother," I add rather pointedly, to make a statement, to get everything out that I want her to know. I've lost all will to be here since this is going exactly how I should've known it would. She is too emotionally exhausting, and I don't need to stay and take it anymore.

A wave of love sweeps over me when I say it out loud, noticing how my smile comes out despite my irritation at her. It spreads across my face without any help from me, tadpole bringing me a sense of serenity from within. My hand instantly moves to cover my stomach gently. Feeling its presence here with me gives me so much more strength. I focus on this tiny joy of my life and gain the strength I need to finish this, letting it flood through me.

"I see." She glances at me and then back at her desk, and my smile fades.

Has she never felt the love for me that I now have for Tadpole? Is it something she's ever possessed for me?

"Is that all you have to say to me?" I ask dejectedly, suddenly tired. The bubbling anger seems to have given up on me, and I find myself sighing instead. I can't do this with her anymore. I don't have the emotional energy to go through this scenario repeatedly.

How often have I built myself up for anything from her and always come face-to-face with this reality? This deflating reality ... This nothingness.

"Well, a baby isn't something I ever thought you wanted. You've never been very maternal or shown any interest in children. It's no picnic being a mother, Emma. I hope you know what you're letting yourself in for." Her tone, one of seriousness, edged with ice. I blink at her in dumbfounded silence, my heart aching, "Is it because of the baby that he proposed?" She asks as an afterthought with a smug expression.

"You never wanted me did you, Jocelyn?" I blurt out, more as a realization than an accusation, and she at least has the decency to let her composure falter, especially at my use of her first name. I don't feel anything about it now that I see it, not a single drop of pain over the fact that she never wanted motherhood or the clinging arms of a child. All those years of keeping me at arms-length, no affection, no warmth, and no protection, all coming together in clear clarity at last.

"I didn't not want you, Emma. I just didn't plan on ever having a baby. I wasn't suited for motherhood but made the most of it." There's no apology in her tone, no trying to soothe my feelings or gently deliver an answer, but there has never been. She looks down at her desk, moving a couple of files, avoiding my gaze.

There are so many things I could say and accusations I could throw at her, but they evade me. Instead, there's nothing but pity and a little sadness. All the fight and will to somehow make her see how she's scarred my life is gone. I have nothing, no inner need to do this and no fight left to push this anymore. With a vague sadness, I realize I don't care anymore.

I sigh and sit up, looking at her fully, willing eye contact.

"You're broken, Jocelyn. Something inside of you doesn't work and maybe never did. I'm sure there's a reason that you're built this way and why you're drawn to men that hurt you. Maybe some of your past is so bad, like mine, you'll never be able to tell me, or maybe you can't be a mother of any kind ... But I'm done." I shake my head sadly, aware that she isn't responding to me.

I stand slowly, my heart aching but no longer ripping in two, a pain that is bearable and will fade in time. She watches me with her large wide eyes and says nothing, no emotion, no protest; just looks at me ... emptily. The same way she always used to, yet it doesn't feel the same way this time.

"You're incapable of being what I need, and I've spent enough of my life trying to get you to love me. That's not a child's job ... That should've never been my burden. Maybe you do love me in your own way, but it's not enough. I want my child to know love the way it's supposed to be, and I could never inflict your sort of indifference and inability to nurture on my baby." I move my chair back, gathering my composure. "I'm walking away, Jocelyn. I'm saying goodbye to the pain you've always inflicted on my heart and the way you always made me feel like everything bad that happened in my life was my fault. Jake showed me how wrong that was." I give her a moment to do or say anything, but I already know it won't happen. She is sitting still and straight with that icy wall up and a blank expression on her face.

"I love you, and you'll always be in my heart, but I don't need or want you in my life anymore. I want this between us to end right here. So, if you have anything to say to me, then do it now." I feel braver. My trembling hands and the aching pain inside me are a sign that I care and always cared, and I can accept that. Because I do know how to love, nurture and protect, and I'm never going to let myself be ashamed of knowing how. I am worthy of having a heart and giving a piece of it to those I love, but she doesn't deserve my love anymore. She doesn't deserve me in her life, and she hasn't asked about my wedding or even congratulated me on the baby says it all. I was never her focus in life, never any part of her world where it mattered.

"I hope you'll be very happy in your new life." Her emotionless, cold words seal her fate. Even if she knew any kind of warmth, she would've never allowed herself to show it. No emotion, no tears, and no attempt to try to change my mind. She and my father are alike in so many ways. They used what they could from me until I was of no value anymore and then left me to find my way on my own; at least he'd been more honest about it.

I was always the one to care for her, protect her, and love her unconditionally, even before I was old enough to understand what she was taking from me. I gave my childhood away to please a woman who gave me nothing in return.

"I know I will be ... I'm sorry." I turn to leave before I cry because I know I'm going to, and that's okay too. I'll grieve for a mother I never had and make a space in my heart for a mother already working her way around it, accepting the woman I am without any expectations. Mamma Carrero will give me what I've always yearned for, and I'll give her a grandchild I know she will smother in real love. Jocelyn Anderson is the only one losing anything, and she doesn't even care.

"I hope you find happiness, Mom. I hope you find your Jake because God knows you need him just as much as I did. Everything that happened, everything I endured, none of it was my fault. I know it without a shadow of a doubt, but I don't need you to acknowledge it anymore because I see it for myself and accept it. I own my past because it brought me here to him.... I forgive you." I smile sadly, the wave of tears rolling down my cheeks.

She swallows hard, a tiny break in her wall, a flicker of something as she watches me, but it's only a small drop of raw emotion in an ocean full of false affection. It's the only reaction I'll ever see. But it's not enough, and it's far beyond too late now.

"Goodbye," I whisper, letting the tears fall, letting it hurt because this is what I need to do to let her go. I turn and leave and don't look back. I don't stop, and I don't feel regret. And she doesn't stop me.

My heart aches, and I know I'll probably grieve for her at some point, maybe sooner than later, but I need to do this for my happiness and my future with Jake. I need to do this for a child who will look to me to learn what love is, and I am doing this to make sure they'll never know anything but real devotion and a real mother who would die for them. A family who will shelter and protect them every step of the way.

I'm lighter, walking down the stairs to the main hall, like a part of me has sprung wings and flown away. I feel like I've let something go, despite the tears streaming down my face and the ache in my heart.

Claire raises her head, acknowledging my return to the foyer at the bottom of the stairs, with a confused look at my emotional demeanor.

"Hi again, Emma," Claire blanches, concern etched on her face. There's no reason to explain anything to her. She wouldn't understand it anyway. I'm not the only one my mother puts false walls up against, pretending everything is okay when it isn't. I look at her and smile weakly.

"Pregnancy hormones," I reply with a light smile, gently grazing the top of my small bump, highlighted by the sundress I decided to wear today. Claire's face suddenly beams with happiness.

"Oh! Congratulations, Emma!!" She swivels off her chair around her desk and comes to give me a small hug; I reciprocate. She's not my mother, and having a little tadpole seems to soften my heart long enough to let Claire embrace me.

"I thought there was a certain look about you!" She smiles, pulling out of the hug to look at me. "You look absolutely radiant. Motherhood obviously agrees with you already." I can't help but smile. She has more joy for my announcement than my own blood.

"Thank you, Claire." She goes to sit back down but turns to face me as I head toward the door and my freedom from this place and my mother.

"We'll see you soon then, Emma!" She calls out. I stare blankly at her, not daring to correct her assumption, and wave.

"Goodbye, Claire." I smile faintly.

I push the door open with one hand and pull out my phone with a heavy sigh, slowly inhaling as I inhale fresh air.

I'm okay. I really am okay.

I text Jake, asking him where he is, letting him know I'll come to him. I need the air and the walk. I need the time to myself to let all that happened in that room sink in. I want to walk to him smiling, to show him that I'm much stronger than I ever have been.

She never fought for me and told me she loved me, but then she never did.

I'm not the one who is broken or unlovable. She is. Yes, I am scarred, but I'm healing, and I've finally found my way into arms I know will always be waiting for me.

Chapter 27

Jake is watching me over a mug of coffee in the small café. My tears have finally stopped. I'm not heartbroken, just resigned and letting go of all that pent-up emotion; part of me is relieved. There are no other words for it. His eyes never leave mine, and his arms are aching to hold me, but he knows I need a moment to let my body, emotionally, mentally, and physically, settle. I want to get through this without any outside help. It's just something I need to do.

My Jake grounding me, always understanding what I need. He listens intently as I repeat every word from my encounter, holding my hand and letting me cry. He has wiped my tears and been the rock he always is.

"You don't want her at the wedding at all? No visits when the baby comes?" He's watching me closely, trying to understand my decision, wanting to affirm what and who I want in our future. I shake my head.

"No, as far as I'm concerned, both my parents are dead. I have my family, and its surname is Carrero." I link my fingers through his on the table and tug his hand closer to me, wanting him nearer now that I feel stronger. He lifts our linked hands to his face, tenderly running my thumb across his jaw, always so caring and there whenever I need him.

"You'll be a Carrero soon, *Bambina*. You're the daughter my mamma has always wanted. She told me." Jake's fingers rest on my bottom lip as I smile at him, and he smiles back. His adoring eyes locked on mine, mesmerizing me with their green beauty. I hope our child will have Jake's green eyes, the kind that draws you in and steals your soul with love, compassion, and kindness like his.

"I love your family, even Giovanni." I giggle to see Jake frowning at me, a look of 'really?' running across his face. He shakes his head as though I've seriously lost the plot.

"My father is ... complicated." He sighs, looking out across the small café, still no closer to seeing his father in any other light than the man who hurt his mother.

"Of course, because I know nothing about complicated parents." I roll my eyes and giggle again when he tugs my chin forward, leaning over to kiss me across the table. The gentle brushing of his lips quells any lasting hints of sadness inside me. He sits back down but doesn't let me go.

"I know he's the strong silent type who thinks it's weak to show so many goddamn emotions, but he is allergic to any sort of affection." Jake frowns harder, a mild irritation passing over his sexy mouth. He doesn't like talking about Giovanni in any way. If anyone has any allergy, it's Jake and the topic of discussing his relationship with his father.

"I'm sure your mother disagrees; she was manhandling him under the table ten minutes before you proposed." I let out a stifled laugh at the mortified, gaping expression startled across Jake's beautiful face. He looks torn between being physically sick or hurting someone.

"No, she wasn't!" He shakes his head, frowning and grimacing to remove the image from his mind, then lets me go so he can use both hands to scrub his face. "I don't even want to know." His voice is ridiculously cute. He sounds like a child completely traumatized by catching his parents canoodling.

"More of your daddy in you than you care to admit, Mr. Carrero. Your mamma and papa are obviously still very young regarding their libido." I smirk at him wickedly, trying to contain the laughter in my throat at his obvious discomfort, and then jump when

I see that mischievous grin coming my way. He rounds the table for me, and I high-tail it out the door. He is a little terrifying. We've already paid, so he catches up to me quickly in the street, swinging me into his arms.

"I'm taking you back to our hotel to wash that mouth out and apply some discipline for saying disgusting things." He's smiling, but I think I may have scarred him for life. He still has a rather pale hue and an unamused expression on his face. I hope he never actually witnesses any of his parents' shenanigans first-hand, or Jake will need to join Daniel and me in therapy; that would be cozy.

"What kind of discipline?" I lift an eyebrow, snuggling in closer, arms snaking around his neck and pressing myself close. This could be interesting. Jake's kinky side has been toned down since our reunion, but here's hoping it makes a grand comeback.

"Depends on how frisky you get between here and there ... I could be persuaded to tie you down or maybe work you into some seriously aggressive, angry sex." The lust-fueled promise in those eyes has me squirming against him, unable to contain the way they light my insides on fire. Promises of lingering memories have me all out panting.

"Or both ... you've never angry fucked me while I've been tied up." I grin naughtily as he turns from serious to boyish, chuckling, his brow lifting in surprise.

"I'm seriously starting to worry about what I've done to you, *Miele*. What happened to my sweet, naïve little ice maiden? When did you start calling it fucking?" He kisses me on the nose adorably, but I will not be swayed. I start kissing him seductively and sucking in his bottom lip with a bite.

"Keep doing that, and I'll fuck you right here in any fashion you want," Jake growls at me, and my inner core self combusts. I can't deny an invitation like that ... and move in for a steamier kiss, wrapping myself around him tighter and higher. I don't care who is walking around us or that we're standing in the middle of a busy street. He has always taken my pain away, knowing instantly what I need to help ground me. Right now, I can't imagine anything I want more than a crazy angry release and a lot of kinky fun with him to forget about her and everything that coming here symbolized.

"Lucky I parked the car so close," Jake growls again against my mouth, sliding down to cup my butt and pulling me off my feet. Pinned to his taut body as he strides purposefully towards it, carrying me with him, not giving a crap about the heads turning our way.

* * *

I'm breathless, exhausted, and most definitely satisfied, staring at the hotel ceiling while Jake channel-hops on the TV aimlessly. He's sat up with his back against the headboard and a sheet at his waist, a little flushed and most definitely perspiring, showing signs of a lot of exertion for once. His hair looks ruffled for the first time ever because I ran my hands through it crazily when we had crazy sex. It is a good look on him.

"Your stamina seems to be failing you, Mr. Carrero." I grin at him, lying flat on my back and stretched out in the afterglow of an afternoon of kinkiness. I'm sprawled, luxuriating in how I feel right now. He smirks down at me and tweaks my nose.

"I've still got it, baby. You're just catching up to match me, took you long enough." He settles on some loud macho movie and slides back down beside me. "Want to order room service and stay here all night?" His fingers trace patterns on my collarbone softly as he leans over me on one arm.

"I wasn't aware we had other plans while in Chicago." I point out, snuggling into him, entangling our limbs under the sheets.

"I thought you could give me a tour of where you lived and grew up, but I don't want you here. I want you out of this place and back where you belong. Back in the Hamptons, getting our new house together." He places a hand on my face, stroking my cheek, bringing his nose closer to mine so we share air. Those hazy green eyes are coming to draw me in like they always do.

"I agree." There's nothing here for me in this city anymore, and the plan was always to stay one night and leave in the morning when I'd seen her, starting our journey to our new home directly from here. I am closing the door not only on her but also on this city and all its memories.

"Food, movies, and more sex ... Sounds like my kind of night, *Bambina.*" He kisses me slowly, then pulls back to look at me again. I can't resist the urge to reach up and tangle my fingers in his hair, tugging it a little, so he leans toward me, kissing me at the invitation.

"Better make the most of it. Soon our nights will be filled with feeding, crying, and a lack of sleep." I grin and watch as that filters through his over-sexed Carrero brain. The little flicker of a frown as he contemplates life with a baby.

"That's what grandparents are for, and often." He smirks again, and I can't be mad at him for that, as it's another thing I'm looking forward to. How loved my child will be in this crazy family of people. Not just Jake's immediate family but the extension of people who flock to the Carrero home every couple of weeks; cousins, in-laws, and all the others who live around too. Plus, our extended circle of friends will adore our little one as though they are blood relations.

"We really are going to be okay, aren't we?" I stroke his face gazing at those beautiful eyes, losing myself in them and daydreaming, bringing Jake's words back as a reminder that I should always trust him.

"I told you, didn't I? I would move mountains to make sure of it. You're my world, this ..." he cups my stomach, "...is my world. I would move heaven and Earth to protect you both. You changed my entire life, Emma, for the better. I don't think you realize how much you've given me." The seriousness in his look and the way he's lingering over my abdomen sends a sweet ache into my soul, and my voice catches in my throat.

"I haven't given you anything but me, and you've given me all of this." I wave my arms around at the five-star hotel room, the ring on my finger, and then run a hand down my stomach. Finding his hand there, I entangle our fingers. "You gave me the fairy tale, the perfect sexy man, the crazy opulent lifestyle, and the happy ever after, Jake, all I gave you was some scared girl so afraid to love." Tears fill my eyes.

"That is the most amazing gift you can give anyone. Having you is more than all this combined. You saved me from myself, from an empty life of parties, fame, women, and booze, and driving myself into the ground with work. You gave my life meaning and feeling. You gave me a purpose and completion, Emma. I know it took a while to stop and realize that I had it all, but we're here now, and I promise this is only the beginning. This will only get better. We have much more to look forward to, and this baby will change everything."

I'm bowled over by the intensity of Jake's gaze and every word he's saying to me. His voice is husky with emotion, and I can't breathe with how much I need him now. "*Miele,* I didn't save you. You saved yourself and me in the process. I only showed you the way."

Tears prick in my eyes over the way Jake views what we are, but he couldn't be any more wrong. He saved me from me, emptiness and loneliness, and fear. He has given me the strength I pretended I always had, unlocking the doors to let me deal with my past. He gave me love in many ways; in return, it enabled me to love myself and heal. He truly is my world, and I have everything I could ever need or hope for in this room.

"I love you so much, so very much. I never want to hide or run or lose you again. I swear I'll always try my hardest to tell you everything I'm thinking and feeling and never shut you out or make you think I don't need you. I can't breathe without you." I sigh tearfully, and Jake's eyes mist up too, holding me close. My words tumble out in a way that I can't control, and I can't help but smile. I think back to PA Emma, she would have been verbally frozen, unable to say a word, but here I am, letting every single thought in my head pour out uncensored for him.

"I can't wait to marry you, to have you as my wife ... I want you. I want the world to know you're mine and see how proud I am of you. I worship the ground you walk on, Emma. You're my everything." Jake kisses me hard, passion spiking between us. I can't say anymore. My throat is full of tears, bursting with intense emotion, and my heart is cracking under the pressure of so much love. I wrap myself around him greedily, holding tight and committing this moment to memory.

This moment is too precious for sex or talking, so we hold each other tenderly, stroking hands and kissing; erotic but slowly and sensually, heightening our feelings for one another.

Chapter 28

"Home sweet home." Jake walks past me through the open doorway, carrying the cases into our new multi-bedroom two-story Hamptons mansion, excitement bubbling over me.

There are sheets and tools everywhere. Amid the chaos and noise of power tools, sawing, and banging, workmen wander around doing seemingly important jobs.

"I thought they were decorating? Sounds like construction." I point out, with a raised eyebrow, looking at Jake suspiciously.

"I kinda okayed some minor changes in various places," Jake smirks at me, and my eyebrow raises higher. He doesn't even try to fake guilt over his admission.

"What happened to the agreement that I would choose the décor? And oversee any refurb!" I narrow my eyes as he ducks under a low-hanging cable to avoid my scrutiny, and I catch a tell-tale mischievous grin pasted on his face. He is shameless.

"Baby ... *Bambina*, I was never going to be easy to live with. I don't get why you're so surprised." He walks off fast with a backward wink, and I shake my head after him, a little exasperated.

No, I wouldn't expect anything else. This is who he is, and for the most part, I like this side of my Cocky Carrero.

Two workmen wander past, and I catch them looking me over, eyes skimming my legs as they carry a large sheet of wood, leering at me and passing smirks to one another in quiet agreement. I lift my chin defiantly and glare right back.

"I suggest you keep your eyes on your work, or you'll be finding them scanning the classifieds for another job," I snap, and both men immediately look away, moving off quickly, acting sheepish. There is no way I am putting up with wandering, sleazy eyes in my own goddamn home. I have realized, through Jake, that men do not have the right to objectify me anymore.

"Saved me the job of doing that." I'm hit with Jake's low growl and realize he's leaning in the doorway watching me. His hand sexily on the jam above his head, stretching out his sculpted torso, a hint of skin peeking from under his lifted shirt, and smirking at me with those sexy devouring eyes.

"Maybe it's about time I started doing it for myself." I point out and smile as I slowly cross the marble hall and slide into his waiting arms, nuzzling my face into a chest that screams of home.

"I might allow that occasionally, not every time, though. I get a kick out of growling for a fight and claiming what's mine." He buries his face in my neck and kisses it slowly, teasing me into submission. The noise all around us completely kills the mood.

"Maybe we should take a tour and see what has been done." I look to the ceiling as he slides me loose, taking my hand and leading the way across to the marble stairs, equally curious to get an eyeful of our new home.

"Our bedroom should be done, and our en suite ... Lounge and kitchen were on the list of completed rooms too, so all of this is everything else. I've been told they'll only be here 9-5 until it's done, not on weekends." He points out, and I'm glad to know this invasion of sweaty men and decorators will be gone soon. I don't relish being stuck here with a bunch of men I neither know nor trust.

"What are you having redone that needs all these carpenters and ... Is that a crowbar?" I ask, shocked to see the large metal pole lying dangerously mid-way up the stairs. Jake scoops down and picks it up with an angry frown on his handsome face, hanging it on the banister to the side.

"Those idiots need to be more damned careful; you could have fallen over that! ... I'm having a couple of the extra rooms switched from bedrooms to something we'll have more use for, and the library and office knocked out into one space for us to have a place to work together." He's still glaring at the metal bar hanging between the rails as he guides me past a pile of sawdust on the next step. The workmen are carelessly untidy, something that bothers me. If they're going to be here from 9-5 for five days of the week, in my home, they could have the decency to sweep up now and again. Or at least move a goddamn crowbar so I don't fall over it!

"So ... Exactly how long do we have to endure all this mess and noise for?" I squint at the men below, walking around carrying what looks like a granite worktop into a small side room.

Tell me again, why we moved in so quickly?

"It looks worse than it is. The house mostly needs paint and paper and our choice of a shit load of furniture. This crew should be done by Friday, neonata. These are all temporary contractors." Jake waves a hand across the milling workers and continues leading me slowly and carefully up the minefield of the stairs. One hand on my back and the other holding my hand in front of me as though I'm elderly and fragile. He sometimes makes me feel like both when he's in protector mode.

"Mr. Carrero, Miss. Anderson!" The gushing friendly voice of Monica Briggs, the interior designer, comes at us from the top of the stairs, and she starts floating toward us in a puff of Chanel number five and a red shift dress. I choke as she gets close, trying to ignore the cheek kissing thing she does to Jake, leaving nasty rouge lip tar across his chiseled cheekbone, whorishly marking my man yet air kissing me from a distance.

Hmmmmmm.

I reach up and immediately start wiping her mark off his face with my thumb and throw a rather snippy glare in her direction.

The only bitch marking him will be me!

She seems unphased by it, and I resist the urge to elbow Jake when I catch that half smirk on the corner of his mouth as he watches me having a little green-eyed moment, amused by my possessiveness over him.

Yeah, Mr. Carrero, you think that's funny? I know you wouldn't like it if some guy was giving me marks all over my face!

"Miss. Briggs, we're finally home and eager to see what's been done." Jake's in charming mode, all Carrero suave, and sultry-voiced, with his smile reserved for clients and shoulder-rubbing rich folks.

"You must let me show you then." She gushes, leaning down to slide her arm through his, but I step up beside him quickly so she's met with my rather close cleavage; at least she has the decorum to look mildly uncomfortable. She smiles tightly and moves back awkwardly, a small rise of red creeping up her neck.

Yeah, I'm the woman of this house ... Back off.

Jake slides an arm around my shoulder, swooping in to kiss my temple in a show of adoration. His way of telling her to move away so fluently that she probably doesn't realize it. He's doing what needs to be done to get her to understand he's not interested. It must work as she seems to have remembered her place and smiles, stepping back further to let us continue, gesturing up the stairs towards a lot more noise, raising an eyebrow at Jake. I let him lead the way, pulling me along at a casual pace.

Upstairs, the sound is far worse than the mess, and I can see that a lot has been done despite the tools and sheets all over. The long, wide hall has plastic covering the thick carpet, and an array of glossy white doors stand open to let light fill the area from each room. It's like a corridor of doors.

She leads us across the walkway, dodging plugs and wires, to our master bedroom, which is close to the start of the main landing, and I'm met with the vision we created on design boards and high-tech computer software. My breath catching, dreamily, at the image of perfection before us. The reality is much more breathtaking than the view from a computer screen.

Neutrals, softness, and a cozy large leather bed with a million cushions artfully placed in the center of a huge suede-covered wall. Plush carpeting in a soft mink, fur rugs, and a chaise longue at the bed with a lot of beautiful furniture and seating dotted around. It's a complete haven, a room fit for reading in, lying around, and relaxing in, or long romantic nights of passion by candlelight. I can already envision lazy Sunday mornings with Jake in this room, wandering around half dressed or just nakedly christening every surface I can see.

The view of the sea, beyond the large wide windows facing us, is perfection.

"It's gorgeous." I breathe, letting go of his hand to walk forward and trail my fingers over a furry throw on the back of a beautiful armchair in the softest camel-colored fabric. Immersing myself in the peaceful serenity of this room and catch my breath as I spot a large, traditional, dark wood crib nestled in a nook by the en suite door near the bed. Jake has obviously chosen this. It looks like it belongs there, perfectly suited to the old meets new style and cozy features of the room; the wood matches our bedframe. I turn and smile at him with watery eyes and a lump in my heart. His returning smile tells me he knows what I've spotted; a special moment passing between us that Miss. Briggs. is completely oblivious to.

"What do you think, Mr. Carrero?" Monica is almost kissing him with her pouty voice, but I'm too absorbed in the vision around us and the emotion of that little addition.

"If Emma loves it, then that's all that matters. I love anything she's picked out." I smile without looking around, knowing he's trying to shut down Miss. Briggs, in all her flirting fury. He's equally irritated by her amorous attention. A while ago, he admitted to me that the female adoration he receives is tiresome and annoying, even more so since meeting me.

"Oh ... you have no opinion?" She sounds disappointed at his lack of interest in her pet project. She probably thought that her work would somehow mean more to him, with this being his room. She's obviously forgotten that, as a man, Jake has an extreme lack of interest in soft furnishings, especially when there is an equal lack of high-tech gadgetry in the room. She seems to be blanking my existence.

Stupid hoe.

"Well ... Honestly? There's a bed and many places to prop up my sexy as sin fiancée, so yeah, I love it." I snicker at the smirk in his voice from behind me and can visualize the one-shoulder shrug he's probably giving her.

I snort and cover my mouth to hold back the giggle trying to escape, warmed by his hand running up my back softly as he comes to me, brushing the back of my neck lightly and kissing the back of my head.

Monica seems to be at a loss for words, and I can't help but side-eye him with an indulgent grin, complete adoration, and tingles for my 'reason to live' standing beside me, but I shake my head at him, sighing.

Mr. Carrero, when will you ever behave? But I love you for it.

"If you'd like to see the alterations to the games room and the home cinema you asked for?" She cuts in a tad frosty. I roll my eyes. Some things will never change with Jake, including his love of all things manly and his Xbox room for when Daniel comes to play.

Do men ever really grow up?

"We can look around later when you all leave for the day. We're going to unpack and get acquainted with this room first." Jake turns and throws her his best panty-dropping heartthrob smile. I know without looking, she's probably swooning and close to fanning herself. I jump when he grabs my ass, possessively and dramatically, in full view of her line of vision. "Need to christen the bed after all." He adds cheekily with a wink. I guarantee her face has turned fuchsia.

I sigh and continue staring out the window, knowing full well he's having more fun shocking the poor woman than is necessary, purely making a point at her expense. When she retreats amid a fumbling flurry of words and shuts the door quickly, he turns back to me to catch my impatiently arched brow.

"Remind me again why we hired her?" I stare at him pointedly. I am sure there are probably a million other men who could've easily done the job with less of the eye raping of my fiancée.

"Because she was available for an immediate start, and she has a great reputation." He slides his arms around my shoulders and props his chin on my head, joining me in looking out the window.

"So, Friday, you say?" I sigh, the noise of loud hammering and screeching cutting through the room's tranquility, irritating me immensely. This is hardly the homecoming to a new life I'd imagined when driving here.

"Well ... she promised on the phone. No more construction after Friday, just a lot of decorating and moving men to deal with instead." He kisses me on the nape of my neck and runs his fingertips across my collarbone, sending tingles in every direction.

"Great, just what we need." I sigh heavily, pushing out the overwhelming urge to turn and molest him, which is currently running through my bones.

"The old PA Emma will love bossing around all those sweaty men, and Miss. Briggs. and you know it. You were always an intimidating force in full PA mode." His mouth has decided to linger on my throat, and the warm waves of longing are becoming distracting.

I suppose I can't argue with that. Overseeing, organizing, and making things perfect is what I excelled at when working at Carrero Corp. I'm sure this will be far more enjoyable than anything I managed when I worked there.

"I suppose. We could always stay next door if I can't stand it." I beam at him when I say it; having the Carrero home less than 200 meters away makes me stupidly happy and the only thing taking over my rising hormone levels.

"We could, *Bambina.*" He smiles as he lets me go and wanders toward the room's inner door, near where we're standing, and opens it. He reaches inside and flicks on a bright light in the en suite. His eyes scanning the inner room with a look of delight.

"Oooh," I say loudly when I spot the sparkling coffee-colored floor from the doorway and venture closer. The bathroom is in matching neutrals with the biggest jacuzzi I have ever seen and so many shiny chrome taps and knobs that I am completely clueless about what they are for.

"I know what we're doing for the next hour." Jake winks and yanks me into the bathroom with him, a mischievous twinkle in his eye, finding no protests from me.

Chapter 29

Wandering around, getting my bearings long after the men have packed up and gone for the day, helps this feel less like a dream. The tools are tidied away in piles against the hall walls, the masses of dust brushed to one side, and all that remains is the plastic protecting the floor and the canvas sheets covering delicate pieces of furniture from Jake's apartment. The aura of moving in settling around me, making me grin in excitement.

Jake is busy exploring the rooms and checking for things he wants to alter, being his usual commanding self while I wander this beautiful house, absorbing the feel of it, realizing that this will be our home from now on. It's helping me, making me feel less like a guest in an expensive show house. It's big enough that if Jake and I should ever need space, we could wander in two different directions with no hope of seeing one another.

The house is eerily empty and silent. The staff is still away until all construction work is completed. For now, Mathews is living in the pool house while his self-contained annex is decorated, ready for the arrival of his wife. Jefferson is being allocated to the city when Jake flies back for business, and his cars moved here, so he doesn't require a driver. However, Mathews will happily still chauffeur Jake when I don't need him.

The plan is to sleep here, in our new room, and oversee the

decorating, picking out furnishings and furniture with Monica. We can eat and escape to Sylvana's when we need to, but we need our own space to start this new chapter of our lives. The freedom to relax and have intimacy when we feel like it, without prying eyes.

"Emma?" Jake's voice echoes down to me from the top of the stairs, making me smile. There's something extremely homely and domestic about his voice calling through this house, looking for me, sexy and husky as always.

"Down here," I call back, padding into the kitchen to admire my shiny new appliances. I'm surprised to find a fully ready-to-use kitchen, stocked cupboards, and a bursting refrigerator. Sylvana's trademark Tupperware in the huge double steel doors and shelves, all labeled with heating instructions, she has thought of everything.

Jake strolls in, looking seductive in sweats and a T-shirt, and I'm still in an over-fluffy bathrobe from swimming around that huge tub with him. He immediately heads to the coffee machine that looks like the one from his apartment, but this one is chrome instead of black. This added touch to the kitchen must be one of his choices. The coffee maker has a small place in his heart.

"Mamma says she has a bunch of info sheets for you from her counselor friend and some insight on how to become one." He smiles over at me while preparing the machine, all sexy shoulders and tensing biceps, completely distracting.

"We should go over in the morning." I yawn, trying to drag my gaze off his beautiful body. We arrived late in the afternoon, and the 'unclean' soap fun took considerably longer than an hour. Tadpole and I need food and sleep, in that order. This baby is ruining me. I am such a tired lightweight these days.

"Yeah, I told her it would be tomorrow." He glances at me, and I nod gratefully. The soft look he's giving me makes me feel content; he knows I need some rest just from looking at me.

Jake is running things with Carrero Corp. in his own way; a trip once a week back to the city until he's happy Margo and her new staff are competent enough to take over, then he's planning on fortnightly trips to check up on things until after the baby is here. The idea of having weeks of blissful homemaking with Jake while waiting on our little tadpole is my idea of heaven. I thought we'd never get to this point. The baby's nursery is one of our first projects to tackle together now we're here.

"I just want to get things sorted and settle in properly," I beam. "It feels like this is the last hurdle before life can start." I run a hand over my stomach affectionately, a small bump starting to firm up and extend slightly, another sign bringing this reality back to me.

"It will be soon enough, *Bambina*. If I have to pay them triple time to haul ass, I will. I want nothing more than to start feeling at home here with you." Jake slides a mug under the machine, catching the hot liquid as it pours out.

"Home." I sigh, gazing around the expansive modern kitchen with a touch of emotion. That's what this place is; home to start a family in. To fill with memories, where I belong with him, a new chapter, and a fresh start to forget everything from before.

"Home is anywhere you are." He suddenly nuzzles into me from behind and nudges his groin over my backside suggestively.

"You're still as insatiable as ever." I giggle, his hands coming around to slide inside my robe in true smooth Casanova fashion, his mug discarded at the machine.

"Do you blame me? You're still as fuckable as ever." His hand is heading south on a mission, thanking my inner stars for my lack of underwear as he kisses my neck and moves in for the kill. His hands skim my nakedness and yank the robe open, so he can access me undeterred.

Moving around to my front and into me, he slides his arms around my waist underneath the fabric of the robe, delicious skin-on-skin movement, lifting me onto the kitchen counter in an easy maneuver. His mouth comes to mine, teasing me into erotica as his hands skim my naked upper body. Jake moves his groin firmly between my legs, his tongue sliding into my mouth, catching the back of my head in his palm so he can pull me into his kiss. I have zero capability to stop things from heating up while in this very compromising position.

I groan as he pulls back, sucking my bottom lip, moving into kissing me passionately, his hand smoothing down my naked abdomen, meeting the apex of my thighs with a welcome moan.

His phone vibrates across the countertop beside me, making me jump and giggle as he pulls back slightly with a lusty expression to retrieve it. He curses under his breath and throws me a naughty half-smile.

"Saved by the bell." He growls, his voice low and sexy. He still has his hand between my legs, cupping my warmth gently while he retrieves his phone and sticks it to his ear.

"Jake Carrero, speaking." He leans in and kisses me again slowly, that tongue dipping into mine mercilessly despite the phone almost poking me in the face.

"Uhuh." He props up his phone with one shoulder and returns to running his other hand over my exposed breast, leaning in to trace his tongue up my neck and send a thousand tingles through me. He doesn't care that he's in mid-conversation with someone.

"Thursday?" He sighs, looking at me with a flicker of annoyance crossing his face. His hand between my thighs is extracted as he takes his phone and swaps ears, a look of agitation on his boyish face. 'Business Carrero' moving in to kill his libido. Something must be wrong at work, and disappointment washes over me.

"Fuck's sake, Margo! Can't they do a fricken thing without me standing over the top of them shouting fucking orders?" He lets me go fully, stalking toward the huge wall of french doors, and glares outside. His body is rigid but divine as hell and tense as he pushes a hand to his waist, fisting it there in agitation, looking completely intimidating, like a gladiator about to embark on a war. I guess things with work aren't rosy today. He has a few large developments he's overseeing, so his stress levels have been up and down.

"One night ... We kept the apartment ... Yeah, arrange to have my flight there Thursday and home Friday morning first thing. Jefferson is still in Manhattan, so he can pick me up at the airfield." He almost barks the orders at her, and for a moment, I'm relieved that this is no longer our relationship. As much as I loved working with him and love him in general, I don't think I could tolerate the bossy ass he can be where work is related ever again.

"Sure, I'll see you then ... I will, Margo, thanks." Jake hangs up and sighs in irritation, sliding his phone onto the counter beside me where I'm still perched with legs dangling freely, my robe pulled back together.

"Problems?" I enquire gently, sliding my robe sash across and tying it in a knot. He frowns and walks over, tugging it out of my hands, so the robe gapes open, pulling the belt completely free, and tossing it over his shoulder onto the floor with a childish look on his face.

Oh boy.

"Same shitty headaches; a contracts oversight needs signing off and delays on the building we purchased for another sports complex. I need to fly out for a night, baby. I'm sorry to leave you here, but you still can't fly, and this needs to be sorted quickly." He leans in, kissing me on the cheek tenderly, bringing his body firmly between my legs and that undeniable warmth of his. It feels like home.

"It's okay, I'll be fine, your mother is next door, and Mathews is here on guard duty. I can wander around daydreaming about color charts and throw cushions." I wrinkle my nose at him, receiving his sexy smile as a reward, making my smile wider.

"Get used to domestic bliss, *Bambina.* There's going to be a lot of that as soon as we get this place Emma-worthy." He kisses me softly on the forehead.

"Emma worthy?" I giggle at him and run a hand across his gorgeously rough jawline. "Don't you care how our house turns out?"

"If you two are in it, then nope; happiest guy alive and easy to keep content." His hands find my abdomen, his fingers running gently across my sensitive skin and around my hips slowly.

"You're impossible." My skin tingles under his expert touch.

"Sexy too." He winks at me.

"Hmmm, big-headed with too much ego, more like." I retort with a playful push on the hard expanse of tight chest before me.

"I earned the ego because I know I'm sexy as hell, baby, and your sweet ass knows it." He links his arms around my waist underneath the robe, tugging me forward, so we're almost connected at the groin.

Ah, he's back in Casanova mode and being his delightful cocky self again.

"What will I ever do with you." I gaze adoringly at his face, my arms sliding about his neck, that feels so strong and very edible.

"Go with it ... Margo says hi, by the way." He mumbles as he finds his way back to my throat by tracing his tongue across my collarbone. It takes all my willpower not to let my head drop back and sag beneath Jake's roaming hands, instant submission to his touch, like always.

"Mm." I close my eyes to the sensation, and it's all I can say to respond. My inner self gets hot at his attention, and tingles erupt within my entire body.

His phone vibrates harshly for the second time across the countertop, and I groan this time in irritation.

"For the love of fucking God." He lifts an irate face and grabs the phone looking at the screen before putting it to his ear, scowling at me as though, somehow, it's my fault. I mock scowl back and giggle when he tweaks my nose.

"Hunter, this better be fucking good. I was in the middle of something." He snaps down the phone, a devilish look and wolfish smile appear on his face as Hunter correctly pinpoints what kind of busy he is.

"Yeah, I was ... Why aren't you doing the same thing and leaving me alone?" Jake isn't snapping anymore; he sounds boorish and tantrummy, both normal Carrero traits, so I relax, knowing this is probably a social call.

"Okay, mate, calm down and breathe." Jake's eyes soften, and once again, he lets me go. This time I'm quick to slide down for my sash and tie up my robe. I love being accessible but being nakedly on show while he walks around the kitchen talking to Daniel isn't my idea of comfortable. The expression on his face is making me more concerned than horny right now. He no longer looks chilled; Jake sighs and eye rolls at me, making me break into a smile.

Whatever it is can't be that bad if Jake is implying that Daniel is a drama queen.

"Look, if you're reacting like this, then maybe you should hold off for now. Get your head around it first?" Jake pauses to listen, then moves the phone away for a second.

"Daniel wants to ask Leila to move in with him when they get home, but he's having a panic attack in their hotel bathroom over it." He lifts his eyebrows in complete deadpan seriousness, not even bothering to cover the mouthpiece when passing on the details.

"Poor, Daniel." I sympathize and watch Jake's face intently.

"It's not a heart attack. It's a panic attack. Stop being a fucking girl." Jake has his bossy unamused face on and his male 'no sympathy, no-nonsense tone' laced in his voice. I shake my head at him and walk forward, stealing the phone from his ear gently. Sometimes bull in a china shop comes to mind with Jake and his sensitivity toward Hunter's romantic problems.

"You're unbelievably hostile for a guy who is usually all love hearts and roses with me." I slide the phone to my ear with a raised brow and a schoolmistress look.

"Daniel, it's Emma." I at least sound friendly and hope a lot more sympathetic to the poor guy's current situation. Jake grabs my ass hard and breathes into my neck as he steals a kiss. I quell the urge to yelp.

"Men don't do 'roses and hearts' chats with each other, baby." He moves off smoothly, and I throw another indulgent look his way. He finally walks to the coffee machine and takes a sip of the coffee he left there.

"Emma. I ... can't ... fucking ... breathe." Daniel is panting and gasping. He sounds like he's in serious distress. My heart immediately goes out to him. He sounds nothing like the playboy master of control he normally is.

"You don't need to do this right now, you know? It's early days, and she won't expect it, so stop pressuring yourself." I suggest, hoping to at least get his breathing back to normal.

"I ... love ... her." He pants, and I cringe at his efforts to gain control of his breathless fear. I know what that crushing panic feels like. I've had many panic attacks in the past.

"She loves you too, but it doesn't mean you need to follow

Jake's example and push her at a hundred and fifty miles per hour."
I raise an eyebrow at Jake, and he narrows his eyes right back with a
scowl. When I jokingly remark about the speed at which he
maneuvered our relationship, it always ignites a bristling face from
him; he hates being criticized, but it makes me giggle at him.

"Hey!" He pouts at me, and I blow him a kiss.

"I ... I ... can't ... lose ... her." Daniel seems to get a little hold on
himself for a moment. "I .. need .. her. She ... needs. me to show her
... I'm serious about us. I can't think of how... else to do it ...." As
though a little self-clarity has distracted him from his crippling tight
chest as he seems to regain some verbal control.

"You can only do what feels right." I soothe, wandering away
from Jake toward the fridge, turning my back on him, my eternal
hunger pushing my feet to scope out the munchies.

"What if she says no?" He gasps, his breathing still shallow and
his voice hoarse, but he seems to be normalizing. He's talking more
freely now.

"Then it means neither of you is ready, and that's all; it doesn't
mean she doesn't love you to death or want a future with you." I
can't help but turn and look at Jake over my shoulder with a
sarcastic smile, but he frowns back at me knowingly.

"Yeah, yeah. Point made." Jake shakes his head at me and
jumps off the counter back to the coffee machine to fiddle with the
knobs, obviously unimpressed with the coffee it produced the first
time. I shake my head at him and sigh at his beautiful body.

"Are you mooning over Jake right now?" Daniel asks rather
pointedly, with a haughty tone, despite distracting Hunter to an
almost even breath, and I reply guiltily.

"No ... Well, maybe." I blush at being caught, and Daniel lets
out a long, slow exhale.

"I want this. I'm just terrified." He sounds so young and
vulnerable. It reminds me of the lost-looking boy who sat on our
couch when Leila broke up with him, the boy who is slowly
becoming a friend to me ... of some sort.

Who ever thought that would happen?

"Then tell yourself that she loves you. Remind yourself of why you're asking her." I croon softly, aware Jake's messing with the damn coffee machine, making it look complicated to work, with a frowning and confused look glazing over his face. I think it's more impatience than anything.

"I want her ... every day, every night ... I want to be able to call her and be like, *hey, babe, I'll see you at home.*" Daniel sighs heavily. "Fuck, I sound as soft as Jake right now." At least he's calmed down now and hasn't noticed that his attack is over; talking about Leila calms him without him even realizing it.

"Yep, you kinda do. He's a sucker for love too." I smile at Jake's wide strong back and flutter my lashes as he glances over at me, all manly attempts at nonchalance disappearing.

"Should I be concerned about you two on the phone?" Jake glares at me with his *I'm starting to get jealous* tone. I stick my tongue out at him.

"Tell Jake he's an asshole for turning me into this fucking mess with all his talks of *the one* and *happy ever afters,*" Daniel growls down the phone at the same time as Jake growls at the phone in my hand.

Men don't talk soppy to one another? Right then, Jake.

I sigh with exasperation at being caught between two pig-headed males.

"Jake, you've ruined Daniel's life by pointing out he loves Leila," I say drolly, eye rolling again. Daniel is a drama queen.

"Stop dicking about, man the fuck-up, and just propose, Danny. It's obviously heading that way." Jake says loudly for Daniel's benefit, and there's a sharp inhale of breath and sudden silence on the other end of the cell.

"I think you just caused him to have a cardiac arrest, Jake" I look at him deadpan, hearing the smallest whimpering of hesitation from Daniel. "Oh, never mind. I hear signs of life." I smile wickedly, and Jake continues to glower my way. He's still not in control of that little green-eyed monster growing inside of him, but he's trying to rationalize his stupidity.

"You think that's what she expects so soon?" The fear in Hunter's voice is back with a vengeance, and my heart melts.

"Honestly ... No. Leila knows you better than anyone, and I think she won't expect that for a very long time. Stop overthinking this." I smirk at my reflection in the steel refrigerator door at the irony of my sentence.

When did I stop doing that?

I glance back at Jake and catch the same smirk aimed at me as he thinks the same thing.

Yeah, okay, smart ass.

"No, no ... You're right. Leila's fucking amazing and supportive and ... Fuck. Fuck. She won't want that yet; I don't want that. Emma, I want that. Why wouldn't she want that with me?" The confused turn around in Daniel's tone has me almost giggling.

Daniel is either having some mental breakdown, or he's truly head over heels for that girl and has no control over his emotions.

I catch his heavy breathing coming back.

"Daniel, breathe and stop. You're driving yourself a little crazy. It's too soon, and Leila probably does want that in time. Right now, you're just trying to show the girl she can trust you and have a future with you." I remind him. "She doesn't need anything like this yet, just you to keep proving you love her, and she can trust you." I sound like Sylvana, imparting soft wisdom in hushed tones.

"Trust her. She knows what she's talking about." Jake cuts in. He's had enough of his best friend monopolizing me and swiping the cell from me, propping it on his ear with his shoulder. He manhandles me onto the countertop in a very dominant way, walking me backward toward it with a slight thud.

"Hunter, man up and stop being a pussy. Ask Leila to move in and get off the fucking phone." Jake isn't exactly friendly, but he has a tone of warmth in there somewhere. He yanks open my robe and runs a hand down my abdomen, obviously giving up trying to be patient.

"Go find your girlfriend and fuck her, trust me. I'm sure even you can handle asking her while having sex to take your mind off the fact that you're an emotional cripple." I grimace at how Jake handles Hunter, but I can't be mad since his hand is expertly moving in places that have me writhing. I have a weakness inside me for him that he knows all too well, and I'm instantly submissive putty in his hands; no arguments from me.

Oh, God.

I squirm against his delicious hand between my thighs and watch his transparent green eyes change, glazing over to dark and hazy, his pupils dilating. Excitement rushes up over my body at his lack of patience and control.

"...currently trying to seduce my fiancée and get you off the goddamn phone ... Good plan, let me know how you get on ... Just not anytime soon," Jake smarts in a lust-filled angry tone and hangs up. He goes to continue his advances up my thighs but stops, realizing something. He tosses his phone into the hall with a crashing thud as it breaks into pieces, echoing around the house.

I guess phone shopping will be on the list tomorrow.

"Jake?!" I giggle, but my breath is halted with a sharp tug of my body to his, and my robe falls open fully. I go limp with desire and can't do anything except gape at his mouth as it moves closer.

"Any other asshole interrupts this, and I'll rip heads off." He growls and moves in with the look of a killer animal devouring its prey.

Chapter 30

"Mathews is nearby, and I'll only be gone until tomorrow, baby, and you know Mamma will come to check on you if you don't show face." I'm getting the paternal-type lecture from Jake as he gets ready to go to Manhattan. He's looking sophisticated in a flawlessly tailored dark suit and, for once, a tie; one of his clients is sharing his flight to get business out of the way quickly, mid-air.

"I'm sure I can look after myself for a night. You know, I did handle some independence before I had you." I smile sarcastically as he frowns at me.

"Workmen finish up this afternoon, a day early, so by tonight, you'll be chaos free." He continues, ignoring my jibe. He's on a roll in *bossy commander business mode*, and I revert to PA Emma to listen patiently while he gets it all out of his brain. I remember one of the first things Margo told me about Jake when I started to work for him; she told me he likes information to be repeated back to him and tasks relayed vocally in order of importance. It's nice to think I'm at the top of his list, even subconsciously.

"Good. I plan on a lovely bubble bath, an annoyingly sappy movie, and an early night in our luxurious bed." I lean up and kiss his cheek.

"That sounds much better than going back to work," he grumbles.

"Jealous?" I utter sweetly, leaning in to kiss him goodbye on the mouth this time, always aching to have that intimacy with him.

"No, just wishing I was part of your evening plans, baby. I can't even Skype call this time because I want to get through everything to get back home tomorrow morning. I'm going to miss you a lot." He runs a hand down my jaw and ruffles my hair before the obligatory kiss on the forehead and leaves.

My goodbye waves are rudely interrupted by the chaos of noise starting for the day in the house somewhere behind me. I sigh inwardly as the screeching sounds of a power drill and instant hammering over my head start echoing around the emptiness.

One more day of workmen and chaos and noise, just one more day. You can cope with that.

We've been here a few days and spent most of it locked in our room or the lounge: another perfectly decorated room or next door. We have avoided most of the hired staff renovating and tried our best to escape from Monica when she repeatedly tries to show Jake around the developments. She doesn't seem to take no for an answer and certainly doesn't seem to be phased by his pregnant fiancée hanging on his arm every time they enter the house. I've told Jake repeatedly, much to his amusement, that I think she's one of those older women cougars you hear about, preying on young hot rich men.

I need to grin and bear it for today, and then they'll be gone, dragging all their tools and mess and chaos with them out of my way. I want to start adding some homely touches to our castle finally. I wrap my arms around my shoulders and hug myself, unable to stop an internal squeal of happiness.

I wander through the rooms toward the kitchen in my robe and catch two men walking from the library to the dining area: carrying boxes. I sigh in agitation and avoid eye contact, instinctively pulling my robe tighter around my body; for more comfort. At least, for the most part, they keep out of my way. One of them seems to have an eye for me, though, but it's nothing I can't handle. I've only noticed it the past day or so, and since they're leaving today, I can deal with a couple more hours of this crap, if anything, just to prove to Jake that I can.

I can't seem to settle here yet because of it all. My nausea runs high at the stress of moving into the house and all the upheaval. The constant drilling and banging and heavy sounds drowning out any peace for me mean I can't sleep through the day because of it, so I doubt my little tadpole can. This tidbit brings my annoyance at the workmen boiling up inside me. It tilts my brain off focus with fierce protectiveness. That's why I'll be glad when they leave.

I swallow it down in agitation and walk to the kitchen to fix myself something to eat. I've found that I love cooking since I have all the time in the world to leisurely stand around in this beautiful chef's dream. Sarah would love it. I'm sure she'd be proud of how domesticated I've become, knowing my way around a kitchen. I like not having a cook until she returns at the end of the week. It's somehow enjoyable making meals with love and caring precision for Jake and me to enjoy.

Maybe I'll follow in Sylvana's footsteps and cook for my own family once or twice a week as she does.

Soon the noise of drilling and male chatter and laughter annoys me enough to send me to my room for refuge. At least in here, I can turn on the TV or run a bath and lock them all out. The large hall echoes around downstairs and amplifies it to incredibly ridiculous proportions. Somehow so much louder today. The bed still smells of Jake and has retained some of his body heat locked between the sheets, so I curl into his side and wrap the blankets around me to drown out the chaos and nap.

I am exhausted enough to try to get some sleep. I'm too tired to exchange pleasantries with the workman today, and even Monica isn't around for me to roll my eyes at.

Thank God.

Her overly eager eye fluttering and sexy smiles at Jake every five minutes slowly bring out inner violent Emma lately. The woman simply has no scruples at all. She reminds me of the bored rich bitches Jake and I would meet at every event, those who hung on him and his every word despite their husbands standing close by.

The downside to a popular hot man!

Even here, the noise is too much, and I give up. I haul my restless body out of bed and resign myself to getting dressed, every intention of spending today in the solace of Sylvana's kitchen, hoping for some inner calm and serenity ... if not for me, then at least for the baby. If I can avoid the last day of banging and hammering, surrounded by strange men, then I will. I'm uneasy here without Jake, so seeing his mamma with her gorgeous welcoming heart will be a comfortable break.

I swear maxi dresses were made for the comfort of pregnant women; in one fell swoop, I'm dressed and ready to get on with the day since I am begrudgingly forced out of bed by the invasive chaos. I tap down the stairs of the stairwell and slip my feet into the ballet pumps I have lying by the entrance to the living area. I can't seem to go anywhere downstairs without a layer of dust settling on my feet; at least after today, that should hopefully be over. I pick up my bag, drop my cell into it, and then leave.

"Miss. Anderson?" One of the burly men calls to me as I'm walking for the door through the main hall downstairs.

"Yes?" It's unusual for them to address me directly. I turn sharply. Jake normally deals directly with the workmen while Monica and I focus on the décor, blissfully ignorant of the construction work going on; that's Jake's kind of thing.

"We should be out of your hair by noon at the latest, ma'am. Just wondering what you'd like us to do with the keys if you're not back?" He regards me with a relaxed, business-like expression, and my insides instantly calm. No danger here. Old Emma always rears up inside me when I face unexpected, strange men.

"Drop them next door if I'm out. I'll either be there or close by. Sylvana is my mother-in-law, so that's fine." I smile gratefully.

"Sure thing." He nods at me and lets me on my way, walking out into the warm day, and I chew my lip a little. I didn't know they'd been gaining access with their own key the whole time. I assumed Mathews or someone at Sylvana's had been letting them in and out, which bothers me a lot. Those random men have keys and access codes to my house, and it's grating on my inner calm, old Emma showing face and trying like hell to point out the dangers in it, in a rather disturbing way, through visions of what those men could do to me. I'm glad to be leaving and relieved that this is their last day.

I'll ask Jake to change the locks and the codes when he's home. That'll make me feel better. How could he have forgotten to tell me that the contract workers have full access to the house? Maybe it's just something that richer people are used to.

I sigh inwardly and head to my second home, a huge smile on my face and a rumbling stomach despite having eaten. Sylvana's cream cannelloni are singing to me across the grassy lane, as is a morning curled on the couch with her like yesterday. Cocoa mugs and daytime soaps, chatting our boredom away. This new way of life is starting to agree with me.

* * *

I leave Sylvana's, not realizing how late in the evening it is, and let myself into the house, the entrance hall is in complete darkness, so I clap my hands to switch on the lights.

Jake and his gadgets.

It's eerily quiet and peaceful in here now I can see my hall minus a lot of tools and mess and protective sheeting. I blink around appreciatively, place my bag on the uncovered side unit, and sigh with annoyance when I notice that damn crowbar. From here, you can spot it between the rails. The workman who left it on the stairs in the first place obviously hadn't realized that Jake had moved it, so here it is still in my house, hanging halfway up my banister where Jake left it.

Every other tool in the place is gone, just not that. Given the color of the vertical dark metal railings, it's easy to miss a crowbar hanging dejectedly beside them; similar in color, it would be easy to slip from eyesight at every other angle in the house but this one.

I head for the stairs to save my beautiful wooden handrail from the ugly metal bar, but my phone ringing distracts me, drawing me back to the entranceway. Jake has kept in contact a few times today, and I spoke to him on my cell at his mamma's before I came home, so it's probably him making sure I managed to walk the fifty yards back home without injury or getting lost. I walk to my bag and fish it out, seeing Mathew's name flash up on the screen. It's strange for Mathews to ring me, so I instantly inhale like something's wrong, internally tensing.

"Hello?" I ask in a friendly tone.

"Miss. Anderson, good evening. I'm just calling to inform you that I'm on my way back."

Oh, of course.

He's been out collecting some things I ordered from a nearby home décor boutique. Sylvana sent him to get them earlier since I was at her house for the day, and he was hanging around waiting for something to do. Since Sylvana has security at her home, it seemed a waste not to let Mathews out for a few hours. He's probably only been gone an hour at most, anyway.

"Okay, that's me home now, so I'll probably go upstairs and take a bath. You can retire for the night." I smile as I say it, so he'll get warmth in my tone. Mathews has a fatherly quality that is growing on me; he makes me feel safe in the same way Jake does, and I'm starting to wonder if that's why Jake has entrusted me into Mathew's care because he knows that I feel this way about Mathews. So, in a way, it's like Jake is watching over me even in his absence.

"Very good, Miss. Anderson. I'll check the house and lock it up before I go to my quarters. Have a good night." His friendly yet efficient tone is as close to unprofessional as I'll ever get with him; the man is all business.

"Good night," I breathe softly and hang up, remembering suddenly that we never got the keys back. The workmen must've forgotten to bring them to Sylvana's or taken them home ready to bring in tomorrow. These contract workers are so incompetent. Their inability to follow instructions and keep a clear workspace irritates me. I call Mathews back immediately.

"Miss. Anderson, is there something else?" He sounds very business-like and professional again instantly, never missing a beat.

"Yes, Mathews. The workers have finished here but didn't leave the keys as instructed." I sigh heavily, irritation creasing at my forehead, and I look around, overwhelmed at the high-tech door locks and fan-dangled things that I don't know how to operate. Those keys do everything.

"I'll deal with it, ma'am. I'll collect them before I return; may I suggest, in the meantime, you can arm the house with the code 101? It's a temporary alarm that can only be bypassed with a code that only Mr. Carrero and I have." He is smooth and efficient, and his no hint of worry instantly makes me feel better.

"Thank you, yes. I shall do." I smile, knowing how safety-conscious Mathews is and the thought of that little bit of extra security makes me feel better; at least I won't have to mess with the crazy-looking boxes on the door I assume are locks.

I wander to the digital panel on the inner wall of the entrance and arm the alarm, ensuring the doors and windows down here are shut securely first, then grab my bag and head upstairs in a much more relaxed mood.

I can't stop yawning lately, good old pregnancy fatigue has been my worst enemy, and I can't even imagine trying to work like this. All I do is sit around, eat, sleep, or have sex. It isn't very good when I think about the person I used to be. I know people often talk of baby brain, but I didn't think it affected someone this early. Jake has ruined me for the real world; returning to it will be hell. It's strange, I never imagined I would ever submit to being some pampered billionaire's girlfriend ... fiancée, but Jake is the king of pampering. He does treat me like his queen.

God, I love that man.

I know it's temporary, though. Once this little bundle comes and gets a little older, I intend to pursue a new dream, a new career. I have no reason to live life this way indefinitely. There is still a huge part of me that wants my own achievements, my own worth proven to myself by myself. I want to leave some worthwhile mark on the world and a legacy for our children. I want to be more than just a billionaire's wife. I think I owe it to myself.

I get upstairs and pad toward our bedroom, clapping for the lights, but they don't come on. I'm standing in complete darkness with little light coming through into the hallway of doors, the moonlight peeking through the bedroom windows of one open door, splashing little slivers of light through but not enough to see much. I kick my shoes off by the top of the stairs and leave them lying there to feel my feet along the ground, trying to find my way while my eyes adjust. I clap louder, trying to remember where the sensors are in case I'm not close enough.

"Oh, for fuck's sake!" I snap and clap again, but nothing happens. I don't know where the manual switches are up here. I'm standing in the hall between various rooms' doors, with no windows in the hall in front of me. It's too dark up here to try running my hands around the walls, and I'm internally cursing these God-forsaken workmen. It's just my luck to finally have the house done and empty for a stupid fault like this to show up. Jake will have to call them back tomorrow to fix the damn things, and I'll have to endure another day of them invading my space.

Carefully treading my way across the carpet, my palm runs along the smooth walls slowly until I reach the handle of my door and slide my palm around it to grip it. I know there are switches by the door and at least four lamps in the room. Plus, the huge picture window will allow the moon to cast some light, and I'm sure it'll be much better than standing in a dark hall.

"Don't fucking breathe." A harsh, heavy growl lashes into my ear, hot breath assaults my face, and the metallic smell makes me gag as I freeze like a stone-cold statue; an arm comes around my throat at lightning speed, and my mouth is covered cruelly, blocking out my ability to squeal. Everything inside me thuds with a sickening terror, and my blood turns to ice in my veins.

A rough hand crushes my face, bruising my lips against my teeth. I'm pushed forward against the door with force, my body pinned hard and heavy with a thud so that I don't have any time to react. The solid weight of a big man crushing against me cruelly and restricting my breathing brings sheer fear and consuming panic through my foggy brain. I'm imprisoned with dead weight and can't move a single muscle. My feet, planted on the floor, are pushed far apart with a kick, and a man's disgusting wide body and legs are forced right against me from toe to head. His erection forced up against my ass, making me still and complaint with sheer faint fear. I can sense the aggressive violence pulsing in the air around me, crackling like stars in my vision.

I can't breathe, see, or move, but I can smell, all my other senses in utter chaos. My heart thuds hard as my hands claw at the wood in front of me, instinctively looking for anything to grab. But my sense of smell invokes a memory that has my knees trembling and bile lifting from my toes, a cold sweeping wave of panic and realization hitting me hard.

I smell him.

I know him.

I choke on my own terrified tears as it creeps through me.

Ray Vanquis is here with me all alone.

Chapter 31

My body is temporarily shocked by the fear, and I can't move. His rough hands painfully and cruelly grope my breasts from behind as he keeps me pinned against the wall, immobile.

My mind races back to the desolate horror of my teenage assault and how he exerted power over me in Chicago. My body is trembling involuntarily, and my mind is constantly racing to the miracle inside me and my maternal need to protect it against all odds. This isn't just about me anymore; I need to find the strength to save my child from what I know is coming.

He will take what I denied him a few months ago and back when I was a teenager; payback for Jake for beating him. He will ravage my body sexually in ways that will devastate my mind emotionally, but I can't give in to this. I must search deep inside myself for safety with my baby, wrap my body around us, lock us both in, and let my mind detach. I can't fight someone like him, I could try, but I know he would beat my child from within me, and it matters more than the damage he could ever inflict on me.

"Remember me, darlin'? I didn't forget about you, my little whore. You and I have some catching up to do." He snarls against my   ear,   pushing   a   hard-erect   lump   into my ass and roughs up against me, straining through his rough jeans. His rancid breath is heating my face and making my skin crawl in disgust. My heart pounds through my chest, and all I can do is squeeze my eyes shut, trying to will Jake to know I'm not okay, for some sixth sense to make him feel my need for him, mentally calling for help, attempting to keep my body from unraveling at the panic building inside of me. All rational thought is fleeting away, and I know I am completely and helplessly about to be abused. Ray succeeding where previously he failed.

I know it's pointless trying to call for help telepathically. Jake flew to Manhattan. He's an hour by plane, four hours by car, and not due home until the morning. Mathews is on some goose chase for keys, which could be just as long. I am alone, but Ray knows he doesn't need long to inflict lasting damage on my soul. He only needs a few minutes to subdue me, even if Mathews is heading back. This will take me away from Jake, remove my ability to handle a man's touch, and inevitably take my life from me. I try to flex my body, to get some purchase but the biting grip and heavy pressure collapsing me into the door takes my breath away. If I fight against him, he will push me down with more aggression, and I can't let him hurt my child.

My baby girl! I know it! My little Mia, maybe ... Mommy will protect you, my sweetheart. We'll hang on in here. Just listen to my voice; we're going to be okay.

She is the one thing I must protect no matter what he does to me.

"What do you want?" My voice is small and shaking as his hand uncovers my mouth while he changes his grip position, my palms are flattened to the cold door in front of me, and I'm trying my hardest to claw back some sense of calm to my fevered mind. I'm so terrified I can barely breathe, but strength is chanting through my fear-addled brain that my baby needs me to stay calm.

We're going to be okay, baby girl.

"Your rich prick boyfriend and I have some unfinished business, and man, I have been patient, waiting and watching. Did you feel me, Emma? In your house? Watching you from afar? Did you feel me near you and sense the way my cock hardened for you anytime you passed me?" The smell of his breath on my face makes me choke as his dirty mouth comes to my cheek. I try to recoil from him, but the biting grip on the back of my neck pushes my face hard against the door. His disgusting slimy tongue makes its way up my cheek, and his hot sour breath assaults my senses. I gag as a huge bolt of nausea lifts in my stomach, lurching repeatedly.

I gulp down my tears, fighting back the cold wave of terror. Then it clicks in my brain; he was the man watching me from the shadows, the one whose eyes I could sense on me occasionally! The one lingering around that I'd noticed the last couple of days. He'd been here, among the workmen, all along. He's probably the one they trusted to return the keys to me. My gut tried to warn me, tried to tell me that something was off about him. If only I'd voiced something to Jake at the time, Ray would've been found out.

Jake, I'm sorry. I'm so sorry. My baby ... our baby. I'm sorry.

"If you hurt me, he'll kill you. He won't just come after you, Ray. He will fucking kill you, slowly and painfully, and enjoy every fucking second." I snarl between clenched teeth willing myself to sound braver than I feel. I am trying so hard to get my body to draw in some strength to stand stiffly instead of the mush of Jell-O I am right now. I know I shouldn't be antagonizing him, but my inner fight is finding her feet at the thought of those clear green eyes, his sexy natural smile, and our beautiful baby girl. My inner strength urging me to protect them both.

Mommy's got this, okay, baby girl? I've got this.

"Baby, I want him to know what I do, to see what I've done to you. I want to know the agony he's in when he's looking for you and knowing I have you, and I am fucking every part of you until you bleed." His raspy threat ends with a hard bite on my ear, sting, and warmth oozes instantly down my neck. I scream in pain impulsively. The sound muffled as his fingers bite back at my mouth, crushing me to silence again.

My inner rage kicks out, and I try to elbow him, my leg thrusting back in sheer defiant hate, only meeting with defensive blows. The pain, kick-starting that inner teen rage, lashing back to fight and to be free, never to be his victim again.

He laughs, grabbing the back of my skull and, with alarming

force, pulls back my head, smashing me forward into the door with a bone-crushing thud to my forehead that draws instant nausea up my throat and blood into my mouth as my teeth pierce into my tongue, my nose collides with the door and heated liquid runs down over my mouth.

The sensation of darkness hits me before any real pain does, and I feel overwhelming dizziness as my body buckles in front of him. My bones melt instantly, and I have no idea what is happening to me. He's knocked me senseless but not completely out, and he slips me over his shoulder limply and effortlessly.

I'm fighting with my consciousness to wake up and failing. There's a dark haziness over me, I know what is happening, but I cannot do anything about it. My body temporarily paralyzed, and my willingness to fight locked inside my head. It feels like I'm dreaming, and all pain and fear have slipped aside. I can hear harsh whimpering mewls coming from somewhere and realize it's my own voice. My inability to fight back and the fear inside me blow up dramatically, but I have no strength or courage to do anything.

He is carrying me toward the stairs, effortlessly taking me from this house with an aura of satisfaction; my limbs are heavy, and I have a slow, tingling sensation coming into my fingertips. I'm sure I will throw up, the beginning of retches and jerks of a stomach getting ready to empty itself. I start tingling and aching in my legs as I realize my body is coming out of the shock that his assault placed it in. I'm slowly, so very painfully slowly, able to move my fingers, fighting the huge weight of my limbs to lift them.

I whimper and reach out, trying weakly to grope at the closest banister to me as we pass. Every jolt and nudge is painful in my abdomen as my body bounces on hard shoulders with every step downward. I'm trying to hold on, but my weak fingers slide with no grip, still not completely responsive. I slump and try to inhale slowly, trying to regain strength in my body as the mental fog in my brain starts to clear. My head aches heavily as it begins to come through.

His pace is slow and steady. He's enjoying the build-up to taking me from my home, getting a kick out of his dominance. His cruel, vindictive game of building my fear, knowing I'm helpless. He planned this, thought about every step, and now he's relishing every second. His body odor and sweat wake my senses up, gagging and retching. The undeniably strong stench of a man used to physical work and lack of hygiene.

"I've seen how weak pretty boy is over you. I'm going to enjoy sending him the videos of what I'm repeatedly doing to you. I'm going to enjoy this much more than you are, sweetheart! I have so many inventive ways to fuck you. I just hope you live long enough to torture him into insanity." He laughs again, almost to himself, his comments more of a smug self-assurance in an evil sadistic way than a confession of his plans for me. It makes me realize how deeply he has been fantasizing about this, thinking it through, every step planned for precision at how to get back at Jake and me, serving punishment on a man he's no match for and a girl who evaded his demands twice.

He's taking me somewhere ... somewhere he's prepared with cameras and God knows what else. He intends to rape, torture, and probably beat me; violence has always been his turn-on, and he wants to inflict pain upon Jake in the most demonic way possible. He's seen Jake's love for me, and he will use it as a weapon knowing Jake can never physically touch him. He's a coward and a twisted son of a bitch, a man who can only dominate women that are no match for him.

Fight for God's sake! Get up and move, Emma!

That inner voice claws at me, a wave of fear running through my stomach for me and little tadpole. He'll kill us both for sure, and if he doesn't kill me, he'll kill the innocent life that grows inside me. She would never survive repeated rape and torture, and killing my baby will end me too. Even if I survive this, I know I would never survive the loss or the knowledge that I didn't protect her. I am her mother; I need to protect her always.

Emma, you are not your mother. You can and will protect your daughter from Ray. You can do this.

Baby girl, sweetheart, Mommy is here. I'm here.

A surge of anger and some deep unearthly protective rage rush from somewhere inside me. My arms strain out as my hands grasp the railings, desperately trying to latch on. My palms slide on the wooden surface, but I try again and grasp on, gripping hard onto my lifeline, tugging us to a sudden unexpected halt, mid-step. It earns me a massive searing smack across my legs and butt, and pain and burning sensations flash across my skin in agonizing pain. I yelp but grab out again, catching further down the banister in the hopes of doing it again, each time delaying him so that maybe Mathews has a chance of getting here in time.

We're almost halfway down the huge sweeping staircase, closer to the door, and probably a waiting car to take me, never to be found alive again. If I let him get me out there and take me from this place, all is hopeless. No one will know where to come and find me. I'll be his to do with as he pleases, and I can't let it happen.

Jake won't survive this. It'll kill him. It will destroy him. The beautiful soul that makes him who he is will be devastated and broken forever.

I try to picture him to give me strength and courage. His beautiful face and powerful body, that calm demeanor but passionate heart. He and our baby are my body, soul, and reason for breathing. They are my whole world, life, and future, and no one has the right to take that away from me or to take me away from them.

I close my eyes tight in determination, and with a slow, steadying breath, I grab at the smooth wooden rail, resolving to hold on to it with everything I am.

My hand connects with something loose on the smooth surface. It slides and rattles against the railings as I'm tugged onwards in our descent. It's cold and heavy, and my fingers have grasped it before I can contemplate what it is.

The lights are off down here, he must've killed them before following me upstairs, and I can make out the solid object I've caught in my palms. We're still moving, so he mustn't have noticed it. He's too engrossed in his thoughts of what he will do to me once he gets me into his car. My eyes dart open in surprise at the sudden weight I'm gripping onto ...

What is this ... Long and thin and heavy ...

My breath catches in my chest as my scrambled brain makes sense of it, suddenly clicking my thoughts into place.

The crowbar ... The crowbar!

I yank it up harshly, lifting it as high as I can above my head, positioning myself with my abdomen crushing against him, giving me balance and arching my back and head as high as possible. I stretch my arms to full length and extend the bar upwards for a fully heightened swing. I bring it down with the sheer force of hatred and self-preservation, teen Emma engaging my brain and taking control.

Take this fucker!

The crowbar connects with the base of his spine instantly with a magnificent self-satisfying crack, a body-vibrating shudder runs through him to me in a flash, and suddenly I'm flung backward at his shock of the connection. I am flying slowly down the stairs, disconnected from him, and surprisingly fearless. He cries out with a deep throaty gurgling scream of pain echoing around us in the dark space.

I hit the stairs sharply at an odd angle, tumbling backward as my ankles turn under me, the stomach-churning crunch and burning pain in my left foot lurches through me. I yelp loudly, gripping the bar as tight as possible because my life depends on it. I catch it across steps, trying to stop myself from sliding backward down the steps, my butt wedged over the edge and my head pressed to a wall from behind. I'm balancing crazily below where he is on the stairs, and my senses are finally coming to me, my body on high alert. This is my one chance at saving both of us, and he'll have to pry this bar from my cold dead fingers to get me to relinquish my weapon.

He's falling toward me in the dull light, brighter down here nearer the white marble hall because of the wide long windows and white reflective flooring. He trips down the steps trying to regain balance, attempting to catch the handrail with one hand while his other is on his back. He's moaning out loud, grappling and struggling to regain his equilibrium as I shuffle backward to get some purchase on the floor with my butt and legs, trying not to wince at the pain coursing through my body, pushing away the searing agony.

I am ready and waiting as soon as he stumbles close enough,

sheer fury coursing through me, fear giving me strength; my body numbs out the pain as adrenaline spikes in my blood.

I swing as hard as I can with both hands grasping the bar at the base, right at his knee level, giving it all I have left.

The crushing, gnawing sound of crunching, snapping, and splintering bone echoes before his scream, and he crumbles over the top of me like a sack filled with deflated air. His heavy weight crashes down on me, winding me. His big arms and disgusting stale sweat entangle me in panic and jolt my body down with his. He's pulling me off balance and down the last few steps in a tumble as we roll the last distance in an entangled mass of limbs, grunts, and groans. His sheer smell and feel brought back nausea in my throat and the realization I am about to throw up ...

My stomach is my only concern and my child within. I curl into a ball, holding tight with the bar in my arms against my breast, one hand protecting my baby, and fall into darkness with him at astounding speed. My eyes are closed, willing myself to hold on tight to what is most precious to me. The vision of Jake and our baby in my mind giving me the strength to keep going.

Our harsh marble floor landing is softened by his body at the base of the stairs, and we suddenly stop. I uncurl around him, realizing I'm on top and can get away if I shuffle backward on my butt. He's too focused on grappling at the floor, writhing in agony and whimpering pathetically. I'm empowered by the groans and moans coming from his hunched-up body and drag myself away from him, turning on my knees with only the thought of getting away, crawling to safety, and getting help. His vice-like grip comes out to catch my broken ankle, causing excruciating pain to course through me, resulting in a high-pitched scream. I bite out and catch my breath, trying to hold myself together, but I'm not stupid. I'm still holding the crowbar, clutching onto it with the fury of a woman unleashed. I know what I must do. I know he will keep coming for me, keep pursuing me unless I disable him properly. I bring the bar down with perfect precision and great clarity over his skull and the force of a desperate and terrified woman.

There's a deafening thud, an echoing and eerie silence as a

breath escapes him, and then nothing. His body lies motionless, his hand on my ankle drops loose over my injury, and I hastily kick it away with my other foot.

I'm crouching at an odd angle, still gripping the bar so tightly that my nails have pierced my palms, breathing so hard it's painful and making me dizzy. I turn to stare at the bulky form in the dusky light, and something inside of me snaps. All fear and flight go out of me, and emotionless clarity and sense come over me; a dark sense of quiet, calming stillness, followed by a moment of completely detached pause, and I listen to the long slow, steady breaths from his almost lifeless body.

If I leave him this way to go and get help, he could get away, wake up and run, or catch me before I get anywhere. He will never stop coming for me if I always run from him.

I hold up the bar and contemplate hitting him again, but he doesn't appear to be conscious, and I know in my heart I don't have the stomach or the willpower to kill a man ... Even him ... Even if I could justify it to myself and the world, I could never look at myself in the mirror the same way again. Jake would never look at me the same way, and how could my child?

I scramble around on the floor, trying to find something to help me figure out what to do. The pain in my ankle is hot and burning through me intensely, but I push it down and claw my way across the space, dragging my leg behind me like an injured animal, slowly and surely. My head is a scrambling mess, my emotions all over the place, and a hard tension growing in my pelvis is making my body rigid. I can't begin to analyze how I feel; I'm just spurred on by the breathless anxiety of knowing that I am not out of danger yet. He could wake up at any second, and my body's pain is weakening me with every movement.

A sticky liquid blurs my vision on my face, and my mouth is full of the taste of blood. My head is pounding and swelling across my brow at an alarming rate, bringing back deep nausea and dizziness. My body is giving up on me, and I need to save myself before it does.

My eyes wander to the phone on the unit, and I crawl to it,

yanking the cable right out of the wall like a crazed woman, biting into my hands and slicing my palm with the strength of my force. I pull it from the base of the phone stand and crawl back to him. I'm determined to do this, the overwhelming trembling of my body going into shock is slowly creeping up from my toes, so I need to be quick.

I've never restrained a person this way before, but sheer fear and adrenaline have me looping his hands behind his back and tying a multitude of complicated knots as tight as I can. I don't care if I cut off all circulation. The feel of his rough skin is making me recoil internally, and the stench of his musky body is choking me, but I keep tying the cord, hoping that this will be enough.

His breathing is shallow, so he's alive, and I can make out dark liquid oozing onto the floor by his head. I injured him in the way he hurt me, and somehow, it starts a tiny spark of strength deep inside me, a calm that sweeps up through me, giving me focus and determination.

I take a deep breath and sit back to look at my handiwork, calming my crazy body and reeling thoughts. He's strung up at the back, and I've run out of cords to do more. I hope it's enough, and his knee is too smashed to be able to use his legs should he want to come to get me.

I need Jake. I need help. I need the police. Get help, Emma ... Go.

I realize my phone is in my bag upstairs, and I must've dropped it with his assault. There's no way I can muster the ability to get up that steep, winding staircase, and I've just disabled the only landline nearby.

Fuck's sake, Emma. Well done.

Stupid. Stupid. Okay, look around, Emma. Look! What can I find? What can I do? How can I get help?

I grab at my temples and knock on my head, trying to think. My eyes wandering around the room, desperately searching for something to help me get comfort.

Calm, Emma, be rational. Sylvana is right next door.

The street ... Get to the street.

I try to get up, and my ankle gives out completely, another sharp agonizing pain, wooziness hitting me with ferocity and dampness now coursing down my chin as a fresh wave of blood pulses further down my face. I'm shivering. My body is shaking so badly that my hands are becoming unusable.

I trace the warmth of the liquid up to my forehead and realize he's cut my head open with the force of my collision into the door upstairs. My brow is swelling, and my hairline is crusting with blood.

"Jake is going to fuck you up!" I snarl at his motionless body, suddenly enraged at what he's done to me, what he intended to do to me! The anger I used to harbor kicks free and claims me with a fury I normally keep locked up, like some seething crazy past Emma.

This will not be over if the police take him away. He will bide his time and come back. He'll wait in the shadows again until we least expect it and lash out in a new, more horrendous way.

I look down at my stomach and recoil in sheer fear and terror.

He will come for our child ... I know he will.

Something in me tells me he would, that his level of patience and craziness means he will be a threat forever, one that even Jake can't keep us safe from.

I need to get to Sylvana. She will know what to do. Mathews will come back, and he can do something with this piece of shit while Jake comes to me and figures out what to do. Jake always knows what to do.

With more determination, I try to stand again to walk out of this house, but my ankle bites at me in pain. I crumble in screaming agony; nausea washing through me so fast I can't contain it, and I throw up on the floor, finally giving up the contents that had been threatening to expel all along.

I lean back in disgust and grab at my swimming head, spitting blood and sick out of my mouth, and use my sleeve to wipe at it. I clutch at my stomach as a tremor of ache courses through my lower abdomen, a prickling of anxiety at the fear that my baby might be damaged somehow. That this physical encounter has hurt her. The ache hits again, low and winding, like a punch in the gut, and it strokes panic in me once more.

The sheer force of deep-rooted fear at the possible loss of her hits me, consuming everything but the need to get help for her ... For my baby.

He will not take you from me. He cannot win.

The tears start pouring down my face, and I can't take much more of this pain soaring in my heart; every aching assault on my abdomen comes in waves and is like a piece of my heart being sliced away.

I lift my chin defiantly and drag myself onto my knees, moved by the power inside to get my child the help she needs to stay with me. My belly is aching and twisting inside of me, and tears flood my face, diluting the blood and mess and leaving a trail across my shirt and neck.

My arms are aching, and my body is shaking violently. I crawl purposefully, ignoring everything else but the need to save her, my beautiful little green-eyed girl. I want to see her smile back at me. I want to hold her in my arms and know the smell of my little one against my face. The feel of her delicate skin and soft breaths. I won't lose her now; I'll grip onto her harder than I'll ever grip onto anything in my life.

I crawl to the front door, trying to haul myself to my feet to reach the handles, crying with every single effort and calling out in pain. My eyes are screwed shut, and my fists are clenched to get my body to move upward.

I won't let him do this to me. I won't let him destroy any chance of happiness or take away our life in this way.

I reach up, hauling at the handle in one last desperate effort, trying to get enough purchase to open the door and shove myself up further against the screaming pain.

I connect with the handle and tug. The door opens enough to catch my fingers in the crack and sob out loud in relief, grappling manically and slumping back down onto my knees, somewhat relieving my ankle's excruciating pain.

I pull the door back as far as I can against me, shifting my weight out of the way to accommodate the door's opening. It is less than a second before the alarm engages at the disruption.

My home turns into some flashing beacon of lights and wailing sirens, overwhelming my senses in a terrifying assault. Crying for help in deafening proportions, I make out the blurred lights near the front door, blinking in time to the brain-fogging ringing around me. Knocking the last of my senses into oblivion.

I did it. I signaled for help, and now I want to lie down, curl around my child, and hold onto her for a little longer. My body is giving up on me while my brain tries to find the calm in the chaos around me.

Stay with me, sweetheart. Hold on for just a little longer. They're coming. Daddy will come. Please, baby ...

Chapter 32

It all happens so fast that it's like a dream, the car sweeping past as I gaze out of the open door hazily, distant enough to be a blur but close enough to see it turn this way. Headlights turn to blind me painfully as the house alarm wails become almost unbearable. My consciousness gives way as the pulsing aches and ripples through my abdomen course along my legs and up my front, making my jaw ache. The warmth between my legs causing my heart to break and silent tears to pour down my face. I can no longer move or cry, immobilized and cradling her to me, begging her to stay. My head is foggy as the ache devours me slowly, like a wave of numbness moving in.

It's just the two of us cocooned together in a safe little bubble of non-reality, holding on in the hopes of coming out of this okay, of never being parted.

The blur is Giovanni running toward me, a dark expression of concern on his face and his familiar wide shoulders, like Jake's, grounding me. I focus on nothing but him and try to breathe as his face of safety gets closer, relief sweeping through me as heavy fatigue takes me over.

Now Mathews' face is close to mine. I must've closed my eyes for a moment. Nausea, dizziness, and blurry vision heighten as my body rises away from the cold hard ground. I don't know what's happening anymore. Human warmth around me, the smell of distant aftershave, and mixed voices. Familiarity in some weird distant way.

"Emma! Emma."

I hear my name, but it's far away ... so far... my baby girl and I want to sleep.

Yes, sleep and wake up in Jake's arms and the beautiful smile I call home.

* * *

My head aches so badly that I'm afraid to open my eyes, my throat stings, and my whole leg is throbbing. My abdomen feels like nothing, just cold calm numbness. I'm too hazy to experience any emotions inside me. Woozy and sick, disorientated, and I have no idea if I'm dreaming or dead. The pain is too much for me to push through to open my eyes, and my body feels so heavy and unresponsive that I'm not even sure I can.

There's a low gentle noise seeping into my thoughts, tenderly stirring emotions that I am trying so hard to cling to. The sound is fading in and out of my mind; every time I try to follow it, it seems to move further away. I feel like I'm at one end of a long dark tunnel, and everything else is over there, at the glimmer of light in the distance; if I move toward it, I can hear it a little clearer.

I pull myself along the dark, cold space, moving closer to the light in the far-off distance, straining to listen and hoping that if I do, my eyes will open and let me see where I am. The silence starts to recede as I urge along toward the muffled noise, bringing it louder into my subconscious and the notes vibrating around my brain. The faint melodic notes of a familiar song tugging me toward the light and the warmth that now seems to be trailing across my cheek. Something so familiar and inviting, begging me to turn toward it. Tiny notes of a song I know and the soft touch that I need with emotions connected to fuzzy memories that are just out of my grasp. I need to try harder.

I strain forward, the heaviness becoming tranquil, helping my mind stay tuned. I recognize the melody instantly; the beautiful soft words of "Halo" come through the haze toward me and a soft, gentle breath crosses my brow. Jake's words, his songs, explaining to me how he feels in a way he thinks he never can.

My emotions rush through my heart at finding this small piece of joy in my dark prison. The familiar intoxicating smell of his body and soul and the touch of his fingers across my lips as he tries to draw me out to the light to be with him.

"Emma, *Bambina* ... I'm sorry. I'm so sorry I wasn't there for you. Come back to me, baby ... Don't leave me, please ...."

Jake! Jake, my sweet Jake. You're here. You found me. I love you.

His low husky tone is wracked with anguish and pleading, reaching out to me, and I want to stretch out and console his voice. I want to open my eyes and draw him into me. His voice is drowning in pain and aching for me, and I try desperately to reach out to him. My mind is too exhausted, it wants me to go back into the darkness, but I won't submit. I won't leave him. He needs me. I can hear it in the pain that tortures his voice. He needs me to make it all okay for him.

I did it, Jake. I fought him off. Ray was here at our house in our lives, but I fought him off, and I won. I did it for us, for you and our baby. He can't hurt us anymore.

"I love you, Emma ... I can't do this without you. I'll never survive. Please? I need you to try for me. Just try to come back to us ... I'll never let you go and never let you out of my sight again."

I'm trying, baby. I swear. I want to tell you everything. I want to be with you forever.

Jake's soft voice pulls me upwards against the tide of heaviness trying to consume me. His hand, a graceful, gentle stroke of tenderness, runs across my face, and I beg my subconscious to open my eyes and tell him I'm here. I'm trying so hard to be with him. Consumed with painful emotion and overwhelming sadness at whatever this is, trying to keep us apart, I want to fight so hard; fight for him and us. I feel like I'm stuck in a dream and losing time whenever the darkness draws me back in.

I awaken to the flicker of light again, still trapped in my tunnel, and a song takes over, its volume increasing, and his soft, warm breath and gentle lips graze mine, starting my body with a jolt and a surge of energy. The light comes closer, and within grasp, so I beg him to kiss me again and wake me from this nightmare properly. It's like I'm holding my breath, waiting for another touch, but his mouth moves away, the soft breath fading, along with his smell, and I know the kiss isn't enough. I'm sliding backward, the darkness inviting me in, peaceful on my senses and helping my confused and dazed mind recuperate.

"Emma, you need to open your eyes for Mamma. They said you could do it, so I know you can. You just need to try to find us again."

Sylvana.

Her soft feminine voice is so close that I can almost reach out and touch it. Her homely, welcoming, warm tone is waiting to embrace me as soon as I leave this darkness. But it keeps clawing me back, and the moments feel like days. The seconds could be hours. There seems to be no concept of time in my mind, just the changing of the music every time my subconscious brings me around from another wave of enveloping darkness.

"Emma, you listen to me now...This is not on! You get your ass up, and you wake up, you hear me."

Leila ... sweet, feisty Leila, how much I love you.

The soft crying dampens her haughty tone and fiery rasp through her voice as her gentle tiny fingers cup mine, and I can smell her sweet perfume. The aroma sliding up my nostrils, trying to awaken all my senses.

"Move over, Leila, let me in.... Emma, it's Sarah, honey. Listen to me. They said if we talk to you that you know ... Maybe you'll hear us. We love you. We are all right here with you." There's sniffling, and the shifting of bodies as the skin on my arm tingles with goosebumps at her tender stroke. "Don't let that bastard win, baby girl. Don't let him take you from Jake ... from us."

I try so hard just to do something, say something or respond somehow, but I can't.

"Can I just be alone with her?" His broken voice comes through to me, and I try again so hard to reach for him, to will my voice to work. He needs to help me; I need his strength because I'm too exhausted to do this alone. I need him to draw me out from this place that holds me still and motionless, suspended and floating like I'm drifting away on the water. I don't want to be here anymore.

The music comes closer and louder, something new that makes my heart ache. The one song that is always going to hold my heart. Bringing me back from another brief trip into oblivion. I have no idea how long I will go there for.

"Say you love me ...." His voice is closer than the music and in perfect sync, his fingers are trailing my face, and he stops singing to lean in and breathe kisses across my closed eyes. Every touch and caress makes it easier for me to move closer to where I want to be. I ache to end this darkness, so I can feel him and run my fingers across his mouth and jaw. I want to open my mouth and kiss his, responding to his song in any way I can. But I'm held captive and can't find the strength I need to pull myself out of this. I need him to help me like he always does.

I need you, Jake. Please save me.

"Emma Anderson, you listen to me ... I'm not going to sit back and watch you fucking sleep for the rest of our lives, you hear me? Where is my PA Emma? She has way more sass than this. She wouldn't lie around like this, doing nothing. Who else will kick my ass in gear when I'm misbehaving? If you don't wake up right now, I'll haul your ass up and make you."

Jake's forceful tone is almost a growl, full of emotion, tears, and aggression. He's trying to find me in here, and he knows that the bossy, domineering asshole he can always be had a way of giving me what I needed, even if it's to wake up and give him attitude back. I get a spike of defiance in his non-gentle tone, yet a surge of deep-hearted love at this version of him. "Listen, *neonata* ... No woman of mine is spending her life lounging in bed, letting everyone fall apart around her ... Enough is enough. It's been days, Emma. Now get up!" His tone is deeper, huskier, and almost breaks. His raw emotions are laced in every word he says, trying so hard to reach me.

I am getting so frustrated at myself that my inner anger rears up. I'm surrounded by the song that gave me two of the happiest moments of my life, when he gave me his all, and yet here I am lying here, my subconscious holding me back from what I deserve. It's like the beginning of our relationship all over again. I'm back to the defiant, closed-off Emma who never let him in, always holding back when he needed me most.

No! I am not doing this to you, Jake. Not anymore, I won't!

The song reminds me that he doesn't always need to be my strength, but a prompt to show me that sometimes I need to be his too. I need to build my own force to find my way back. I need to hold him up and face whatever reality comes when my body wakes up. Maybe that's why my mind doesn't want me to wake up. It's afraid that what Ray did to me will make me hide in the shadows again, that I won't be able to love Jake and let him in the ways I did before Ray tried to kill me. But it's not going to be like that this time. I need to be the one to put the pieces back together in the aftermath of what happened. I need to accept help from others who only want me to feel loved and safe, but I also need to be the one to put Jake back together after this. He will need me to help him get through this. His guilt will eat at him if I don't.

I bite at a tinkle of defiance, growing into something more.

I'm stronger than this.

I push with every ounce of strength and stubbornness within me and aim for the light trying with all my might to break free. I can feel it; every ounce of my being comes together and fights with an almost deafening pain. The exhaustion of trying to wake up is virtually drowning me back down into the darkness. I know I'll only need one push to break the barrier holding me here, that once I leave this place, I'll be free and never return again. The confines of my prison will fall away, and I'll be free.

I CAN DO THIS.

I push with everything within me, all I've got, but reality comes up too fast, and my senses go into overdrive with the sudden explosion of noises, smells, and sounds consuming my brain, and the pain and aches of my body overwhelm me all at once. The harsh lights from the room are blinding even with my eyes closed. From one side, the smell of coffee and flowers rushes up to nose into my brain, and I can feel the softness of a bed under me. My body is heavy, and my limbs are aching too much to move, but I know I can move them if I try. I suddenly feel connected to the heaviness I know is me and no longer floating in some weird tunnel. My face aches, and my eyes are glued shut. My mouth is dry and cracked, and suddenly nausea consumes me.

Yet, somehow, through all of that, I know I'm here with him, in his reality and not in some dream-like state anymore on the other side. I can hear the hum of machines, the noise of something blowing air in and out, and the mumbling sounds of hushed voices passing by in the distance.

"I just don't know what else to do, baby." Jake's voice breaks and tears me in two. The sound of defeat and broken-hearted pain is so obvious, I can almost sense his body sagging close to me, and I can hear his breathing so very close, the smell of his aftershave and just him luring me out of my haze.

I blink my eyes and become brutally aware of the bright white crisp surroundings and agonizing light over my head, buzzing like an electronic device about to explode. Blinking harshly to try to adjust and fighting the will to close them once more as pain envelopes my skull.

Warm heat envelops my right hand securely, a touch I'd know from anywhere, and it brings my full focus and attention straight to the one person I want to see and feel right now. My eyes flicker once more before finally being able to open enough to see things. I gaze down at my hand before taking in my surroundings.

His large tanned hand grasps at my lifeless delicate one, and I look so pale in comparison. He's holding on desperately, fingers entwined softly, dwarfing my hand inside his. That strong forearm exposed his olive skin and hints of tattoos along his inner arm under the rolled-up sleeve of the shirt I saw him put on the day he left the house. It's rumpled and wrinkled, and my eyes follow the length of his arm up to his beautiful face.

My Jake. My beautiful reason for fighting to hold on.

The sight of him makes my heart explode in my chest, as though we've been apart for months, and I'm only just seeing him. He's sat on a chair, slumped forward with his face in his palm and facing the floor. He's still wearing the same clothes he wore the day he left for the office, minus his tie and jacket, but his hair is a mess, and his face is unshaven; his posture is screaming with emotional agony. He looks completely awful and ridiculously delicious; I couldn't love my little lost boy any more than I do right now. His brave attempt at domineering when it's obvious he's anything but. He looks broken beyond belief.

I clear my throat at seeing that gorgeous, beautiful sight, the man who makes my heart soar and suddenly feel so safe; with him so close, I know I'll always be protected.

His head snaps up at the noise, and I feel like I've been slapped. All thoughts of chastising him are gone as soon as I lay eyes on the face that means the world to me. He looks devastated. His eyes are bloodshot, red-rimmed, and tired. His face is ashen and drained of all life. Seeing him this way hits me in the gut, a mirror image of the broken Jake who betrayed me so long ago.

"Emma, *Bambina*!" He jumps to his feet, his palm hitting a button on the wall, and he starts cradling my hand against his face. His eyes are wild, he doesn't know whether to cry or smile, and he's unsure if he should even be touching me. Hands hovering in case he hurts me, unable to conceal the trembling of his body. "Jesus, baby, oh God, Emma ... I didn't think you were going to wake up." A single tear escapes his eye and slides slowly down his face. "I've never been so scared ... I couldn't breathe." He leans in, kissing me softly on the mouth, and I take great delight in being able to enjoy it. I lift a hand to his neck to pull myself closer to him and lose myself completely in everything that is him. He pulls away and gently strokes my hair, a slight, tensing throb running across my face at the touch.

"Jake." I croak softly. My voice is weak and hoarse and almost non-existent. I'm suddenly so tired, and my emotions start to tumble out of me as a tear escapes and rolls down my face. The pang inside my abdomen hits me as though somehow being conscious reminds me of my baby, we'd been apart in my dream world, but now that I am back here, I can feel her clinging on ... somehow, I know she's still connected to me even if she's so very weak.

"I'm so sorry, baby. I'm so fucking sorry ... I should've been there. I should've known. It was so monumentally fucking stupid of me to have not done a major background check on the people I left in our fucking house ... I should've made sure, back in Chicago, he would never come back." He's rambling, all emotions set loose, eyes brimming, and body trembling. I grip his fingers to try to bring him some comfort, trying to calm him with my touch. I want to be the strength for him that he is to me, the one that helped me come back from the darkness.

"Jake ... stop ... please ... This isn't your fault." I grate out painfully as soft, gentle tears fall down my bruised and aching face. I flinch when his hand brushes them away, my face aching more with every second my eyes open. I can't ignore the awful painful agony in my foot and glance down to see some tent monstrosity over the top, keeping the blankets from touching my leg. I'm guessing it's in a cast.

Jake leans in and kisses my forehead to calm himself, breathing fast and seemingly unable to take in that I am awake.

"Ouch," I yelp, and he recoils.

"Shit ... I'm sorry, *Bambina*. Fuck ... Oh, baby, I'm so fucking sorry." Jake breaks down again and cries over me, leaning down to lay his head on my neck, making my heart ache right through my chest for him.

The doctor appears in the doorway with a professional smile reaching his eyes as Jake's gentle hands cradle me close, never once letting me go. I could lie like this with him connected to me forever.

"Miss. Anderson, welcome back. Let's take a little look at you now you're awake."

Chapter 33

I smooth my hands down my ivory wedding dress. It's classy elegance, and the understated top is lined with a simple sleeveless fitted bodice and tiny pearl detailing. It has a full wispy floating skirt and layers and layers of chiffon puffing out to a full-length cloud of loveliness. It's a fairy-tale princess dress that matches beautifully with the elegant engagement ring twinkling on my hand, sparkling in all its glory.

I admire my flawless natural makeup in the mirror, touching up my nude lipstick. My tawny hair is wild and curled in its loose, romantic style, tiny tendrils hang around my face, and I appraise my reflection with pride.

I look beautiful! I feel beautiful and serene. There is no fear whatsoever.

I look like a woman hopelessly in love, about to marry the man of her dreams.

I am that woman.

I slide on my satin ivory stilettos that almost mirror the shoes I used to adore so much. It feels weird to be back in heels after so long, and I turn around, hearing movement from the room behind me, alerting me to tropical blue eyes catching mine in the reflection as I straighten up.

"Oh, my God, Ems ... God, you look stunning," Sarah holds

back a tear, touching her eyes with a tissue and waving her hands to save her mascara from running as I watch her in the mirror behind me. She's wearing her fitted aqua bridesmaid dress, and her messy blonde short hair is pinned up in a loose half-up style like mine, and I'm overcome with a huge surge of love. Her bright blue eyes are heavy with emotion as she watches me intensely in a way that has my heart lifting with excitement.

"It's happening, Sarah." I smile widely, a tremor of passion rippling through me. My nerves are tingling, my stomach is fluttering, and my knees are turning to mush. I spin around, lifting my delicate veil, and let my eyes skim that flawless silhouette in the mirror, flat stomach once more and a body that looks like it never changed. I'm hit with that familiar tug of emptiness at no longer feeling her life growing within me.

The vacuum of emptiness inside never leaves me, but I smile to myself weakly and push it down, lifting my chin defiantly, looking like old PA Emma, yet so different in so many ways. This is my happy day; no tears unless they are ones of joy. I remind myself that I'm not going to cloud this day with running make-up and emotional breakdowns unless they're related to taking my vows.

"Oh, my God, Emma." Leila bursts into tears when she sees me sliding into the room behind Sarah. They only left me for a few minutes so that I could step into my dress, yet they're acting like this is the first time they've seen it too, even though they were the ones who helped me choose it.

It took me endless shopping trips to find the perfect one and constant boring fittings with selfies that Leila just had to litter over Instagram. I banned Jake from using any social media the entire time we planned the big day for fear of trending posts giving away ideas of which shops I was heading into and people snapping sneaky photos of me trying on gowns in shops. Leila saw them on more than one occasion and promptly chased them off, but pictures would still find themselves all over the social media sites. After all, the world still loves their Carrero hotty, and his hashtag on anything wedding-related seemed to top the bill weekly.

"You're ruining your make-up." I chide Leila softly, but she shakes her head and smiles back through a wave of tears. Her eyeliner is already making a quick exit down her face.

"Daniel likes me looking like a train wreck nowadays ... Will just turn him on seeing me with mascara down my chin again." She sniffs, and Sarah starts fussing with the hankies, cleaning Leila's face up in a desperate attempt to salvage her perfected makeup. Leila is so hopelessly cute when she cries, and I agree with her on the Daniel point. The boy clucks around her like a mother hen anytime she bursts into tears. Daniel is turning as hopeless as Jake nowadays and never far from his lady's side; gone is the Hunter of old who partied and messed around with women galore. Leila is his world.

"I think the fact that you've done nothing but cry non-stop since he got you pregnant means he has no choice but to love that train wreck ... Invest in waterproof mascara." Sarah chides, and I watch as Leila runs a hand over her bulging bump. I am hit with another hint of rising tears and a small tug of envy. Her growing bump is twins, much to Daniel's shock when they found out she was even carrying. That day I thought we needed an ambulance for him since he passed out in the doctor's office.

I run my hand over my own flat stomach automatically with a sharp internal pain in my heart, the familiar wave of emotion I get every time I realize there's nothing there anymore. I was warned that it would take a long time for the feeling of emptiness to go away, and maybe not until I try for another child, but even the thought of having another baby brings fresh tears to my eyes. The hormones are still messing with me even now. There is gut-wrenching heartache at the emptiness of my body, so I try to push it aside mentally with a deep inhale, slowly letting it back out.

"Guess I'll have to marry him now then, huh?" Leila dabs her face with Sarah's tissue and sniffs a little to reel in her tears. "He's asked enough times, and I'm only saying no because I'm such a mess all the time. Why would he want this?" Leila sighs back her tears again and tries to limit the damage to her face with a compact, squinting at it disapprovingly, then dabbing manically over the streaky areas to fix it. I predict it will happen many more times today.

"You're asking me?" I look at her with a knowing expression, saying you 'do remember the crazy mess I've been this past year?'

My recovery from a head fracture and small brain bruise was a big ordeal and included a very long and messy recovery. I had a lot of counseling to deal with my past and the emotional aftereffects of what Vanquis did to me. Recovery involved rehabilitation in getting past some of the brain damage I incurred from the incident, such as impaired balance, bouts of severe low mood, and awful headaches for months on end. My crying and psychotic behavior consumed me these last few months and tested everyone's love around me. It has been a very trying period in my life, and Jake has been my absolute rock throughout, the perfect fiancée with the patience of a saint.

Now I'm throwing myself into my new path and studying to become a counselor for abused children within Sylvana's charity. I want to be a beacon of hope and a hand to guide children to a better life. I want to do for the Sophies" of the world what Jake did for me. It was hard to study and go to classes, still seeing my therapist weekly to keep on top of everything while aiming for a new future. Jake supported me in everything and finally let some of his authoritarian side relax.

"Well, Leila, you'd better hurry up because my wedding is in a month, and you'll be the only single one of our trio." Sarah has given up on salvaging Leila's make-up and instead hands her a wet wipe. It's a safe bet to say Leila has looked better, but it's no surprise that her cute face can pull off the smudgy look any day of the week.

I gaze at Sarah's flawless, happy face and smile at the radiance I see reflected at me. Marcus surprised everyone by proposing to Sarah, rather publicly, at her birthday bash, which Jake organized for me as a thank you to Sarah for being my friend. The proposal was beautiful, and I admit that Marcus is right for her. Sarah was bowled over, not only by my public appreciation of 'the girl who loved me when no one else did and persevered anyway' but the sheer spontaneity of Marcus's proposal. She didn't see it coming at all. None of us did, except maybe Jake. I'm sure Marcus had a few whispered conversations with Jake to organize the whole thing.

"Okay!" Sarah turns to me and takes a deep breath. "Ready?" She holds out an arm to me bossily, the only one who seems to be organizing things today, and I tilt my head with a final breath. I don't feel any nerves or inner doubts I'd been expecting to sweep over me when this moment arrived. Instead, I feel impatient knowing he's out there waiting, picturing those devastating green eyes smiling back at me and his unbelievably kissable mouth.

"Feels like I've been waiting for this for an eternity." I smile and allow my best friends to guide me from the room, one on each arm, out into the hallway. They pick up my dress to avoid catching it on the door.

We make our way down the hall, and I'm met with the almost unemotional face of Giovanni Carrero. He extends an arm to me with a smile and a nod, his eyes appraising my dress, and I slide my own into his. He smiles wider and brighter, inclining his head approvingly. This is about as far as the man ever gets with any real show of emotion, but I get it. I know him better nowadays, and I smile, sighing with indulgence at the father-in-law who is so completely loveable. It has taken some time to figure out this rogue enigma, but I'm sure I have some understanding of him now. After all, we're similar kinds of people. The type to be more reserved in affection than Jake and Sylvana and subtle in how we show it to those who don't know us well.

"Ready to walk me down the aisle and present me to your son?" I nudge him gently, a little affectionate grin on my face and that huge warmth runs through me when I see a little softening of his stern focus. The subtle tells that underneath the cool Giovanni exterior beats a warm and loving heart.

"Of course. I can imagine nothing more I'd rather be doing today." He winks, smugness appearing on his face, and I shake my head at him. He reminds me so much of Jake at times, but I know neither would ever admit to it.

"Glad you feel that way." I lean up and plant an impromptu kiss on his cheek, with no qualms about bestowing loving affection on my family members, even the males. From the corner of my eye, I catch his eyebrow twitch, much like Arrick's, showing a betrayal of flat emotion. My happy heart is too full of warmth and excited energy today, and it must be rubbing off on him.

"Well, I didn't go to the bother of losing an assistant and sending her back to my son on a whim." Surprisingly, he winks at me because he's not a winker ... and that's twice now, but I'm more astonished by what he said.

"What?" I blink at him nonplussed, thinking I maybe misheard him and can't quite compute what he's saying. I blink at him while gripping his arm tightly and look confused.

"My son was in pain and hiding from what he wanted most," he says so factually, looking down at me, "I put you back in his path, so he would stop being a coward." Giovanni grins, and all words leave my brain in an open-mouthed silent gawp, realization dawning on me so suddenly that I am rendered speechless.

He sent me back to Carrero House? Making me believe that he would fire me if I didn't ... an ultimatum that led us to where we are now.

Giovanni is admitting to maneuvering me back into Jake's building so that we would end up back in each other's arms, the crafty jerk he is. He giggles like a schoolboy at my shocked expression and pats my hand tenderly over his inner elbow. That self-confident effortless look on a man who always sees all and knows everything.

"No need to thank me, Emma." He raises his brows in an almost smug manner, and I clear my throat, finding my voice, still shocked that if he hadn't done that one simple thing, then I wouldn't be here today, with him, getting ready to do this.

"You sent me back to him, so he would? So, we would? How did you even know?" I am completely blown away by his confession, emotions brimming to the surface and a deep aching pain in my heart, so touched by a man who always seemed indifferent toward me. We're still standing in the hall as the two girls mess about nearby with their dresses and hair while we wait for the rest of our party. They haven't heard any of Giovanni's confession since they're further back, and neither is paying attention to my almost tearful expression.

"He's my son. I see everything. I know him even if he doesn't like to admit it. You were actually a very competent assistant." That wily look and lift of a satisfied smile have me shaking my head at him again in complete disbelief. Giovanni is a sneaky man, but I absolutely love him for every sneaky, underhanded card he has ever played in the final happiness of his son. I squeeze his arm and throw caution to the wind by throwing my arms around him instead, giving him my best version of a Jake hug that I can muster. He tenses for a second awkwardly, Giovanni is not a man who does public displays of affection and then hugs me back, a solid sort of fatherly hug for just a moment, but it means the world to me. He lets me go and straightens his jacket, returning the mask of effortless grace and poise I know only too well.

"Move down the hall a bit. We'll wait for Sophie nearer the door ... She better hurry up." Leila huffs impatiently, gently pushing us, bossy pants back on and face flawless. She's checking the time on her wristwatch and frowning at Sarah, who is looking up and down the hall for any sign of our missing bridesmaid. I don't expect anything else from Sophie nowadays, the girl is a fifteen-year-old ball of fun, but we all adore her mercilessly.

Giovanni leads me out of the hallway toward the larger area outside the main hall doors, a brighter and airier half-circle room with ceiling windows letting the sun stream in. I lift my chin a little with each step, my heart expanding more with the realization that this really is it, and it's really happening. The Carreros are making me one of their own, and I am getting my Jake for an eternity, never to be parted again.

This crazy man is taking me as a daughter with his terrifying family and secrets I'd never like to guess at or even know.

Like what exactly he did with Ray Vanquis after he handed me to Mathews.

Not that I want to know, and I've never pressed Jake about it, either. Giovanni took care of things because I am family and the less I know, the more I can pretend it never happened. Jake never speaks of Vanquis either, and as much as I know that Jake would've never been involved in anything like that, I also know he's probably relieved that his father swooped in. I don't want to know if Vanquis is dead or alive. All we got was a promise that Vanquis would never return. Giovanni assured us of that, and I've learned that his word is his bond.

Jake changed toward Giovanni after that. He no longer disapproves of his father's less-than-legal ties, especially when they swoop in and deal with a problem over Jake's head. Jake couldn't exactly take a moral high ground with his father's dealings when he told his father to do whatever needed to be done to keep his family safe.

The relationship between them is far more level now because of it, changing with every passing month, and I'm happy to see some genuine bond building on both sides; I'm sure Sylvana feels the same way.

Here I am, arm in arm, with the man possibly capable of making a human disappear to the waiting arms of the man who spent a lifetime misunderstanding him. Now the two have some mutual bond because Giovanni saved me in place of his son. He won Jake over by saving the one person in the world who mattered to him the most ... Me.

We are a family. All of us.

My heart catches in my throat as we reach the double doors that hold my life inside and pause to wait. My heart and happiness await me; I'm about to take that step inside and finalize it very soon. Just a few more minutes of waiting, we will be going in there to end one chapter of my life and start a new one with the person I adore more than anything in the universe. My heart growing with excitement, and my nerves rising in anticipation, even though I know I have nothing to be frightened of.

"Do you think she'll be in there, Emma?" Sarah whispers behind me, and I shake my head, already knowing who she means without asking. Nothing registers in my heart at her question, not a flicker, no feeling about knowing my mother won't be among the sea of friends and faces in that room to watch me marry my soul mate. I am long healed from the absence of her in my life. I feel a sense of freedom, much like the day, over a year ago, when I walked out of her building.

She never made contact again, even when the papers reported my near-death experience and four-day coma at the hands of an intruder at 'Billionaire Business Entrepreneur Jacob Carreros New Family Home.' The media had a field day with that story and ran it for weeks, even long after my exit from the private care hospital and back home. My mother never graced me with a phone call or even a text or email that whole time. I didn't have a single visit from her in my several weeks in recovery in the private hospital, not even a bunch of flowers or a get-well card. I ceased to care about her at all. It only helped me move on.

"Are you okay about it?" Leila soothes in, and I turn to my girls and nod honestly, smiling happily. I am worth far more than any effort she ever put into my life, and I am surrounded by people who genuinely care, showing a real kind of love and affection, not some cold shadow of an attempt at it.

"Wait! Wait." Sophie's panicked voice is coming at us anxiously, and she appears, down the hall, looking a little flustered. Her dress is barely zipped up, and her hair is already working loose. She's rushing down the hallway with Mrs. Huntsberger in tow, looking every bit like the wild teen she has become lately. The poor woman looks flustered and tired, chasing down that energetic girl and trying to bring calm to the chaos of the child she loves so much.

"That's what we were doing." Giovanni winks at her, and Leila and Sarah start fussing with her hair to calm the wildness that is Sophie nowadays. She is fast taking Leila's place as the 'wild child' and is excelling at being more than a handful lately. Sometimes she's exhausting, but we all love her dearly, and we all understand that this is Sophie's way of dealing with her past, much like it had been Leila's ...

Teenage girls!

"Is that everyone?" Giovanni smiles at me, and I nod back at him, taking another steadying deep breath. Nerves overtaking me, not because I have doubts, but because this is the most important day of our lives and I am tingling with suppressed excitement. I am finally becoming a Carrero ... Mrs. Emma Carrero. Jake's wife. I can barely stand still with the urge to burst through the door and get to him now that we're all assembled in the right positions. The girls take their places behind me; Sarah is fixing my veil at the back and fluffing my dress one last time; Leila handing me my simple, eloquent bouquet of lilies and beautiful tropical flowers, and I close my eyes to take a moment for myself.

With a deep breath, Giovanni opens the door that throws open my view to the sea of people who mean everything in the world to me. The room is fit to bursting with standing guests all waiting patiently, looking this way, and the immediate melody of music echoing toward us.

Christina Perri's ' A Thousand Years' plays down the aisle, and I frown back at Leila with a half-smile on my face. It's not a song I would've chosen myself.

"Sophie picked it," Leila mutters, rolling her eyes. "She's a *Twilight* fanatic, and we drew straws." Leila and the others fought over the job of head bridesmaid almost ruthlessly in the run-up to this day, and drawing straws became commonplace for decisions. I let them squabble over who picked my wedding march song while I focused on my studies. They took away my wedding stress by organizing most of it between them.

"Nice ... I suppose it fits." I giggle at Sarah's eye roll and disapproving look at Sophie. The girl just shrugs mischievously with a huge smile.

The music drifting over me brings my attention back to the front, making me emotional, and for the first time, I listen to the words of this very beautiful song. I take a deep breath and gesture to my father-in-law-to-be that I am ready, so we move forward. Slowly and surely, held safe in his gentle embrace, we walk down the aisle together, followed by my beautiful girls.

The room is huge with high ceilings, and the smell is overpowering with the array of a hundred flower arrangements placed on every wall and row of seats. Beautiful garlands at every high-arched window and colored sashes act as a walkway to my red-carpeted aisle. It's a glorious and stunning wedding venue, made more magnificent by the people standing and watching me with beaming happy faces as I pass by.

I scan the aisles as we walk on and take in the faces as we go, the Carreros at my left in their droves. Now, people, I consider myself close to. Rows and rows of beautiful Italian-looking people with big smiles, most of whom I've only briefly met in these past few months. Then there are all Jake's friends. He seriously has too many people in the world that he classes as family or friends. I feel like I'll never get to the end of all the people he knows.

On the right are those from Carrero Tower and Carrero House that worked alongside me and knew me when I was a different person. I am not ashamed that they sit in place of my family because they are all here with me, watching me walk down toward him, and he's all I need.

I catch sight of some of my favorite women on the right-hand side of the aisle. Margo is wiping a tear from her eye and nudging Wilma in her side as both woman wave to me. They're blowing their noses and crying as Donna throws tissues their way. My crazy trio of motherly hens. Donna's mascara is pouring down her normally flawless face. I spot Rosalie waving from behind a very handsome man, grinning wildly and looping her arms with him, a look of radiant happiness on her pretty face. I beam back at them with a tiny wave before moving on in time to the music, slow steps, with Giovanni leading the way.

I catch sight of the Huntsbergers, my new extended family sitting close by, and smile warmly at them. The row of adopted children and Huntsberger father looking so proud of his family. Ben and his baby son are near the end of the row. He is cuddling him proudly and looking every bit the doting dad. He is now his sole parent, seeing as Marissa lost all interest in a baby she had no purpose for anymore. She went under the communication radar soon after giving birth, not that I'm complaining. I'm happy that Marissa stopped being our problem, and we'll likely never have to deal with her again.

The girl Ben has been dating for the last six months sits beside him in the row and smiles my way shyly. Grace is everything Marissa isn't, and she dotes on little Adam as much as Ben does. We've all started to become friends recently, and she seems to be looking like a permanent fixture in Ben's life. A new mummy for the most beautiful little mini-Ben you could ever see. It's obvious Ben has found his *Emma*, and Jake has regained some sort of friendship with him over the last few months. Hunter is a little jealous that someone is moving in on his bestie in a very manly 'bromance' way, and it's endearingly amusing.

Jake's staff from the Manhattan apartment are sitting nearer the front as part of the family. Nora, Jefferson, the array of security guards, and of course, good old Mathews, another of my heroes that never leaves my side nowadays. He is like a guardian angel and makes my life in our Hamptons home safe and secure. He rarely leaves my presence when I go anywhere. Jake didn't need to ask that of him. He naturally became a father figure to me and took it upon himself to always watch over me in a very protective manner since he felt like he failed me when Vanquis came after me.

He hauled ass to a hospital with me and saved my life that night. I was suffering from a bleeding brain injury caused by the blow to my head, which would've been my end if Vanquis had managed to take me from the house as intended. I only lived because of the fast-medical attention given to me because Giovanni and Mathews showed up when they did.

I catch his eye and smile warmly as he and his wife grasp hands, and I swear I see a tear. It tugs my heart and makes me smile widely. I would trust my life under his care and protection for an eternity, and I never doubt my safety when I am with him.

My eyes scan the room as I walk the long white aisle, rows of white benches edged with wildflowers and lilies, and my eyes can't help but travel the last distance to the most beautiful thing in the entire room, getting achingly closer ... That gorgeous man smiling my way. I'm drawn to him and know that once I meet his glorious face, I'll never turn away for anything in the world ever again.

He's watching me walk toward him with his steadfast green gaze and attractive smile, giving me courage and grounding me to him in the way he always does. He looks every bit the billionaire playboy in a flawless navy suit and gray cravat and waist sash, perfectly tailored and groomed; every bit the man of my fantasies. He can pull off the groom-to-be look effortlessly. His calm façade not failing once as he stands gazing at me in his usual casual yet cocky pose. I smile back radiantly, my heart swelling with pride at the picture he makes, and I quell the urge to run the last few steps and jump into his arms.

He's standing between Arrick and Daniel, holding the most precious little blue-eyed bundle of mischief in his arms near his face. My chubby-legged little heart, my tiny perfection of blonde curls, and happy smiles that can make my whole day better with a mere sigh. They're beckoning me to come and finally join them in name and make our family unit complete. The most enticing reason to ever walk toward anyone ever in the whole wide world. These two precious faces hold my entire universe. My little girl, so like me and almost three months old already, adoringly gazing up at the daddy who is as smitten with her as I am.

Jake pulls her to his face and kisses her tenderly on the forehead, hugging her one last time before handing Mia to Sylvana with a beaming smile. He's unable to conceal the adoration of a daddy, rarely separated from his daughter since the day she was born. She's as much his world as she is mine. Our reason for living.

I reach instinctively for my little one as we close the last gap, my heart swelling with overpowering love, and my stomach aches with pride at that flawless piece of perfection held in her grandmother's arms. I kiss her tiny little head, inhaling Mia's unique smell with closed eyes, and take a moment to make her laugh for my enjoyment, a sound that brings my heart to unbelievable swelling completion.

She always has laughter for her mother, a smile, and a cheeky little face. I coo at her, biting my lip with overwhelming love as her grandmother moves aside. Jake and I watch her go for a moment before turning back to one another. Our eyes lock, filling with tears as we take each other in and realize what this moment is. He looks as stunning as the first time I ever laid eyes on him, and I can't help instantly longing for him, despite having been with him for as long as I have.

Giovanni releases me to Jake and takes Sylvana's arm to help his wife and grandchild back to the waiting seats. They are amazing, loving grandparents and spend as much time trying to steal her from us as Leila and Sarah do. Everyone loves Mia to death and fights over her affections endlessly.

I turn to look at the men before me. They look gorgeous, the three most handsome men you ever saw, and I know Leila will be behind me bawling her eyes out the sight of the man who has been begging her to marry him for months. Daniel is well and truly changed, and Leila is close to giving in and trusting him for once. The boy is smitten; the wild party animal with an endless stream of porn stars, booze and drugs is long gone. He treats her like his princess and bought her a house almost across from ours in the Hamptons. I'm rather proud of how fast Hunter is becoming another domesticated good boy, much like Jake.

The fiery nature of Leila and Daniel's relationship still exists but in a much healthier way, despite her sometimes-violent outbursts, and he's sticking around for an eternity. She never has anything to worry about with him again, and I feel Hunter will be a surprisingly good daddy. He's already amazing with Mia and little Adam; after the first shocks of learning he was going to be a father wore off.

Jake's eyes hold mine, his hand slides into my fingers, and he pulls me toward him with a determined tug and a naughty smile on his handsome face. He doesn't wait for permission but kisses me fully on the mouth. His lips molding to mine and cupping my jaw so he can get as close as possible while naughtily gliding his tongue, passionately, across mine. He puts an arm around my waist and brings me to meet his body with another tug. I'm not sure full-on tongue is appropriate, but I have no chance of resisting given the way he kisses; I never could. His kisses always have the ability to make me forget where we are.

"I think you're meant to wait for the 'you may now kiss the bride' bit," Daniel smirks at us when Jake pulls back and fixes my lipstick with his thumb. He throws Daniel a defiant smile looking like the cat who got the cream.

"Fuck off. I can kiss her whenever I damn well please … It's a perk of being hers." Jake grins, his effortlessly 'I'm hot, and I don't give a fuck' smile that melts my panties on sight. He turns back to me, almost ignoring the uneasy shuffling of the man above us, ready to take us through our vows. "Sorry, Father," Jake mumbles apologetically. "She's irresistible, and I can't help it." He smiles up at the poor priest with a decidedly unapologetic look. The man just nods with a rather blushed face and rattled expression. I guess he doesn't like his service being played out backward. I nudge Jake with my bouquet to tell him to behave, but he only winks at me and earns himself a sigh.

Jake has never cared about making public displays of affection, and he isn't going to change now; the small titter of laughter running from the audience confirms it. I can't say that I'm mad, this is the guy I fell in love with, after all, and this is part of him I wouldn't change for the world.

"You look breathtaking, *Bambina* ... woman of my dreams. My angel." He lifts my hand and kisses it, his eyes never leaving mine the whole time. The man in black uses throat-clearing coughs to bring us back to attention and back to the reality of the few hundred people staring at us, patiently waiting on the end of Casanova Carrero. I glance at Jake as he moves me to stand before him, taking my hand in his and holding it tightly.

Daniel moves to one side, pulling Leila gently with him to stand at the step below us, fingers entwined, kissing her on the cheek lovingly and proudly.

"You look stunning, baby girl," he whispers at her, and I catch the rise of color in her cheeks, and a small giggle escapes the lips of a completely smitten girl. I have no worries that the wedding is coming since I know Leila is ready to put him out of his misery and say yes the next time he asks. I'm sure it won't be long, as asking her to marry him has become a fortnightly habit until she does.

Arrick takes his place behind them and smirks, looking from us to Sophie as she sashays into the space next to him, taking his arm with a cheeky grin. She is becoming a cute and feisty little woman, developing so fast it's terrifying, and Arrick is probably the only one she ever listens to nowadays. They have an almost sibling bond. His calm Jake-like nature cools her jets when others fail to get her to listen. They look adorably cute side by side, and he's whispering something in her ear that makes her giggle. She adjusts her dress to smooth it down before using her hip to bump into him and grin his way. He reaches up and tucks a stray hair behind her ear, and they look our way like an innocent pair of teens who could do no wrong. It's hard to believe there's a five-year age difference between them, especially when they stand side by side and look like the most adorable couple ever.

Sarah finds her place next to Marcus, who has wandered over from the side, looping his arm in hers with a smile and a gentle kiss on her cheek. They look like the ultimate example of happiness, despite turbulent ups and downs, which now seem forgotten, and he looks good for his part today. I smile at them all with such an embracing love in my heart. They are my new family, and I wouldn't have this day any other way. They make it as much as Jake does.

Now it's only Jake and I standing on the top step. The others have taken their places on the podium below us, and we turn to face the man who will join us forever in vows and love and step up to meet him. Jake keeps a firm hold of my hand and pulls me to his side, close enough so no one else will hear. His strong body makes me weak with his mere touch as he leans in closer and turns his head my way with a flash of those bewitching hazy greens.

"I love you, *Bambina*." He throws me a sexy wink and a Carrero Casanova smile then tilts his head to lean down to me, rubbing his nose against mine in the way that Jake has perfected.

"I love you more." I lean up and kiss him on the nose cutely, dying to be alone with him, to see what he's hiding under that sexy tailored suit and cheeky grin.

We turn to face the voice of the man who will join us in marriage and feel nothing but love, devotion, and certainty, standing hand in hand with bodies touching. Without a doubt in my heart, I tell the man of my dreams that I'll be his forever.

A note from the Author

I hope you enjoyed my book; it would mean a great deal to me if you took the time to leave me a review. My reviews are something I regularly and actively read, and I appreciate you taking the time to leave me one. x

Find the Author online

You can find L.T. Marshall across all social media, and she regularly interacts with fans on Facebook.

Facebook fan group

https://www.facebook.com/groups/LTMarshallFans

Website: ltmarshall.blog
Facebook: facebook.com/LTMarshallauthor
Twitter: twitter.com/LMarshallAuthor
Instagram: instagram.com/l.t.marshall

Made in the USA
Monee, IL
25 July 2023

39860470R10247